*continued on next page . . .*

## Friends and Lovers

"Hip . . . crackles with wit and all the rhythm of an intoxicatingly funky rap. . . . Dickey has an eye for detail. A fun read."
—*Cincinnati Enquirer*

"[A] sexy, sophisticated protrayal of hip black L.A. . . engaging, dynamic." —*Publishers Weekly*

"Recommended. . . . Dickey uses humor, poignancy, and a fresh, creative writing style . . . connects the story line to believable real-life issues." —*USA Today*

"The language sings. . . . It flows . . . fluid as a rap song. Dickey can stand alone among modern novelists in capturing the flavor, . rhythm, and pace of African-American speak." —*Sun-Sentinel*

"Speaks directly to the heart . . . bittersweet, honest, and soulful."
—*Dallas Weekly*

## Sister, Sister

"Dickey imagines [his characters] with affection and sympathy. . . . His novel achieves genuine emotional depth." —*Boston Globe*

"Vibrant . . . marks the debut of a true talent."
—*Atlanta Journal & Constitution*

"A hip, sexy, wisecracking tale." —*New York Beacon*

"Bold and sassy . . . brims with humor, outrageousness, and . . . affection." —*Publishers Weekly*

"One of the most intuitive and hilarious voices in African-American fiction." —*St. Louis American*

# cheaters

ERIC
JEROME
DICKEY

NEW AMERICAN LIBRARY

New American Library
Published by New American Library, a division of Penguin Group (USA) Inc.,
375 Hudson Street, New York, New York 10014, USA
Penguin Group (Canada), 90 Eglinton Avenue East, Suite 700,
Toronto, Ontario M4P 2Y3, Canada
(a division of Pearson Penguin Canada Inc.)
Penguin Books Ltd., 80 Strand, London WC2R 0RL, England
Penguin Ireland, 25 St. Stephen's Green, Dublin 2, Ireland
(a division of Penguin Books Ltd.)
Penguin Group (Australia), 250 Camberwell Road, Camberwell,
Victoria 3124, Australia (a division of Pearson Australia Group Pty. Ltd.)
Penguin Books India Pvt. Ltd., 11 Community Centre, Panchsheel Park,
New Delhi - 110 017, India
Penguin Group (NZ), cnr Airborne and Rosedale Roads, Albany,
Auckland 1310, New Zealand (a division of Pearson New Zealand Ltd.)
Penguin Books (South Africa) (Pty.) Ltd., 24 Sturdee Avenue, Rosebank,
Johannesburg 2196, South Africa

Penguin Books Ltd., Registered Offices:
80 Strand, London WC2R 0RL, England

Published by New American Library, a division of Penguin Group (USA) Inc.
Previously published in Dutton and Signet editions.

First New American Library Printing, May 2001
20   19   18   17   16

REGISTERED TRADEMARK—MARCA REGISTRADA

LIBRARY OF CONGRESS CATALOGING-IN-PUBLICATION DATA:

Dickey, Eric Jerome.
Cheaters / Eric Jerome Dickey.
p.   cm.
ISBN 0-451-20300-3
1. Afro-American men—Fiction.   2. Dating (Social customs)—Fiction.
3. Young men—Fiction.   4. Betrayal—Fiction.   I. Title.
PS3554.I319 C47 2001

813'.54—dc21          00-066831

Set in Sabon
Designed by Leonard Telesca

Printed in the United States of America

TO MRS. VIRGINIA JERRY
love you always
thanks for picking me up
when others wanted to put me down
all you've ever asked
was for your family to be happy
and to stop borrowing money

your grandson
EJD
(now loan me a dollar, please?)

# part one

## Borrowed Nectar

# 1 Stephan

*"How many womens you got now, boy?"*

When I was in the third grade, my daddy came to visit us. I marveled at how dapper my old man was. Head to toe, he was always clean. Daddy leaned back in our tattered, creaking love seat, then glanced over my elementary school report card. He grunted as he puffed a hand-rolled cigarette. My old man was bland about my attendance being perfect, nonchalant about my conduct being above satisfactory. He even showed a touch of enthusiasm about my finally making the honor roll. After a few draws, he put his unfiltered smoke out in the red tin ashtray with one powerful twist of his wrist, took a gulp from his leather-cased flask, sipped a time or two, then yanked me tight against his side.

He put his face close to mine and grinned. "You hear me, Stephan? C'mon, you can tell me. I'm yo' daddy."

I shook my nappy head like I was lost.

Daddy's gold tooth shined when he whispered, "How many womens you got now?"

If I told him I had one, he'd call me a sissy. Two, a punk. A punk was an upgraded sissy, I thought. A giver, not a taker. But still not a real man.

"Got me three womens now!" I bugged out my brown eyes and smile-lied, using eagerness to pump it up and make it sound real.

"Good." Daddy smiled, gripped me with his callused hands, and pulled me up into his lap next to his damp face. Mississippi's humidity kept his roan complexion dank. He beamed and said, "Then you a man now, nigger. We mens."

I smiled at his acceptance.

"When you gets to be a big boy, you know what you 'pose to do to womens, doncha?"

I shook my head.

He whispered, "Find 'em. Fool 'em. Fuck 'em. Forget 'em."

I didn't know what he meant, but the words stuck in my head.

Momma came into the room long enough to ask Daddy, "Where's yo' wedding ring at? Why ain't you got it on?"

He grinned, winked at her, then started tickling my stomach. Momma looked outside at the passenger in his car, looked back at him, picked up her Bible, held it tight to her chest, then walked into the kitchen with her eyes closed. Walked like a woman gone blind. Her lips moved, like she was praying for strength. Each step was lead heavy.

After Daddy watched our black-and-white television's fuzzy picture for a couple of minutes, he reached into his pocket and gave me all of his loose change. Then he swaggered to his Buick Wildcat and drove off with some high-yellow woman. A woman in a big pink hat. The lady who chain-smoked and stared at our house every second he was inside. His Wildcat kicked dirt clouds and spat pebbles back at us as he sped away. I waved. He never looked back.

As the dust faded, I shook my pocket. Smiled at the rich noise it made with each jingle. It rang like a child's fortune. I wasn't sure why he gave me the reward—if it was because of my grades or my womens. Either way, I was a whole dollar richer.

Momma never said anything about his dropping by off-and-on to visit us unannounced and leaving an irritated female in the car. Almost every time a different nameless female. He'd been gone all summer; that was the longest he'd stayed away. And now when he dropped by, he never hung around but a few long minutes. He never cut his car engine off. Right before he grabbed his fedora—his signal to us he was about to leave—he would try to kiss Momma on the cheek. But she'd always move and twist her face into an evil look. He'd laugh, then try to hand her a fistful of crumpled-up money. She wouldn't take it. On the way out, he'd give up a wry smile and drop the wrinkled greenbacks on the faded coffee table.

After he left, Momma always went into her bedroom, turned off the light, and closed the door for a long time. Usually the rest of the night. Quiet. She'd always be withdrawn for a few days.

Even when Daddy's game was weak and he was cold busted with another babe, Momma always let him come back. It seemed like it was inevitable. All he'd have to do was say he was sorry, I mean real fucking sorry, confused by love. Look sad. Pitiful. And be humble, on his knees right in front of Momma and his two sons. A real, stupid humble. And, if he could manage it, cry. But he never overdid the crybaby routine. That would ring out as contrived. But he cried like a man standing before his savior confessing his sins. Then left the walls of salvation, hit the liquor store, and rolled into an all-night juke joint.

My sweet mother was a real woman. A sensitive woman who more than anything believed in family. Why did she keep taking him back when she knew he was a dog? Most women got this thing called compassion. It doesn't make them foolish, just more forgiving. More capable of trying and hoping things worked out.

The day Daddy told me I was a man was the last time Momma let him see us. She'd had enough. Enough of him. Enough of the pretty women he kept on his arm. That was the last time he set foot in our house. The last time Daddy held me in his lap.

I remembered thinking I'd be like my daddy. A real man. I wouldn't be a punk neither.

Darnell and Dawn knocked on my door around nine. Dawn never used my doorbell and banged like I owed her money. I had slipped on my spandex shorts and T-shirt almost thirty minutes ago when I got up to turn on the ceiling fan. I'd left my racquetball racquet and cross-trainers in the living room by the front door so they'd know I was ready.

Dawn was an almost six-foot-tall, borderline full-figured, scratchy-voiced sister from Brooklyn. Her arrogant eyes were the first thing I saw through the peephole.

Darnell was a little over five-eleven, chestnut complexion, slight receding hairline, built like a linebacker, arms almost as big as my legs, his belly getting a little on the pudgy side.

They were dressed in matching baggy black shorts and oversized T-shirts, the sleeves rolled up to the shoulders.

"Hey, babe," Dawn said in her typical tart tone. Her assertive East Coast accent rang out. We hugged. "You smell nice."

I said, "I took my weekly bath."

"Good. I was going to talk to you about that."

"Whuddup!" That was Darnell.

Dawn rolled her eyes. She hated it when he got too stupid too soon. She stretched and said, "You ready?"

"Hold up. I need to see a man about a horse," Darnell said. He headed toward the bathroom.

Dawn went to the kitchen and made herself a huge glass of orange juice, then peeped into the bedroom.

She whispered, "Who's this one?"

"Samantha."

"Have I met her before?"

"I think so."

"Where?"

"I think you met her at Kenneth Hahn Park when my momma and Pops had that family picnic. Last year when my sister Jackie came home from Spelman for spring break."

"If you're talking about last year when I met your other two brothers, then nope, that was a tall, tanned girl with long brown hair that I met. She was my partner when we played dominoes and we whooped everybody, including you and your momma."

I reminded her who that was when I said, "Brittany."

"You tell me. You need to make 'em wear name tags."

I said, "Well, act like you have met Samantha, then."

"You ain't shit."

"Love you, too."

Samantha had driven down from L.A. at four this morning, came by to get some loving before sunrise.

Dawn shook her head and walked back into the kitchen. "She's not going with us?"

"Nope. She'll probably sleep until we get back."

Samantha moaned, rolled over, almost opened her eyes.

Dawn stepped away from the bedroom door. I moved into the bedroom, eased the door up behind me. "Hey, sexy."

Samantha cleared her throat, pulled the sheets up over her bare breasts, said a weak "Who were you talking to, Stephan?"

Samantha's dark nipples were like beautiful blackberries sitting on top of small, elegant mounds of chocolate-coated joy. Her twenty kisses were juicier than a ripe berry, twice as sweet. I ran my hand across her short, curly hair, massaged the back of her neck. "You heard Dawn," I said.

She lifted her head. "Who's Dawn?"

"Darnell's wife."

Samantha yelled, "Hey, Dawn. Stephan told me about you."

"Hello, Samantha," Dawn called out from the other side of the door. "Nice to see you again. Didn't mean to wake you."

"It's okay." Samantha waved one of her hands in the direction of the voice. "Stephan, what're you doing?"

"Saturday morning racquetball."

"That's right."

"You want to go?"

She sighed. "Can I stay here until you get back?"

"Why don't you come work out? Sleep later."

She cursed. "You have an extra racquet?"

"Of course."

Which was good. I didn't want to leave her here in my space all by herself. She might do a Columbo and go through my condo from ceiling to carport. Find something that she didn't need to find.

She kissed me. I put my hand under the sheets, slid my finger inside her, made her moan. Slid my digit deeper until I couldn't slide it in anymore. Used two fingers. Moved them in and out in a slow, stirring rhythm. I knew how to wake her up.

Samantha wiggled and pushed my hand away. "Don't start something you can't finish."

I smiled. I yelled, "Dawn, Samantha's going with us."

Dawn yelled back. "Okay. I need some female bonding."

We all laughed.

Samantha whispered, "Have I met her before?"

"What?"

"She said it was nice to see me again. I've never met her."

Samantha had a false smile on her questioning face.

I smiled, ignored that question. "Hurry and get showered."

Samantha's eyes changed, became sultry, and she asked, "Is that door closed all the way?"

I nodded.

She pulled my hips up to her face, reached into my spandex, and pulled out my penis. Moved it up and down, kissed it like it was a newborn child, slid it into her mouth like she was easing that baby in its favorite cradle. I gasped and made a *mmmm* sound. So warm. So good. Her eyes were on me as she licked around me, then slurped, pulled me in deeper.

Dawn drove us down the hill to L.A. Fitness, where she had reserved a racquetball court. We played doubles, first couples against couples, then the guys against the dolls.

Dawn was as vicious on the courts as she was in her real estate office. Aggressive, smooth. Hardly moved, but when she did, it was with a definite athletic rhythm.

Samantha looked studious and dangerous because she crouched low and wore protective goggles. She'd calculate where the ball was going to land and be there before it knew where it was going.

Darnell played too hard. He ran into the wall a lot and hit the ball damn hard, so hard every shot had the power of a kill shot, even from back court. Whenever he missed a shot, he'd look at his brand-new racquet like it was defective.

I'd find out each of their weak spots and concentrate on playing that angle. Dawn's backhand was inconsistent and sucked from deep in the court because her racquet kept bumping into the wall, cutting her return short.

Darnell would get mixed up on a three-wall shot. I'd use the back wall for awkward returns and mix it up with ceiling shots to try to break their rhythms.

Samantha wasn't as agile and swift on the court as she was in bed.

Me and Samantha won the first game by two. Dawn and Darnell won the next two without a lot of effort.

When we switched partners, guys against dolls, Dawn said, "Samantha, let's kick these bitches' asses."

Darnell chuckled and bobbed his head. "It's on."

I shouted a warning, "No mercy for those who menstruate."

Grunts, bumps, and curses: It sounded like a war.

Me and Darnell struggled and won a game, beat Dawn and Samantha by three points. The last game the dolls beat us by four.

We had thirty minutes left on the court, but we were all beat because each game had lasted almost twenty-five minutes.

Silliness took over and I staggered, overacted, like I was trying to catch a second wind. I sat and tried to stretch my already worn-out muscles. The sounds of rubber balls bounced off the walls; the screech of tennis shoes echoed around us.

My T-shirt was soaked from chin to waist because I had kept wiping my face on it. We crashed on the hardwood floor, Dawn next to Darnell, Samantha and me across the court, sharing a bottle of Sparkletts water. My back was on the floor, feet up against the wall. Samantha sat with her legs spread apart, and she stretched side to side, then face to the floor.

Dawn said, "Shit, Samantha. If I was that flexible, I'd have a baby by now."

We laughed.

Darnell said, "If you'd stay in bed on a Saturday morning instead of dragging everybody down here, you'd have a baby."

Dawn countered, "If you'd come to bed instead of typing on that damn computer all night, you'd be a father by now."

Samantha said, "I'm all against the wall and worn out. I used to be able to play hours on end. I must be getting old."

Dawn smiled. "We used to close out every party we went to."

I said, "I know that's right. Party all night, hit Fatburgers, then make it home just in time to go to church."

Samantha laughed. "Is this what being thirty does to you?"

Dawn asked, "You have any kids, Samantha?"

"Thirty with no babies."

"Just like me and Darnell. I'm damn near thirty-two and no heirs. If I have to wait until I'm thirty-five, I'll be in that high-risk category, and that won't be cool. Not at all."

Darnell sighed. "Don't depress Samantha, sweetheart."

I was picking up bits of chastisement from my friends, but Samantha didn't know them well enough to know that Dawn was dead serious.

Samantha laughed. "I'm cool. That's why I stopped my biological clock at twenty-five. I'm in no hurry to give up my freedom."

As she was talking, Dawn went after her husband. Darnell scooted away from her. She slid after him and started tickling him. Darnell's damn ticklish. She climbed on top of him and kissed his face. Even though they fought, they had years of something that I envied.

Samantha was watching them, smiling, then looking at me.

Her eyes were gleaming for affection.

Six months ago I met her on Pico at Roscoe's Chicken 'n Waffles. The place was crowded; both of us were alone; our eyes had mutual interest, some curiosity, so I asked her if she wanted to share a table. She smiled, said sure, we did, and we talked nonstop. That communication drew me to her. Very articulate, well read, up on all the political activities in the neighborhood. Neither of us wanted to end the conversation. More like she didn't want to stop talking. Women always make it easy for a brotha. All that crap about running your mouth and macking harder than Max Julien ain't the move. The secret of conversation is to get a woman to talk, then listen and absorb. They'll tell you who did 'em wrong, what they want, raise their eyes to yours in a soft and tender way that asks if you can meet those demands. All a brotha has to do is pay attention, nod his head a time or two and, when she's through, let her know that whatever the last man did, he'd never do that.

Minutes later me and Darnell were in the locker room, butt naked on opposite sides of the communal shower. A couple of other guys, one white and the other Asian, were in there too, but they weren't talking much. I rinsed the liquid soap off my body and stood underneath the waterfall of cool and cleansing water.

I asked, "When you gonna have some more of that story for me to read?"

"The next day or so. I'm only getting to write a paragraph here and there because work has had me tied down. And the moment I get home, Dawn starts whining for attention."

"Women will suck the life out of you."

"I know that's right. Giving a woman the attention she wants is another full-time job. But work is taking up most of my time. I'm getting ready for a hearing against Northwest out in Palm Springs. Plus I'm doing some unlawful detainers for a friend of a friend who's trying to evict some tenants out in Rialto. The tenants haven't paid a dime in rent in over a year."

"Don't wear yourself out. Finish that book. That could be a million dollars you sitting on."

Darnell smiled at my encouragement, then asked, "You talked to Jake?"

I said, "Yeah."

Jake is another one of our running buddies. He's a fireman out in L.A., near my folks' house.

That was when I remembered and told Darnell about the ski trip. On Valentine's Day Jake and his fiancée are hitting the local slopes and had extended an invitation for all of us to tag along. I would've told Darnell sooner, but I didn't want to bring it up in front of Samantha. If I was kicking it with her this weekend, I'd have to kick it with Toyomi next weekend. But if I finally catch up with Brittany, never know what I might do.

Darnell said they had plans for Valentine's Day. He was taking Dawn an hour across the Pacific Ocean to experience a few golden sunsets at Catalina Island. Their romantic weekend, the glass-bottom boat ride there and back, the five-star hotel room and champagne brunch, were already hooked up.

He asked, "Jake tell you those dreams were back?"

I let some water run over my face, into my mouth, then spat it out. I didn't want to get into talking about Jake's dreams. They were too eerie, so demented it made my flesh crawl just thinking about them.

I changed the subject, asked what him and Dawn were getting into today.

Darnell replied, "We're going to catch a couple of movies at the AMC on Fullerton Road. What you doing?"

I turned my shower off, grabbed my green towel. "Trying to get rid of Samantha."

He laughed a bit.

I shook my head, said, "When she comes out here, it's hard to get her ass to go back home."

"That girl likes you, that's all."

"I like her too."

"Yeah, but if you're seeing eight or nine other women, how will you ever know if that relationship has potential? You have to focus on one. They start to cancel each other after a while."

I ignored his calm expression of righteousness. "I know she's going to try and stay until Sunday night or early Monday morning, so I'll tell her I'm going up to see my momma. That way I can just follow her home, then bounce over to see my folks before I come back out this way."

Darnell chuckled.

I said, "What's funny?"

"You got your game laid out. You've got a backup plan for your backup plan. If I had your hand, I'd throw mine in."

I laughed. "If you got Dawn, you've got the best hand."

"Grass is always greener."

I said, "Not when you're taking care of your own lawn."

"With all the lawns you're tending to with that weedwacker of yours, how would you know?"

I laughed and finished drying off. After I got dressed I used the pay phone hidden in the locker room to make a few phone calls. Had to check a few traps. It took me twenty minutes to get Toyomi to cool off, but when I told her about the ski trip for Valentine's Day, everything smoothed out. Pretty much. She was still filled with disappointment. She'd get over it as soon as she saw me.

We stopped by Mimi's restaurant in Industry for coffee and lunch. Two hours after that I was following Samantha up the 10 freeway into the heart of Los Angeles. We dropped her car off, then rode deeper into territory that owned cool breeze after cool breeze. She wore shades she'd bought in Venice Beach for five bucks, a leather backpack-style purse, sandals, no bra, a Bob Marley T-shirt over a short red dress, no panties. We hung out on the promenade in Santa Monica, drove the coast north toward Malibu. Rode until the sun was setting, then parked, had sex in the car. Samantha was moving her backside round and round, up and down, right on Pacific Coast Highway, with traffic whizzing by.

We ate seafood dinners at Gladstone's. Walked out into the darkness and let the sand rise up in between our toes.

Back at her place, we oiled each other down, massaged each other while the soulful voice of Rachelle Ferrell lulled us.

As I slept, I drifted back to my childhood.

Smelled Daddy's cologne.

His cigar.

Heard a dollar's worth of lies jingling.

Felt that chill again.

Sorta missed my old man.

Sorta.

Wondered if there was a heaven for him.

# 2 Chanté

A little boy cried out, *"Daddy."*

That rudeness was right outside my condo, at three in the morning. The child sounded like a fire engine and probably woke up the city of Diamond Bar.

*"Daaadeee, Daaadeee . . ."* It was a little girl's voice that time. It was faint, like a cry in the wind.

Michael quit dipping and probing, stopped chanting how good my love was, quit moving his hips like he was shuddering on the inside. I think he'd stopped before I had heard the cries.

I was about twelve strokes from a nuclear orgasm when I realized the crumb snatchers were on my front porch.

*"Daaadeee, daaaadeeee, daaaadeeeeeeee . . ."*

My hips screeched to a halt. The cloud I was on evaporated, and I lost the buzz I had from the chablis I had sipped on while we partied in downtown L.A. at Little J's.

He pushed up on his elbows and snarled, "Shit."

I opened my eyes.

His were already open. Wide open, just like his mouth.

He stared through the candlelit room toward my front door. Toward the voices who were howling woeful noises for their daddy.

The sensation of being kicked off a mile-high cliff toward jagged rocks raced through my body, put a choke hold on my soul. I gasped so hard I thought I was about to suffocate myself.

Through candlelight, the aroma of black love incense, and Etta James singing a sultry song about burning down the cornfield, I stared into his eyes.

He panted. Blinked. Trembled. Didn't get off me. Or all the way out of me. But it would've been impossible for him to wiggle over an inch because my fear had me clinging to him.

"Michael, who in the hell is that. . . ."

"I—I—I . . ."

I knew one thing for damn sure: Those rugrats sure in hell weren't mine. First off, I'm a sista. Mostly. My grandma was Native American, and everybody else was full-blooded Negro, so yadda yadda yadda I'm a sista. So the crumb snatchers had to be screaming for the cocoa butter-complexioned naked man who was on top of my naked body, the one who was going to love me until the new sun shattered the old darkness.

The girl squealed, *"Daaaa-deeee, come home, please."*

They were knocking at my door and ringing my bell. A cavalry was out there.

A sista cried out, *"Michael Clifton Davidson."*

Hell, no.

I panted, fought the dizziness, said, "Michael, who is at my door and calling out your name like they've lost their mind?"

The woman must've heard me, because she raised her voice. *"It's your wife, Michael. And your children. Sidney, Rachel, and Jordan. Could you come here, please?"*

He was so scared that slobber slipped from his mouth and splattered on my neck. I closed my eyes as tight as I could. I was livid as I grumbled, "This isn't happening to me. Michael, please, tell me this ain't happening to me."

*"Daaaadeeee, Mommeeee said to tell you to come back home."*

My nails dug deep into his back. I sent all my anger to my fingertips and tried to dig down to his bone. He wailed and rolled off me. The hysteria in his eyes, the deadly scowl swelling in my face—nothing had to be said.

I wanted to kill him, probably should have, but I was in too much shock to move.

*Children. Wife.*

On my dresser, next to the condoms and Irish Cream massage oil from Victoria's Secret, were two dozen long-stemmed red roses. Not a two-dollar arrangement from the Mexicans hustling at the freeway off-ramps, either. Michael had sent another dozen long-stems and a super big box of See's candy to my job this morning.

All of a sudden I felt naked.

Cold, sweaty, and naked.

Like I was in the middle of a voluntary rape.

"Michael, you ain't shit. You lied, you lied, you lied."

"Chanté." He jumped up and grabbed his clothes off the floor, bounced like a kangaroo and tried to get his pants back on in one good hop. "It's not what you think."

"Well, I don't think that's UPS at my damn door."

Before I could catch my breath, Michael dressed and exited without saying a word, tripping over furniture in the dark.

I grabbed my white satin robe, raced behind him, snatched up the garden of roses he had given me, and threw them at his ass. The glass vase bopped him hard upside his head. Water splashed over his rayon shirt, stained my off-white wall. Somehow the vase didn't break when it hit the floor and rolled back toward me. He cringed, grunted, staggered and stalled for a moment, turned his six-foot-two frame around, and curled his thick lips inside his mouth. Those dark green eyes tightened, became fire, burned down on me like he wanted to attack me.

He weighed almost two hundred, and I don't weigh but one thirty, but I kicked the vase out of the way—that shit hurt the hell out of my toe—balled up my fist, stood still and firm, got ready to break a nail or two. My hair came loose, hung and dangled, swayed all across my face and down my back. I was a wolf. I snarled, showed my teeth, got ready to claw, chew, howl, and go for broke with this no good son of a bitch.

"Daaaadeeee, daaaadeeee, daaaadeeee . . ."

"Michael, don't make me act ugly out here."

He rubbed the knot that was growing on his head, turned and swaggered in the direction of the voices of the bounty hunters who had tracked him down. I wailed out a few curse words, yanked the roses from the floor, ran up behind him, pushed him as hard as I could, then slapped the back of his head forty-eleven times with the rest of the bouquet.

He kept moving. Rose petals fell like confetti.

I caught my breath in the hallway, lowered my head. God. I went through pain and agony with Craig Bryant just three months ago. Seems like yesterday he messed me over. Why again? Why so soon? I'm only twenty-seven years old. Can't some of this agony be spread over the next seventy years?

By the time I got myself together well enough to go spy out the living room window, Michael had picked up one of the children, a little girl wearing flowered footed pajamas and ponytails. The child hugged his neck and looked back at my ruptured life. Michael also held the hand of a thumb-sucking little boy. A long, tall woman in a gray housecoat and Bugs Bunny slippers trudged behind him and carried another snoozing, diaper-sagging rugrat, a baby dressed in the colors of Africa.

I yanked my front door, thinking I was about to say something profound. His wife turned and gazed at me. She was tore up, head to toe. I took inventory of the deranged, dark-as-the-night-is-long woman in a housecoat and rollers.

One of the kids asked, "Who's that lady, Daddy?"

Michael talked as he rushed. "Get your butt in the car."

"Mommy, don't cry."

"Hush. Get in the car with your daddy."

Mrs. Michael slowed and stared back at me.

Both of us had a Soul Train of tears running down our faces. My middle-class multi-ethnic neighbors were either outside or peeping out their windows.

Michael's dysfunctional ass rushed his two into his Lexus and screeched up Diamond Bar Boulevard toward the freeway. His mate for life strapped the toddler into a car seat, then crawled into her Volvo wagon. She shot one last glare back toward my asylum. It was one of those crazed scowls that said two things: He's mine; I know where you live.

She had been through this before.

I dabbed my eyes, tied my hair back, blew out candles, picked up rose petals, tried to figure this shit out. Michael had played me bigtime. I met him last month at Borders bookstore in Montclair. Both of us were in the itty-bitty black folks section of the store. We started chitchatting, exchanged business cards, and since that day he'd been sending cards and flowers. Guess he was spending his household income driving out from the Valley, taking me to lunch at the Cheesecake Factory, and to dinner at California Pizza Kitchen. Has never forgotten to call. Gave weeks of passion. Perfect in every way.

Except his Alzheimer's kicked in and the bastard forgot to tell me he was married. And I would have to be all romantic and get freaky with him a week before Valentine's Day. But hell, it had been three months since I got me some.

Now this fool—talking about myself—realized why Michael never answered his phone when I called; he had given me a voice-mail number. That's why it always went *beep-beep-beep* at the end of the outgoing message. A damn pager.

When I had told him that I wasn't fond of the freeways, that bastard had kissed my eyes and said, "You know, with all the carjackings and freeway shootings and drive-bys, I don't mind coming to see you."

My little red buggy did have its own problems, the kind that could leave a sista stranded in the middle of the night, so I didn't argue with those warm and kind words.

I feel it changing. My heart. It's getting cold.

Roses were tossed in the trash. I yanked the sheets off my bed, crammed them in the trash, too.

I stood in the shower, tried to scrub and scrub all of him off me. It was hard to scrub away a memory, but just like I'd been doing since Craig wrecked my world, I tried. I mixed some hard California water with my bitter tears, tried to scour away what everybody had left behind.

God. Let me stop crying. Let my head stop hurting. Make my body stop feeling so heavy.

*   *   *

At daylight I still had my arms folded across my breasts, pacing from room to room, talking to myself, cursing from wall to wall.

I closed all of my venetian blinds and collapsed in the middle of my bed. I dialed my job at Moss Adams, one of the largest accounting and consulting firms in the U.S. of A., got ready to leave a message with the head cheese and tell them that their favorite double minority was sick and disabled. Then I realized it was Sunday morning. I didn't have to work today.

My head was jacked up.

I'm too smart for this kinda madness. I have a B.S. in accounting from Cal Poly at Pomona. But I guess there are some things they just don't teach a sista in college.

By ten a.m. Ma Bell had been chiming. Fifteen times in a row. When I finally answered, Michael whined and whimpered, tried to apologize, begged to come over. I told him hell no.

"How did your wife know where I lived?"

"The card you sent me. She found it."

"Divine intervention."

He begged, "Drive up to Fullerton Road, meet me at Mimi's Café so I can explain my predicament."

I chuckled. "Predicament?"

"It's complicated."

"Let me simplify it for your lying ass. You're married. You were married when we met. You slept with me when you knew you had a damn wife waiting for your dick to get home. If your memory is that damn bad, start taking a handful of Gotu Kola every morning while you feed Cream of Wheat to your busload of rugrats. Is that simple enough for you?"

"So, we're not going to be together on Valentine's Day?"

I hung up, soft and gentle.

Blew out so much air I thought my lungs were about to collapse. The phone rang again. I answered cursing, making threats that involved a sharp knife and a short penis.

A pregnant pause. It was so quiet I heard a fly buzzing around the room.

A friendly voice that flowed like a poem said, "Chanté?"

"Karen?"

"Damn." She paused. "What happened this time?"

I repeated, "This time."

She repeated, "This time."

I stood up, gradually became aware as I struggled to gather my senses. "I'm sorry. Thought you were that nigga Michael."

"How did Michael get demoted into the depths of Niggaville?"

I didn't say a word. Didn't say a goddamn word.

Karen said, "Don't tell me you slept with him?"

My insides felt ruptured. Sometimes she was super caring. Other times she was the queen of chastisement.

Noises of shame and disgust were flowing from my mouth.

"What's wrong?" Karen asked over and over. "You there?"

Karen was comforting, questioning. I couldn't breathe. I inhaled, my body locked up until my face turned blue, then I exhaled hard enough to make my venetian blinds sway.

I answered, "I just went through this crap with Craig."

"That's why I was calling." She sighed, then anger peppered her tongue. "He's back. I saw Craig walking around the mall."

"When?"

"Five minutes ago. He was passing through Mervyn's."

A new hostility came to life. "Who was he with?"

"Nobody."

"He see you?"

Karen stalled. "Chanté, he had the nerve to come over to my register."

"He ask about me?"

"No." She hesitated. "But he had the nerve to ask me out."

"When he asked you out, you said . . ."

"I went off on his ass."

I rubbed my forehead hard enough to start a fire.

Karen asked, "What did Michael do?"

The sound I made, well, it had to be the wail of a bear with a box of salt being poured on an open wound.

I'll never come out of these blues alive. It's always heads they win, tails I lose.

# 3  Darnell

"Darnell, how long're you going to be up, sweetheart?"

I didn't answer. Dawn used the word *sweetheart* like it was a substitute for other curse words. Maybe it was her hard New York accent that made it sting. I stopped typing on my PC because she'd wrecked my train of thought. Had to stop and massage my temples. Felt stress coming on strong. I felt my ideas thinning out. She knew I was in the middle of something, and she knew she was disturbing my creative process, wrecking my flow.

It was after midnight. The first few minutes of Monday.

A moment later Dawn appeared in the doorway. The hall light allowed her six-foot frame to cast an eight-foot shadow across the wall that held all of our laminated degrees, on my proclamation from the city, darkened the wall nearer to the side with her desk. My desk was nearer the window. At night I clicked off all the lights and worked by the illumination of the PC. The darkness all around me blocked out the outside world, made me feel focused in the fantasy that I was creating.

"Darnell? How long're you going to work on that book of yours?"

"Another hour or two."

"No, Darnell." Again, the way she said my name sounded like an abomination. "I mean how long. You've been doing this one for over a month. The other book you wrote is over in the corner collecting dust. You have a job. Your degree is not in writing books, for crying out loud."

"You want to read what I'm working on?"

"It's late. We have to get up early. I'm going to bed."

I turned back around, trying to find my place in the story, trying to get back into the characters. Trying to get back into character. Dawn was still in the doorway. I felt her presence the same way I saw her restless shadow moving side to side.

"Darnell? Sweetheart?"

Again I rubbed my temples. "Yes, honey?"

"I didn't marry a book writer."

"Did you marry a man or an occupation?"

"You know what I mean. You're an attorney. You have a good job. We have plans to do other things. You're thinking about quitting your job to write a doggone book—mind you, that you do not have a degree in journalism—"

I cut her off. "Grisham, Clancy, Files, none of them have a degree in journalism."

"Sweetheart, I hate to burst your bubble, but you're not Grisham, Clancy, or Files."

"And before Grisham there wasn't a Grisham."

She said, "I'm just being honest. What, am I supposed to put having *our* first kid on hold just because you have a writing bug up your ass? And if you quit work to investigate this new avenue, until you get that *lump sum* check from a yet to be named publisher, do you expect me to pay the mortgage on this three-bedroom house, foot the bill for two car notes and insurance, pay for electric, buy food and clothing, do all of that on what I make selling real estate? You know how my job is. You know about its highs and lows."

"We could cut back."

"Cut back? You mean, move out of Walnut and go back into Los Angeles? I don't think so." She shifted side to side. "Baby, I love you. You went to Whittier Law School, and I supported you; now you're an attorney with the FAA, and I still support you. And as far as the FAA goes, you need that job so we can pay back the student loans that enabled you to become an attorney."

We'd been over all this before. "Did you read the five pages I gave you day before yesterday?"

"It's in my briefcase with the other stuff you gave me."

I hated the way she referred to what I did as *stuff*.

But still I asked, "Have you looked at any of it?"

She turned to walk away. "No."

I said, "Stephan thinks it's good. He liked the suspense. Said that he could *see* the people and everything."

"When did he stop hoeing around long enough to become a critic? What did Jake say about the stuff you wrote?"

"Jake doesn't read fiction. What did you think?"

"I was reading my Sue Grafton novel. I'll get around to reading yours. Why don't you turn that computer off?"

My head was throbbing. "In a minute."

"Stop running up our electric bill and come to bed at a decent hour for a change. In the old days, nighttime used to mean something to married people. Something special. It's a shame when a woman has to beg a man to be her husband."

"And it's a damn shame when a man has to beg his wife to be his friend."

"I didn't marry you because I needed a friend. I have plenty of them. I married you because I wanted you to be my husband."

"Or just because you wanted a husband."

"I wanted you to be my husband; I wanted to be your wife." With that, she left.

I tried to get back into the groove of what I was doing, but that groove was gone. I tried to get focused. That lasted five minutes.

Pictures that Dawn and I had taken on our honeymoon way back when were on the wall between our desks. I looked at them. Looked at us.

Me and Dawn met at church. Faithful Central. Singles Bible study. That was when all of us—Jake, Stephan, Dawn—were living in L.A.

I'd come in church late because I'd been working out with my buddies at the gym, sat next to her, and when it came time to find the scripture in the Bible, it took me forever to find the passage in Corinthians. Church wasn't one of my playgrounds, and outside of Easter, it hadn't been my parents' favorite place. Seemed like everybody else was in Corinthians, reading along, and I was still flipping pages. Dawn peeped over at me struggling, smiled. She leaned close to me and whispered, "It's in the New Testament."

"Oh. Thanks."

I struggled a few more seconds.

She added, "Between Romans and Galatians."

I fanned through Luke. John. Acts. Still lost.

She said, "First Corinthians."

She leaned over and helped me. Helped me find my way the rest of the evening. We ended up in the parking lot, discussing the Word. We were so in sync, like two of God's instruments playing the same tune, harmonizing in faith. She had me engaged before I could protest. Back then she claimed her goals were to become a real estate broker, open her own office. But she's stopped chasing that dream and settled for working at someone else's office. And after she found what she'd come to church to get, church wasn't as important. Just the three W's of the wedding—when, where, and what time. I thought she was in love with me, but deep down I've always felt she was more in love with being married, with the white picket fence, two-car garage image of marriage.

Eight years of being career-driven people, of having shifting priorities, of working and studying on weekends, Sundays included, has changed us both.

This world has changed us like it changes everything.

She interrupted my thoughts of yesterday, of yester-her and yester-me: "Darnell. Sweetheart. Baby."

I heard Dawn down the hallway in the bed. Shifting around.

I clicked the PC off.

Forget about my dreams deferred.

I went and put my head on my wife's bosom.

Gave her the attention that she deserved.

Became her husband.

# 4 Stephan

Valentine's Day.

By nine a.m. we were all at Mountain High, skiing the blue runs on the east resort. Blue means intermediate slopes.

Jake was a little ahead of me, whizzing around fallen snow boarders. His fiancée, Charlotte, was right behind him, skiing down the groomed track like a serious snow bunny. Charlotte's in her late twenties, about five-foot-five, slim and trim. About the same height as my girl Toyomi. My woman for the day.

Jake pointed toward the advanced run. The one labeled Wildcard. "We're going to hit this black diamond run."

I said, "Can you handle it?"

Jake smiled under his shades. "Man, please. After Sun Valley and Vail, this whole mountain is a bunny slope."

We laughed. I planted my poles at my side, pulled off my mittens, then reached inside my jacket and pulled out my camera. They shuffled close enough to hug. I took a few pictures.

Charlotte beamed like a prom queen. "Game for the moguls?"

Moguls are those bumps in the ski run that test the hell out of your skills. And your knees. My muscles were aching a bit, and I didn't want to get sloppy and do a Bono into a pine tree. I waved the ambitious pair toward the downhill run. "Go on. I'm going to wait for Toyomi and her friend Shar."

I watched them dive into that run like they were born on snow. Jake and Charlotte looked so good together. The smile she had when she was with Jake was pure joy and happiness. And while Jake was with her, you'd never know he had more women waiting with warm sheets than Toys R Us has Barbie dolls.

I hope he appreciates what he has.

I'd stopped halfway down Goldrush. Stood at eight thousand feet. In smog-free air. Surrounded by mountains frosted in pure white snow. All the pine trees stood like proud snow cones. Overhead, blue skies with very few clouds. The view spanned all the way out to the dry desert of Palmdale and Lancaster. Snow and sand. The dichotomy of the moment sucked me deep inside.

"What are you looking at?" Toyomi did a couple of quick and sassy turns, stopped on a dime a few feet from me, and sprayed a ton of snow on my boots and skis. When it came to skiing, she thought she was the next Picabo Street.

Again she asked, "What're you looking at?"

My eyes were on the snow. Watching the sun reflect off the whiteness. At this moment I felt like snow was Mother Nature's way of telling people to slow down. Telling me to slow down. I should've told Toyomi that, but I didn't. Instead I gave her my best smile and said, "Looking at you. Let me take your pic."

After the snapshot, she said, "You're sweating."

"Thermals have me a little toasty. Ready to roll?"

Toyomi said, "Wait for Shar. She's right behind me."

"She fall down?"

"Yep. Her ski came off, and she was struggling to get it back on. Oh, look, Steph, some more black people are up here."

The hills were packed with Anglo and Asian, quite a few Mexicans. Toyomi pointed at six sistas who were traversing their way down the mile-and-a-half Goldrush run. Good-looking sistas in attention-grabbing colors: yellows, reds, light blues. Body-tight ski suits made the women in winter wonderland look good.

They stopped, eased up their goggles, and smiled down the hill when they saw me. One of them waved.

In a heated tone Toyomi asked, "And who is that?"

"Who?"

"That bitch who waved at you?"

That was the side of her I hated. Her eyes darkened. I smelled insanity on her breath. I asked, "Why does she have to be a bitch?"

"Because the bitch waited until she thought I wasn't looking to wave at you. Why couldn't she wave at *us*? That's what makes that bitch a bitch. Who is she?"

"I have no idea. Just black people waving at black people."

"That was more than a wave."

I asked, "How would you know?"

"I'm a woman and I know women."

Toyomi maneuvered down the hill and stopped close enough to me so she could take off her sunglasses and get a kiss.

She whispered, "Happy Valentine's Day."

I told her the same. Told her the same thing that I had told Samantha last night. The only way I had slipped out of Samantha's arms was by telling her I had to work. Last night she went all out: strawberries and champagne being licked off every part of me. That's why I was so damn sluggish. Five hours of sleep and three hours of driving can slow a man down big time, no matter how much orange juice, ginseng, and yo'himbe he's ingested.

I tongued Toyomi down and told her happy Valentine's Day.

The same thing I might tell Brittany later on tonight.

Out of the three women I spent time with, Toyomi was the main one. The one, relative to the other two I entertained, whom I really cared about. We'd been seeing each other a little over a year. Thirteen months and some change, to be exact.

Underneath her black ski suit, mittens, and earmuffs, Toyomi's a small-waisted, perky-breasted, healthy-butted, half-Black, half-Japanese sister I met on-line in a Net Noir chat room. After e-mailing and sending each other photos, we met face-to-face at a scanty club in Redland called Whiskey Creek. Shot eight ball and nine ball half the night in that honky-tonk atmosphere. Ended up gambling for kisses. She's a fresh twenty-four. Just got her first white-collar job two years back. She'd had two lovers since she turned nineteen. Inexperienced in sin, but a quick study and a perfectionist who aimed to please her man in any and every way possible. Her plus was her minus too, because she was too intense and clinging.

Toyomi had brought her best friend, Shar, along. Shar didn't have a date. Her purple bib and red jacket appeared in the distance, swooshing side to side, maneuvering around a few fools who had fallen. She caught up a minute later.

Toyomi dropped her pole, and as she bent to pick it up, Shar stopped near me. Right up on me. She touched the butt of my bib with her pole and smiled. She always gave me this wanton gleam when Toyomi wasn't watching. Shar's tall and always pleasant to talk to and more than a fantasy to behold from any angle—front, back, side to side.

By the time Toyomi raised her head, Shar was gazing off in another direction. Acting like she'd never noticed I was there.

I asked Shar, "What happened to your date?"

She shrugged. "We broke up last week."

I already knew that. Part of me just wanted to hear her voice. I told them that Jake and Charlotte were ahead of us.

Shar said, "Which way we going, good people?"

I yanked out my map of the mountain, checked out the trails, and suggested. "Let's cut over to Sepps's this time. We haven't done that run. It's long and not too steep."

They took off before me, carved their trails in the snow. I took it easy and followed their snow-powdered scents.

Toyomi was in front, kept her skis parallel, planted her poles before she turned, dipped those hips as she moved with a passion. Always moving with a passion.

Shar's tall frame moved with equal hunger.

Toyomi's a bona fide, bodacious, fine-ass woman, but I couldn't keep my eyes from wandering to Shar. Couldn't stop imagining. And that's a damn shame on my part. Yep, over and over I've caught Shar looking at my buns, smiling. Waving a match in front of my kerosene. Every time I've seen her, those baby brown eyes have owned that same glare of imagination that mine had been trying not to broadcast for the last year. Shar's called my place looking for Toyomi a few times, and we've had some nice conversations. We've discussed her boyfriend. The problems they've had. Sex. And, as far as I know, she's never told Toyomi that we've said more than a hi and bye to each other. Whenever she's near Toyomi, she paints the impression of this thick, uncrossable line being there.

I wondered what would happen if both of us became victims of space and opportunity.

After we rode the bus to the west resort and skied most of those trails, we came back to the east side and headed for the lodge, Angeles Crest Café, to get our grub on. Hot dogs, hamburgers, fries, Mexican food, all of those smells were in the air and made my stomach grumble. Luck was on our side and we caught an empty table outside in the sun. It was about forty degrees, no breeze. Crowded. Not another empty table in sight.

We'd loosened our boots. Unzipped our jackets. Pulled the beanies, headbands, off our heads. Steaming hot cocoa and bottled water were on the round iron table. Sandwiches were being devoured.

Toyomi said, "Charlotte, I'm glad I finally got a chance to meet you. Stephan's been talking about you for over a year."

Yep. This was their first-time meeting. Charlotte had met a couple of the other women I kicked it with, but never Toyomi.

Jake asked Shar, "You work in R&D with Toyomi?"

"Nope," Shar answered. "I teach high school math. I'll leave that engineer stuff to Toy and Stephan."

Charlotte tugged off her gloves and liners. That was when Toyomi saw her engagement ring. "I forgot Stephan told me you were engaged. When's the wedding, Charlotte?"

Nobody answered.

Shar was sitting between me and Jake. I felt her leg pressing against mine. There was plenty of space, but she was right up on me. Felt her warmth radiating through my bib. Shar told Charlotte she wanted to see her rock, leaned across me, put her body all on mine, rubbed up against me as she said how beautiful the marquis was, then sat back down, her leg still up against mine. She ignored me, pretended what she'd done was no big deal. She was focused on Charlotte when she asked, "How long have you two been engaged?"

Charlotte sort of smiled at the questions, but uneasiness sprouted in Jake's expression. Lines grew in his forehead. His fingers came down his roan complexion and stroked his black goatee. He did that methodical move over and over. That was his nervous-trying-to-look-cool move.

Charlotte answered, "We haven't actually set a date yet. We've talked about it, but, well, you know how it is."

Shar said, "You must've just got engaged."

"Not really." That slight smile was fading from Charlotte's face. A weariness from answering that question a million times since that ring had been planted on her hand. "We've been engaged almost a year. To be exact, a year on the twenty-fifth of this month. But who's counting?"

The women at the round table shared a womanly expression. I felt them transferring information in silence. Jake felt it. I know he did because we were communicating without words too.

Toyomi said, "I've been with Stephan longer than you've been engaged."

Silence interrupted us. In silence there was judgment.

Then Shar piled on another question. "How long were you and Jake together before he popped the question?"

Charlotte said, "Six months."

More communication and judgments in the absence of sound.

A longing was living in Toyomi's eyes.

I didn't say anything. Just chewed my turkey sandwich and let them talk. Felt like my head was in a vise grip.

Toyomi and I had been on the ups and downs. Mostly the downs. She was becoming too intense. She started off as a midnight run. Just another B.C.—booty call—to be made on weekends. A movie. Dinner. Maybe party out her way. Then some serious boot knockin' that had the neighbors banging on the walls with jealousy. Things clicked and what we had was almost a bona fide relationship.

Charlotte patted her man's hand, then got up from the table.

Toyomi asked, "Where you off to?"

She held on to her smile. "Bathroom. This is the part I hate about skiing. Standing in that long line, then having to wrestle with all of these doggone clothes while I hold myself up and try not to let my booty touch the filthy toilet seat. Moments like this make me wish I was a man, 'cause there are plenty of trees out here. I'd whip sling-a-ling out and mark me some territory."

The women laughed a naughty girls' laugh.

Toyomi stood. "I'll walk with you."

Shar followed Toyomi, saying, "I gotta go too."

The women headed toward the john, did their female bonding ritual as they strolled across the wooden walkway.

As soon as they were out of hearing range, Jake let me know that he needed some male bonding as well. The bad dreams were back. He has these nightmares that make it hard for him to sleep. He's been having them off and on for about a year now.

He sipped his cocoa and said, "It was just like the other ones, man. This time I opened my front door and saw a kid, a cute little girl, light-skinned, wavy hair, about sixteen. And she just kept following me around, looking like she wanted to bite my motherfucking head off."

Jake never curses around Charlotte. Always a gentleman in her presence.

I askèd, "Which head?"

"Both of 'em."

We chuckled. Not long or strong. Fear seasoned his laugh.

I asked, "Any idea who the girl in your dream is?"

"For a while she looked kinda like Brenda."

"Who?"

"This freak I had this thing with when I was at Crenshaw High. Man, I had forgot about her. Think she was fifteen, or fourteen back then. But, hell, that's almost fifteen years ago. I can't remember everybody I've hooked up with since then."

"Sure you're not dreaming about Brenda?"

"Hell, naw. I barely remembered Brenda, until that kid that looked kinda like her popped up in my dreams. And she had eight or nine of her friends with her. Some of 'em looked about her age. One or two might've been in middle school. Or elementary. A couple of brothers about her age, about as tall as me, were staring me down, frowning like they were about to shank me. One of the brothers was pushing a baby carriage."

"That Brenda, the one who you think that one of the girls looked like, did she do something to you?"

"Naw. It wasn't like she was my girlfriend or nothing. We just got busy a few times back in the day. It's not just her."

"What?"

"Well, all of the kids, all of 'em look familiar, but I can't remember who they are, or who they look like when I wake up. But it's the same people in every dream. I'm pretty sure of that."

I said, "But they never do anything to you, right?"

"The way they look at me, man, it scares the hell out of me. Sometimes their faces change and they start to look like somebody else, or each other. I run; they follow. If I'm in a room, they close in on me, kinda like Michael Jackson and those freak, weirdo, dancing zombies did Ola Raye in that 'Thriller' video. I run all around the house. Well, it's not really a house. I think that it's a hospital."

I said, "A hospital? You never told me that."

"I just figured that part out. Could be a doctor's office. I'm sure about that. It's white and sterile. Too much light sometimes. I can't tell, 'cause you know how dreams are all clear in some parts, then fuzzy in others."

I yawned, rubbed my eyes, and listened to the fear of a six-foot-one firefighter. I said, "What else you see?"

"This time there was a man, might've been a woman, in a mask."

"What, they're trying to jack you?"

"No, no. It's like, I dunno, maybe like a surgeon."

I waited.

He said, "Maybe not a surgeon. But I know it ain't the Lone Ranger. Whoever it was, they were dressed in black, standing there with their arms folded, watching the whole thing."

He shut down for a minute.

I said, "Maybe it's time for you to slow down and jump the broom with Charlotte."

He massaged his goatee.

After we made a few more runs up and down the mountain, we called it a day, changed into our after-ski gear, and began loading up the vehicles. Charlotte and Jake had ridden with me. Toyomi had chauffeured Shar out from Palm Springs. I dropped my skis off at my car and asked Jake to secure them in the ski racks on my roof, then walked down to the opposite end of the lot with Toyomi and Shar to help them get loaded up.

Toyomi kissed me. "Am I going to get to see you tonight?"

I said, "I have Jake and Charlotte with me. You could come by my place."

"You know Shar's with me."

Actually, this inconvenience was a preplanned convenience. I had an all-night date planned for later on. But I played along.

I gave her my warmest smile, told her how beautiful she was, said, "The important thing is that we spent today together."

"It's a lover's holiday. That's why I want to be with you tonight. Skiing is fun, but I'd rather have something, you know, more romantic. One on one."

"Me too."

"Well, when are we going to get together?"

"Maybe next weekend. But you know I have to go kick it with my momma and stepdad on Sunday. We're doing the family thing up at Coley's Jamaican restaurant."

"That's what I love about you. You have a beautiful relationship with your mother. You don't have all of those issues other men carry around. That's important to me."

Another kiss. I said, "You better get on the road."

Toyomi's face bloomed like a rose, but her eyes housed a ton of disappointment. Leaving me was the last thing she wanted to do. She let out a soft cry of distress. "I don't like this."

"Like what?"

"The geographical distance between us. Sometimes I need to see you more than on the weekend. And lately it's been more like every other weekend. Any idea what we can do about it?"

I didn't feed into that conversation. When she loosened her grip, I became busy securing her skis to her car roof. Then I let my hands stay active packing her and Shar's boots and poles into her trunk.

Over the last year, sometimes Toyomi has had the severe PMS moodswing crap. Today she was super sweet, the moods weren't swinging like Tarzan through the jungle. Under the bright skies and snow that was blanketing everything my eyes could see, she was the way I loved her to be. But in a heartbeat she'd flip out and we'd have vulgar arguments about irrelevant bullshit. And I had to be honest and ask myself if that was the kind of woman I wanted to kick it with for the next sixty years. The problem was that usually a brother didn't find out who he was really dealing with until after the morning after. After the sex has happened and the best behavior has faded.

Toyomi gave me another good-bye hug, holding me closer than Siamese twins, her short, thick fingers rubbing up and down my back. Her back was to her childhood friend. Shar raised her shades, winked, darted her tongue at me, then smiled and eased into Toyomi's brand-new Subaru.

In my ear Toyomi whispered, "Charlotte's ring is very nice."

If she only knew. Charlotte refused to make love to Jake before they got married. That was why after six months of heavy petting he dragged his blue balls over to Charlotte's mother's house and proposed. And as soon as she had that promise of forever on her finger, the morals softened and her vow of celibacy disintegrated like a cracker in boiling water. Hard to stop the sexing once the can of carnality has been opened. If her morals hadn't weakened, they'd've been married a year ago.

That doesn't make her a bad person. At least not in my book. I have a lot of love for Charlotte. She's ambitious. Speaks Spanish and works her ass off. Independent and gives Jake a lot of space. A lot of rope. I don't think I've ever heard her bitch about anything. She is the kind of woman that I'd love to be with in that eternal kind of way. Which was why I wished Jake would recognize what he has before it's gone.

Toyomi kissed me again, then finally eased inside her car.

The tires of her Subaru crunched across the melting snow and ice as she gave me that good-bye wave and those longing eyes.

# 5 Chanté

This year Valentine's Day ended up being just another day. I'd had enough of watching the women at work running to the guard's desk, then coming back with an armload of flowers, balloons, and smiles. Bragging about how their beaus were taking them to a Love Jazz festival at UCLA tonight.

That was why at noon I said enough was enough, took my butt home, and romanced myself. I picked up a bouquet of flowers from the florist in the mini-mall across the street, gave myself a nice long bubble bath, then watched my soaps while I pampered my dark and lovely skin with a much-needed facial. *One Life to Live. General Hospital.* I laughed all afternoon. It was nice to see somebody whose life was worse than mine was.

Karen and Tammy came over later in the evening; no roses for them either, so that said a lot about their love lives.

I'm a year older than Karen, but my round face and soft eyes make me look younger. My girl is only five foot four—three inches shorter than me—and weighs a hundred pounds when she is soaking wet. Maybe what I'd been through, or was going through, made me feel so small.

Tammy showed up a little while later. She's an Amazon: five eleven, one hundred sixty pounds, the complexion of Irish cream, ample breasts, golden streaks in her light brown weave—oh, I could go on and on describing that statuesque diva.

These are my girls. My sistas. My friends.

I didn't have any real food because I wasn't a culinary queen unless I was in the mood, and I wasn't, so we decided that we'd stop counting calories and order a pizza. In the meantime, I raged while we held hands and ran across Diamond Bar Boulevard to Lucky's grocery store.

Tammy was pushing the cart while Karen sashayed like a vixen and helped me pick out my goodies. Tammy's face reddened as I told her the story. Her voice had a touch of anger when she said, "His wife had his kids out at three in the morning?"

"Yes, the heifer did." I threw some apples, grapes, grapefruit, and oranges into the basket, right next to the jar of prunes Karen had tossed in. My insides felt locked up; I was so upset I knew I'd be constipated for a month. I added, "The skank was in rollers and house shoes."

Karen stormed, "That's disgusting and irresponsible. What kind of sista would expose her children to that?"

Tammy sniveled, "Please tell me he wore a condom, Chanté."

"*Huh-ell yeah.* You know I made him wrap that pickle up. And the fool didn't even snatch the jimmy off before he ran out."

I described how his rugrats were yelling like nitwits, and acted out how Michael lost his mind, was naked and tripping over every damn thing, stuttering and shaking, and we cracked up.

Karen's laughter shut off in mid-stream, and her lips curved down. She stopped in her tracks, a very dramatic move, then said, "What's wrong with this picture?"

We were heading toward the liquor section of the store, and up ahead was a tall, lean, dark-skinned brother holding hands with his tanned, blonde-haired, blue-eyed dream. She had on aerobic clothes, the kind of leotards that flossed the crack of her butt.

Tammy was putting three bottles of Asti Spumante in the basket when we saw them laugh, giggle, share a kiss, pat each other's backside, then push their baskets our way.

My eyes and Karen's eyes went toward the couple; then we looked at each other and tsked. Tammy didn't help us out in the Department of Righteousness. She actually backed off a step.

As we passed Karen said, "Hey, O.J."

The brother stopped and frowned our way.

Karen stood firm, did a slight neck thing, and said, "Oops. I thought you were somebody else, *black* man. My *brother.*"

He looked like he wanted to say something, but the Bambi he was with pulled him right along. The silver earring in her tongue clacked against her teeth when she said, "That's okay, honey. Just ignore her. She doesn't know any better."

Karen obstinately said, "Tell him to ignore the fact that skinheads up in Lancaster are still assaulting black men with machetes. Or are you helping him close his eyes and ignore that reality as well?"

The white woman was speechless.

The next thing I knew, homeboy's full lips had balled up like a fist. It looked like some mess was about to blow up, but he just shook his fat head and moved on. Back to the plantation.

Tammy exhaled like she was glad a ruckus didn't break out on aisle nine. "Karen, that wasn't necessary."

With a nod and a sigh, I agreed. "It's not like he was cute. He looks like a cross between Dennis Rodman and Shaq."

"This is Chanté's neighborhood," Tammy said. "This is where she shops every day of the week. If you want to act a fool in Riverside, then do that. But respect Chanté's space."

Karen said, "It must be an epidemic. Everywhere I look, I see that shit. At the DMV, at the mall. How can a black man—who came from a black woman—chase everything but a woman who looks like his mother? The brother has deep issues."

"You have issues," Tammy snapped, her voice barely above a whisper because a few multicultural people were passing by. "How can you go to church on Sunday, then be prejudiced on Monday?"

I answered for her, "We're Americans. That's what we do."

Karen chastised, "Tammy, you're light-bright-and-damn-near-white, so you're not going to bear witness to the truth."

Tammy's eyes said that she didn't like that joke, not at all. It went deeper than Karen's remark. Tammy never talked about her family. They live a few hours away, and not once have we met them or heard her say that she was going to visit them.

Tammy retorted, "I'm too busy trying to pay my own rent to be worrying about who's dating who. I have a life."

"That's very Republican of you," Karen fired back.

I chided, "Karen, you have a strong black man. Victor."

That was the pet name Karen had given her vibrator. Her over-the-counter, Mandingo-strong, chocolate-colored, D-battery–powered lover who had the hang time of the Energizer Bunny, but had about as much personality as a Black and Decker screwdriver.

Karen's eyes broadcast her ill feelings for what I'd said. "And since you went there, Chanté, there are a few issues I feel obligated to discuss with you."

"What *issues* do you feel obligated to discuss with me?"

She nodded, sucked her teeth. "It can wait."

A little while later, we were back at my condo. Karen had pulled out a Glad bag full of weed before the door closed.

I said to Karen, "What's up with the illegal activity?"

She retorted, "Don't worry. I'm not going to funk your place up. I need to step out for a minute and get my head right."

I surprised everybody when I said, "It's cool, this one time. Maybe we all need to get our heads right."

I looked at Tammy, checked her reaction. So did Karen.

Tammy groaned, "Oh, God. Last thing I need is peer pressure."

I called across the street to Rudy's Pizza and Pasta and ordered two medium vegetarian pizzas. We huffed and puffed and moved my oval wrought iron and glass coffee table aside, then spread out a red, black, and green Mexican blanket on the cream carpet.

I was in one of those moods where I longed for days gone by. Wanted to go back to when Now and Laters were a meal, Josie and the Pussycats were the bomb, and getting my hair wet at a water plug was better than a trip to Six Flags. Wish I could be that little girl with skin the color of C&H brown sugar who disliked boys, and loved for her daddy to tickle her until she almost peed in her granny bloomers. Kickball. Pac Man. I missed it all.

But those days were memories that colored the back of my mind, so the best I could do was get my girls to help me drag my old Magnavox record player out of my storage closet. I found my favorite music collection, funky tunes my momma and daddy used to dance to, and we pow-wowed to the sounds of an old, scratchy Ohio Players album. Did some old dances and roughed it. No glasses, drank Spumante straight out the bottle, and ate pizza out the box. This was our buppie town camping trip.

Tammy took a hit, gagged a bit, then passed the potent J my way. "Damn, I don't believe I'm doing this."

"That makes do of us." I choked. "I mean, *two* of us. Now I see why I haven't smoked any of this mess since high school."

Karen said, "Well, after your last batch of relationships, a J or two won't seem so bad."

Tammy was in salmon-colored satin PJs. Mine were emerald. Karen's, vermilion. We were barefoot, satin dolls.

We got tipsy as hell. Buzzed. Speech slurring.

Tammy leaned and swerved. "Well, I'm tore up. So I know we ain't going to Shelly's to party tonight."

I shook my head. "No can do. Last thing I need is to be in a room full of couples who're gonna be grinding on each other and sucking face."

Karen nodded. "I think we're in for the night."

I went back to venting about Michael, tried to pretend it didn't hurt so bad by making it sound like I was the winner in the ordeal.

That I was Miss Billy Bad Ass when his wife showed up on my doorstep. I tried to convince them and myself.

With a mouth full of pizza, Tammy said, "Well, don't sweat it. You still have Thaiheed ringing your phone off the hook."

Karen raised a brow. "That's a new name. Who's Thaiheed?"

I hesitated when I saw that disapproving look in Karen's tight, red-rimmed eyes. "I met him a while ago. He lives in Upland."

That culture-free desert town was about fifteen minutes east.

Karen inhaled, then asked, "What does he do?"

"He's an engineer at a Fortune 500 company in Irvine."

Karen passed me the J, then spoke in a judgmental sort of way. "This gets to the heart of what I wanted to talk to you about."

I matched her tone. "Which is?"

"You need to slow down. I hope you're not going to stop seeing Michael today, then start seeing this Thaiheed tomorrow."

Tammy horned in. "Karen, Chanté shouldn't stop living her life because of a fool. It's called moving on to the next episode."

"What I'm giving is from my heart. All I'm saying is I have nothing but love for my sister. She's a queen, of Mother Africa, and I want her to start acting like one. We were by her side when Craig did her wrong, and now Michael."

Karen meant a lot more than she was saying. In between the lines I felt my character being questioned. Miss Better Than Thou always did that. I started to feel uneasy.

I responded, "Thaiheed's just a friend."

Karen tsked. "That's what you said about Michael three weeks ago. And here's a news flash: men and women can't be friends. Somebody is always going to want to take it to the next level."

"Fine. Then help me figure out why men treat me like this, and I know I'm a good catch. I'm single, live in a condo, have a good job. Hell, my finances are straight. I have a degree. I know what to do with money. With my portfolio, I should be a black man's dream woman. *Any* man's dream woman, to tell the truth."

"This *condo* and your *good job* and that *portfolio* won't do you any good if you end up suffering from dementia in an AIDS hospice," Karen added, in a Maya Angelou tone of reason and responsibility. "Our bodies are flowers. Don't let every bee that buzzes by pollinate your garden. Your body is a temple; treat it as such."

All of this moral criticism was from the Queen of Get High.

I sniggered at that Negress, but not a damn thing was funny. My inner spirit was being smacked around right now. "So how am I supposed to know when a brother's lying?"

"Get a damn clue, Chanté. You're the stupidest sista with a degree that I know."

From my soul rose a cringe that made me tremble. *"Ouch."*

My dark eyes stared at Karen, shooting her the look that a sister gives when somebody has gone too far. The bitch had insulted me under my own roof.

The two seconds of silence felt like an eternity.

"You need to have somebody tighten you up," Tammy told Karen. "Couple of orgasms will give you a new attitude."

Karen retorted, "I can do that myself, fuck you very much."

My voice was shaking as I said, "Vibrators don't count."

"Much better with a man," Tammy sang. "One of these days you're gonna stick that thing in you and get electrocuted."

"If I met a halfway decent brother, I'd still be in a relationship." Karen scratched her breasts. "Bastards make promises, come too quick, and have the nerve to look at you like you're the one who has the problem."

"Even though he was a dog," I said with a mouth full of pisstivity and pizza, "Craig always made me come first."

"For real?" Karen's face asked me if I was lying.

I nodded once or twice. "For real. He had a slow hand."

Karen looked amazed. *"Always?"*

"Yep, always." I frowned. "And a buck-fifty dick."

Tammy raised a brow so high it looked like the arch at McDonalds. "What's a buck-fifty wee-wee?"

I used two fingers as a ruler, spread them apart to show my girls what I meant. "A dollar is six inches long. He had about a buck fifty. And a two-dollar tongue."

Tammy's eyes bucked. Karen's tongue rolled out like carpet.

I said, "But that don't make him a man."

Tammy shouted, "That makes him a mule."

I was absorbed in the bitterness of the memory. I told Karen, "I don't believe Craig asked you out."

Karen's brow rose in offense. "So, what're you saying?"

"Nothing." I tunneled my hands through my hair, shook my head. "Drop it."

The bastard had disappeared from my life, then came back without even a simple phone call, then had the nerve to ask Karen out. That hurt so bad I forgot about Michael and his bounty hunters. Well, not forgot. It was just that a new pain had muffled the other one.

Then quiet fell over us. A smothering kind of silence.

I don't know what they were thinking, but my mind was on Craig. Thinking about him was enough to break my spirit.

I met that fine brotha when I was partying with Karen and Tammy out in Moreno Valley at this club called Pinky's. Moreno Valley—Mo Val—is another one of the Inland Empire's desiccated, one-mall-for-everybody, one-club-for-black-people kind of towns. A good place to go watch tumbleweeds get tangled up. The only reason I went out there was because I heard 92.3 FM saying that KKBT was going to be out in Mo Val for a Friday night shindig.

Craig touched me, talked to me, made my heart ricochet. That feeling of getting weak all over took hold. I fell for him while Brian McKnight crooned his one last cry. I believe in love at first sight, but that's another thing I'll be giving up for Lent. Craig was tall, funny, ambitious—at least he talked a good talk—and in the Air Force, forty-five miles east of where I lived.

For a year we had dinners, sex, and movies—most of it at my expense because he didn't have any money-management skills.

The last time I saw him, it was on a Monday. We were in his stuffy room on base. After we had finished the loving, he said he was going to rent a car on Wednesday, November 11, Veterans Day, on my birthday.

"Yeah, Smoochiez," he'd said. He always called me Smoochiez. He said it was because he loved the way I kissed. Told me that my lips were so arousing. He held me. "I want to take my baby to dinner at the Shark Bar in Hollywood."

I beamed. "Mmmm. Sounds good."

"Then we can shoot over to the Shubert Theater on the Avenue of the Stars to see *Phantom of the Opera*."

I asked, "You serious?"

"Does this look serious?"

He showed me the tickets.

He gave me that crooked grin that made him look so suave and sexy. "Front and center, so close that when the Phantom passes by, you can reach up and snatch that little mask off his face."

I was so elated that when I left Craig at midnight, I floated the forty-five miles from Mo Val back to Diamond Bar.

Wednesday I took a vacation day to get myself together. I hit Nordstrom. Tried on a million outfits. Found a hip-hugging black sequin dress that had the right cleavage to pimp out my twin 36C cups. A little sumthin'-sumthin' that nobody else would have on. I got a manicure and pedicure.

I didn't know what to do, wear my hair wavy, blow-dry it and make it straight, or pin it up. I ended up putting my do in spirals that hung down and framed my face.

After all was said and done, I finished dressing a little before four. Craig was supposed to be here at four-thirty.

The next thing I knew, the sun had gone down.

Six o'clock became eight became nine-fifteen.

By then I was tired of pacing back and forth from phone to door to window, so I finally wiped my eyes and admitted to my well-dressed self that I had been stood up.

I had seen the tickets, so somebody was having a good time on my birthday. I speed-dialed Craig again, but this time there was no answer. His stupid answering machine was turned off. He always turned it off when we made love. Told me the only sounds that he wanted bouncing off his four walls was me.

I changed into ripped, dirty, baggy jeans, a wrinkled rayon blouse, and a Recycle Black Dollars baseball cap that Karen gave me. I ended up all alone at In-N-Out Burger, eating a greasy double-double hamburger and sucking on a strawberry milk shake.

It was 11:47 when I got back home. No notes on my door. The only new message on my machine was from Karen and Tammy. They were partying hard at Shelly's, and had stopped getting their groove on long enough to call and sing me a tipsy version of Stevie Wonder's Happy Birthday song.

Tammy yelled, "Enjoy the play."

Karen added, "And Craig."

"Get that freak on!"

"We'll bring you your birthday presents next week!"

Tammy yelled, "Love you!"

"Tammy, don't yell in my ear."

"Sorry."

Karen laughed, yelled, "Kisses! Love you!"

Other than that dose of friendship, which generated a half-hearted smile on my rigid lips, no messages were on my machine. They were having such a good time, I didn't want to call them and muck up their night.

11:59. Too mad to cry. Too hurt to sleep.

A couple of days crept by, and I still hadn't heard from him. I had called a hundred times. No answer, day or night. Anger turned into worry. Some of the UFO creatures from the X-Files could've swooped down and kidnapped him. He could've fallen and hurt himself. Or had a car accident and been in a coma. Or worse. If something tragic had happened, it wasn't like my name was on a slip of paper to get notified. I wanted to make sure he was okay, just to ease my mind, so I prepared for bad news as I sped back out to his dorm or barracks or whatever they called those funky little rooms on base.

The bastard had transferred to Germany. He had received his orders, his TDY, two months before my birthday.

No Dear Jane letter. No phone call. Not even a postcard good-bye. I hate it when people leave without saying good-bye.

For months, at least twice a week, I had felt his tongue moving up and down my thighs, called his name in more octaves than Mariah Carey. And let's not talk about what that relationship had cost me. I ran my Unocal card up driving all the way out there, my Visa had been used and abused, and my phone bill was sky-high.

He'd left my body exhausted, mind fried like a piece of chicken at Golden Bird. I should've seen it coming.

But I never do.

Stillness made the music feel louder. The Ohio Players were singing a sad lament of hopefulness, chanting that one day they were gonna be free from love, lies, and a lifetime of suffering.

We listened. Sang along. Mostly Tammy, 'cause she can sing her ass off. She took us there, made us live inside those words. By the time the melody ended, the air in the room was serious.

Tammy's tone was that of a hushed secret, saying this was just between us, between friends. "Let's be real."

A chill ran from my skull to my toes. I said, "Okay."

Karen nodded.

Tammy asked me, "I mean, let's be *real*. What are you afraid of, Chanté? I mean, I'm worried about you. I hate seeing you hurt so often. It hurts my heart when you're like that."

So much love was in her voice. Always so much love.

I paused. Let the song change. Now the Ohio Players were lusting over a sweet, sticky thing. My breath eased out of me, made me feel like my soul was collapsing on the wing of a sigh.

Finally, my voice was that of a nervous whisper. "Growing old alone. I'm not needy, but I like having somebody who complements my existence. I think I'm above average. My biggest fear is growing old, being alone, and being broke."

Tammy nodded like she was on the same page with me.

Karen remarked, "Chanté is so codependent it's pathetic."

My hand went to my neck, rubbed a bit. Karen's words were like an arctic wind, and its stupefying chill numbed me. That callous cow.

My voice was very weak, unsure. "I'm not codependent."

Karen fronted me hard. "What's the longest you've gone without being with a man?"

I straightened my back and leaned forward. My body was strong, but my voice was still too soft. "But love, whatever love really is, comes and goes faster than I can handle it sometimes. Faster than I can understand it. I love being in love, and I love making love when I'm in love."

Karen clarified, "Having sex."

"Okay, I love having sex. I'm not going to fake like I can sit around and not want to feel what I feel when a slow hand—a hand that's not attached to my body—takes me there."

Indignation floated in Karen's eyes. I was pushing the right button.

Karen leaned forward on her elbows, crept into my space. "I didn't ask you about love. I specifically asked you what was the longest you've been without a man."

I stayed eye-to-eye with Karen's intoxicated hostility.

Tammy did her best to increase the peace. "Change the subject. Let's play a game of spades or dominoes or something."

"My cards are on the table," Karen said to me. "I mean, damn, you gave it up to Michael. Seems like Craig was just over here. Shit, my sister, sometimes I wonder how many dicks have been inside of you."

That insult jarred the hell out of me. I warned, "Don't go there, Karen."

The heifer kept tormenting me. "Tell the truth, Chanté. How many men have been inside of your basement?"

Nobody can hurt you like a friend.

Karen's face knotted up. "Unless we're talking about the wrongful imprisonment of Mumiá Abu-Jamal, or something relevant like disabling Prop 209, I don't need to hear anything else about men. Damn men. Our existence, our reality is much more than that. At least it should be. Brothers aren't our problem; *we are our problem*. Instead of having a pity party, bitching and blaming, moaning and mourning and licking open wounds, we need to have a forum on empowerment. We need to be discussing why we keep ending up in the same damn place, year after year."

Another slice of silence before Tammy chuckled uncomfortably, "We've had too much of this sin juice. And whatever them Colombians are putting in these herbs ain't no joke. This mess'll make you loco like a mofo."

I cut off Tammy's political and peaceful move, said, "Karen, since you're giving it out, can you take some criticism?"

Her red-rimmed eyes turned on me, her tone grim. "What?"

I said, "Why don't you go back to school? Get your degree from Riverside Community College, then transfer to Cal State."

Tammy shifted, touched my arm gently. "Chanté, let's change the subject. I don't like it when y'all get hostile like this."

Karen waved Tammy's puppy-dog expression away, and I saw an inferno behind Karen's dark brown eyes. "It's all right, Tammy. So, Chanté, my friend, what's the bottom line?"

I cleared my throat. "All I'm saying is, if a brother stepped to you and said the exact same thing, didn't know where he was going with his life and didn't know how he was going to get there, be honest, would you get serious about him?"

"I do not even like this conversation," Karen snapped.

Of course she wouldn't like *this* conversation. She's been engaged three times, married zero. Her unused wedding dress is still hanging up in her itty-bitty no-bedroom apartment. That chiffon and silk memory is taking up most of the hallway space. That damn thing is suffocating to look at.

I said, "I'm not trying to hurt your feelings, Karen—"

She interrupted, "I answered your questions, answer mine."

"What question?"

"How many men have been down in your basement?"

Tammy said, "Don't be crass, Karen."

I didn't answer.

Karen hissed, went into the bathroom, closed the door.

Shame was in my peepers when I looked at Tammy.

She whispered, "What you just did was fucked up."

"I was just trying to have a conversation. We're supposed to be friends, so we're supposed to look out for each other."

Tammy said, "Do me a favor."

"What?"

"Give me a thirty-day notice before you start to chastise me. I want to make sure I have Johnny Cochran present."

Tammy went on defending Karen, reminded me that she was all alone in this world. A couple of months after she was born, Karen's daddy was killed in a pool hall fight over fifty cents. That was back in St. Louis. She has five brothers and sisters, but none of them talk, and she doesn't know where any of them are. She came from that kind of family. When Karen was in elementary school, her momma ran off with some man and sent her out here to Rialto to live with a great-aunt. Her aunt had a stroke when Karen was seventeen and died less than a month later. She ended up in a group home until she turned eighteen.

"All things considered, she's doing fine."

"But she could do better."

"One way or another, we could all do better."

I don't know anything about Tammy's family, but I do know that she has a dream beyond standing behind somebody's cash register and wearing a name tag for the next forty years.

Nope, I wouldn't go off on Tammy. She's too cool. Too real. Second, she understands me from the inside and doesn't judge me from the outside. And I don't mind loaning her money. She's trying hard in

Hollywood. I'm proud of her. She landed a major part in a CBS sit-com, but the comic who was the star was killed in a car crash right before they started taping.

Karen came out of the bathroom and went into the kitchen, took a cube of ice out of my refrigerator, wrapped it in a paper towel, made a noise like she was meditating, massaged her eyes and forehead. We made eye contact. Stared at each other. She tossed the ice in the sink, came over to me, hugged me, kissed the side of my face, then sat back down and grabbed a slice of pizza.

I spoke just above a whisper. "Sorry, Karen."

She nodded. No matter how much evil stuff Karen has ever said to me, I've yet to hear her say she was sorry. It's always me apologizing to her.

I said, "You okay?"

Karen was solemn. "Just sensitive about a thing or two."

More silence breezed by.

Karen's voice softened when she asked me, "You okay?"

I surrendered a smile. "Just sensitive about a thing or two."

The side of the album ended, so I scooted to the stereo and turned it over. Put the needle on side two.

*Stupidest sista with a degree.* I didn't have *common sense.* I'd been poked in my eye with a blazing nail. All I did was give her the same hostile love, point out her faults, and that wanna-be Erykah Badu heifer folded like a cheap picnic table.

It wasn't our first time going at it like that, and it probably wouldn't be our last. To tell the truth, to me it was childish. Sort of the way rugrats in school go at it, swear they'll never be friends again, but by recess they are buddy-buddy. That's why an hour later it was business as usual and we were watching videos on BET, laughing, yawning.

Then we were calling hogs.

I woke up in the middle of the night to the irritating sound of the scratched album repeating the same lyric: *Roller coaster of love. Say wha— Roller coaster of love. Say wha—*

My bladder screamed like a monkey set on fire. I pulled the comforter off my head, used the edge of the sofa to pull myself up.

Karen was sprawled out on the sofa, hugging my body-length pillow, her dark shoulder-length mane tangled and in her face.

Tammy was across the room on the carpet, in the fetal position, a psychedelic scarf covering her long brown weave with the golden streaks, my plaid Mexican blanket pulled up over her chest.

I tipped over, clicked the record player off, squeezed my legs tight, staggered to the bathroom, and relieved myself in the dark.

With the sound of my liquids breaking water I was dizzy, but I mumbled to myself, "The next time things are gonna be different for me. Fuck trust. Play the game the way they play the game. Play the players before I get played. From now on, heads I win, tails they lose."

# 6 Stephan

Eager. Sitting out on my car, underneath a Valentine's moon, I had been waiting almost an hour. I'd just paced up and down Town and Country Road, the private avenue inside the beige stucco condominiums called Phillips Meadow, when Brittany's red Capri hummed around the corner. Her drop top was down. Hair bouncing when she screeched into Phillips Meadows, ran a stop sign, and hit the speed bumps full force. I'd been beginning to wonder if she'd be able to make it, if she couldn't get away.

She parked in space 260, my extra spot that was underneath the pine trees and wealth of greenery that crept up the hill toward the 60 freeway, right behind my Mustang's spot in my carport. She smiled and sang, "Sorry it took so long."

"That's okay," I said. "You're looking good."

"Thank you. Happy Valentine's Day."

"It is now."

Trying to catch Brittany was like trying to capture the wind with a net. Me and Brit had a one-on-one relationship back in the day, only I made a bad choice and fucked that up. She has a man, but from time to time she's mine.

Brittany's skin is the color of a new penny, dark freckles under her light brown eyes; she's my height with her heels on.

She rustled around in her car, stepped out barefoot, threw her hose on the front seat, then put her sling-back shoes on. She moved like she was hungry for attention. I was famished. My soul was anticipating, getting aroused with the thoughts of poetic intimacy and middle of the night conversation. She gave me a deep, brief kiss, then caressed my crotch.

"Put your top up." I nodded at her car.

"Can't stay."

"What's up?"

"Tony wants me to follow him to Santa Ana so he can drop his car off at his sister's. He caught me off guard, and I couldn't think of an excuse."

"Santa Ana? All the way to Orange County?"

"She doesn't have a ride to work and won't get a rental, so he's letting her cheap butt use his car this week."

I glanced down the road, the way she'd just driven in the complex. "He's not following you, is he?"

"I told him I couldn't remember where his sister lived, so I'd have to follow him. Right before we got too close to your exit"—she laughed—"when we passed the 71 and were coming up on Phillips Ranch Road, I slowed down and let a couple of cars get in between us and jumped off the freeway."

"You did what?" I laughed.

"I'll tell him I got lost. It's dark. My sinuses were bothering me, so my eyes are blurry. I'll tell him I accidentally started following the wrong car."

"Somebody's gonna be mad."

"I'll say I'm pissed because he drove too fast, play that quiet mad role, you know. Pout like I was scared. Then he'll apologize. I'll forgive him tomorrow or the next day. He'll be happy to see me smile again."

"That sounds fine."

We kissed and groped at each other all the way up the stairs. Laughing and snickering. We stopped tonguing long enough for me to put my key in the lock, but then she grabbed my hand and prevented me from opening the door.

Brittany licked my lips, then licked her own lips. "Here."

I felt the warmth from her wanting. "Here?"

We were on my porch, a dim light overhead. Across Town and Country Road the windows in the condos of Country Park Villas faced us. Cars passed off and on. We were positioned in front of my neighbor Rebecca's front door.

"Scared?" She started unzipping my pants. I shook my head and smiled. The only thing predictable about Brittany was her unpredictability. As many times as I'd been with her, even when we were a couple, we'd seldom loved in the bedroom, hardly ever got all of our clothes off. It was always primitive and bold.

She turned around, hiked up her leather skirt, tiptoed, pulled me close, got comfortable, gripped the iron railing. I ran my hands up her side around to her front, under her silk blouse, and unsnapped her bra.

In the next heartbeat, we found our rhythm.

It was on.

Kleptomaniacs, stealing passion we knew somebody else thought was exclusively theirs.

I slapped my hand over her mouth to smother some of her moans, but I couldn't do anything about the vibrating rail. In the midst of our motions, I played lookout and lover at the same time. I stood firm. Cars drove by. My eyes glossed over while I watched bedrooms facing us, wondering if any of the darkened rooms held Peeping Toms. Intensity grew with each slow in and out, with each bump and grind. I got so turned on, became overwhelmed by the tingle in my groin, the swelling and hardening of that part of me, working my hips against her soft backside, feeling her become a moaning fire, listening to her hum out that sweet feeling, that I was too excited to care if the entire community watched us over a bucket of popcorn.

Clicking noises came from downstairs. A door opened. Heavy feet scraped against concrete. We slowed, or rather I slowed. The more I slowed, the harder Brittany pushed and grabbed.

"Don't stop," she whimpered. "I was just about to—"

"Wait," I whispered. I tried to back the limousine out of the garage, but she reached back and stuck her nails into my butt. Pulled me back inside. Again I whispered, "Hold on."

She shuddered, made a *mmmph* sound; her face glowed with orgasm.

I covered her mouth. "Shhh. Shut up."

She wheezed and panted. Then she was moving again, swirling, pumping.

From ground level came clicking sounds from two locks and a dead bolt. My graying Hispanic neighbor, Juan, walked out below. He had his gas company uniform on, a sacked lunch in his hand.

I wrapped my arms tight around Brittany, straightened her up from her doggie-style position, adjusted our clothing the best I could with her still wiggling like a worm, made it look like we were snuggling under a full moon and a cool breeze.

"Did you?" she puffed.

"No."

"Good."

We acted like we were being playful while we watched the stars. Me still inside her, throbbing and ready to get back to my sensual dance. Brittany giggled and Juan looked up when he passed, but didn't slow his stroll toward the carports.

Juan said, "Stephan, how are you, my friend?"

"Hey, Juan," I said.

*"Hola, mi amiga."* He waved at Brittany, then looked at his watch. "How are you tonight?"

"Fine." Brittany moaned.

Chills went all over my body.

"On the way to work?" I asked quickly.

Brittany leaned back and kissed me. I felt her hips, pushing back into me, sly and rotating toward her destination.

"Yep." He yawned and moved on. "They put me back on third."

"Too bad."

He waved without looking. "Still got to make that money."

Juan stepped out of sight. Brittany bent over, purred, growled, began pushing harder, aching and shaking like she was making up for the lost seconds. I moved her from the rails to the stucco walls, put our backs to the other condos. I put my hand over her mouth, smeared her dark lipstick when I tried to suffocate her sexy sounds, but she bit my hand and laughed. A quick minute later, she became rigid. Then one of her knees buckled a little bit; her eyes squinted like she was concentrating on squeezing out the last drop of pleasure. She threw her head back, bumped into mine, them smiled and let all of her inner air go free. She relaxed back into me. With her mission accomplished, I wanted to do the same. I was about to follow and match her satisfaction, but she threw her hand back and grabbed my hips, stopping me with a soft plea: "No."

She faced me, wrapped a leg around me. She loved to hold me, kiss with a passion, and steal my breath while I orgasmed. She got off on my erratic breathing. Shit drove me crazy.

A minute later, we were laughing, panting, adjusting our clothes and wiping our sweaty faces.

She tucked her blouse in. "I gotta run now."

"Already?"

"Yep." She snapped her dark satin bra back together. "Gotta go, gotta go, gotta go."

"Want a towel?"

"Nah."

"No time to kick it for a few?"

"Next time."

She fluffed her hair and put more lipstick on while I walked her to her car. More like followed her swift pace. She barely kissed me on my cheek and hopped in without a hug.

I asked, "When will I see you again?"

She winked. "I'll call you."

"When?"

"Soon."

She sped off, never slowing at the speed bumps. I watched her become smaller, listened to her four-cylinder engine fade into the night. At the end of Town and Country Road, she screeched left, fled up Rio

Rancho Boulevard. Fifteen minutes had passed since she pulled up. Under a star-filled sky, on Valentine's night, a thief in the night had been ripped off by a thief of the night. Lipstick was smeared on my hand where she had bit me. The wetness and aroma on the front of my pants was all I had to convince me that she, or somebody, had been here. This was already a memory.

Each time we did this, I never knew if it would be the last time. A relationship like this couldn't go on forever. We almost had something a few years ago, but now we were just good old-fashioned fuck buddies.

NQA, NSA—No Questions Asked, No Strings Attached.

I roamed back upstairs. My keys were dangling in the lock.

Even though I hadn't known how to tell her without coming across weak, I'd really wanted Brittany to stay. For more than just the sex. I wanted company. I needed to feel connected, to somebody who used to know me better than I knew myself. Part of me wanted to grip on the shreds of the old relationship. The forever connection we had until I let her go because I thought I'd found a better woman.

I was exhausted, but I couldn't sleep. Didn't want to dream. I had a feeling that nightmares like the ones Jake had would plague me all night long. I didn't want to sleep alone, and I didn't want to wake up by myself. I needed some warmth.

I gave up Brittany for what I thought was real love. It still feels like yesterday, but six or seven years had slipped by since I messed around and fell for Michelle. A cocoa brown–complexioned, long-haired sista who could've passed for Janet Jackson's twin sister. Well, stunt double, at least.

The sista was fresh out of Berkeley and had gotten disengaged right before we met. She told me about the relationship, how they'd basically just grown apart. As high school sweethearts they were compatible, but as adults with several hundred miles in between them, they didn't have much in common.

After I met Michelle, my attention shifted like the wind. I tried to keep my carnal account with Brittany open as long as I could, but a brother can't be in two places at the same time. I could pull it off and see two or three people on Christmas, because that was twenty-four hours and that could be worked out. The hard holiday was New Year's Eve. It had one moment at midnight.

I spent that holiday with Michelle. By that point I was spending all of my time with her. Hiking, jogging the river trail, catching movies, sitting in parks reading to each other, deciphering Shakespeare sonnets, doing all the romantic things listed in *Ebony* and *Jet* magazines.

Brittany called me one day at work.

"Stephan, you've been MIR since Christmas," she said. MIR meant Missing in Relationship. She asked, "You seeing somebody?"

Michelle felt so right, so real, so forever.

I simply said, "Yeah. I met somebody."

She paused. "That serious, huh?"

"It's getting there."

"Why didn't you say so?" She didn't raise her voice. Her tone was still sweet, mellow. But it sounded like she cared about me more than I'd given her credit for. She went on, "I'd much rather hear the truth from you than somebody else." A pang was in her voice, underneath the lightheartedness. "Let me know how it works out."

"I will."

"Stephan, six months from now you'll be calling me."

"You think so, huh?"

"You have my number, so don't be a stranger."

Back then I was living in Cerritos, thirty minutes south of L.A. That was in the early part of January. By February, Michelle had moved in with me.

The wind shifted in July, right after Independence Day.

What was predictable became unpredictable.

She disappeared on a Friday. Didn't call on Saturday.

Sunday morning she crept in with a stiff smile and stood over me and my bowl of Froot Loops. She didn't have a regular smile, but an I-hope-you-can-take-this-neutron-bomb-I'm-about-to-drop-on-you smile.

She hemmed and hawed, so I started the conversation with a hard tone. "Where have you been for the last two days?"

She shot my mood down by cutting to the heart of the matter: "Vince and I are getting back together."

"Vince? The guy you was engaged to?"

She nodded.

I swallowed my spoonful of Froot Loops. "You're bullshitting me, right?"

She shook her head.

"When did you and Vince decide to get back together?"

"I think, I mean, well, Vince, I care about Vince, and I, um, maybe might want to try and get back together with him."

"You've been in contact with him?" I scooped up another spoonful of cereal. I was surprised at how smooth my movements were, at how tame my voice sounded. "You two talked about this?"

Her eyes said that her mind was already made up. This was an FYI session. Not open for discussion. She made it sound so simple. I'd had more trouble at McDonald's making a decision between a Big Mac and a Quarter Pounder.

In a flash, I thought back over the entire relationship, tried to find a flaw, determine which moment changed what was so loving into bullshit like this.

All I could do was ask, "Okay, tell me. What did I do?"

"Nothing." Her voice cracked, lips moved for a few moments before more words found their freedom. "You didn't do anything."

She sobbed her way into the bathroom.

Something had been going on right in my fucking face. I hadn't noticed the funk because I was too busy making everything smell sweet.

Michelle hurried and packed a small overnight case. When she stopped at the door, she looked at her feet and said, "I'll come by and pick my stuff up while you're at work."

Just like that. Gone.

Three days later, she called a little after midnight. I was wide awake. Hadn't slept much since she left.

"Stephan," she said, "I need to see you."

Michelle showed up at my door in her Morris Brown College sweats. Twitching, rocking, waiting for me to signal that it was okay for her to come inside.

I said, "Come on in. It's cool."

She looked different. The kind of change a person had when something tragic had happened to them. I didn't ask what she'd been through.

Michelle stared at everything wide-eyed, like it was the first time she'd ever been inside the apartment.

"Can I sleep on your sofa?" she asked. "I just need to regroup. I'll leave first thing in the morning."

"Take the bed. I'll crash on the sofa."

By the time I made my pallet and laid down, she had changed. She stood in the doorway in my plaid pajama top. The top was unbuttoned so I could witness the rise in her breasts, her long legs.

She watched me. I watched her.

She walked over, took my hand, led me to the bedroom.

No real passion. Too much pain. Contrived lovemaking. It was hard to pretend that it was cool, because every time I gripped her hair and pushed myself deep inside her, I imagined that somebody else had done the same thing last night. Maybe only a few hours ago. She was giving me the same motions and moans she had been giving somebody else. I wasn't loving her, I was stabbing her. She accepted the pain.

We finished and lay next to each other like strangers.

I still cringe when I think about it. What was messed up was that I was unable to surrender to a good thing like Toyomi, but I could stand out on my porch, underneath cobwebs and dust that had settled into the grooves and crevices of a stucco wall, and love in the moonlight with Brittany. But after Michelle I'd stuck to safety nets.

Samantha.

I needed to get a grip on myself and realize what a good thing she was. Samantha always welcomed my noon visits, didn't reject my midnight calls. She was always happy to see me.

Two in the a.m. Still couldn't sleep. I decided I'd call her and see if she'd let me swing by and cuddle up with her. I could pack a bag and RSVP some affection forty freeway minutes away.

Her phone rang twice. An exhausted voice answered. A voice too deep to belong to a woman. I hung up. I had the right number. I'd programmed her digits into my phone's speed dialing.

That hurt. That pissed me off.

I called back. The dude answered again. Picked up and answered like it was his phone, like he had the right.

I hung up.

No need to deny what was up.

I needed a bigger net.

# 7 Stephan

Upper-middle-class Baldwin Hills was where my people lived. A mostly black but still multicultural neighborhood. I drove to my folks' two-story stucco house located in the mouth of the cul-de-sac named Don Diego. Palm trees. Exotic shrubbery. A castle-high view of planes cruising into LAX.

Once a month on Sunday we had family church at FAME, followed by a mandatory "Soul Food" day at Momma's house. Ever since she saw that *Soul Food* movie, she wanted everybody to get together at the house, for no particular reason. I guess my momma likes to keep tabs on her dysfunctional family.

The children had put up a volleyball net in the backyard, and my older brother's three teenage children—Akeem, Ronda, and Nathan Junior—along with about six of the neighbors' children, were jamming CDs on a ghetto blaster when I walked around back, following all the jubilant noises.

My chocolate, Michael Jordan–bald, goatee-wearing stepfather,

Pops, was at his grille dressed in his greasy chef's hat and ragged knee-length jean shorts with sandals and black knee-high silk socks. He was wearing the Walkman I gave him for his last birthday, listening to some old-school Jimmy Witherspoon blues, no doubt. He moved his headphones and took his King Edward cigar out of his mouth, waved at me when I walked through the gate.

Pops said, "You know it's almost Monday now, son."

"It's barely two." I shrugged. "I got tied up."

He shook his head. "You better settle down. People dropping dead left and right out there."

"What makes you think it was a woman?"

"What make you thank it wasn't? You dabbling in ho soup."

"See, you wrong. You know how far I live from here."

"Forty-odd miles. Ain't nobody told ya to move all the way out there in the middle of no-man's-land."

"My job's out that way."

"They got jobs up here. You should be up here near your family. That's what's wrong with Negroes. Everybody moves away from each other. You don't see the Koreans and the Chinese doing that. They stick together, help each other out. That's why they ahead."

"When the helicopters stop hovering overhead at night, when fools stop cruising and clogging up Crenshaw on a Sunday night, I'll move back."

"Suit yourself. That Toyomi done called out here about twenny-hunnert times looking for you."

"What she say?"

"Call her. What you thank she said? A few other ones been ranging the phone off the hook too." He ordered, "Make 'em understand that you don't live here no more, and not to be calling here every other minute."

"Yes, sir."

He said, "Dabbling in ho soup gonna catch up with you, one way or the other. I done seen many a men get they life taken away over some foolishness. Yes, indeed. My own brother was gunned down over a no-count woman."

"Yes, sir. You told me."

"But you a grown man. So you thank. Just don't brang any of that ruckus up here on my property. Keep it out of your momma's house. She done seen enough in her lifetime."

I knew he was referring to my daddy. He always did.

He had on a too-bright, too-busy Bermuda shirt that was so ugly it almost looked good over his pot belly. Barbecuing at his grille. And I do mean *his* grille. It'd take an act of Congress signed by God to get him to let somebody else barbecue.

Pops and Momma have been married over fifteen years. Might be closer to twenty. Since my younger sister is in college, it has to be closer to twenty, maybe more. In between celebrations, I've lost count. Me and Pops have never gotten along. When I was growing up, he either ignored me, or was impatient with me. Made me feel like an outcast. He never mistreated me, just didn't seem to care too much for me. Minimal contact. Few words. A lot of discipline. Momma knew how I felt about him, how he felt about me, and tried to love me more herself to take up the slack.

Momma stepped out the house, snapped out my name, and gave me her classic impatient frown. Her worn-out house shoes flopped with each quick step. She took off her reading glasses and started fussing while she rushed over to kiss me. "Where the doggone sodas I told you to bring?"

"In the car. I'll get them out in a minute." I kissed her face on her crow's feet. She lightened up when I squeezed her.

"Well, we ain't gonna be eating in your car. People are in the house as thirsty as I don't know what. Toyomi called five minutes ago and wanted you to call her when you get here."

"I'll call her. Why you got your hair pinned up?"

"And before I forget, Brittany called last night. My hair's up 'cause it's hot as hell be damned out here. I might go over to Cynthia's shop on La Brea and get it cut off next week. Might get it cut short and styled like Nancy Wilson's."

"Momma, please don't let Cynthia cut your hair."

"Why you men always want a woman to have long hair while y'all have yours all cut down to the bone?"

"Because it looks good."

"I ought to get a bald head like Jeremiah got. Now, go get them sodas before everybody dries up."

I hugged her. "Yes, Momma. Where everybody at?"

"Junior at the shop on Crenshaw. He might have to work till eight, so him and Darlene and the twins might not be coming over. You know how funny Darlene can be, and Darlene'd have to drive because Junior still got that restriction on his license from that accident when he ran into the back of that white woman. I told that boy about riding around with no insurance on that car. He can't drive nowhere but to work and those A.A. meetings. And you know how funny Darlene is about riding at night, especially coming into L.A."

My short, buffed, no-neck, mahogany-flavored brother Nathan stuck his head out the back door. He still had on dark suit pants and a white shirt. "What's up, stranger? Why wasn't you in church with everybody else?"

"Overslept. Y'all need to stop expecting people to show up for eight o'clock." Especially when I'm wrapped around some warm legs. I waved, then gave the thumbs-up. "I like the beard."

He grumbled, "Lisa said it makes me look distinguished."

"When you start listening to Lisa?"

"The day we got married."

"Nathan!" Momma called out.

Nathan cut her off. "I'm gonna send Jackie a birthday present." He was referring to our baby sister.

"On time," she added. "Y'all hear me?"

"Yes, Momma," we both sang at the same time.

"I'm going to pick up the wife," Nathan said. "I'll be back in a little bit."

"Stephan, hurry." Momma pushed me in the direction of my car. "Boy, go get them sodas before I dehydrate. I hope you didn't get none of those cheap generic drinks like you did last time. If I wanted something that tasted like water, I'd drink water."

Momma could talk forever when her children and grandchildren were at home. She always made everything more urgent than it was. I ran my hands against her salt and pepper hair as she adjusted her sky blue sundress over her petite figure. Momma could eat a horse and not gain an ounce.

Momma sashayed over to my stepfather to inspect. Pops tried to run her away from the grille by raising his spatula, but she didn't budge.

He said, "Was I in your way when you was in there making that potato salad and beans and cole slaw, was I? Now, get on back in the house 'fore I get mad and burn up everythang."

She pinched his cheek and held it. "Hurry, snookums."

"Unass me, woman," he said. "Get back in the house and make yourself useful."

She didn't move until she was good and ready.

So much noise, so much life was here.

We lollygagged awhile. A few neighbors dropped by. But my attention was on my mother. On the woman who had allowed her second husband to stomp on the memory of my father and cart us from Mississippi to California. My loving momma, Faye Ann.

Four children, two fathers.

Momma loved both of our dads enough to last a few lifetimes.

In front of other people I've had to tolerate her talking about Daddy.

She said he was too pretty, too conceited. He felt more husbandly obligations to the women he wasn't married to than the one he was. That last sentence was a quote from Momma's mouth. What she's told anybody who asked about my daddy.

I didn't tell what happened after that day Daddy left with that high-yellow woman on his arm. The following day when we came home from school, Momma was sitting on the porch in a rocking chair, holding a revolver in her lap while she watched a pile of gassed men's clothing burn in an oil barrel. As the fire died, she dropped in more brand-new shirts and ties and casually went back to rocking.

Nathan asked her where Daddy was, but she just sat in the chair, rocking and staring out into the yard. Each time a car or somebody looked like they were about to turn in, she cocked the gun and sat up. I thought she was getting ready to shoot a robin or a sparrow or something. You know, go hunting down by the old creek like we'd do sometimes. I kept my lips tight and watched Nathan so I'd know what to do. He talked to Momma for about thirty minutes, then gave up. We stood in the quiet for about ten minutes, when all of a sudden she turned to us and smiled. "Hey, snookums. When y'all get home?"

Some days stay colored in your mind. The next morning I woke before dawn, just in time to see Momma leave the house, dressed like a queen and smelling rosy, the way she did on Sunday mornings before we all went off to church. She was distant, in a trance like she had been the day before on the porch.

She didn't come back home until late in the evening, after the sun had gone down and the cicadas were clacking in the trees. Me and Nathan had caught some june bugs. We had tied sewing thread to their legs and were making them fly in circles when Momma walked up, smiling and too normal. So normal that she scared us. We were about to make a break for the woods on the other side of the road. She picked us up and danced while she kissed us, cooked dinner, fed us cookies and cream after dinner, helped us with our homework, sang us to sleep.

We found out what happened through word of mouth—and in a Southern town the word spread faster than a hurricane. When she got up that day at the crack of dawn, she had pressed her hair, styled it, dressed in her best and brightest clothes, and headed the five miles up to Daddy's job at the lumber yard. She stood out in front and sweetly called him out. He stepped outside, madder than hell and swearing words hotter, followed by his best friend, Jeremiah Mitchell. All of their coworkers stopped working and dashed over for the show. Daddy was holding hands with some full-figured, long-haired Creole woman.

Momma's voice was ice. "You ever coming back home?"

Before she could get an answer, the high-yellow lady walked out and threatened to break Momma's neck for coming to see her man. Spat on Momma.

Momma took two steps like she was leaving, then pulled her revolver out of her purse and started firing.

People tripped over each other, jumped, dove for cover behind piles of wood, trees, each other, and mounds of dirt. Six rounds, reload, six more rounds. She didn't hit anybody. Didn't really try because we all knew she had the skills. She shot at Daddy and his woman, let them know who they were dealing with.

Daddy's woman was so afraid, she snatched my old man in front of her, and they tripped. She fell, pinned him down. The woman prayed, screamed, kicked, cried, apologized.

Momma aimed at her. "I don't appreciate you spitting on my dress like that."

Screams, prayers.

Then she turned to my daddy.

Screams, prayers.

Momma said, "Be glad you the father of my children. Just be glad of that."

Without flinching, Momma fired five rounds into his brand-new Buick Wildcat. The engine, radiator, the lights, tires, and what windshields she didn't shoot out, she broke out with bricks.

When she finished, she looked at him. "Don't come back."

He asked, "What about my clothes?"

She pointed the gun at him.

He backed away.

Momma sighed. "Y'all have a nice day, ya hear?"

A few days later, Jeremiah Mitchell showed up at our house. Momma greeted him at the door with her revolver drawn, not saying a word. He just eased down two big bags of groceries on the old, rusted lawn chair we had on our porch, tipped his hat to her, then walked to his car and slowly drove away.

Once a week, real early in the morning, we'd wake up and bags of food would be between the screen and front door. If it had ice cream in it, he'd tap on the front window with a coin so we would wake up and put it in the icebox. And we had an icebox, not a refrigerator. By the time somebody got to the door, he'd be pulling off.

One morning Momma caught him outside putting two bags in the swing. With the gun pointed, she snapped, "Tell him I don't want his charity no mo', and take this back to him."

"Missus Griffith," he said. "He ain't the one who been sendin' you the supplies."

"Who sent 'em then?"

"They's from me, ma'am."

"Why?"

"I don't mean no harm by it," he said through the ragged screen door. "But, Miss Faye Ann, I know you going through some hard times, and I done seen what Duke done put you through. Firsthand. He out there living sweet with that no-count siddity excuse for a woman, and you done fell on hard times. I can't stand to watch you and them boys suffer on the count of his foolishness."

"Why?"

"Because I always thought highly of you, Miss Faye. Always have, always will. As far as I could see, you always was a real good woman. I know you ain't got none of your people in these parts to help you out. Now, I 'pologize if I done 'fended you, but I just try to do right. If you don't mind, ma'am, I'll be on my way now."

Momma invited him to stay long enough to stand and drink a cup of coffee. We saw more of Mr. Mitchell, every now and then coming by in the afternoon or evenings, bringing her this or that, running her here or there. Fixing this or that.

Almost a year after that, I woke and he wasn't in the living room, but his car was outside. Momma's bedroom door was closed. It hadn't been closed since Daddy left. I tried to peep through the keyhole, but she'd put tape over it.

At first I didn't care for this new man in our house. But I began to look forward to his car being outside. Got used to him taking me and Nathan for a ride every now and then. Got used to the laughter coming from the other side of Momma's locked door.

Still, I missed my Daddy.

Momma and Mr. Mitchell married. He adopted us and changed our last names from Griffith to Mitchell. Eight months later, my sister Jackie was born. The next year, Jeremiah Junior.

They tell me that trouble caught up to my daddy. He did a midnight run north, kept running until he landed in Canada. That was the last Momma heard of him before we received a death notice in the mail. Cirrhosis of the liver.

I never talk about it, but that family history hasn't been easy for me to deal with. I didn't want some other man to be my daddy. I didn't want some strange man coming in our house trying to tell me right from wrong.

# 8 Darnell

Our phone rang, jarred me out of a dreamless slumber.

Dawn woke up and rumbled, "What time is it?"

I glanced through the darkness. Red numbers glowed on the digital clock. I said, "Few minutes after three."

Dawn cursed. "On a Monday morning? Somebody better have died, calling here this time of the friggin' morning."

The phone was on my side of the bed, so I picked up. I left the sleep in my tone when I answered, "Hello."

A husky voice spoke up, "It's me."

"Jake?"

"Yeah." He sounded frazzled. "I wake you up?"

"Three in the morning. What you think?"

"Damn. Sorry. I didn't look at the clock."

"Don't worry about it."

Dawn sat up for a moment. "Everything all right?"

I told her who it was. She made a frustrated sound and pulled a pillow over her head.

Jake said, "I pissed her off, huh?"

"Don't worry about it," I told him. Dawn mumbled a few words, told me to take the phone into another room so she could get her sleep. I headed for the office. On the way down the hallway, I asked him, "What's up?"

His voice vibrated, had a disturbed tremble. He said, "Dreams. Those dreams again."

His chills came through the fiber optics loud and clear.

"You at the fire station?"

"Glad I ain't. I wouldn't want them to see me like this."

It sounded like a bad connection. Clicking was in the line. The crackle was soft, barely audible, but it was there.

I lowered my voice and asked, "You with Pamela?"

A beat passed before I heard his ragged breath, then his words: "Not tonight. I'm out your way in Chino."

"At Charlotte's?"

"Yeah."

I asked, "Where's your Florence Nightingale?"

" 'Sleep. She pulled a double at Pomona Valley Hospital."

I cleared my throat, sipped the glass of water I had left on my desk, sat down. I said, "Those crazy dreams are back?"

"Yeah. Every time I close my eyes, that Stephen King shit starts up. Man, I didn't mean to wake you, but I just have to talk to somebody when those dreams come down."

I told my friend, "Slow down. Everything's all right."

"Them fucking dreams are getting worse. Shit, all of them fucking bastards were chasing me through the fire station this time, up Crenshaw and shit."

"Any of 'em look familiar?"

"Yeah. And most of 'em were coming out of the ground, popping out of coffins."

Jake sounded weary. The nightmares he'd been having were starting to wear me down as well.

But he was my friend.

I clicked on a light, left it at a soft setting.

He gave me the details.

It made no sense to him. Made no sense to me.

I told him, "Charlotte's phone is still clicking."

"It was okay a while ago when I called home and checked my messages. It started that clicking then."

"Speak up. Your volume's low."

"I switched phones two or three times, and it didn't make any difference. She said that GTE is coming out next week. They might have to replace some wiring."

"Where's she?"

"I got me some of that, and she rolled over and went to sleep." He puffed. "She's getting better, but still, a bad performing and a nonfulfilling woman drives a man to stray."

"You know you ain't right."

"If I could get her to pump her narrow ass and talk dirty like Pamela, hell, I'd marry her tomorrow."

"It should be more between you two than sex."

"It is. Just not after midnight. If I hadn't stayed at Shelly's so long, I would've went to see Pamela. Should've. She does some booty-licking shit that drives a nigga crazy. But after Charlotte rides off to work in the morning, I'm going to hook up with Pamela. Now, she always answers the door in satin and silk, runs a brotha's bath water, rubs him down, ain't got no hang-ups, tries to turn a brotha out every time she sees him. I try to do some real shit with Charlotte, and she gets all tense."

I said, "Work with Charlotte. Buy some Kama Sutra books, check out some erotic movies and watch 'em together. Maybe try some nude yoga, give each other oil massages."

"Man, Charlotte is almost thirty years old. What am I going to look like trying to teach her what she should already know?"

"You're gonna look like you love her as much as she loves you and wanna share some serious gifts. It should be different with your fiancée. Make it spiritual. Hell, I thought what you liked about her was that she hadn't been around the block."

"Yeah," he sighed. "I know. Be careful what you wish for."

I said, "People pray for rain, then complain about the flood. They pray for it to stop raining, then bitch about the drought."

"I know you ain't trying to lecture me."

"Charlotte's not the same as Pamela. What's the point of holding on to Charlotte if you keep on doing wrong?"

Jake sounded better. The phone was still clicking, but his voice was clearer. I wasn't getting through to him though. I wanted to say that nobody could gamble forever and never lose. Coming from me, it would sound sanctimonious. I'd be the first to admit that I'm a creature of contradictions. In one way or another, we all are.

He said, "I hope I get some sleep before Tuesday."

"What's going on Tuesday?"

"I'll be co-teaching a class on fire and emergency medical services. I can't function on no sleep."

"Get some rest."

"Still shook up." Jake sighed. "Man, sorry to wake you up, but these dreams, man, damn, they mess me up so bad, I have to talk to somebody for a few minutes."

He was searching for somebody on this earth that he could trust with the weight on his soul. And that was either me or Stephan, but Stephan didn't take too kindly to middle-of-the-night phone calls from Jake. The talks about dreams left bed-hopping Stephan just as rattled.

Most of Jake's anxiety crept back as he said, "There's another part I ain't told nobody about."

"What?"

"This part scares me more than anything, because it makes it feel so real."

"What part you talking about?"

"One of 'em looked like my momma, another looked kinda like my daddy."

Carefully I said, "Maybe you just miss your folks."

His voice softened. "Fifteen, almost sixteen years. God bless 'em. I miss 'em all the damn time. Man, Momma made the hell out of a pineapple cake. She made me one for every birthday. Made it from scratch."

"I know that's right."

"Yeah. Miss 'em all the time."

Jake's parents died in a fire at their house in L.A., off Crenshaw on Sixth Avenue. That was when he was fifteen. When he was tall and skinny. Before he buffed up. Bad wiring set their house ablaze. The bars on the window turned their home into a deathtrap. His daddy had barely saved him, dragged him out on the lawn, then he went back for his mother.

I said, "Your folks were good people."

He chuckled out some sadness. "They had their problems."

"Everybody does. I understand that better than anybody."

"One girl that had me cornered, I swear she looked like she was Daddy and Momma put together. She had their features."

I closed my eyes and pretended we were two old men resting on a wooden porch down somewhere where peace came to roost, imagined that off-and-on click on the phone line was the sound of crickets chirping, talked to Jake for a while.

It sort of reminded me of the old days. Law school, marriage, and a ruling wife like Dawn, all of those things have made me unavailable for my friends for a long while. But whenever I was stressed, Jake was always a phone call away.

But I had to go to work in the morning, so I couldn't stay up all night and baby-sit him. After he'd calmed down enough, I babble-babbled a few more minutes, then got ready to let him go.

I asked him, "What you going to do?"

"Call Pamela."

I said, "You ain't worried about Charlotte waking up?"

He chuckled. "She sleeps like a log. Don't even wake up to go pee in the middle of the night. Pamela pees about ten times a night. That pisses me off because she wakes me up every time. But she likes to get some in the middle of the night. Then there's Charlotte. Man, after Charlotte gets to sleep, don't even think about waking her up to make love."

"Maybe you should try. Kiss her neck."

"It wouldn't be worth it. It takes her too long to get off. I just don't feel like working that damn hard. Pamela don't take but a hot minute. If I'd have known that Charlotte was gonna sleep the whole time, I would've gone by Pamela's tonight."

We talked about five more minutes.

When I pulled the covers back to crawl into my bed, Dawn said, "Tell Jake not to call here this late anymore."

"He was having some problems."

She repeated what she'd just said.

# 9 Chanté

Thaiheed is cute, heading toward handsome. He has an oval-shaped head, keen gray eyes. Hypnotic eyes. Conservative haircut, thin mustache. Stands about five foot eight, so he's barely taller than I am, meaning I have to wear flats when we go out. Nice runner's build. Doesn't eat pork. Spiritual.

The brother knows how to treat a woman. He took me to lunch three times in a week. When the weekend rolled around, he called and told me that he was going to the Shark Bar in Los Angeles. So me and my girls—Tammy and Karen—wanted to get out of the Pomona valley, and we went up there to hang out in a place packed with Hollywood celebrities.

Thaiheed was so glad to see me. I told him that a sister was feeling a little parched, hadn't eaten since lunchtime, and brother man pulled out his plastic, paid for everything: dinner, drinks, dessert, even bought me a rose.

Tammy peeped at the bill. "*Dayum*. We did some serious damage up in here."

Thaiheed smiled. "I got it covered."

Karen leaned in and asked, "Are you going to at least leave the tip?"

I shook my head. "Hell, no. Let the man be a man."

Karen's broke ass didn't argue. Neither did Tammy.

After the financial and emotional loss I had from dealing with Craig and Michael, I had a new agenda, so that was the way it had to be. From here on out, my coin purse was glued to my hip.

As the old cliché goes, one thing led to another. He was convenient and a gentleman. By the end of March my body needed maintenance before I spontaneously combusted with stress, so I spent the night with him. It was a decent exercise in sexual healing, not the best. He was a little too tame for my liking. After that he was ringing my phone off the hook. The next weekend he drove me south and rented a five-star suite at an exclusive beach club down in Del Mar that faced the Pacific Ocean. We hung out in San Diego all day Saturday. Blouses, shorts, silver jewelry, shoes—I had him buying me everything my eyes touched.

That was cool. For a hot minute.

Something negative always happens, usually when I get comfortable. Some asshole always has to spit in my Kool-Aid.

The next weekend I was at his apartment in the city of Upland—a two-exit municipality in the Inland Empire—and his phone jingled in the darkness. His answering machine came on, the volume loud enough to hear the outgoing message. Before the beep, he crawled over me and snatched the cordless phone off the hook. He stretched, yawned on his way into the hallway, said a few things. I was tired, but his mumbles and my curiosity woke me up. He clicked the phone off, cursed. Scared me. That anger was a side of him I'd never seen before.

I pulled my face out of the pillow. "What's wrong?"

"That was work. They need me to come in ASAP."

My eyes went to the digital clock on his oak dresser. It was barely six in the a.m. I put my hand over my mouth, covered my morning breath. "At the crack of dawn?"

He tried to explain to me that one of the Encore systems had crashed and they needed him there to bring it back on-line.

"I hate it when they do this," Thaiheed complained. "They couldn't get in contact with those white boys."

"What you expect? It's early on a Saturday morning."

"Something told me not to answer the phone."

It didn't bother me, not in the least. I had other things I wanted to do today anyway. Somebody I wanted to see had finally called. More like finally called back. So all Thaiheed did was save me from having to make up an excuse to raise up out of there.

I didn't mean to be tacky, but I said over a yawn, "You get time and a half on weekends, right?"

"Yep." He calmed down. Gentleness was back in his face. "Time and a half on weekends."

"Mo' money, mo' money, mo' money. Boeing just laid off eight thousand. Be thankful you're not in that group."

"I need to learn to be more positive like you."

With extra dollars going into his pockets, I let him know what I thought he should do. "Save all of your overtime money and put it into a separate money market account. Maybe use it as some investment money. You know, expand your portfolio."

He checked his watch a couple of times, glanced out the window. "What's up with you today?"

"Might drop in on a couple of open houses. I want to see what people are selling their condos for in my complex."

"Thinking about selling?"

"Thinking about trying to get a bigger place, then rent mine out. If it's in the same complex, it'd be much more convenient for managing. You could help me with some of the handy work."

"Cool."

He kissed me, tried to ease on me before I was warm, but that wasn't about to happen. I made him slow down, put my palms on top of his head, and pushed his mouth down south, held him hostage down there and let him gurgle in my goodness for a few minutes.

Yes, when it comes to oral love, it's better to receive than to give. 'Cause you know I wasn't giving up nothing but hard times and bubble gum, and I was fresh out of bubble gum.

After he left, I wasn't sleepy anymore. My body was still tingling, aching to cross that threshold one more time, so I touched myself, massaged slow and easy, and made that explosion come and go over and over. Doing that makes me feel so guilty, maybe because I always feel like I'll get through squealing and squirming and look up and see somebody gawking down on me.

I showered, cleansed my face, lotioned, let my hair flop, put on one of his CK T-shirts, and sat in the wicker chair in his living room. I played a Nina Simone CD I'd brought along with me, clicked the Magnavox on, and watched the *X-Men* cartoon while I worked on my second bowl of cereal. A commercial came on. Then the phone rang. I debated whether to answer.

It could be Thaiheed.

I picked up on the fourth ring, just as the answering machine clicked on. After the outgoing message finished, I cleared my throat, tried to sound like a man, and said, "Good Morning."

"*Bee-yatch!* What 'cha doing answering my eff'n phone?"

I laughed. "Tammy, you know you can't disguise your voice."

"Scared you, didn't I? Tell the truth."

"I knew it was you."

Tammy laughed. "Girl, *X-Men* jamming this morning."

"Sister Storm got it going on. You call Karen?"

"She's getting dressed. She has to be at Mervyn's when they open."

I asked, "You alone?"

"Bobby came over last night, helped me with my French. He's in the bedroom, in a coma."

We talked, laughed.

The phone let out an abrupt high-pitched squeal, put terror in my heart, and I screeched. "Stupid answering machine must still be on."

Tammy said, "Hope we didn't say nothing juicy."

I thought about it for a moment, then couldn't remember what we had talked about. And I didn't want to take any chances. My conversations were my conversations.

I yelled for her to hold on. The tape was rolling and recording. My machine was different, and I couldn't figure out which button to push.

I picked up an extension and asked Tammy.

"Push the dot," Tammy shouted. "The circle."

I did. The machine stopped. The shrilling did the same.

I asked, "What did we talk about?"

"You know I can't remember anything that's not in a script."

"I say anything about calling Craig?"

She sounded surprised. "When did you call Craig?"

"I didn't."

"Oh, God. You're dating Mr. Disappearing Act again?"

I wanted to kick myself for letting that slip. "I should erase the whole thing."

"Might erase something important."

"This is true. What, then?"

"Push the arrows that point to your left, make it rewind, then push the one single arrow pointing forward to make it play."

The machine clicked, whirred, did the Cabbage Patch, and when it clicked to a halt at the beginning of the tape, it began to play.

> *Hello, Thaiheed. It is me. Uh-mmmmm. I'm cooking fish. If you're still hungry, I'm still hungry. For you. I know I do trip, but you do trip, too. Talk to you. Bye.*

"Whoa." I jumped off the bed. "You hear that?"

"Sister wanted to fry a lot more than some fish, too. Move your ass closer to the phone and turn the volume up."

> *Click, beep!*
> *Hello, Thaiheed, this is Albert Cohen from work. We're making up the weekend schedule, and per your request, you don't have to work any weekends this month. Karl Banks will cover for you.*

My eyes fell on his wrinkled sheets. And I thought about the damp sheets I was left to wallow in the morning Michael had been reclaimed by his wife.

Tammy's soft voice asked, "You all right?"

"I'm cool." I sucked my teeth. "This ain't nothing new."

> *Click, beep!*
> *It's time for you to freak me, baby. Thaiheed, this is Peaches,*

*your one and only love. I'm at my sister's house. So pop down here and we can spend quality time together. See ya.*

Tammy mocked, "His one and only love?"
I humphed. "Thaiheed has had a busy week."

> *Click, beep!*
> *You know what? I'm right about sick of this mutherfuckin' answering machine of yours. Every time you should be there, it's after nine o'clock. But I'll tell you what, when you walk your ass in the door and you listen to this, pop in and call me.*

I said, "Peaches is a trip."

> *Click, beep!*
> *This is Chanté. I was calling to see what—*

I said, "That was yesterday."
"You okay?"
Quite a few freaky-deaky messages played before my trite conversation with Tammy.
I sighed, "At least I know why he left this morning."
"Why?"
"To keep somebody from coming over. Probably Peaches. After the phone rang, he broke his neck getting ready."
"Chanté, I want you to do something."
She told me how to get Thaiheed's machine to display its retrieval code. Tammy was as scandalous as a politician. I gave her the three-digit code, then she called back and used the sequence, made sure she could play his messages. Made sure *I* could play his messages.
I decided not say anything to Thaiheed. I'd use the code, play back the messages that his verbal pen pals were leaving day and night, and see what was up. It didn't matter, not that much. Bluntly, I like Thaiheed, but I didn't care enough about him for this to hurt.
Time was wasting, though, and I had to get ready for my secret rendezvous. I was going to see Craig Lying Ass Bryant.
I'd tracked him down on base, called him until he finally returned my call, and last week he promised to meet me at the food court in Ontario Mills around noon. I demanded to know why he'd abandoned me like he did. It fucked with me because I didn't know, so I told him he owed me some sort of answer.
I showed up at the meeting spot at eleven-thirty.
At two he still hadn't arrived.

Once again he stood me up. That didn't surprise me.

I kept calling. I knew I should've gave it up, turned it loose, but hell, no. Brothers always got off too easy, so a sister had to make them rue the day we were born. I was gonna harass him until I got some kind of an answer.

So, in the meantime and between time, I kept my eye on Thaiheed. Kept dialing his digits and listening to his messages. A couple of times I deleted the ones I felt like deleting.

Over the next week, I heard messages from Peaches, thanking him for a good time, then calling back mad as hell because she couldn't track him down. Some sista named Nina thanked him for taking her to hear Dr. Khallid Abdul speak on black unity somewhere in L.A., then called back with that sensuous and desperate voice wanting to know if they were going to get back together, or if that was a one-night thing.

They were blowing up his answering machine, and he was blowing up my pager, leaving message after message on my answering machine. And oh, after I saw how easy it was to rip off his messages, I trashed my answering machine and subscribed to Pac Bell's message center. Yeah, I'm learning a little every day.

# part two

## Long Day in the Desert Sun

# 10 Stephan

Damn.

It was three in the morning, and my damn phone was ringing. Like the R&B singer Joe said, a true player never gets a chance to sleep. I didn't have to click my copper-colored lamp on and check my caller ID to see who it was. After knowing Toyomi for over a year, I recognized the frenzied pitch of her ring.

"Stephan." Toyomi sounded sweet, amorous. "Love you, baby."

Outside my window a car hit the speed bumps on Town and Country Road.

Toyomi said, "Are you there?"

"Barely," I groaned. Sleep was all over me. I asked, "What're you doing up this early, or late, or whatever?"

"Missing you like crazy. I'm sitting here, watching HBO, eating a candy bar, lonely as hell, thinking about you."

"Damn, baby. Three a.m. Can't sleep?"

"No." She hesitated. "Steph, this bed is cold without you."

"I know. Wish I was there. What are you wearing?"

"Nothing. Just you on my mind. Baby, we need to talk."

Damn.

No matter how a brother ducked and dodged, every relationship got to a point where a *talk* was needed. Where shit got muggy, the funk couldn't be denied, and had to be clarified. Boundaries needed to be redefined. Or just defined. When it was time to be upgraded from coach to first-class or get the hell off the plane and find another airline.

"Where's this going?" she wanted to know.

"Where's what going?"

"Us. Our relationship. We've been spending a lot of time together, and I want to know, you know, if there is going to be a commitment or if you're just going to keep dropping by when it's convenient for you."

It was early on a Sunday morning. An unseasonably hot Sunday morning that felt like the middle of July. Toyomi was mad because I was supposed to drive out there yesterday, but I called her and canceled after I checked my calendar and saw I had put blue circles around those days—reminding me those were her period days. I didn't need a PMS weekend where any spark could start a fire. I could have a bad time by my-damn-self. So I dipped into my bag of excuses and told her I had a lot of things to take care of in L.A.

Her tone stiffened. "Oh. You didn't mention that before."

"Slipped my mind."

"What you have to do that's so crucial?"

I told her that the Los Angeles Black Business Expo was going on this weekend, and I wanted to make some contacts. "It's time for me to pass out my résumé."

"Uh-huh."

"I heard through the grapevine that some of the smaller commercial companies in Culver City, Los Angeles proper, and Santa Monica are looking for experienced programmers."

"L.A." A lingering pause. "The opposite direction of where I live. That would be another hour west of where you live now."

"Forty-five minutes."

"We'd be three hours from each other, in no traffic."

"Well, yeah. But I'd be near the beach. Near my family."

"You don't like your family."

"Just my stepdaddy. I love Momma, my brothers, and my sister. Don't exaggerate."

Her tone had shifted like a cheap house during an earthquake. "So, you're considering Los Angeles?"

I said, "Just checking out my options."

"When did you decide to check out your options?"

"When my job gave me a slamming review, told me I was at the top of my game, then dropped me a lousy three-percent increase."

"Well," she paused and chewed, "that's pretty much standard."

"It's bull. That was an insult, like getting a demotion for doing excellent work."

Toyomi sighed. "Have you looked for anything out this way?"

"It gets up to a hundred and twenty degrees out there in the summer. And that's in the shade. Cactus shrivels in that heat."

"It cools off at night."

"Yeah, it drops to a hundred and nineteen."

"So, you haven't even considered looking out my way?"

I groaned, closed my eyes, massaged my forehead. How could anybody pick a scorching desert over a cool beach, a calm place where the temperature drops at the start of every golden sunset?

She wasn't letting go. "You left L.A. because of the drive-bys and helicopters flying overhead all night."

"Ear plugs and a bulletproof vest would take care of that."

"Not funny, Stephan."

For the last three years I'd been designing firmware for a small company in Brea, writing ancillary programs for testing out flight hardware. Brea is south of Phillips Ranch, down the 57 freeway in Republicanized and used-to-be bankrupt Orange County.

She kept at it. "So you might move back to L.A."

I let that drift into the land of the rhetorical.

She chewed on her candy bar, slow chomps like the chocolate had become gooey and thick, paused like she was hoping for an invitation to move toward the Pacific Ocean as well.

She proclaimed, "I don't like what's happening between us right now."

"Well, what's wrong with what's happening between us?"

"Nothing's wrong. I don't want to waste my time."

"We're not wasting our time."

"You know how much I love you. I've told you that. It's just that you live all the way in Pomona."

"Phillips Ranch."

"What's the difference?"

"Twenty thousand dollars a year."

"Not funny, Stephan. I'm ninety miles away in Palm Springs. And these long distance bills are just too high."

"Toyomi," I said, "I've asked you to get on-line, and we can do instant messages and chat over the Net for free."

"Typing messages back and forth is so impersonal. I have to hear your voice. I at least need that much of a connection. But you should see my phone bill, Stephan. I've spent over a thousand dollars just calling you in the last six and a half months."

"Well, my phone bill is high, too. You've put quite a few collect calls on my tab. Every now and then you'll call collect. Then your buddy Shar calls out here for you, collect."

Toyomi said, "That's a lot of money we could spend on other things. Vacations. We could use that money on more ski trips, like to Vail and Idaho. Or to the jazz festival in Maui. Anything instead of giving all of that money to the phone company. Not to mention that my rent is five hundred ninety a month and your mortgage is over eight hundred."

"It's after three. Can we talk about this in the morning?"

"Five more minutes. Let me give you something to sleep on."

I exhaled in the darkness. "Okay. Let's wrap this up."

"If we put our money together, that's almost thirteen hundred. If we were smart, we could be living in a three-bedroom house with a garage and backyard for less than that."

*We?*

She kept talking. "I need to see you during the week, baby. I want to hook up with you. I'm not saying get engaged or nothing like that. Just maybe we should live together for a while and see which way this is going. Spend some time together. It's been over a year, and we should move to the next phase."

Phuck. Capital P-H-U-C-K.

That's not on the blueprints, ain't in the plans, and due to my reluctance to commit one way or the other, the conversation went downhill quick, fast, and in a hurry.

Long story short, Toyomi introduced me to Mr. Dial Tone in midsentence. I groaned out the stress she'd blanketed my peaceful night with, stared at the erotic art by Merryl Gaye that decorated my cream-hued walls. I was waiting for the phone to ring because I knew she'd call right back. Ten minutes went by. I rolled over and over and ended up staring at my rotating black ceiling fan. I watched it go in circles, eased back to sleep. Thinking. In a relationship where you love 'em but you still need to let go. That's where I was. Coasting. That's exactly what I'm doing. I'd call her after I woke up and, you know, find the right words and phrases and justifications to rationalize continuing what we had, keeping it the way it was. To keep it coasting.

By ten in the morning, sunlight was gleaming, but my vertical blinds were still drawn. I was in my queen-size bed, on top of my green and gold comforter, flicking through the channels on my twenty-six-inch TV trying to find a decent college B-ball game to watch, when the phone rang. My caller-ID said the number was unavailable. I picked it up right before the machine kicked on.

"Morning," I said.

"Collect from Shar to Toyomi," the operator said.

"Uh-huh," I mumbled with a lot of attitude. That's another reason why my phone bill was hitting the ceiling.

The operator asked, "Do you accept the charges?"

"Yeah."

"Hey, dude," Shar sang with her usual melodic flair. "Put Toyomi on the phone for a minute."

I said, "She's not over here."

"You're joking, right?" she said. "Yesterday morning after softball practice she said that she was driving out there, and she wanted me to call her."

"Call her for what?"

"She wants me to meet her. She saw a coat at Burlington Coat Factory, and I wanted to get a Nike sweatsuit. She said you found one for under fifty bucks."

"Yeah, I did," I said, then told her, "Toyomi's not here."

"Hmmm. She wasn't home when I called. Her car wasn't in her stall when I drove by. Maybe she's on the way to your place."

Discomfort eased into my chest. I was wondering where she could be. Felt a twinge of jealousy. She was happy with me, but she was unhappy at the same time. It didn't take a rocket scientist to figure that out. At three a.m. she was lonely and frustrated. Maybe if she couldn't be with the one she loved . . .

Then I remembered the days I had circled on my calendar, and that insecurity went by in the blink of an eye.

I brought to light, "She always calls before she comes over."

"Why she have to call?" Shar laughed. "That's silly, considering you two been hard-core dating since the day you met."

"Well, if she drives out here, it'd be nice for me to be here, don't you think?"

"Give her a key. She could come and go—"

"Anyway," I cut her off. If I gave Toyomi a key, half of her life would be here by nightfall. More like the other half, because she already has a stock of books and plants and clothes here and there. This territory has been well marked. I diverted the conversation. "You and Chuck back together?"

"Nope." Shar sighed like she was lonely and brokenhearted. "And we never will be. I've been interested in somebody else for a while. Very interested."

I asked, "Who's the lucky brother?"

"I saw him Valentine's Day."

"You were with us Valentine's Day."

"I know."

We paused.

Her voice went soft and sweet, with a side of innocence. "It don't matter. He's seeing somebody."

We talked about other things. She told me she'd broken up with Chuck because he wasn't consistent. She'd call him in the middle of the night and he'd be on the other line. That pissed her off because he'd never let whoever he was talking to go, meaning she was at the bottom of the scrotum pole.

She'd tell me something about Chuck, I'd tell her something about Toyomi. I clicked the TV off, and for ten or fifteen minutes we were yawning and comparing notes on bad relationships.

"Toyomi wants to move in with you?" She laughed like the idea was absurd. "That girl is not leaving Palm Springs."

"Yep," I said. "She called me at the wee hours of the morning with that nonsense."

"She is sprung."

"I know."

"What you decide?"

"Shar, look," I said. I tried to explain that looks attract me to a woman, but personality and character are what keep my head next to her bosom. Toyomi was a knockout, but there was more to beauty than having more breasts, thighs, and legs than a bucket of KFC. I confessed, "It's hard for me to feel relaxed around her. Feels like I'm walking on eggshells."

"Stephan, we must be twins. That's the same way I felt about Chuck, the same questions I had been asking myself."

"I feel for you, Shar."

"Then what?" she asked. "Toyomi's my girl, but she does get on my nerves from time to time. It's different with me because, thank God, I ain't the one sleeping with her. How long do you think you'll be able to handle Toyomi's funky attitude?"

I sat up and said, "It'll play out. We'll eventually go our separate ways. That's the way they all go, I guess."

Shar quieted and cleared her throat. "Stephan, would you creep around if you found somebody easy to talk to, easier to get along with, somebody you had something more in common with?"

"Why you ask?"

"Stephan, when we went skiing—I shouldn't say this . . ."

"Don't be shy."

Shar said, "You're a good-looking man."

"You're a beautiful woman too."

All those winks she had passed on over the months, all that touching when nobody was looking, had come to this. The recipe was on the table. A secret love was in the making.

It felt so wrong, but I felt so human. So carnal. This flesh and blood was craving uncharted flesh and blood.

I wanted her to make the first *real* move. Maybe all of the moves. Maybe open the deal I'd be more than anxious to close.

I felt vibrations, the sounds of somebody coming up my stairs. Shit. I had a feeling that was Toyomi. Enough time had gone by, so she could be here right about now.

I told Shar to hold on while I checked.

Through my peephole I saw Rebecca, my neighbor. She's an older sista. Her head was in a scarf. She had a housecoat on. For the sake of good Negro images, I hoped she hadn't been running around the neighborhood dressed like that. I hadn't heard her go down the stairs, just felt the vibrations from her tiptoeing back up.

I rushed back to the phone.

Shar said, "Let's stop acting like nothing is going on between us."

"Okay," I said. "Five minutes of honesty. Agreed?"

"I was hoping for more than five minutes."

"Whatever you need."

"Stephan, I feel the energy. I see the way you look at me," she said intensely. "You bump into my breasts, touch me."

"I see you peeping too." My voice dropped an octave. "Can't help but notice how you stare."

"Really?" She giggled. "Thought I was being discreet."

"Really."

"God, Stephan. I never told you, but your cologne turned me on so much, I went out and bought some for my ex-knucklehead."

"Did you?"

"I'd give anything to see you. Alone. For a while."

"Sounds good to me."

"So," she released some air, some tension, "what're you going to do about Toyomi?"

"What are you saying?"

"Toyomi's my girl. I want to see you, but I don't want any conflict. If this got out, it would mess it up for everybody."

I agreed with that one hundred percent. "Any suggestions?"

Her voice lowered. "I'm getting wet thinking about you right now, so what do you suggest?"

"Wet?"

She said a bewitching "Like a bowl of soup."

"What flavor?"

"Come find out."

My voice was thick, filled with seduction. "Really?"

"I'm not joking." She moaned, like she was warming her love up. "Come see me. You can come this morning, then leave later on this afternoon. If you park in my garage, no one will ever see your car."

"I'd love to park my car in your garage."

"You just don't know how bad I want you to."

We shared childish laughs.

I said, "Damn. I feel the same. Hmmm."

She made a sexy, orgasmic sound, put some melody in the air when she said, "I'll unplug my phone and be all yours. Then when it's over, we pretend it never happened."

"What if it's better than we think it will be?"

"If it's half as magical as Toyomi says it is, 'cause she describes it to the teeth, tells me that you have some serious skills, then, hell, I'll have to have some more of that wand."

Flaming butterflies were flying circles in my belly. My hand slid down between my legs, held on to my penis. It was getting stiff, tingling. Leaking the beginning of love juice.

"Stephan, baby, come see me. I got my nerves up to say all of that, so please don't leave me hanging from a tree of shame."

I closed my eyes, felt so fucking weak with desire. "When?"

"Mmmmmmmm. What's good for you?"

"I'm free all day."

She hummed, then asked, "What about Toyomi?"

"What about her?"

"Would you feel guilty making love to me?"

"Does it matter?"

"I mean, if you love her, I don't want to, you know."

"I don't love her."

"Mmmmmmmm. It's almost ten-thirty."

I said, "I could be there by noon."

Shar grew quiet like she was considering, contemplating our proposed indiscretion. Already I envisioned her long, soft brown legs wrapped around me, those hips rising and falling while I grooved in and out of her valley, made her shout, her svelte frame clad in something sheer, sinful, and sexy. The thought of us made me warm. So damn warm. Felt my hardness coming on strong. It was time to shit, shave, shower, and get there before she changed her mind.

Crying came from nowhere.

Wails.

Shrieks like somebody was in the last moments of labor.

I was rattled, damn near shouted, "Shar?"

"Stephan," another voice bellowed. "You ain't shit."

"Toyomi, that you?"

Toyomi snapped, "Who the hell you think it is?"

Shar snapped, "You're on a three-way, Stephan."

I moaned a long, drawn-out *"Shit."*

"Toy," Shar shouted, "I told you, I told you, I told you. This no-good nigga dragging you around—"

"Shar," I exploded, "shut up! Toyomi, don't listen—"

"—got your life on hold, waiting for him to come through—"

"Stephan, I don't believe you said some mess like that—"

"Toyomi, baby, please! Don't let her play you like that."

"—and he don't give a damn about you. And you know if he was trying to screw me, he's already screwing somebody else."

"Toyomi, wait. Baby, listen—!"

"Stephan," Toyomi cried. "I don't ever want to see your ass again. I'm burning every damn thing you left over here."

"Toyomi—"

"Quit begging, you stupid bastard," Shar snapped out. "Toyomi, hang up and I'll meet you at your town house."

"Toyomi, baby, hold on, wait, I'm coming over."

"Now you wanna come over?"

"We need to talk."

"If I see you, I'm gonna fuck you up fuck you up fuck—"

"Toyomi," Shar crowed in that adamant tone. "Hang up. *Now.*"

Toyomi shrieked. I think she dropped the phone.

Shar yelled Toyomi's name. Toyomi didn't answer.

I hung up, kicked the covers to the floor, fought off the trembles, yanked on some dirty gym clothes, and grabbed my keys. The next thing I knew I was on the 60 freeway, eastward bound.

I tried to gather my thoughts, find a notion of what I should or could or would say when I got there. Think of what to do to keep Toyomi's roughneck cousins from kicking my ass into the middle of the next century. Nothing came to mind.

But I knew what I'd do if I got my hands on Shar.

*Fuel level is low. Fuel level is low.*

Mad as hell. Nauseatingly dry heat blew through my window across my face. I was so pissed I had driven for thirty miles without so much as a glance down, didn't realize I was riding on empty until the warning voice was activated, and then I was so deep in thought I barely heard it. I saw the gas hand was sleeping on the other side of empty, the digital warning said I had five miles to go. Up until then I had been cruising at a little over 90 m.p.h., whipping from lane to lane like a psychotic speed racer, passing everybody on the freeway like they were standing still. I was on a mission.

*Fuel level is low. Fuel level is low.*

First I saw a Mobil, then a '76 sign standing taller than the sky-high palm trees in the distance. I jumped off the freeway in Riverside at the 3rd Street exit, saw an Arco AM PM on my right, and pulled into the lot.

When I stopped, I realized I didn't have my wallet.

Mustang was on empty.

No cash, not even a dime in my ashtray.

Broke as a joke.

Thirty miles from home. Not enough gas left to get back to Phillips Ranch. Definitely not enough to drive seventy more miles to Palm Springs.

I backed up to two Pacific Bell pay phones under a tree and used my calling card to phone Jake. Had to put a finger in my ear because the traffic blaring from the freeway was as loud as thunder. I could hardly hear myself think. No answer. Same thing with Darnell. I paged both of 'em and put in 9-1-1, then waited an hour for somebody to call back. Nobody did.

Hot asphalt. Burning oil. The kind of heat that rose and gave the illusion that there were puddles of water in the road.

Heat was screaming at me.

Laughing.

Cursing me.

Fuck Palm Springs. I had to get out of here before I lost my mind.

Samantha was always reliable. I called my dependable one. She wasn't home. Had to leave a message.

Damn.

I couldn't remember Brittany's pager number.

Pops would tell me that it served me right to suffer.

Double damn.

I parked and waited it out in the desert heat.

# 11  Chanté

Thaiheed wanted me to meet him for breakfast. He'd been calling, paging, calling. Getting on my last nerve.

We were hooking up at BC Café in Claremont, ten minutes from my crib. A moms and pops eatery where the food was always slamming, so the place was packed from opening to closing.

Thaiheed was in jean shorts and a tank top, waiting out front along with about thirty other starving people. He pulled his round shades off and did a double-take when he saw me.

He blinked and said, "Chanté?"

"You expecting somebody else?"

"Damn. Look at you."

"What do you mean?"

"Your hair is all bushy . . ."

I nodded. "Sexy like Lisa Nicole Carson's do."

"And it's lightened . . ."

"That it is. Good for you, you're two for two."

His eyes were all over the new me. Everything had a meaning. The golden color of my hair was that of spring, when things changed. My orange and red sarong was as radiant as the uncontrollable fire inside me. A tattoo of a butterfly on my shoulder represented my evolution, my breaking out of my cocoon.

His eyes were patrolling all over me. The brother was about to drool on himself. "Your dress—"

"Something wrong with my sarong?"

"It's kind of revealing."

"Negative. Not revealing, *uninhibited*." I put some ethnicity, some real flavor in my words. "Problem wit dat, partner?"

"You seem so different. You've changed."

"Negative. Not changed. I've evolved."

He complimented me on the ten silver bracelets on my left arm. He'd bought them for me down in Tijuana, but I guess he'd bought so many presents, he couldn't keep track of what he bought for whom.

He said, "You've been hard to catch up with."

I pushed my lips up into an oh-well smile.

Minutes later, I was chowing on blueberry pancakes and home fries when my pager hummed. It was in my purse. Thaiheed didn't notice. I excused myself to the ladies' room. It was Craig calling.

I stayed in the shadows and made a quick phone call. I'd been trying to reschedule a meeting for weeks. He said today was the only day he could see me. Bastard was dodging me and still playing games.

I sashayed back to the table, told Thaiheed, "Thanks for the snack."

"You leaving?"

"I'll get back to you later."

He shifted, took a few breaths, looked upset. I didn't care. I'd been checking his answering machine. He was with Nina on Friday, saw Peaches last night. Thaiheed's a silly rabbit who needs to learn that tricks are for kids. He never erased his damn messages. His ego probably loved to replay the voices swooning over him.

Thaiheed said in a rush, "Let's kick it. We haven't been together in over two weeks."

I put my hand on my stomach, cringed. "Cramps."

The waitress put the bill on the table, left the tab in the center, in the neutral zone. I slid the invoice over to Thaiheed. I took out my lipstick and started freshening up my face. Wondered what Craig's first reaction would be when he laid his eyes on the new me. Wondered what my reaction would be when I saw him. My nerves were bubbling in the pit of my belly.

Thaiheed asked, "Want to catch a movie or something?"

"Bad cramps. Bad, bad cramps. I'm about to die over here."

Craig wouldn't meet me out this way, so I had to make a forty-mile journey out to Mo Val. In the heat. I'd rather head toward Manhattan Beach instead of roasting in Montclair. Hell, by the time I made it to Mo Val, I could be on the sands of Redondo Beach sipping on a tall glass of lemonade.

I needed to go east, but Thaiheed made it to his truck before I could get out of the lot, was riding right behind me, so I had to drive west and fake like I was heading back toward my crib. Damn. That meant I had to take the long way and add an extra ten miles to my trip.

But that gave me time to think.

The world I was living in, well, I could wrap my ass up in a sarong and get tattoos from my arched eyebrows down to my golden toenails, but that wasn't going to change what was inside me.

Wouldn't change my heart.

I guess what I'm saying is that it takes a whole lot of energy for me to pretend that I'm somebody else.

Hold on a sec.

I smell something.

About fifty minutes have gone by since I ditched Thaiheed. I'd changed from the 10 to the 57 and was zipping out the 60 freeway, doing eighty. I crossed the 215 freeway, so I wasn't far from UCR— University of California at Riverside.

Something's on fire.

My car started shaking and coughing and gagging like an old man with emphysema; it lurched like it was trying to throw up some bad Chinese food. It slowed down, and my stomping on the accelerator and screaming *Go stupid car go* didn't help, not at all. Everybody and their momma was hopping out of my lane and buzzing by me so fast. Fumes shot from every which-a-way, sounded like everything underneath the hood was falling out.

Traffic was in every lane, and I could hardly see the road.

My poor old buggy was about to explode.

I managed to talk my red car into limping toward the next exit. By then it was steaming, jerking like an epileptic trying to do the Humpty dance. When I finally made it into an Arco parking lot right off the freeway, my car collapsed right in front of a green car and blocked some brother in.

I don't know what the brother thought of me when I jumped out, but I know what he saw: a frowning woman with a wild, uncontrolled, Bohemian hairstyle that jutted out about two feet.

I snatched off my shades, ran to the front of the car, and cursed out that inanimate object, flapped my hands because I was flustered, then struggled to get the hood open. The damn thing was so hot I had to snap my hand back. Then I screamed because I thought I had broken a nail. I shook my head. Me and machines.

While I was doing my pain dance, the brother stepped out of his car. Brought his mad and greasy face into what had to be the dry heat of hell. He moved toward me like he had road rage. I cringed, glared him up and down, checked out his wrinkled T-shirt over those biker shorts. The closer he came, the more my brown eyes widened like that woman's did in the movie *Psycho*.

I scurried back, gave him room.

"Excuse me." I said that with a blend of panic, fear, and anger. "Do you know anything about cars?"

He checked his watch, stared east toward Palm Springs, ran his tongue over his teeth.

Then he sighed, nodded.

Minutes went by.

I said, "This heat is making me feel like a french fry under a McDonald's heat lamp."

He hadn't said a word since he started mucking around. I watched him sweat, wipe his head, and maneuver around under the hood of my poor car. I wondered where he was from. The plate on his car had a black Crenshaw Motors frame, so he had to be from way out in L.A.

He mumbled something.

I asked, "What's wrong with it?"

He fanned vapors out of his face, poked around here and there. He did that again and again. Made me nervous.

I fanned myself, bit my lip. "What's wrong with it?"

"Hold on a sec," was his tart response. I hardly made out what he said because he mumbled like he had a speech impediment.

"What are you doing to my car?" I asked.

He stood up and wiped the sweat from his forehead. His face softened up a bit, and for a moment he had a boy-next-door appeal. He said, "I thought maybe you broke a belt."

"Did I?"

"Busted radiator hose."

"Damn diggity damn." I groaned. "Busted, huh?"

"Yep."

I asked, "Is busted worse than broke?"

"Sometimes."

"I don't have to get a new engine or nothing like that, do I?"

"Nope," he mumbled. "You have tools in your car?"

"Uh, no," I said. "Why would I?"

He walked toward his car. "I have some."

I peeped at my watch, then looked at the pay phones.

Mr. Mumbles took his time about walking to the trunk of his car. My roll-on deodorant was draining with each drop of sweat. I wanted to step underneath the shaded area for a moment, but then I'd feel like I was acting ungrateful. I didn't feel comfortable with Mr. Mumbles. One thing I did know for sure: at some point he'd try to get my phone number. I was already thinking up a fake name and a wrong number.

I checked my watch.

He peeped over the trunk of my car and mumbled something.

I said, "What?"

"Are you in a hurry?"

I dragged my hand across my hair. With this heat, my scalp would be peeling like Corn Flakes before I got home. I said, "Sort of. I was supposed to meet somebody for breakfast."

"Call him and tell him you're gonna be late."

"Who said it was a him?"

"Then call *somebody* and let them know what happened."

He slammed the trunk, moseyed past me, stopped in front of my car, dropped down a handful of tools and a jug of antifreeze.

I asked, "Are you a mechanic?"

"Nope. Software. I design software."

I tsked. "An engineer."

He shook his head. "Nope. Not an engineer. I design software."

"Well, you sure you know what you're doing?"

He didn't answer. I think I irritated him. I backed off. Minutes passed. Mr. Mumbles motioned for me to come over by him.

He said, "Let me show you what happened."

I didn't care, so long as it got fixed, but I went over.

He pointed. "Rip in your hose. Not big. I could duct-tape it and that might hold you until you made it to where you could get it fixed."

I reached and touched the hose, faked like I knew what he was talking about. He bent it and made the wound more obvious.

I asked, "Expensive?"

"Few bucks."

I bit my lip, smeared my chocolate lipstick all over my pearly white teeth. Last thing I needed was another bill.

I asked, "Hard to put on?"

"Clamp, a couple of screws."

"Will a mechanic charge a lot to fix it?"

"You're a woman. He'll overcharge you."

I swayed from side to side, wiped away the dampness on the back of my neck. Confronting Craig would have to wait. I fretted at the possibility of the car getting too hot and melting the silver duct tape before I made it back home to Diamond Bar.

I asked, "If I buy it, can you put it on for me?"

He stood up and spied around for a moment. A row of lines came across his damp forehead. His mouth creaked open like he was just about to answer when the pay phone started ringing.

"Hold on a sec." He ran toward the phone booth.

I was about to yell to him, but I stopped. Stopped and watched his broad back and round butt, his calf muscles flexing and releasing as he jogged. I mumbled, "Damn, partner."

Sweat rolled into my eye. My makeup was oozing down to my chin. So much for looking cute as a button. Karen lived right up the street, less than two miles away, but I knew she wasn't at home. She was on her feet behind a cash register at Mervyn's, slaving away the weekend.

Enough was enough.

I reached into my car and snatched out my purse.

"Soda?" I yelled at Mr. Mumbles and pointed toward the mini mart. I wasn't sure if he heard, so I did the sign-language move, mimicked like I was drinking while I walked backward.

He lowered the phone long enough to wipe the sweat from his face. "Yeah. Get something with no caffeine."

Beggars sure are choosy. I asked, "Chips?"

"That would work."

Him smiling made me feel at ease. I should've smiled back, but it was too hot to waste energy. Besides, if you smile at a brother, he thinks he's in like Flynn.

Inside, I savored the coolness and took my time. It felt like I was being watched. In fact, I knew I was. I glanced up and saw the big security TV-screen-thing that had me and everything I did on it. There were a baker's dozen people in the store, but the camera was focused on me. The only black in this building in the boondocks. A big red sign over the top of the screen read SMILE. I flipped it off. I pulled the juice out of the freezer, rolled it over my neck and arms and breasts. Mr. Mumbles was still yakking on the phone. I bought an Arizona Kiwi Strawberry and an Arizona Mango, searched for something with low-fat, couldn't find a damn thing, so ended up grabbing a bag of Ruffles. I hate depending on people for anything. But moments like this were when a sista like me needed a man with strong hands around.

Back at the car, I gave him the Kiwi Strawberry and chips. He gave a shamefaced expression and said an uneasy "Thanks."

"Waiting for somebody?" I asked, and opened my Mango.

Seemed like I was talking to myself. But then again, there wasn't a wall to shelter the noise from the freeway, plus we were facing the off-ramp. The street behind us had endless traffic. He probably didn't hear me.

I asked, "You don't work here, do you? Stupid question. If you worked here, you wouldn't be using a pay phone."

"Ran out of gas." He blinked out of his trance. "That was somebody I paged earlier, trying to get him to come rescue me, but Jake is up at Magic Mountain with his fiancée."

"That's at least three hours from here."

"I know. Want a chip?"

That was when we actually looked at each other. His almond-shaped eyes were attractive. Curly eyelashes gave that part of his face some sensitivity. I have a thing for eyes.

I took a chip, then said, "You ran out of gas?"

"Left my wallet. I'm broke and stranded."

"Let me buy you some gas for helping."

He thought about it. "Only if you let me pay you back."

I smiled. "Nope, that's not right."

"It'd make me feel better." He almost smiled. "I mean, you don't have a major problem with your ride."

I pointed at my sick-mobile. "Can you put the radiator hose thingee on for me?"

"I'll tell you what. We'll do it like this: hook me up with three dollars' worth of gas, a loan. Then I'll run you to a parts store and get you a hose *thingee* and put it on for you."

*Fuel level is low. Fuel level is low.*

When I heard the car warning and looked over at his gas hand, I felt a helluva lot safer because I knew he wasn't lying.

"You know, you shouldn't let your car get below a quarter tank," I said. "I read that in a book when I was at the dentist. It said something about it can mess up the engine."

"I know. I've got a bad habit of riding around on E."

"You better get Triple-A."

He laughed.

Cute smile.

Very cute smile.

And those thick eyebrows were definitely a plus.

He pulled up to the self-service pump, and I sashayed inside and handed the attendant my Visa. Mr. Mumbles was pumping the gas before I made it back to the car.

I smiled. "Put in ten dollars' worth."

"We made a deal for three."

"Already paid for."

"Then I owe you ten."

"No."

"Yep."

"If you insist."

"Thanks."

"You're welcome."

He let his windows up and turned his air conditioner on full blast. Lord, that sixty-degree breeze felt better than a head-to-toe Swedish body massage. All I needed was a big cup of raspberry lemonade from Hot Dog on a Stick and I'd be in my own corner of heaven. I smiled with the sensation, relaxed, and flipped the radio from station to station, went channel surfing. Outside of oldies on 100.3, hip-hop on 92.3, and jazz on 94.7, he had R&B stations 102.3 and 103.9 programmed in his box, and those were black L.A.-based stations that didn't get picked up out this way, so he must live out west in the urban areas.

I hoped he wasn't a rapist, or one of those fools who liked to hack people up and leave body parts in ten states. He did have duct tape, and rapists use the hell out of that shit.

But Mr. Mumbles seemed cool.

My mind turned to Craig. Wondered if he'd already left. I shouldn't go see him, but I had too many unanswered questions. Too many open doors that needed to be closed.

Out of the blue, I asked Mr. Mumbles, "You ever break up with somebody and leave without saying good-bye?"

"What?"

I repeated my question and waited to see if he would answer me this time. Guess I was reaching for a man's perspective on my female problems. Daddy had never told me it would be like this out here. Didn't tell me about all the lies and back-stabbing. But my people were cut from a different cloth.

Mr. Mumbles finally answered, "Not that I can remember."

"I take that as a yes."

"I've been in relationships that faded into the sunset."

"Faded into the sunset. I take that vague answer as a manly yes." His answer pissed me off, the lack of forthrightness, but I didn't let it show. I said, "Why do people do that disrespectful crap?"

He mumbled, "Don't know. A coward's way out."

"Plain old shysters."

He shrugged. "I guess."

A red light later, I said, "Well, I believe in closure."

"So, you're late for a date with closure."

"Yeah. No. I was going, but I don't know."

He told me, "You're going."

"How do you know?"

"You've checked your watch every other minute."

I said, "You've been checking your watch quite a bit too."

A moment passed.

I asked, "And what has you so distracted?"

No response whatsoever. I hate it when men do that shit, ignore a woman, answer when they feel like answering.

At Super Kmart, while he was getting the hose and radiator fluid, I strolled down the aisles, picked up a cherry fragrance to hang from the rearview mirror. His car smelled fresh, like wild cherries, so that made me want my car to smell good too. I browsed through the seat covers, picked up a nice cream-colored pair that was on sale, but I tossed them back when I read they were imitation sheepskins.

"Imitation?" I said to myself. "What is a fake sheep?"

Mr. Mumbles came strolling down the aisle, holding a black hose and a yellow jug of antifreeze.

He checked his watch, said, "Ready?"

"Yep." I checked mine too. "That's all I need?"

"Yep."

I followed him. Watched his backside the entire time.

Back at the service station, the sun had moved a little more, so the amount of shade had dwindled. The two short palm trees near the street didn't have enough shade to cool off a housefly. I stood in the handicap parking space and watched him work, knowing I wouldn't remember a damn thing he did. The heat from the blacktop was creeping up my legs, all across my butt.

He took the busted hose off, cut the new one down to size.

I went in the mini-mart for a second, came back, put another Kiwi Strawberry in his reach, then sipped on my grape slurpee and stared across the lot at the only patch of shade. The sun was dancing on top of my head. I wasn't wearing sunblock, so my flesh had been beat into the Land of the Sunburned. My panties stuck to my butt, and I tried to wiggle them free. Didn't work.

He asked, "Why are you shaking like that?"

I fanned myself. "You wasn't supposed to see that."

"I saw it. Why don't you wait in the mini-mart?"

I dabbed my nose. "I'll keep you company. We can talk."

He said, "Okay. Talk while you sweat for no reason."

I fanned myself. "Why don't you talk first?"

" 'Cause women talk the most."

"That was sexist."

He added, "Especially black women."

"And that was racist."

He countered, "No, it's not. Women are conversational to the nth degree. You're better communicators. Am I lying?"

"Sexist, racist, and feminist. I should be offended. Especially since you think black women talk too much." When I said that, he stopped working. His brown eyes passed over me, head to toe, then toe to head.

Immediately I asked, "Why are you gawking at me like that?"

He asked, "What nationality are you?"

"What do you mean, what nationality am I?"

"At first I thought you were Mexican, but you don't have an accent. That pretty much rules out Puerto Rican too. You could be East Indian, but since you don't have a dot on your forehead, I doubt it. I could be wrong."

"Negative on the Mexican. Double negative on the Puerto Rican. I'm black like you."

"You might be black, but not like me."

"Well, seventy-five percent anyway."

"That twenty-five percent of whatever else you have hanging from your family tree is showing today."

"That twenty-five percent is American Indian. How could you even look at me and think I was Mexican?"

"Who said I was looking at you?"

"I saw you looking at me."

"If you saw me looking, then you had to be looking at me."

"I wasn't looking at you."

He asked, "Aren't a lot of Mexicans derived from Indians?"

"Derived?" He was getting on my nerves. "Some Mexicans are derived from Indians. But I'm not related to any of those Mexicans. Or the ones that are derived from Spain either."

"I didn't say anything about Spain. Mexicans derived from Spain are more fair-skinned. You're not fair-skinned."

"I'm not dark-skinned either."

He said, simply, "Never said you was."

The little patch of shade across the lot was looking better than a beach of jet black sand.

He wiggled the new hose in place, said, "You got quiet."

"Didn't want to be a woman and talk too much."

"Sounds like I pushed the wrong button."

"I was just trying to be civilized and talk."

He said, "We can talk. You start the conversation."

I asked, "What kind of woman do men want?"

"That's a switch."

"You're no good at picking a decent conversation."

He responded, "And you are?"

"Answer me, please. But we don't have to talk if you don't want to."

A second later he replied. "Generally speaking?"

"Yeah. Generally speaking."

He thought a sec, then answered, "That special perfect one."

I laughed. "That's a Chanté Moore song."

"You kinda look like her."

"So, you think she looks Mexican?"

"She's mixed with something."

"You're a trip."

He said, plainly, "Chanté's beautiful."

I wrinkled my brow when I heard him say my name. "What?"

"Chanté Moore's beautiful. I saw her in concert in Hollywood. Epitome of fine. Still remember that red dress she had on. Seems like she had a good personality to boot."

I chuckled at his observations. "And you think I look like her?"

He didn't add to the vague compliment, if that was a compliment. All he did was pick up the yellow jug and pour some in my car's radiator. Made me feel transparent in more ways than one.

Mr. Mumbles wiped his forehead with the back of his hand, left a black streak all over his face.

He kept on, "Hair. Body. Face. A brotha would like to find it all in one place, but it's scattered everywhere."

I didn't hide my disgust. "Typical."

"What's typical?"

I told him, "Stay shallow and keep fantasizing, partner."

He repeated, "Oh, so I'm shallow?"

"Maybe. Time erodes everything that's beautiful. What about the parts of a person that are closer to the soul?"

"Uh-huh."

"I'd like to meet somebody who has intelligence, caring, spirituality, and morals."

"Now you're the one fantasizing."

I fanned myself. "No, I'm being real."

"So, you'd date an intelligent, caring, spiritual, ugly man."

As I laughed, I felt moisture stains growing underneath my armpits. My panties were flossing the hell out of my butt. If I didn't know better, I'd say the heat and sweat had made my thong shrink. It felt damn tight. Too tight because when I took a step, I heard a squeak.

He asked, "Why are you wiggling like that?"

"You weren't supposed to see that."

"I did."

"Watch the car, not me, please."

He asked me, "So, outside of wiggling in place, what are your bad habits?"

"You mean in a relationship?"

"Okay, in a relationship."

I shifted, asked him, "Why?"

"Okay, don't answer. You're the one who wanted to talk."

"Trusting too soon," was my answer. I'd pretty much tell him anything. This was like a candid conversation on an airplane with someone I'd never see again. I asked, "What're your likes?"

He said, "Walking in the rain, kissing, cuddling, dancing."

"Sounds pretty physical. Dislikes?"

"Cauliflower."

"I meant about a sista. What turns you off?"

"Chronic halitosis."

Again I chuckled. Something about the distant vibe between us didn't feel so distant. I didn't like that. Not at all. I was talking too much. Another one of my bad habits. I told Mr. Mumbles, "It's too hot to be having this conversation."

"Some of your ancestors worked in this heat. They sweated under the hands of a man with a whip and sang spirituals."

"Gee. I never would have known. Thanks for the history lesson." I wiped a stream of sweat from my neck. "If I'd been a slave in Egypt, Georgia, or Mississippi, I would've been a house nigga, underneath an air conditioner, watching BET."

He said, "I'll be done in a minute."

My pager went off twice, back to back. The first beep was from Thaiheed. The second was Craig.

I went to the pay phone, called Craig, told him I was having car problems, and asked him to meet me out this way instead.

Then I went and cooled off in the mini-mart.

Ten minutes and a bottle of Sparkletts water later, Mr. Mumbles waved for me to come back out. Everything was in place. I started the car up, and he inspected and quadruple-checked whatever he had done and made sure everything was running.

He said, "No leaks."

"Looks good."

Mr. Mumbles put the half-empty fluid container in my trunk, threw the old hose into a trash bin, then went to the men's room to scrub his hands. When he came back, his shirt had greasy smudges from where he'd rubbed up against the hose. Blotches were under his eye from where he'd wiped his face.

Bit by bit, my eyes fell on his left hand.

On his finger.

The one next to his pinky.

No ring.

No visible line.

I thought, Damn, he's nasty as hell, but he's cute.

He'd be too short for Tammy. But not Karen. I could hint that I have a single girlfriend who lived three minutes away. Karen needs to retire Victor the Vibrator and hook up with some flesh and blood. He seemed pretty cool. Nice, dependable eyes. A real job.

Maybe he was exactly what Karen needed in her life.

But then again, if his résumé was as real as he pretended, Karen might not be the kind of woman he needed in his.

"Well, everything should be okay now." He said that as he scratched his face. His short, dirty nails came down over his damp flesh and made an abrasive sound on his stubble. "New radiator hose. Your car is filled with fluid. You're good to go."

"Yeah." I sighed in relief. "It's running a whole lot better. It felt real rough earlier before it started smoking."

"It was low on fluid. Get your oil changed. It's pretty dirty. The Jiffy Lube sticker in your windshield says you're six hundred miles overdue for your service."

"Okay." I was unquestionably surprised. "Thanks."

"No, thank you. Without your help I'd still be stranded."

"Guess we helped each other."

With a smile he agreed. His warm expression made me respond with a softhearted grin. The kind that reminded me that underneath the makeup and sweat and frustration, I was my daddy's little girl. I didn't want to respond to him that way, but I couldn't stop it. His eyes brightened and the corners of his lips curved up a little bit more, made him look like his mother's little boy.

I said, "Kismet."

"What's that?"

"Destiny. It means inevitability. Like our being here at the same time was meant to be. So we could help each other."

Now that was my shot at flirting. Very subtle, but it was out there.

He nodded. "Kismet. Cute."

And that was all he said. Oh, well.

We grinned at each other and said nothing for a moment. That shy feeling was all over my musty body. He broke away from our moment of chance, from our split second of amusement and satisfaction, drifted over to his car and crept inside. After he started his engine, he waved and gave me the thumbs-up.

I gave him the same signal of positivity.

He drove away.

I didn't know his name.

He didn't ask for my number.

Nothing off color. Not one of those mumbles came close to resembling an indecent comment or unwelcome advance.

A nice guy. A real nice brotha.

He hopped on the 60, heading back my way. I was right behind him until we crossed the 215/91 interchange, was about to speed up and try to catch him, maybe pull up beside him and thank him again, then ask him to pull over at Market Street so I could get his number. But Mr. Mumbles sped up and exited at Rubidoux Boulevard. He zoomed away and left me in the two lanes of heat and smog. I thought he was long gone, but I saw him zip right back on the freeway, heading in the opposite direction. I should've hopped off and tried to catch up with him, but I let it go.

Craig was waiting for me.

# 12 Stephan

My mind wouldn't let it go.

In my head, Palm Springs was still screaming.

The air conditioner was working overtime, but the heat was getting worse by the mile, like riding into the mouth of an oven. A stale odor was under my nose. I smelled like an old pork chop.

An hour later I had zoomed past hundreds of gigantic white windmills along the mountainside, a beautiful sight when you're not too frenzied to enjoy it. I exited the 10 freeway at Monterey Drive and pushed deeper into the inferno, crossed Dinah Shore Boulevard and saw a digital sign in front of Wells Fargo Bank that said the temp was 111 degrees.

I let the window down, turned my air conditioner off to save gas. Desert air bum-rushed me, forced coolness out.

My throat was dry, my stomach turned and bubbled. Had to play this by ear. Try to be rational, stay logical, and contradict whatever was dished out.

After all, Shar had called me and solicited my services, right? That was entrapment. I never made any advances. Just answered her questions. That was all I did. I never said I'd sleep with her. Just said I'd come by. That was open to interpretation.

"You don't actually think I'd sleep with your best friend, do you?" It sounded silly, but I practiced saying that like it was a new Easter speech, contorted my face to emphasize how ridiculous the situation was. "And remember, Shar said she'd been looking at me, right? I'm the one who was playing along. She's pissed because she broke up with her man, and she don't want you to have anybody."

Yep. I'd convince Toyomi that I was playing along and I was going to let her know what kind of friend she had. We'd talk. I'd be real sorry. We'd smooth things out.

Toyomi's car wasn't in her designated stall. But my clothing—suits, drawers, ties, jeans, condoms—were sprawled across the asphalt, spray-painted in red, some of it shredded. Tire tracks were over everything. Three Italian suits I'd bought at Al Weiss's shop in downtown L.A., shirts, everything was ruined.

I jumped out of my car, tried to find something salvageable.

There was a crash. A bottle broke and rang like a gunshot.

My heart pumped.

Another explosion came before I could recover from the first.

A bottle crashed near my feet and splashed fluids all over my legs. Glass bounced up, almost hit my eye. Another smashed into my car window. The next missile slammed into the side.

Toyomi was on her balcony, her hair in a ponytail, underneath her motionless wind chimes, wearing short Minnesota pajamas, slinging bottled Cokes.

"I told you not to come over here, didn't I?"

"Toyomi, chill out for a minute!"

Neighbors rushed out into the heat. The old and wrinkled were clacking their false teeth and shaking their heads.

She bent over, and when she stood up, two more bottles whizzed out. One flew past my car, the other short.

Ray-Ray—her twenty-year-old, too-big cousin with the bald head, nose ring, and head-to-toe tattoos—came out and glared down. The same scowl and hate that lived in her face was etched in his.

I shouted, "I was just playing along and I was going to—"

"Stop lying!" That was Shar screaming from inside the second-story condo. She stepped out on the balcony and pulled Toyomi by the shoulder. Toyomi stumbled backward a couple of steps, then jerked away.

My smoothness dried up. All I could say was corny, soap-opera crap: "Toyomi, come talk to me—"

"Toyomi, come inside," Shar said, and gripped Toyomi. "Forget about him. You don't need him. He ain't about nothing."

Shar stared down on me. In that moment when nobody saw her looking, her angry stare turned into a smirk. I swear to God she giggled. By the time Toyomi faced her scandalous friend, Shar's bogus anger was back, harder and stronger than before.

*"Leave me alone, Shar!"*

I shouted, "She knew we'd been having a hard time—"

Toyomi countered, "When did we start having a hard time?"

"He ain't worth it, Toyomi." Shar rolled her eyes at me. "You heard what he said. Don't let him play you like that."

Toyomi had a bottle in each hand. Breathing heavily. Her ponytail had come loose, allowing her hair to dance with anger. With wide eyes she screamed, "I don't want to see you."

Toyomi, Ray-Ray, and Shar. Not to mention all the white people who were watching us. Everybody was sneering at me like I was the bad guy.

My insides were loose, as blubbery as a sea lion. That was how it felt one moment, but the next I ached for freedom, like I was clamped in the jaws of a great white shark.

I had lost.

Enough of yelling up at her balcony. This was about as useful as trying to cut down a redwood tree by shouting at the damn thing.

I eased back into my car and started driving away. A bottle bounced off my trunk, another barely missed my window. I floored it, screeched, and bounced over a speed bump. Four bottles crashed on the sides and in front of my ride at the same time. Toyomi didn't throw all those by herself. Not that quick.

My fingers were throbbing. I was disoriented, dazed.

A half mile outside her complex, I pulled into the lot at the College of the Desert long enough to check out the damage to my car. Dents. A window was cracked like the Liberty Bell. I leaned against my car for a moment, my head down, fingers massaging my temples. Until I stung. The heat punctured my skin like needles. I moved on.

Turned my air on low. Drove slowly up Monterey toward the freeway.

I stopped at a red light at Country Club Drive. Spent that time wondering how something so much in control could flip the script. Guilt swooped in, covered me in huge waves.

Then my car was bumped from the rear.

I'd been rear-ended and almost knocked out into traffic.

This day was going every way but the right way.

I was ready to get out cursing until I looked behind me.

Toyomi.

Fuming and biting holes in her bottom lip. Revving the engine of her Subaru. Her eyes hotter than the Chicago fire.

We were the only cars in the intersection. Nothing approaching from the south. Not a damn thing on the north side. But a steady flow of cars were zipping east/west. People at the Mobil gas station on the right weren't paying attention. Neither were the people at the Sav-On mini-mall.

She backed up, bumped me again. Not hard, but hard enough to show she was borderline psychotic. She let down her window and slung a bottle. It bounced off my hood, rolled into the street. Her car door flew open. She ran up, slammed her fist into my window.

She screamed, *"Ouch!"*

"What's wrong with you?"

"I hurt my hand," she huffed. *"Open this door!"*

My insides were shaking like I had malaria. I'd never seen a sista look that vile.

*"Stephan, how could you do this to me? I loved you."*

Traffic slowed.

My pulse had the pace of a wild stallion. I sped through the red light. She jumped into her Subaru. Ran the light. Chased me the way they did Rodney King.

My Mustang was up to eighty when I whizzed through the intersection at Frank Sinatra Drive. I hoped that after a few miles, she'd think about what she was doing and back the fuck off.

She didn't. I crossed Gerald Ford Drive; she was still in pursuit.

I had a feeling she wanted to kill me. The thought of death rushed into my head. A not-so-pretty image of a crashed Mustang, a beautiful fire, smoke that could be seen for miles, came to mind. That and me pleading for mercy while Toyomi stood over me out here in Timbuktu, laughing as she toasted a marshmallow in the flames.

I put the pedal to the metal.

I couldn't go out like that, not on a barren road on the edge of a tourist town populated by old white people who liked to golf and play shuffleboard between Bob Hope specials.

Toyomi's headlights flashed on and off nonstop, like deranged eyes. Her car stampeded like it was possessed.

She caught up, jumped in the lane to my right.

Her stare challenged my existence down to the bone. I tried to tighten my mouth, exude sheer madness, wanted to come across like I wasn't scared shitless, but I don't think it worked. My sweaty forehead and quivering lip were a giveaway.

She screamed. Curses rattled from her thick lips.

She grabbed something.

Bottles flew out of her window like migrating birds. The first flock of Cokes were no-hitters; she whipped past me and threw several more so I'd crash into them head-on. Her engineering brain had come to life. I swerved, switched lanes, got behind her, and slowed. She jammed on her brakes, tried to make me rear-end her, but I skidded around her and almost ran off the road.

The woman was serious.

I pretended I was on the Starship Enterprise, and prayed for warp drive.

She became larger and larger in my rearview.

The 10 was two hundred yards away, and I was doing a hundred, too fast to slow this bullet down.

I ran the light in front of Home Depot. She ran it too.

Once over the overpass, the street narrowed, curved real deep, forced me to ease up. A turn came up much too fast. I panted, growled, wrestled with the steering wheel. Found control and barely kept my ride from flipping like a pancake. My tires screeched and vibrated on the asphalt.

Then I was back on the 10 freeway.

I was free. Westward bound.

Home free with jubilation in every beat of my heart.

Then I checked the rearview. Damn.

A mad-ass car was buffaloing through traffic. Lights flashing like Stephen King's *Christine*. Toyomi was on my ass like a motherfucker.

No matter how fast I went, her reflection grew.

With an iron fist I hammered my steering wheel over and over. A thousand times I yelled, "Damn!"

Toyomi accelerated around the four lanes of traffic, caught up, rode my bumper, swerved and switched into the lane to my right, pulled up and matched my speed of 85 plus.

A lopsided, malicious, take-no-prisoners frown was rooted in her face. My toes curled like fists.

She gritted her teeth, veered at me.

My nostrils flared; I winced, swerved away.

With a tom-tom beating for my heart, I scowled over, saw tears flooding from her eyes. She pulled strands of reddish-brown hair from her face, pursed her full lips, showed me the middle finger of love. Her eyes were those of a tiger, telling me to stay the fuck out of her jungle.

Toyomi whisked off at the exit to the Morongo Indian Reservation.

Vanished.

My face was flushed, skin so hot that the torrid air of Palm Springs chilled my body like an Antarctic breeze.

I raised my eyes to the sunny skies, exhausted and aching like I'd run the L.A. Marathon, and said, "Thank you, Jesus."

# 13 Chanté

Craig said he'd meet me at the IHOP right off the 60 at Archibald. Outside of the imported greenery, the area was industrial and barren. One step above being a truck stop in Barstow.

I freshened up. Put on a fresh coat of dark brown eyeliner, cocoa lip liner, and spiced cider lipstick; sipped lemonade, and tried to be patient while I sat in a booth. When you're hot and sweaty, waiting forty-five minutes felt like a month of Sundays.

Just when I thought I'd been stood up again, Craig pulled up. Just like that, sweat spouted on my nose, on my neck. Anxiety warmed my breasts and buttocks too. He was driving a new gray car. I wondered whose car he had borrowed. He disappeared. He must've been parking on the other side nearest Archibald, where I had left my car.

A moment later, he strutted toward the building. My heart quickened. Then he was coming through the front door.

The sun had tanned his caramel skin. I was burnt like toast as well. That was probably why Mr. Mumbles thought I was everything but a sista. When my flesh gets this fried, it does have a tendency to accent the Indian features in my bloodline.

That's beside the point.

Craig saw me. He wiped his hand over his yellow Tommy Hilfiger shirt, tugged his shirt down to his shorts. The quality of his wardrobe had improved. His hairy legs were almost as dark as his brown sandals. His hair was so short he looked bald.

I shouldn't be here. I knew that already.

But bits and pieces of Craig were still floating around inside me, like speckles of litter in a clean pool. As he came my way, I remembered the first time I saw him, and I felt so shy. He read me. But that was then, this now. His ass won't be able to read me, not ever again.

The day a blind man with no hands can read Braille is when he'll know what I really feel.

He sat down across from me and said, "Hey, Smoochiez."

God, I hated that nickname. Used to love it; now I hated it. I wanted to grab his neck and puke down his throat.

I said, "Whose car are you in?"

"Mine." He had a pompous grin. "I bought a Nissan Maxima."

"Brand-new?"

"Yeah." Then he asked me, "So who fixed your car?"

God, I was pissed. All the money he saved when we were dating is what bought that fucking brand-new car. I said, "Craig, let's not start off by pretending nothing has happened."

The waitress showed up and butted in before I could get this party started. She grinned enough to show her silver-capped teeth, asked me if I was ready to order, and before I could answer, Craig rattled off for her to bring him a Rooty Tooty Fresh and Fruity.

She gave him a subtle aren't-you-the-rude-one look, then turned to me and smiled. "What would you like, ma'am?"

I hissed out what I was feeling. "Closure."

Her brows rose in confusion.

Craig didn't get it and was looking over the menu like there was actually a meal called "Closure." I wished there was such a thing. A sista could pull up a chair, take a few bites, pay $5.99, then move on with her life. On a full stomach.

I told her I'd order in a minute.

She left.

I glowered at him. "*Phantom of the Opera*. Dinner at the Shark Bar. You renting a car. Any of that sound familiar?"

His head lowered. "That was a while ago."

"November the eleventh. Which coincides with my birthday. Why didn't you tell me you were TDY'ing out?"

He paused. Then he said, "I wasn't feeling you anymore."

"Not feeling me?"

"Not feeling you."

Those words came from his heart. Told me of the nothing he felt for me then. Which was why it was so easy for him to ask Karen out now. No scruples. No morals. That stung like a hornet's nest inside me, attacking my heart. But if he was trying to read this face, he'd have a better chance of seeing his reflection in the snow.

He raised his head, had a super-cool Maxwell sorta sneer. "I apologize. My head was all messed up."

"So say you."

"Now I've had time to think."

His eyes were on my hair, my blouse. It was cold in there, and my nipples were standing on the mountain waving at people. I folded my arms across my chest, hid them suckers from him.

Craig asked, "Wanna catch a movie or something?"

"No, or as you put it, I'm not *feeling* you."

"All I asked is if you wanted to see a movie."

Sarcasm seeped out. "Of course you did. And we know what you're *really* asking, so cut the bull. I have needs and you're sure not one of them. So this will not be going there."

"You're right. You caught me on that one."

I asked, "You seeing somebody?"

"So, do you want to come back out to the base?"

"For?"

He smiled.

"No, thank you," I said. Part of me did want to win in whatever way I could, even if I had to tie him down and make him chant my name while I did a victory dance and spat in his face, but the part of me that refused to be the same fool twice was large and in charge. "Let me rephrase: Were you seeing somebody else when you were seeing me?"

I reminded him that he'd shown me tickets to the musical. Even when I felt I had all the answers, well, sometimes a sista needed to hear what she didn't want to hear.

He chuckled. A coward's guilty laugh.

Inside I felt my pang swelling. I gave in to the insecure feelings I'd been living with from day to day and asked, "Was it something I did or didn't do to make you treat me like that?"

"Chanté, don't get loud."

"Oh, this isn't loud. You want loud? I can do loud."

"Don't get emotional."

I demanded, "Answer my question."

A white family behind Craig, as well as a Mexican family behind me, and God knows who else, were peeping at us.

Craig said, "The only reason I agreed to meet you *this one time* was so you'd stop calling me at work. The commander—"

"I don't care about your commander. I asked, were you seeing somebody back then. That's all. Yes or fucking no. Answer so I can order and eat and take my butt back home."

He cringed like he was walking barefoot on the sun.

I reassured him, "Don't worry about hurting my feelings. I'm *way* beyond that. If you can be a man and tell the truth, then I can be a woman and, hell, I can take it like a man."

He sighed.

I went on, "You do know how to be a man, don'cha, partner?"

He said, "Yeah."

His pager went off. He checked it, double-checked the time on his beeper against the time on his watch, shifted.

I said, "You took her to see the *Phantom*?"

He bobbed his head.

I added, "On my birthday."

Craig held on to that get-over-it expression.

At that moment I saw something that I had never seen before. I asked, "Have you ever respected me?"

He rubbed his eyes. Grunted like I was working his nerves.

Finally he asked, "You gonna eat?"

"You buying?"

"Okay, whatever. I'll treat you to some eats."

"Sure. It's dinnertime, but I'll grab some breakfast."

He flagged the waitress down. I ordered a Rooty Tooty, a sampler, a number one, number two, glass of juice, and a Sprite.

When the waitress left, Craig tried to lighten up the air at our table. "Damn, where are you going to put all of that?"

"These hips, thighs, and butt don't come from nowhere."

"I know that's right."

The tone in his voice told me that he still had hopes that he could conquer the unconquerable, if only for one night.

My voice had hope too. I asked, "Where's the ladies' room?"

His shoulders relaxed. He pointed toward the front door.

I scooted out of the booth, said, "Have to go potty. I'll be back in a few."

I did a slow stroll, let mystery and arousal lead the sensual sway in my hips. Glanced back long enough to see Craig lusting at the roll of my forward motions. He'd been stirred and was fiendin' for a chance to quench my sexual appetite. Maybe just to satisfy his own. Saw his dreamy eyes on my erotic hairdo that rang of a new wildness, on my colorful sarong that sang a song of a new me, on the butterfly that wanted to fly genteelly and free in a warm and gentle breeze.

He smiled at me. Lusted at everything physical. Ignored the most important parts of me. Disrespected the essence of me.

The nerve of that bastard. First he was dissing me and telling me that he didn't feel me anymore, which meant the thrill was gone. Now his eyes said he wanted to rock me all night long.

I smiled too. But mine was different. Mine was a frown turned upside down. A serious mask blanketing my disgust. My smiling face showed no traces of the evil that was lurking within.

He finally turned his head away.

The bathroom was on my right.

I faked right, ducked around a waitress, made a smooth left, and cruised my body toward the front door.

Again I peeped back, made sure Craig didn't see my deft move.

Outside, I gritted my teeth and dragged my spare house key down the passenger side of his brand-new Maxima, dug so deep sparks flew every whichaway. Since he was sandwiched between two trucks, and I was on the passenger side, he probably wouldn't notice the damage until he made it back to the base. But if he noticed the artwork, who gives a damn. He couldn't feel me, but he'd sure as hell feel this. I pranced back and forth five or six times, went from headlight to tail-light, peeled off gray paint down to the metal, scraped his car to the bone, tried to make it bleed like a ruptured heart.

I strolled to my little red car and went on with my life.

That would have to be my closure. And whoever said don't repay evil with evil can kiss my black ass. I don't feed hungry enemies, and I don't give them water when they're thirsty.

Damn damn damn damn damn.

When I pulled off Diamond Bar into my home sweet home, I gripped my steering wheel and gritted my teeth. Thaiheed was waiting in his truck, blocking my damn garage.

We exchanged cold-blooded stares. I ran over the speed bumps, stopped next to his ride. He gave a weak hand wave. A chill made me consider driving off.

He broke the silence. "Where've you been?"

"You mind moving?"

"Where've you been?"

I blew my horn and screamed, "Dammit, move!"

The bastard took his time. I ran my hand across my hair, over the dried sweat I had just earned dealing with Craig. I grumbled, "I don't need this shit."

Thaiheed moved to an open visitor spot. I parked, slammed my door, then marched over to cut him off. He wasn't welcome here.

"How long you been here?"

"Where've you been?"

"Haven't you heard of calling first?"

"I did call."

"Evidently I wasn't here. So what are you doing here?"

"You didn't answer."

"If I didn't answer, I didn't want to be bothered."

"You said you were sick. I wanted to be sure you were okay."

"I didn't say I was sick, I said I had cramps."

"Sick, cramps"—he threw his hands up—"what's the difference?"

"Look, if you call and I'm not here, that's not an invitation to come over and check on me. Don't *ever* do that again."

"Where were you all this time?"

"I've been where I've been."

The sun had set, so it was cooler, but my 'tude was afire. My sarong was soggy, sticking to my butt, thong was drenched in sweat, still trying to cut me in half.

Thaiheed looked me up and down.

I gave him a shot of sarcasm. "Satisfied?"

With a sternness he said, "Let's go inside."

"For what?"

"I want to check your panties."

"Excuse me?"

"I want to see what's in your panties."

I stepped back. "You're tripping; it's time for you to go."

He asked, "Where'd you go? You didn't eat but half of your break-fast. I've been here since you ran out of BC Café."

"Thaiheed." I ran my fingers through my hair. I said, "Cut to the chase. All month I called your job, and they said you haven't had to work a weekend in a long time."

"Who did you talk to?"

I didn't buy into that setup for a brand new lie. I replied, "So, you were at work?"

He shrugged. "That's what I said, wasn't it?"

"Thaiheed, you know and I know that you've been tipping to see your other female friends."

"I'm not seeing anybody else."

I smirked. "Peaches."

"What?"

"So, partner, who is Peaches? And I'm not talking about Peaches and Herb."

Thaiheed's face was silent and unmoving. Fucking incredible. He was busted and still wouldn't admit it. I'd just learned something else: never confess. Even if they have a bloody glove, ugly-ass shoes, and forty sets of fingerprints, never confess.

"Anything else?" I asked.

No answer.

I walked away.

"Chanté," he said over and over.

I slowed to a stop. "Thaiheed, instead of worrying about checking my panties, check yourself."

A thousand times he said, "Chanté—"

"*What what what*? Why do you keep calling my damn name?"

His eyes darkened, jaw squared up. It startled me, I think I shrieked with my mouth closed. But that off-center expression he had, it disappeared so fast I knew I had to imagine it.

"Don't do this, okay?" he said. "Think about it. After all I do for you, do you think I'd be with somebody else, huh?"

"Thai, you must think I'm half blind, crazy, or just plain stupid. I know what's up, you know what's up."

"There is nothing between me and Peaches."

I gave up a harsh laugh. "Oh, now you remember Peaches."

"She's just a friend of a friend. Ain't nothing to her."

"Tell Nina I said hello," I said. "Ask her how she enjoyed kicking it with you at the World Famous Town House."

His walking rhythm changed, sounded like he stumbled on his anger from defeat at the hands of a neophyte in this arena.

I held on to my burned-out pace and strolled away. No sashay or sway, just a plain old I'm-tired-of-your-lies walk. Too tired to have an attitude, too exhausted to have a meaningless fight, too nonchalant to grieve over another dead-end relationship.

He was moving up behind me. Hard steps that scared me. My body wanted to become tense because something told me he was getting ready to grab a handful of my hair and hit me in the back of my head. I kept on moving toward my door. Step by step, I moved in the direction of safety. He was right behind me. Getting closer. So close that I felt the wind from his indignant breath.

He stopped marching.

I stopped sweating.

I glanced his way long enough to see his gray eyes were soft, peaceful, very apologetic.

He said, "I care about you. I've done a lot for you. Whenever you needed something, wasn't I right here for you? Is this the appreciation I get for being in love with you?"

I clapped three times. "Bravo."

I resumed my soulless strut.

His tone changed. Turned vile. He snapped out a few more unkind things, made a few more quick and hostile steps in my direction.

I didn't know if I should shriek for help now, or just be quiet so I didn't disturb my neighbors, and just bleed and wait for the paramedics to strap what was left of me to a gurney.

A car came into the complex, passed right by me. I waved at the neighbor. That was when Thaiheed stopped following me. I started back breathing and double-timed to my front door.

Inside, I peeped through the venetian blinds. He was leaving. Not a happy camper.

Craig. Thaiheed. I was two for two in their arena. Not a bad day in a fool's paradise. Not a bad day at all.

I showered, lay across the bed on top of my goose-down comforter, naked, television on ESPN, volume on mute, radio on low, watching the ceiling fan, following the rotating blades.

*Womanizer.*

That single word flashed in my head. I jumped up off the bed, covered my breasts to keep them from bouncing, ran up to my loft, grabbed a dictionary. First I looked for the word. The folks at *Webster*'s had Don Juan, philanderer, Casanova, swinger, seducer, and other sweet-sounding, complimentary terms as synonyms for a slutty-ass brother.

Fair was fair, so I hunted for what a bold and audacious sister might be called, a *manizer*. It didn't exist. Whore, prostitute, tramp, Jezebel, bimbo, hooker—plus a few others that pissed me off to no end—jumped from the pages.

I read the inside cover, sighed with pity. "A man wrote this damn book. They can dish the shit out, but they can't take it."

# 14 Stephan

By Monday Toyomi had made about a hundred vulgar phone calls. I didn't respond to her madness. Tuesday she e-mailed me pages of vulgarities. I blocked her e-mail address. Wednesday, via snail mail, I got a box with cards, pictures, pieces of poetry, and all the letters that I'd ever given her, ripped to shreds.

Thursday was quiet.

Friday was tame too.

It looked like she'd come to her senses and grown up.

Until I made it home from work.

I trudged up the stairs around eight-thirty, running late because I had to take my rental car back and pick up my repaired Mustang from the dealer. Shaking my head because my deductible set me back five hundred dollars. I stopped dead in my tracks when I saw a bright red message painted on my door.

THE DOG ASS NIGGA WHO LIVES
HERE AIN'T ABOUT SHIT AND

WILL FUCK YOUR BEST FRIEND
IF YOU TURN YOUR BACK
WOMEN BEWARE
HE AIN'T ABOUT SHIT

A thousand curses flowed from my mouth like lava from a volcano. I changed into Levi's, no shirt. Darkness found me sweating, scrubbing my front door.

My middle-aged, thrice-divorced neighbor, Rebecca, came out in her terry-cloth housecoat, snooping, struggling not to laugh. She has streaks of gray hair, long neck, medium frame. Her head had a peanut shape, sort of like women from Somalia.

Rebecca said, "Stephan, I saw it all. Toyota zoomed up—"

"Toyomi."

"Whatever. She parked under your window this afternoon."

I mumbled, "She knew I was at work."

"Toyota banged on the door for five minutes."

Rebecca saw everything when she glued herself to either the peephole or her patio window, whichever offered the best view.

I asked, "You say anything to her?"

"Heck, no." Rebecca chuckled. "She ain't right in the head. Stephan, what did you do to that girl?"

"Nothing," I said.

Rebecca huffed. "You must've done a whole lot of nothing."

My shoulders ached from scrubbing.

Soap and water didn't remove the paint.

Rebecca continued her cackling, this being the most she'd ever talked to me in the last six months, probably the most excitement her eccentric, agoraphobic ass has had since she helped Moses part the Red Sea.

Rebecca blabbered, ". . . was hitting the door so hard I thought, Lawd have mercy, it's the big earthquake! Because my oak china cabinet was shaking and just a rattling, so I knew it had to be the big earthquake, and I fell on my knees and started praying—"

"Rebecca," I politely interrupted, "you have paint remover?"

"Let me see. Back in a second."

Soap and water didn't work on oil-based paint. I checked my watch, it was after nine. HomeBase on Rio Rancho had closed.

My stairs vibrated as somebody charged up. My heart beat strong. I jerked around, ready to throw down and defend myself.

It was Darnell and Jake.

"You ain't ready?" Jake frowned, then stepped back and let me see his new golden outfit. A thigh-length dashiki and matching kente pants. Roman sandals. He boasted, "Who the man?"

"You the man," I replied, then asked, "Where'd you get that?"

"Charlotte bought it at Kongo Square in Leimert Park."

"You're ready to rule," I said, then wiped my face with the back of my hand. "Give me a few minutes so I can shower."

"You haven't showered?" That was Darnell. He was dressed in suspenders, pinstripe suit, starched white shirt, red tie.

All the time I was trying to block my door, but the writing was too large to hide.

My homies looked at each other, then at me.

Darnell read, "Dog ass nigga . . ."

They looked at each other. Then at me.

My neighbor's door opened. All of us jumped. Rebecca saw my homeboys, lost her smile, touched her undone hair, stepped out long enough to hand me a small can of paint remover.

I said, "Thanks, Rebecca."

Rebecca scurried back into her place.

Darnell said, "What is up with your door?"

One of my shortcomings was refusing to admit when I'd been fucked over. I hated putting dents in my armor, especially in front of my boys. But it was too late to cover this one up.

I stepped to the side. "Read 'em and weep."

They read the writing, then grinned.

Darnell shook his head and whistled. "Which one?"

Jake said, "Man, you *know* who did this without asking."

They cackled like hyenas on nitrous oxide.

"Not just a regular nigga," Darnell barked, stomped his feet, snapped his suspenders, his tie flapping every which-a-way, "but a *dog ass* nigga."

Jake laughed so hard he almost coughed up a lung.

Skin was slapping, sounds from them high-fiving. Using the remover was another bad move. Wasn't thinking. It stripped off a couple of layers of the paint, but all I did was leave spots that revealed some of the same lettering I was trying to remove.

"I don't believe you fell for the okee-doke, man. First Toyomi set you up and you fell for the oldest—"

"Shut up, Jake."

"—dumbest trick in the book. Now she's doing drive-bys on your butt. You'd better check your pots for boiling rabbits."

I was destroying my door. I said, "Damn, this remover took too much paint off."

"It's paint remover," Jake said. "That's paint, it's getting removed, what you expect?"

I asked, "Can you still make it out?"

Jake leaned in. "Looks like *Wheel of Fortune*."

```
T E   O   A S NI GA   HO L VES
HER   A N'T       UT S IT A D
W LL FUC   YOU   B ST F  END
                A K
W ME   B WA E
HE AI 'T         S IT.
```

"I'd like to buy a vowel." That was Darnell.

Jake said, "You need to redo the whole door. Run up to HomeBase and get what you need. Slap some paint on it."

"HomeBase is closed until seven in the morning."

Jake said, "Ain't a WalMart behind this complex?"

"Man, don't nobody care about that," Darnell said and tapped his watch. "It's nine-thirty. You start messing with that door, you'll be out here for two more hours."

I grimaced. My door faced inward, toward Rebecca's, so nobody who passed by could see that humiliation.

Three tears in a bucket, motherfuck it.

I asked Darnell, "Where's Dawn?"

"She went to see her mother."

I asked Jake, "Charlotte gonna meet you up there?"

He frowned. "She was going next door to Valerie's house. Valerie and her sister what's-her-face are having a girls' get-together thing. Valerie is encouraging Charlotte to push for a wedding date. I've got enough pressure to get married as it is, without her sitting around them lollygagging all evening."

Darnell said, "Jake, you better marry that girl."

"I don't like the same old chicken every night."

Darnell shook his head. "You just have to be creative and find new ways to cook that chicken."

"Why don't you go on and I'll just hook up with y'all at the club?" I exhaled some anger. "It's going to take me a while."

They didn't argue. I wasn't in the mood for crowds or entertainment, but the longer I sat around the house, jumping every time a car went by my door, the more unnerved I'd get. By the morning I'd be a wreck, ready for a straitjacket and a trip to a white room with soft rubber walls.

And I wasn't going to be a prisoner in my own home. I could stand fresh air for a few. At a safer place.

I called Brittany. No answer.

I called Samantha, left her a tender message. Told her I missed her like crazy and I wanted to see her tonight.

Heavenly music poured out of Shelly's and washed through the adjacent coffee shop. In the daytime, Rancho Cucamonga was a serene, palm tree–lined bedroom community that was framed by strawberry fields, industrial areas, shopping plazas. But tonight a saxophone, guitar, and electric keyboard made it sound like people were stomping at the Savoy.

Shelly's was a seafood restaurant by day. At night they crammed in a band on the bar side of the room and left just enough room for a few dancers to bop to the groove.

Sistas were ready to party. Sophisticated attitudes all over the joint. Positive energy grooving in business suits, scandalous minis, or ripped and ragged designer jeans.

I just hoped my weariness didn't make me look unapproachable. I didn't want to slide into the room, give up negative vibes, and repel all of the wall-to-wall fineness. Toyomi had tripped out, but ain't nothing better to make a brother forget about a woman than another woman. It was time to start forgetting.

I give props when they are due, so I'd have to admit some of the brothers looked all right. A few could take some fashion tips. One brother had on a decent off-the-rack suit, good cut and it hung well, but his shoes were from the age of the Flintstones. Cheap, unpolished, and cracked.

All of the outside seating was taken, and the inside was SRO—standing room only. I stuck my head in and felt the energy coming through in a surge of body heat.

I saw Jake walking away from the dance floor, following a sista who wasn't responding. She gave a half-ass smile, then excused herself back over to a table occupied by European guys and another group of women. One of the white guys shot an insecure frown at Jake. A couple of seconds later, Jake adjusted his African threads and headed back to the dance floor with somebody else. He saw me and nodded. I waved. His dance buddy in the black cat suit slowed down, smiled and waved back at me like she thought I was waving and flirting with her.

Darnell stood up long enough to wave me down. He was in the far corner at a glass-topped table, underneath a lazy-moving ceiling fan. A full-figured sista was damn near resting in his lap. She owned a nice ethnic shape—small waist and hearty butt. One hundred percent his type. But for him, getting that close to a female other than his wife was out of character.

I grabbed a non-alcoholic beer from the bar and weaved through the vivacious crowd. By the time I bumped my way to the table, I was warm, and Darnell was alone.

He tapped his watch, gave a twisted smile.

I hunched my shoulders in defense, said, "Got tied up."

"It's almost eleven."

"I know how to tell time. Who was that babe?"

"What babe?"

"The one who was keeping your wife's favorite lap warm."

"Don't you recognize her from the Sunkist commercial?"

"Nope."

"She's an actress. A singer too. She's a writer."

"And you're a married man with a beautiful wife."

"She knows that. I was just saying."

I nodded. "Just checking your flow."

"I was talking to her and her friends when we first got here. Talking about writing, music," Darnell said. He pointed at the band. The girl had waltzed up and taken the microphone. Her thick frame was draped in a long light brown dress and pearls. The outfit looked good on her fair skin. She was a little tipsy. He said, "She has a set of lungs on her, a serious range."

I said, "I didn't know she sang with the band."

"She doesn't." He hunched his shoulders. "She asked if she could sing a couple of songs. Standing ovations both times."

"Yeah?"

From the stage the sista smiled; Darnell returned the playful come-on with a wink.

I said, "Darnell."

"What?"

"Knock it off."

When the sista took the microphone, everybody hushed.

"Hello, how's everybody doing?" She smiled, told everybody she was going to sing an old Nina Simone tune, then nodded to the band. Pee Wee clacked his drumsticks as the count. At clack four the band fell into a soft and passionate melody.

She started singing about being the other woman. Her strong contralto voice took control and quieted the room. Everyone listened, hypnotized by her. Even the bartenders stopped making drinks and leaned over the counter. The pain of how the other woman sat and waited, all polished, manicured, covered in expensive French perfume for her part-time lover. Waiting for him, but in reality living her life all alone. Sistas waved their hands, hummed like they were cruising back down memory lane.

Everyone applauded, loud and long. Darnell clapped so loud it sounded like God's thunder.

The thick singer curtsied, blew a kiss, walked away smiling.

"Sister's bad to the bone." Darnell grinned. He was still applauding as he exited the table. "Damn, she can *sang*."

I said, "Where you going?"

He stood there for a moment, staring at that girl the way a man stares at a woman. But it wasn't lust. It was a deeper yearning. He ran his hands over his lips, shuddered like he was trying to shake off the feeling.

He answered, "Watch my drink. I'm going to go check in with the wife. I want to make sure she stays up until I get in."

Everybody hurried over to the singer, touched her and shook her hand. The sister in the diva cat suit walked over and gave the singer a big hug; they laughed, rocked side to side.

The cutie with the booty in the cat suit saw me staring at her every move. She waved at me from the bar. I waved back. She bumped through the crowd and eased over to my table.

She set free a serene smile. "Long time no see."

I repeated, "Long time no see."

"Oh, now you don't know me." She held out her palm.

I hesitated for a moment and wondered where I knew those tight eyes from. Then I saw the butterfly on her shoulder.

I said, "Kismet?"

She said, "That's right. Kismet."

Makeup, high spirits, and nighttime made her look like a different woman. More mature. Less vulnerable.

I reached into my pocket. "Let me give you that ten dollars."

She grinned and pushed my hand back. "I told you I wouldn't take your money for helping me."

"Well, let me buy you a drink. I forgot your name."

"Never told you. I'm Chanté Ellis."

"That's pretty. Chanté Ellis. It has a nice flow."

"Thank you, but only if you mean it."

We shook hands. "I'm Stephan Mitchell."

"Stephan Mitchell." She smiled. "I didn't recognize you."

"I didn't recognize you either. Your hair is different."

"I curled it. And my seventy-five percent must be showing."

We laughed.

I asked, "How often do you change your hair?"

"Often. But you're the one who looks different. Look at you. All jazzed up in a green suit. That's a nice tie."

"Thanks. Guess I was pretty tore up when you met me."

She beamed. "We both were."

We both laughed.

She leaned closer. "I'm not messing up your action, am I?"

"Nah," I said. "I'm here with a couple of buddies."

"I saw you trying to be slick and look at every booty when they walked by. You still looking for that special perfect one?"

"You still searching for your spiritual ugly man?"

She laughed again, soft and sweet this time. "I'm teasing. But you've got to learn to be discreet. Women were checking you out, but you didn't notice."

"Who?"

"I'm not telling."

"You?"

"Don't even go there."

Her singer friend was at a table on the other side of the room with another sista who was dressed in ripped jeans. They all waved at each other. I told her that her friend was good.

Chanté said, "She just landed a part in a play in Hollywood."

"Really?"

"Un-huh," she said with much pride. "We're celebrating. We were going to go to either Club Century or Pandemonium, but Karen didn't want to go into L.A., then drive back to Riverside and drag her butt in to work in the morning."

"Hold up. Your girlfriend's trying to get your attention."

Chanté's friends motioned toward the glass doors that separated the inside from the concrete balcony with the waterfall and greenery. A short brotha wearing Kani jeans was walking in with a thick-boned, young-looking, caramel-skinned sista. She had on a cream, wide-legged pant suit and was clinging to his elbow.

Chanté peeped over her shoulder just as the brother gawked in our direction. Her feminine grin turned into something morbid.

"Stephan, I'll be right back," Chanté said, then bumped through the crowd and went over to her girlfriends.

The brotha and his lady friend stood in the doorway. She was smiling, singing along with the band's version of a Norman Brown–style Janet Jackson remake. The brotha had a constipated expression. She was oblivious to the tension that breezed in on their coattails. They headed to the far side of the room, but she pulled his arm when she saw a table being vacated right next to mine. He fingered his mustache and cut his eyes down at me.

I said, "What's up?"

Not so much as a head bob from him.

His date grinned. "Nothing much. How're you doing?"

"Better than some, worse than others."

Before they could get settled, his date said, "I'll be right back. I'm going to the little girls' room."

When she snaked through the crowd, Chanté's eyes followed the girl like she was prey. Chanté and her friends huddled. A second later she and the petite woman in the ripped jeans hopped off their bar stools and headed in the same direction.

On the way out Chanté cut her eyes at the brotha.

The guy groaned, a sound of fear mixed with anger and depression.

Before long Chanté, her friend, and the girl bumped back through the crowd, laughing. The brotha's fingers had been drumming the table ever since they vanished, not in beat with the music. Chanté's girlfriend made eye contact with me. She casually licked her lips. I nodded. Interest was in her eyes.

Chanté slowed homeboy's date at my table, said, "I want you to meet a friend of mine." Her eyes told me that something was up.

I stood and extended my hand. "Hi."

"Stephan Mitchell," Chanté spoke loud enough for her words to carry a table over. "This is Peaches."

"Hi, Stephan."

Chanté asked, "Are you here by yourself?"

"Oh, I'm sorry," Peaches said as she stepped past me. Her man friend grunted and took his time about getting up from the table. She said, "This is my fiancé, Thaiheed."

Thaiheed's eyes bounced back and forth between Peaches and Chanté. He never gazed my way, not even when we were formally introduced. I was being dissed.

"This is Chanté." Peaches smiled. "And that's Karen."

Karen winked at Thaiheed. "Congratulations on the engagement, my *true*, *strong*, and *righteous* brother. Not many of you around."

Thaiheed and Karen locked eyes.

Karen said, "You have something to say, Thaiheed?"

"So, when's the wedding?" Chanté asked.

"You want to—" Thaiheed tried to say.

"Next June." Peaches blushed. "It sure would be nice to get your friend Tammy to sing me and my man across the broom."

Chanté's eyes were burdened. She took Peaches' hand. "Let's chit-chat for a moment."

"Peaches," Thaiheed tried to grab the other hand, "we just got here. Let's kick back and enjoy the music for a few."

It was too late.

Chanté dragged Peaches through the crowd. Karen followed but gazed back at me two or three times. Smiled a smile of wonderment and wanting.

I had a bad feeling. Not about Karen, about the situation.

"Where you know Chanté from?" Thaiheed asked.

"Met her tonight," I said. I could hear him sucking on his tongue, tapping his foot, again not in rhythm to the music. At first I thought something was up between him and Karen.

"Didn't she say something about you and her somewhere?"

I cleared my throat. "Her car broke down; I helped her out."

Just then Peaches stormed back over. She existed on a different plateau. The sound of her butt smacking the seat when she plopped down definitely wasn't friendly. Not at all. She sounded like a bull snorting right before the charge.

Thaiheed asked, "Wanna dance?"

She snapped, "How long you been knowing Chanté?"

"What?"

"I thought you said you stopped seeing Nina."

People at the closer tables were watching. Peaches dropped the stuff Chanté had given her—pictures of Chanté and Thaiheed. Dropped the photos on the table and spread them around like they were tarot cards and she was about to tell his future.

Peaches pointed at the pictures. "This is you and her at Sea World. See the damn date. Universal Studios. Look at the date on the picture. Raging Waters. Look at the date."

Thaiheed rubbed his face. "Let's step outside. Not here."

"Just take me the fuck home."

Chanté and company were all watching Thaiheed. At first I thought Chanté was crying, but she was holding back laughter. Peaches stormed out like a hurricane, and Thaiheed followed like a gentle breeze, cutting his eyes at Chanté before he exited. Vindictiveness was written all over his face. Chanté flipped him off with a finger so stiff half the women in the room probably got turned on.

Chanté waltzed back to my cubbyhole, sat down and smiled.

I asked, "Boyfriend?"

She laughed.

I smiled. "Why you dog 'im like that in public?"

"Because he's a dog. And a dog gets what a dog gets."

"What does a dog get?"

"Dogged."

The music picked up, switched to an African beat. The percussionist was working overtime. The keyboard emulated a flute.

Tammy was back up, wailing a tune about a "see line woman."
The African Village of the Inland Empire came to life.
People danced in the aisles. Anywhere the spirit hit.
Chanté pulled my hand. "C'mon, show me what you can do."
I loosened my tie and accepted the challenge. "What's this, a Caribbean tune?"

"Another Nina Simone. Tammy worships that woman."

"You don't like her?"

"I like Nina. She sings the hell out of *Porgy and Bess*. Stephan, check Tammy out. She's getting it on loose up there."

Tammy slapped one hand on the waist of her skirt, hiked her dress thigh high while she made some exotic moves. With sweat dripping down her neck over her pearls, she threw down some serious choreography on the music's break. Other sistas accepted her challenge, kicked off their shoes, left the brothas behind, yanked their skirts up a few inches and grooved their way into the impromptu dance competition.

Everybody was dancing close to fornication.

Cheering.

Shouting.

When the song was over and the applause came down, Jake left the girl he'd picked up and came over. Chanté's friend Tammy came over too, fanning herself, sipping on a soda, ignoring all the men who were trying to get her attention, and gave her eyes to Darnell. He showered her with compliment after compliment. Tammy touched his arm, leaning all in his face.

A moment passed. I looked out the window. Brittany was sitting at a table near the fountain that separated this spot from the restaurant next door. Dressed in a black leather mini, black hose, black pumps, lipstick the color of the night. She was with somebody. A brotha who had his hands all on her legs, on her thighs. More people were in that party-hearty group. Her golden hair was straight, hanging down to her back.

I didn't know when she arrived, or how long she'd been watching me. Didn't know she was coming.

She toyed with her golden necklace, nodded.

I nodded.

"You want that drink?" I asked Chanté.

"No," she said. "I'll take a rain check on my ten dollars."

"I thought you said you didn't want the money."

"I changed my mind. I'm exercising my woman's prerogative. As long as you owe me, I'll never be broke."

I excused myself, then walked through the carpeted restaurant section, slipped around the corner toward the men's room, and picked up a pay phone, pretended to be talking.

A couple of seconds later, hands squeezed my buns, then long and slender fingers ran around to my crotch.

I said, "I hope that's a woman, touching me like that."

"Hey, sexy," Brittany whispered. Her voice was as innocent as the smell of the Coco Chanel perfume that surrounded her. "You were dancing your ass off."

"I did my best."

"Who's the cute girl who was all over you?"

"Don't know. Just met her."

"The way she was all over you, I thought you were trying to get a Siamese twin award."

Three sistas came around the corner. By then Brittany had side-stepped and picked up the other pay phone and turned her back to me. The bathroom door closed behind the sistas.

I asked Brittany, "Who you with?"

"My boyfriend, Tony." She made an irritated face. "Going home alone tonight?"

"Yeah."

"Alone alone?"

"Alone alone."

She whispered, "I've missed you."

"I've been calling you. Why don't you ever call back?"

Her lip curled up at the corner. She gave up a one-shoulder shrug, lowered her voice. "Can I come over tonight?"

We stalled our conversation when a brotha came out of the bathroom. Held off talking until another went in.

Brittany said, "I have extra clothes in my car."

"What about Tony?"

She smiled. "I drove my own car. I'll get rid of him."

She hung up the phone and walked away.

I blew a couple of minutes, called and checked my machine.

*Stephan. This is Toyomi—*

I erased that message before it played all the way.

My momma had called. No word from Samantha. I called her one more time. Got the damn answering machine again.

When I got back to the table, the singer was sitting on Darnell's lap, cat-stroking his back.

Jake was back at the bar. Some girl was writing down her number on a napkin.

Chanté turned to me. "Walk me down to the coffee shop. I'm in a cappuccino kinda mood."

"Okay."

"You're buying."

I asked Darnell if he wanted to stroll with us.

He smiled like heaven was resting at his table and said, "You go ahead. I'm cool right here."

Tammy tapped her watch. "Don't be gone long, Chanté. Karen has to work eight hours tomorrow."

I made brief eye contact with Karen. She shot a subtle snarl at Chanté, then switched up and smiled at me. Wanting eyes. She made a disturbed face that said, "Oh, well."

I nodded and headed toward the door.

The beat was still strong. Everybody had loosened up. Couples were dancing closer than close; sistas were rubbing their bodies all over their partners; brothas' hands were creeping down feminine spines drifting toward magical backsides.

These same people would be at church bright and early on Sunday morning, shouting for salvation. The sinner in every man and woman was buck wild and running free.

Chanté grooved with the music, jitterbugged out in front of me. Maybe my mind had been too ablaze with other thoughts and distractions. Too busy to notice the shapely figure enhanced by her cat suit. Her hips dipped and rolled and bebopped a few moves that could set the room on fire.

Nice personality, nice calves, very feminine persona.

But with the capability of being a bitch.

I stumbled into a chair. Knocked over an empty glass.

Without looking back, she said, "Stop gawking at my booty."

"Stop shaking Mother Africa like that."

"Such a man. I bet you're a dog just like the rest of 'em."

"Look who's talking." I grabbed a napkin off a table and wiped the sweat off my neck. "The way you just played Peaches."

"She was asleep. Somebody needed to wake her up."

We lucked out and found two empty chairs outside Rose's Caffe Luna, sat on the concrete walkway, underneath support beams that supported ivy and other greenery used to create slivers of shade in the heat of the day.

People were passing by, so I moved the round table over a few inches for space. Chanté pulled out her white plastic chair, made a craving sound, then said, "The coffee aroma is strong. I smelled it down at the club."

"If it's kicking like that, won't it have you up all night?"

"Coffee makes me sleep," she said. She'd picked up a napkin and was wiping down the top of the table. The table was round and white, had designs in it that looked like short red worms.

I said, "Makes me restless."

"Makes me suck my thumb and sleep like a baby."

That created a sensual image in my mind.

We wiped the sweat off our brows and necks. This was much better. All of that exotic and erotic energy inside Shelly's had thickened the air down there. A more innocent, collegiate crowd was out this way. T-shirts, sandals, shorts. Kids with that surfer-boy look were lounging, flirting, reading Yeats. I bought Chanté a double cappuccino. I had a cup of decaf with raw sugar. No cream; I'm lactose intolerant. Tiredness ran over me. Like mine, Chanté's voice dragged. She looked a little weary.

I asked, "Long day?"

"Long life."

"Get your oil changed yet?"

"Can you do it for me? I'll buy the stuff."

"I could."

"Will you?"

"Depends. Where you live?"

"Diamond Bar. You?"

"Pomona."

"I'll pray for you."

"The Phillips Ranch section."

Her mouth showed she was impressed. Since I didn't live on the roughneck, gang-banging side near Garey High School, it felt like I'd been bumped up into a better category of Negroes.

She asked, "Condo or house?"

"Condo. Have to work my way up the hill into the multimillion-dollar homes that have a panoramic view of Los Angeles."

She raised a brow. "I think the new racist term the media's using for minorities with potential is *upwardly demographic*."

I sipped my coffee, said, "We're upwardly demographic then."

"Yeah. That we are."

Diamond Bar and Pomona were neighboring cities, so no matter what part of the city she was resting her head in, we lived no more than ten minutes away from each other. And that's taking the surface streets. Not that it mattered. 'Cause it didn't.

We kept the conversation shallow, found out that we both went to the same local clubs, like Savannah West and Little J's and the Golden Tail and Tilly's Terrace, even to Pinky's in Moreno Valley, but we'd never met before now.

I said, "Maybe we just never noticed each other."

"True. You ain't my type."

"I'll consider that a backhanded compliment."

"Just wanted you to know where we stand."

"You ain't my cup of tea either."

She said, "Because I can see right through you."

"Because you *think* you can see right through me."

She said, "I think we dated in another lifetime."

"Why you say that?"

"Because you're a chauvinistic jerk."

I said, "No, you're an opinionated *jerkette*."

"Jerkette?"

I said, "Yep, and we were divorced in another lifetime."

"Who got the house?"

"You did. You're materialistic, cynical, and pretentious."

She sipped her brew. "At least we agree on something."

We laughed.

I liked her. Liked her a lot. Something about her personality was pushing the right buttons. And I didn't like for my buttons to be pushed, not at all.

She lived minutes away from me, which was a definite no-no. Too convenient was inconvenient. She tried to act rough around the edges, but she had soft eyes.

I wrote down my number and gave it to her. After I finished my yawn, I said, "I can do it almost any evening. Just call me and either you can come by or I can drive over and hook you up."

"Okay." She yawned too. "I'll make you something to eat."

"Cool."

She saw her friends coming our way and called for them to hold up. They stopped and waved for her to hurry up.

I said, "Bouncing so soon?"

"Yeah. Nice to meet you again, Stephan Mitchell."

"Likewise, Chanté Ellis."

"You have a middle name?"

"Nope. You?"

"Marie. More than likely I'll call you from work Monday."

I asked, "Where do you work?"

"I'll let you know when you need to know."

"Okay."

She laughed. "Ciao."

"You want to give me your number?"

Real quick, she said, "Negative, partner."

She floated toward her friends. Her hips owned a slight sway like a palm tree's leaves in a mild summer breeze. She moved with glee, was charged with an erotic tenderness, but the energy I received told me that deep within her body was singing a song of sorrow. About halfway she turned around, saw I was watching the movement of her mystery.

She said, "Stop staring. I told you to be discreet."

"Stop walking like that."

"It's in my blood. I walk like my beautiful mother." Without looking, she yawned, waved. "I'll call you."

Chanté and her friends blended into the shadows. I heard them laughing and talking at the same time. Sounded like young, anxious girls having overlapping conversations at a pajama party. Then the sounds they made dissipated.

And I was alone with my own thoughts.

A jingling sound caught my attention. A brotha in a yellow silk suit and bright red hat was swaggering by, shaking the loose change in his pockets. For a moment the dry air felt humid, my arm experienced a sting, like a lone mosquito had attacked me, and I was back in Jackson, Mississippi, sitting on my daddy's lap.

More people strolled down the walkway, dabbing sweat off their brows as they crawled into their cars and drove away. A lot of sistas were lingering, exchanging cards and scribbling their numbers on matchbooks or scraps of paper, passing it on to their catch of the moment. Those brothas had shit-eating grins that said they'd had successful nights.

Darnell and Jake came out and stopped by my table, said their good-byes, then hopped in Darnell's car and headed up Haven toward the 10 freeway. Darnell was taking his desires home to his wife; Jake was heading back to his fiancée's house.

The winds picked up, blew some papers, scattered some dust.

I felt anxious. Lonely. So damn lonely.

Brittany and her beau came out of the shadows. I heard her giggles before I saw her. He was holding her hand, laughing like he was the man of all men, walking her out to her car.

While Brittany stood at her drop-top red Capri talking with her man, I downed my hazelnut coffee and hurried past them to my car. In the midst of their hug, she stole a wink at me.

I hopped in my car and headed home.

Didn't wanna miss my midnight snack.

# 15 Chanté

Minutes later I was behind the wheel of Karen's blue car. She didn't feel like driving, so she was in the passenger's seat, changing the radio station. She'd been tight-lipped. Something was bothering her. Tammy was in the back, singing to herself.

"He's cute," Karen said out of nowhere.

Tammy stopped humming and asked, "Who?"

Karen gandered my way. "I was talking to Chanté."

I asked, "Who?"

Karen had *that sound* in her voice. That tone that made me wonder what I'd done wrong this time. Whenever she was buzzed, that chastising side of her woke up. My happiness fled, and a little tension cranked up.

"The cute guy in the suit," Karen said. "He was flirting with me big-time until you pulled him out on the dance floor."

"Was he?" I said nonchalantly, then tried to change the subject. "Tammy, what'cha singing back there?"

Tammy spoke up. *"Ne Me Quitte Pas."*

Karen asked me, "Who is he?"

"Stephan Mitchell." I said that like I wanted to close the door to that subject, then tried to shift the conversation. "Tammy, that song is pretty. What does *ne me quitte pas* mean?"

Tammy answered, "It's French. 'Please don't leave me.' "

I said, "A sad song 'bout a sista begging a man to stay."

Tammy laughed, then yawned. Karen went right back to asking about Stephan, wanting to know where I knew him from, how long, yadda, yadda, yadda.

I asked Karen, "What makes you think I knew him?"

"Because he was holding your hips, humping all on you like you were a fire hydrant, so I hope you knew him."

Me and Tammy laughed.

Karen continued, "Guess you didn't want us to meet."

I said, "What you mean?"

"You saw him staring me down, then you pulled him away when he was getting ready to talk to me. That was kinda foul."

"You saying I was coochie blocking?"

"You did the same thing the night we met Craig. I was talking to him before you ever saw him. Then I turned around for a sec, next thing I knew you were all up in his face."

"I don't remember you talking to Craig first."

"Of course you wouldn't. 'Cause you were up in his face, so close I thought you were trying to replace one of his teeth."

"Children, knock it off already," Tammy said and patted her sweaty forehead. "Wake me when we get to your place, Chanté."

I said, "Wonder what happened to Thaiheed and his ghetto superstar woman."

Karen said tightly, "She's probably screwing him right now."

A few minutes went by. I was on the 10, passed by the exit for the Pomona Fairgrounds, made the transition to the 57 South. Tammy was snoring. She'd nodded off that quick. I think she had too much alcohol in her bloodstream. After that last dance every man in the room was FedExing her a glass of wine.

Karen had closed her eyes. Just when I thought she was nodding off, she said, "Tammy was all over Stephan's big friend."

"He looked like a black Hoss Cartwright."

We laughed.

Karen said, "His other friend kept trying to hit on me too. As soon as we walked in the door, he was all up in my face."

"He was cute. Why didn't you exchange numbers with him?"

"Too pompous. Peacocking around the room, flashing his lady-killer smile like he was Shaka Zulu Billy Dee Denzel."

I cackled, "You see that gaudy pinkie ring his ass had on?"

"And I don't go out with anybody that wears a pinkie ring."

I laughed. "No pinkie rings. No Jheri Curls."

"And no gold teeth." Karen hummed. "Stephan ask you out?"

"Nope. You want to meet him?"

"No sloppy seconds. I can get my own."

I peeked in the rearview; Tammy was asleep with her face pasted against the window. I exited at Grand, whizzed by the golf course, and sped over the hill toward Diamond Bar Boulevard.

I parked in visitors and popped the trunk for Karen before all of us crawled out of the car. And I do mean crawled.

Karen was jumpy. "Why'd you open the trunk?"

I said, "Get your clothes. You're staying, right?"

Karen opened her door. "Both of you can go on up. I'll get my overnight bag and catch up with you."

Tammy stretched. "We ain't in no hurry."

Karen paused, twisted her lips, and said, "I can always come back down and get my stuff in the morning."

I told her, "Get it now. No need making two trips."

Karen was hesitating, acting all strange.

Tammy said, "What you hiding in the trunk, a dead body?"

When Karen saw that we weren't leaving without her getting her gear, she finally opened up the trunk. Barely. She tried to position herself so we couldn't peep inside. I leaned to the right and saw what she didn't want me to see. Tammy leaned to the left and saw, too. A lot of Mervyn's bags were crammed inside, stacked on top of her Adidas overnight bag.

Tammy said, "Somebody has been on a shopping spree."

Before Karen could grab her bag and close the trunk, Tammy had yanked open a couple of the bags. Pants, blouses, makeup, all kinds of goodies were in those shopping bags.

More stuff than Karen could afford.

I asked, "What's all this?"

Karen dropped her gym bag and pulled the stuff from our hands. "I just bought a few things."

As soon as Karen snatched a bag from one of us, either me or Tammy grabbed another one.

Tammy said, "This stuff ain't in your size. And some of this stuff is man's clothes. Who you buying man's clothes for?"

Karen's hand was shakier than her voice. "I already know what it is, fuck you very much. Give me my belongings, please?"

We all looked at each other for a moment.

"That's a lot of new clothes," I finally said. "Karen, if you're that short on money, why didn't you come to me?"

Her brows furrowed. "What are you saying?"

Neither Tammy nor I said a word, but we stood under the streetlight and stared at Karen with worry-filled eyes.

Then I said, "Don't lose your job over this mess."

Karen said, "What, you think I'm stealing from Mervyn's?"

Tammy raised a hand. "I ain't said nothing."

I fumed, "That's a carload of brand-new merchandise. And it don't look like much of it's in your size."

Karen practically jerked the last of it out of our hands, then slammed her trunk and tried to rush us toward my condo.

She rambled, "I'm just making some extra money. *Legally*."

I followed her and echoed, "*Legally*. How?"

"I buy stuff, use my discount to knock the price down, then sell it to people at the sale price, or the regular price. Depends. It puts a few dollars in my pockets here and there."

Tammy said, "Well, if that's the case, why ain't you offered your discount and whatever deal you got to me and Chanté?"

"Neither one of you shops at Mervyn's."

I snapped, "That's a lie, and you know it."

Tammy went off. "How can you tell us that we don't shop at a place that has aisles of makeup and racks of shoes?"

Tammy asked Karen another question or two about that stockpile of goodies. Karen said she was putting it all on her charge card, then paying the card off as her money came in. Her broke ass must've had a helluva credit limit, because she had at least a thousand dollars worth of goods crammed in her car. Her logic was as weak as watered-down coffee.

Tammy continued to ask question after question. I don't know what Karen's answers were, couldn't really hear because a bad feeling had numbed my ears.

I said, "Karen, if things are that bad, talk to me. I have room. You can move in here for a few months or something."

Her face said that she was insulted. She was so hard and so sensitive at the same time. Smart and foolish.

Tammy offered Karen the same kind of help. Karen told us that we were crazy for thinking that she was ripping anybody off.

I let my girls get settled. Tammy was asleep before I pointed her toward the bed. Karen hopped into the shower.

Karen had me so damn upset that I grabbed my keys. I was going to walk around the complex and calm my nerves, but I hopped in my car, let my windows down, and drove. I needed a moment to myself. I sped to where Diamond Bar Boulevard changed into Mission Boulevard in the city of Pomona, saw my gas hand at about a quarter tank, and pulled into a gas station that overlooked the 57/210/10 interchange.

I looked up and saw I was at another Arco. That pulled my mind away from Karen and made me think about Stephan. For a moment. Stephan No Middle Name Mitchell. His face was vague and faded from my mind as quickly as it had come. I imagined I felt Stephan's body rubbing up against mine when we were getting our dance on. It wasn't just that, but it was a combination of his looks, his intellect, him being the kinda man a wish-she-was-old-fashioned woman like me should have in her life that had stirred me up from the inside out. This coffee has been stirred up before, so the sensation that left warm, fuzzy tingles in the pit of my stomach was nothing new. It'd be gone by sunrise. He was definitely wrong for me. Anybody I was attracted to was wrong for me.

I made another stop before I headed back home.

When I parked and walked up to my condo, Karen was on my front porch. I'd seen her outside the moment I turned on Montefino. I'd been thinking about reiterating my offer to her, telling her to pack up her stuff and move in with me until hard times became softer. That was until I saw what she was doing.

I said, "I know you're not on my porch smoking a joint."

Karen had on her housecoat. She asked, "Where you been?"

I raised the bag I was holding. "Went to get some gas, then drove to 7-Eleven and bought some orange juice for breakfast."

She said, "That took thirty minutes?"

"If I was gone thirty minutes, then it took thirty minutes."

"Sure you didn't go by Stephan's and get your oil changed?"

"No. I told you that you can have his damn number if you want it. I went to get gas and OJ, is that all right with you?"

Her eyes said she didn't believe me. She inhaled her doobie.

I snapped, "Put that mess out before my neighbors call the cops. I don't know where you think you are."

"I'm stressed. Have to calm my nerves. I was worried about you. Didn't know if you came out here and somebody kidnapped you or what. Don't ever pull a disappearing act again."

"I'm sorry. Now chill with the illegal activity before the home-owners start writing me letters and try to evict me."

Karen put out her funny cigarette.

I asked, "Where are the receipts?"

"What receipts?"

"For the stuff you're hiding in the trunk of your car."

"Don't worry about it."

I nodded. "Until I see the paperwork for those *legal* packages, don't bring any of that merchandise into my home."

She chuckled like I was pathetic, made a *humph* sound, and followed me inside.

# 16 Darnell

Eleven a.m.

Venice Beach.

A thick layer of fog stretched out before us, covered the mountains, outlined the horizon. It was warm, but a cool breeze came by every now and then. Still, it was one of the prettiest April days I'd ever seen.

Once again I glanced at my clothes, smoothed out my shirt.

Don't know why I was worried about the way I was dressed. My white shorts, Nikes, and red-n-black Chicago Bulls T-shirt was more than enough for Venice. People were walking around half-naked. I was more self-conscious because Tammy was sitting across from me. We were in the middle of a bustling crowd at the Sidewalk Café, at a small table on a patio facing the boardwalk.

Tammy looked so hip in her rectangular shades and yellow lenses. Her lime top was sleeveless, and the V of the cotton material revealed the crescendo of her breasts. The kind that a man had to struggle not to look at in awe. Her jean shorts were frayed. Short, but not so short that they crossed the line of good taste. Silver rings on almost every finger, matching bracelets, and when she crossed her long legs I saw a silver ring sparkling on one of her toes. Chocolate lipstick, clear polish on both her fingernails and her toenails.

Last night at Shelly's, when she and her friends had sat at our table, before Stephan showed up, Jake had mentioned to the girls that I was an attorney and an aspiring writer. That led to a long literary conversation between me and Tammy. She'd been taking a stab at writing herself. Within three minutes you would've thought that Tammy was one of my childhood friends. On the back of her business card she'd written me a note: *I feel you, my brother. And I get the sense that you feel me on a level that most people miss. If it's okay with you, I'd love to get together and share my work with you. And I'd love to read some of yours. Black writers need to stick together. Meet me for lunch tomorrow if you want to share.*

*Share.*

That was the one word that kept me from tossing her note.

At home, there was no sharing of my life.

She asked me about my job. I told her what I did at the FAA was basically fine corporations, individuals, and airlines for violations.

She asked, "What's the most you've sued an airline for?"

"Half a million."

"*Dayum.* Ever sue any celebrities?"

"All the time. Most of them are impossible to deal with."

"Anybody famous?"

I told her about a singer-actress that we'd fined.

Tammy asked, "What did she do?"

"She saw the no-smoking sign, then asked the flight attendant how much the fine was if she fired up. The attendant told her two thousand dollars. Then Miss Thang said that she could afford that and went in the bathroom and fired up her cigarette."

"That's wild. She paid two thousand dollars just so she could smoke one cigarette?"

I nodded. "I hope you don't get like that when you make it."

Tammy said, "Well, with the Grammys, and platinum records and movies and HBO specials, she could afford the two grand."

We ordered and the waiter had just rushed away when out of the blue she asked, "How long have you been married?"

I almost told her that I'd known Dawn eight years. Met her when I was twenty-two and she was twenty-four. I wanted to explain the evolution of my relationship to Tammy. Let her know what allowed me to be here with her at a clandestine meeting in Venice right now.

But I said, "I've been married six years."

"That's a California record."

"It is."

Her tone was lighthearted, spirited. "What does she do?"

"Real estate."

Then I wanted to tell Tammy that my wife didn't love her job. Had no love for her career. But she was satisfied with doing what she had to do to pay the bills. I was ready for Tammy to ask me where Dawn was at this moment, and I was ready to tell her that my wife had an open house, so I had the day to myself. And in the middle of all of that I was ready for Tammy to stand up and walk away.

Tammy held on to her smile. "A lawyer and a real estate agent. You guys trying to be the Huxtables of the Inland Empire or something?"

We laughed.

I asked, "Where's your boyfriend?"

She laughed. "I'm too old to have a *boyfriend*."

"You barely look twenty-five."

Her laugh died mid-chuckle. "I'm twenty-three."

"Oh. Ooops. I'm sorry."

Again she laughed, "Gotcha."

"Yeah, you got me."

She admitted, "I'll be the big three-o soon."

"How soon?"

"In three years."

More laughter.

She touched my hands, patted my flesh with the tips of her fingers. "Thanks for telling me I still look twenty-five. Since I'm tall, have a little size, people usually think I'm older."

Pounds of flattery were heavy on my tongue, but I turned my tongue inside, kept those words to myself.

Tammy confessed that she had told her friends she had an audition, had skipped out on going to the gym so she could meet me. She'd lied. And I'd lied. I didn't know why I did what I did, but I asked her why she created a falsehood, especially since this was supposed to be a business meeting between us.

She said, "Chanté and Karen—I love 'em, but sometimes I need some breathing room. If I'd told Chanté I was heading for the beach, she would've grabbed her two-piece and been in the car before I could tell her I didn't want her tagging along. After all the fussing last night, I wanted to get away from both of 'em."

"They seemed pretty tight last night."

She shook her head like she was weighed down by the stress she carried. "You don't know the half of it. Sometimes when they get together, I don't know what it is, but the tension grows, and the next thing I know somebody's feelings get hurt and they're going at it like an old married couple."

She was serious, but her delivery made me laugh. I said, "And you play referee?"

"Huh-ell no. I pretend I'm sleep. I do that so much they think I'm narcoleptic. Last night they were arguing before we made it to Chanté's crib."

"What about?"

"Stephan."

I was surprised. "Arguing over Stephan?"

"Karen saw him, liked him, wanted to talk to him. Then she got upset when Chanté started freaky-deaky dancing with him. But then again, Karen thinks every man on this planet wants her."

Our conversation changed several times.

The one that hit me a little hard was when she told me, "You're a Christian?"

"How do you know?"

"Christians have a positive energy I love being around."

I felt transparent, said, "And you? Are you a Christian?"

"I'm more spiritual than religious. I go to church at Agape. That's when I go, which isn't often enough."

"Never heard of Agape."

She adjusted her shades, told me, "It's in Santa Monica."

"Me and my wife—" I didn't mean to say me and my wife, but I hadn't referred to myself in the singular in so long that it was hard to do, even when I tried. I said, "When I go, I attend St. Stephen. That's out my way in West Covina."

A wall of religion and righteousness had been wedged between us. After the fun we had experienced last night, that was good.

She asked, "How long've you been writing?"

"I did some short stories before I went to law school. Entered them in the local contest by my house, at Mount San Antonio College. Had one published in a local anthology. But after law school ended and I'd passed the bar, I still had that void. I love law, but I feel like I have a bigger purpose."

"Why did you become a lawyer?"

"My daddy was from Houston, and he always told me that a black man should understand the white man's law. That way he can beat him at his own game."

Tammy nodded. "I know exactly how you feel. I went to the University of Nevada."

"What was your major?"

"Journalism. My five sisters worked in the casinos until they either got pregnant or found a husband, but I knew that welfare lifestyle wasn't gonna be my gig. I grew up in Laughlin wanting to be a news anchor, had to have my face on TV one way or the other. I graduated cum laude, but I've never had a job in journalism."

"How did you end up acting and singing?"

"Well, I always sang in church. Always did plays in high school and college. I came out here to visit a friend, this jerk I was seeing in college, picked up the *Dramalogue* he had in his apartment, and the next thing I knew I was living in North Hollywood, getting headshots, beating down doors for auditions."

Tammy glanced at her watch, saw time was flying, then opened a black and red Eso Won book bag and took out about fifty sheets of paper, all paper-clipped together. She handed it to me.

She said, "Well, here's my little ol' play."

"What's the title?"

"Right now the title is, well, I call it 'Untitled.' "

More lighthearted laughs.

She perked up and said, "Now gimme dat novel you said you've been slaving away on. I see your leather attaché under your seat, so don't tell me you forgot it at home."

"I brought it." I opened my dark brown attaché, moved my stack of *California Lawyer* magazines to the side. I let her know, "A copy of it lives with me twenty-four seven. I live and breathe this story. I'll give you about fifty pages."

"How long is it?"

I hemmed and hawed. "Around four hundred pages. But that's with one-inch margins and double spacing. That's the format that *Writer's Market* said manuscripts should—"

"Yadda yadda yadda. Gimme the whole doggone thing."

"You sure?"

"Gimme."

And I couldn't get Dawn, my wife, the one feminine creature on this planet who should be my biggest supporter, to read ten pages.

I told Tammy, "It's unedited. I know I need to strengthen my verbs, maybe add a line here and there for description—"

"Stop making excuses. If we're going to read each other's work, that's the first rule. No excuses. Agreed?"

"Agreed."

"No excuses. No apologies. Brutally honest. Now gimme."

My mind was on relationships. On my relationship. On the forever that I had stood before God, my pastor, my family, and promised. People leave out the human factor. They forget that we evolve, that we change, that with every tomorrow we reinvent ourselves a million times over. The things we want today might just be the things that we want to forget about tomorrow.

Taking the manuscript, Tammy said, "Your wife is a lucky woman."

"I wish she realized that."

"She will." Tammy patted me on my hand. On my left hand. On my wedding ring. "Why're all the good brothers taken all the time? I'm having a good time with somebody else's dime."

"What about your boyfriend?"

*"Boyfriend."* She laughed. "There you go again."

"Does he realize what he has?"

She sighed, then made a face that said he wasn't all that. "Well, let me put it to you like this. I spend a lot of weekends out in Diamond Bar. Alone."

We talked. Talked about our friends. About how hard everybody partied last night.

She thought that Stephan and Jake were pretty much the same, but to me they're different. Good, bad, sane, or psychotic, Stephan falls in love with all of the women in life. Jake doesn't have a clue what love is. If love came in a pouch and all he had to do was add water, Jake still wouldn't get it right. But both of my friends have a freedom that I envy. I've always been in a relationship. In a monogamous relationship. I criticized their lifestyles, but I lived vicariously through them. Hearing about their sexcapades did something for me.

I asked her, "Can I see you again?"

She hesitated. My abruptness had caught her off guard. She dropped her eyes, lines grew in her forehead. "We'll hook up."

"When?"

She emphasized, "To give each other critiques."

She knew what I meant, but I let it go. I was glad she brought that to a screeching halt.

Somebody walked up behind me. "Darnell?"

A chill ran up my back. I felt like a captured fugitive.

I turned and saw Debra Dubois. She lives next door to Stephan's parents. She was coming out of Small World Books, the mystery bookstore that was attached to the eatery. Slender sister, shoulder-length light brown hair, fair skin, in plain jeans and Grecian sandals.

The biggest surprise came when Tammy perked up and said, "Debra! Hey, girl."

Tammy hopped out of her seat and they started hugging.

Debra told Tammy, "I was thinking about you the other day. We saw your orange juice commercial."

"I'm still in the biz."

Debra asked, "No big breaks?"

"Did a few pilots, but nothing has come through. You know how it is for a black woman in a white man's business."

Debra smiled, but I saw some pain underneath. She told me, "Before the accident, Tammy was going to be Leonard's co-star in his television show."

I didn't say anything.

Debra asked, "How's Dawn doing?"

I said, "She's fine."

That was all I said, which left an awkward moment.

Tammy asked Debra, "How's the baby?"

"Little Leonard is doing fine. He's out there somewhere with Tyrel and Shelby, driving them crazy. Shelby has spoiled him."

I asked, "How's Shelby?"

"Crazy as ever."

We talked, not long, but long enough.

Awkward words in a conversation that no one knew how to end.

Her eyes went from Tammy to me. One of us had to say something, and I was out of words. Tammy perked up and told Debra about the play at the Hudson Theater that she'd been cast in. Debra smiled. Again, her eyes went from Tammy to me. She was asking things in her mind.

She finally left.

Tammy said, "That was uncomfortable."

"Are you okay?"

"Debra knows your wife and my friends."

"Small world."

"Very."

Tammy gathered the pages I'd given her.

I did the same with her work.

I paid the bill. Left a twenty-five-percent tip.

We said distant good-byes.

Last night, in darkness, alcohol, and music, she'd sat in my lap and rubbed my head. Today, in the brilliance of the sun, in a place where there were no shadows, she waved good-bye.

She went north, toward Santa Monica. I turned right, went toward the muscle section of the beach. Strolled through the thick crowds, avoided brothers walking pit bulls, white men with pet boa constrictors around their necks, went beyond the sidewalk comedians, artists, and people juggling chain saws.

I rested on the concrete bleachers in front of the b-ball courts, right where *White Men Can't Jump* was filmed. Sat there, pen in hand, writing down the details—sight, sound, taste, smell—tried to capture it all. I eavesdropped on conversations, wrote down every word verbatim. Later I'd look at it, check out the way people talk in real life, then work on writing dialogue.

Watching shirtless brothers run up and down the full-length court like gazelles reminded me of how skillful I was before I slowed down. I married. I'd added forty-five pounds since I stumbled over that broom. Seeing the hard bodies pumping and grunting and putting on a show with the free weights in the open gym made me wish for a better me.

But I'm not a gazelle.

I'm not a writer.

I'm an attorney for the FAA.

I'm married.

And I've stood before God and made a promise of forever.

But nothing was absolute, and forever didn't last for always. Whether it's a job or a relationship, sometimes the end of forever creeps up on you.

A brother on roller skates, a turban on his head as he played a guitar, whisked backward down the boardwalk.

A brisk breeze ran from the salty Pacific into my face.

A soft voice: "Darnell?"

"Hey, Tammy. Thought you were long gone by now."

She held up my work. I thought she was about to give my labor of love back. My anxiety told me that I'd done something to offend her while we shared our meal.

Tammy said, "Good. This is good."

"You read it that fast?"

"About forty pages. I started reading while I was walking to my car and I couldn't stop. Actually, I never made it to my car. I ended up coming back and sitting in the sand down by where the skaters are clowning. *Dayum.* Your characters are unbelievable."

"Wow." I smiled. "That's a serious compliment."

She sat next to me, inches away. "You write better than I sing."

"Now you're stretching it."

"No joke. I read a lot. I read at least two novels a month, and I've read a million scripts. This is your calling." That smile of hers became nervous and unsure. "I did have to come back and tell you. I hoped you were still down here somewhere, but at the same time I hoped you were gone."

With her last comment we stood and gazed at each other.

She said, "Let's walk. Walk and think."

We passed by a plethora of sidewalk vendors. Walked in silence as Tammy headed toward the ocean. I followed her behind the racquetball courts and gymnastic equipment, trailed her to the three-foot wall that separated the bike and skate trail from the part of the beach where half-naked people were tanning.

She stopped by the wall. I stood next to her, gazed at the ocean like I was trying to see as far as China.

Tammy spoke in a bittersweet tone. "You're married, Darnell."

Softly I said, "I know."

"Why did you say you wanted to see me?"

"Because."

"I'm listening."

"You're fantastic."

"You don't know me. Singing and dancing doesn't make a woman fabulous. It's all show. An illusion. Not real. That's not me on stage. That's Tammy the entertainer."

"Can I get to know you? I mean Tammy the person."

"Get to know me?"

"As a friend."

"As a friend?"

"Yeah. As a friend."

"My friend Karen says men and women can't be friends. Somebody'll always want to bump the relationship to the next level."

"She's wrong."

"Is she?" Tammy bounced her feet against the wall, did it in no particular rhythm. "Your writing is so good I'm considering snatching my work back from you."

I reminded her, "No excuses. No apologies."

"I hate I said that now."

We laughed. Which was good. I thought that we'd never laugh together again.

She released a nervous sigh. "Darnell, I can't tell you enough how much I liked your writing. Especially the love scene. It's *so* erotic. It moved me."

"Thanks."

Tammy said, "So, you think I'm fantastic."

"Yep."

"No one has ever told me that."

"Everybody should. Anybody who can't see that is a fool."

"Well, I was raised in a house full of fools."

"I'd like to meet your house full of fools."

"Be careful." Her tone was dead serious. "I just might drag you out to Laughlin and torture you with their presence."

She pulled a blue felt pen out of her purse, took my hand, wrote her home number in my palm. Wrote slowly. It tickled. The number that was on the business card that she'd given me last night was to her answering service.

Then she walked away. No good-bye.

I stayed on the other side of the wall. Watched her stop at a stand, buy a Smoothie, then once again she went north.

I stared at the numbers in my hand.

My thoughts were heavy as I took the 90 eastbound to the 405 south to the 105 east to the 605 north to the 60 east. It was an hour drive from Venice to the city of Walnut. An hour of solitude as I drove from the coolness of the coast into the heat of the east.

The sun was setting, and Dawn was just getting home. We pulled up in our double garage at the same time. I sat in my car for a moment before I eased out. She had hopped out of her vehicle almost before she stopped.

Her heels click-clopped on the concrete as she walked to the back of her red Range Rover and took out her briefcase, pulled out her open house signs. Her Sue Grafton novel was sticking out of her briefcase. So she'd been reading that during the slow moments of her day. My wife had on a green skirt that hugged her hips and hit right above her knees; beige blouse that was thin enough to show the sexiness of her bra. Her hair didn't look as together as it had this morning, and her armpits were dank with perspiration.

My wife was beautiful. More beautiful than Tammy.

Then she opened her mouth. "Today was such a waste. So damn hot all day. Help me with these groceries. It looks like the neighbor's kid rode that damn mountain bicycle across our lawn again. Last time that happened, the bastard broke two of our sprinklers. Darnell, please talk to them, because if I have to go over there again, first I'm hurting somebody, then they're going to write me a check to get my sprinklers repaired."

She reached for a Vons grocery bag, but I stopped her. I kissed her. First her eyes opened with confusion. She leaned away, gawked at me like I was insane, but I held her face, softly, and let my tongue muffle her negative comments. I kissed her like it was the first time that our lips had met.

She caught her breath, asked, "Darnell, you're messing up my blouse. C'mon, now. Stop. What's gotten into you?"

"Let me be your husband."

And I kissed her some more.

"Darnell, I have ice cream in here. It's going to melt."

The garage door was up and I was inside a warm garage, feeling my wife up like we were sixteen-year-olds.

She whispered, "At least let the garage door down. People are outside. The Asian kids across the street might be looking."

The garage door hummed down and my mouth was on Dawn's breasts. I had loosened her top and taken her softness from inside her satin bra. My mouth was all over her. My hands were exploring, like this was the first time. Touching. Feeling. Squeezing all of the physical things that defined her as a woman.

She started to moan, loosened up, gave in when I pulled her skirt up, and reached to unzip my pants. She shuddered and clung to me when I pushed myself inside her. Pushed as far as I could, as hard as I could. She said a few words to God. Then she cursed, held me, and moved her hips in surrender, allowed me to go deeper, deeper. And we stood there against her truck, being man and wife. With every moan I tried to make her sing, tried to make her dance. I closed my eyes and imagined she was Tammy.

# 17 Chanté

When I woke up the next morning, Tammy and Karen were already gone. It was too late to get down to 24 Hour Fitness for Angela's class, so I rolled over and called Stephan. He'd been on my mind all night.

I asked him, "Were you asleep?"

"Damn right."

We both laughed.

Stephan told me that he had been planning to play racquetball with Darnell and his wife. "But Darnell called and canceled. He said that his wife had an open house today, and he couldn't make it either."

"That's your firefighter friend in the Shaka Zulu suit?"

He chuckled. "The other guy. The big one."

"Oh. The one who was jocking Tammy all night."

"The one that Tammy was jocking."

I said, "Since you've got all of that energy, and I really ain't in the mood for the gym, you ready to change my oil?"

"Give me about an hour."

"Okay." I yawned. "Give me directions to your ponderosa."

He did, then said, "Playing it safe, huh?"

"Playing it safe. See you between noon and one."

I made it to Stephan's around two. He met me out front of his condo, then had me park. He drove me to Wal-Mart to get a filter and oil and whatever else I needed.

When we got back and he parked under his wooden carport, I had a look around at all the Mexican palms and evergreen trees that lined the beige and brown condos. The ones on his side had stalls, but the ones facing his had detached garages. All the buildings were about the same beige shade of stucco as mine. That was pretty much the description of every house, apartment, and building in the area.

I asked him, "Any units for sale around here?"

"Plenty. People are still getting laid off, so owners are bailing left and right. I've seen a few three-day notices tacked on doors. A few have had to get removed by the sheriff. My buddy Darnell did unlawful detainers for one of my neighbors. People moved in, didn't pay rent, then wouldn't move out."

"A lot to consider before you start trying to be a landlord."

"That's why I'll never do it."

We were walking up his shaky concrete stairs when a door opened and somebody at the top stuck her head out. She was in a housecoat and rollers. At first I thought it was his girlfriend because of her frown, but when I took a closer look, I thought it might be his mother. Even closer, I thought grandmother.

"Hi, Stephan." The lady spoke to him but stared at me. "I heard you out here painting this morning at the crack of dawn."

I smelled the paint that she was talking about.

I didn't know why the lady was gawking. Maybe it was my green spandex shorts and oversized pink T-shirt that bothered the woman. Her eyes made me feel like I was butt naked.

"How're you today, Rebecca?" Stephan smiled and introduced me.

I said, "Good afternoon."

Rebecca adjusted her clothes, turned up her nose. "Hi."

Then the heifer closed her door. Closed it hard.

Damn.

I followed him inside and let my nosiness take over. My eyes went on a journey and checked out everything when he stepped out onto his patio. After he came back in with an armful of clothes and headed for the bedroom, I opened the patio door and stepped out, peeped inside the outside storage closet he left open. There was a dryer next to a metal bookcase. A basketball. Deflated football. Tennis racquets. A lot of how-to-fix-this and how-to-make-that manuals were on the glass bookcase in the living room. Electronics books. Computer manuals. Stacks of tattered *Wall Street Journals* and *Daily Bulletins* were withering away in a rack by his entertainment center. Green leather sofa, love seat, and ottoman. Place smelled like potpourri. Beige carpet, white walls made the room look bigger. Stereo in the living room, no television. Plants on each end table and on the kitchen counter. Impressive so far.

No pinkie ring. No Jheri curl. No come-ons.

Karen's voice came to life inside my head, and jarred me: *Stupidest sister with a degree . . .*

"Nice place," I told Stephan. "For a guy."

"Nice comment, for a gal."

"Ohhh, your plants are dying." I pulled dead leaves out, threw them into his kitchen garbage can, searched his cabinets and found a large plastic cup and filled it with water. I watered the plants in his living room, then walked into his bedroom. No waterbed. A love nest with a marble headboard and a paisley comforter. Matching sheets, pillowcases. The clothes he'd just brought in were scattered on the bed. He wears boxers, V-neck undershirts, has a lot of gym shorts and jock straps, so he must work out quite a bit. It's amazing what you can tell about people just by looking at how they live. Plants were on top of his dresser next to *Ebony* and *Essence* magazines. I put the plants on the floor and pulled out a few more dead leaves.

I said, "These ferns and spider plants and the ones with the red leaves need light. I'm moving them by your window."

He called out from the living room. "Make yourself at home."

"Ha, ha."

His bathroom was clean, had shades of green color-coordinated towels. A woman must've helped him get this organized. That had to be why the place had so much warmth.

"How can your crib be so clean and your plants so dead?" I asked. "You have a cleaning woman?"

"I'm just lacking in horticulture skills."

I asked, "You have food?"

"Nope. Not a crumb."

"I'm hungry," I told him. There was something about him I liked. Before I knew it, trust took over and I was going against the grain of my heart. I bit my lip. "Why don't you follow me home? I can cook something while you change the oil."

He stuck his head in. "Where in Diamond Bar do you live?"

I hesitated, thought about reneging on my offer, then said, "In Allegro. The condos behind Vineyard National Bank."

He said, "You're at Diamond Bar and Grand."

I shrugged. "It's getting hot outside. You'd have to work in your carport. I have a garage, so you won't have to work in the sun."

At my condo, Stephan finished changing my oil in about thirty minutes. When he stepped out on my sun deck and said he was already done, that surprised and impressed me. Seemed like every time I went to the dealer for an oil change, it took them at least half a day.

My photo albums were up in my loft, so while I finished getting everything together, he browsed through the pictures of my life. He saw me in ponytails, braces, high school, prom night.

He brought the albums down and sat at the kitchen table. "In most of these you look like a JC Penney catalog model."

"You calling me a nerd?"

"You look so damn wholesome. Australia. Switzerland. Germany. I see you and your folks have been a lot of places."

"What about you? You ever been away from North America?"

"Jamaica. Cabo. Canada a few times. Never off North America. Unless you consider Hawaii getting off North America."

We chowed on turkey burgers and chattered like black buppies. I told him that my mother used to be events coordinator at a museum back in Chi-town, but she quit so she could trot the globe with Daddy. "I pretty much grew up in the museum."

He asked, "So, you like museums."

"Yeah. Haven't been to one in a while, though."

"Wanna roll? There's an exhibit I want to check out."

Stephan drove me into the city of Lost Angels, took me down on Museum Row to the Los Angeles County Museum of Art. We checked out Rhapsodies in Black, a phat showcase of art from the Harlem Renaissance. We spent a couple of hours perusing paintings, sculptures, photographs by James Van Der Zee, Walker Evans, Carl Van Vechten.

I asked, "You heard of these people?"

"Hadn't heard of Micheaux. Says he made over forty films."

"Me either. Tammy knows all about stuff like this."

"Hell, I thought Spike was the first brother to make a film."

"Wasn't Melvin Van Peebles the first?"

We laughed. Both of us were living in Joke City.

He was so warm. So easy to talk to. So polite. Those almond eyes, thick brows, curly lashes, those strong features that sang of eroticism and intellect had me staring at him like he was the best piece of art in the whole building.

I loved wit and sarcasm. Conversations that flowed as easy as the Nile. And there was nothing like a connoisseur of culture.

We were maneuvering around a crowd when somehow our hands ended up side by side, then intertwined as we stopped at exhibit listening stations.

We passed by a collection of photographs from the Negro League—Baltimore Black Sox, Atlanta Black Crackers—and I asked him, "What's your favorite sport?"

He responded, "Kissing."

That caught me off guard.

I came back, "What position?"

"Sixty-eight plus one. What's yours?"

Again I came back, "Eighty minus eleven."

Walking and having fun, slipping in double entendres, indulging in intellectual conversation that masked erotic desire made me feel like Europa and he was my tall caramel Zeus, wanting to carry me to the island of Crete and do some freaky-deaky things to me.

Stephan checked his watch. "I need to stop by Baldwin Hills."

"What's up there?"

"My momma. If I come out here and don't stop by to say hello, she bitches."

"So, Stephan No Middle Name Mitchell, you have parents."

"A mother and a stepfather. Three brothers. A sister. Me and my oldest brother's daddy died a long time ago."

A volleyball net was up in the backyard. Music was blasting from a boom box. About eight kids were having fun.

Three children ran to Stephan before he made it into the backyard. He introduced them—Akeem, Ronda, and Nathan Junior. Stephan told me the rest were the neighbors' children.

All the kids ran back to their fun. All except for Akeem. He stared like he was viewing a rare flower, smiling like he had a crush on me. He was an elementary-sized brown-skinned boy with teeth too big for his narrow face. He said, "Whussup, Uncle Steph?"

" 'Sup, 'Keem?"

"That crazy girl from Palm Springs been calling out here—"

Stephan cut him off. "Go play, 'Keem."

The little boy smiled at me. "Uh-oh, Unca Steph done pulled him another hottie."

I corrected him, "My name is Chanté, and your uncle and I are just friends. We live by each other."

"Baby, you all that. Can I be your man? I got a Big Wheel parked out front, and we can roll down to Crenshaw and get a bean pie."

"*Go play, 'Keem.*" Stephan raised his voice at him, then popped the rugrat upside the head. "Nathan Junior, come get your brother before I hurt him."

We walked around back, following all the jubilant noises from the ghetto blaster. This peach stucco, Spanish-style home was real nice. Tucked in a cul-de-sac, so they didn't get any traffic. They had a serious view of L.A., from La Brea all the way out to the HOLLYWOOD sign.

Even with that, the air was so cool it felt like a different world. Shit, I almost hated that I'd have to drive east, because once we made it on the other side of downtown and crossed the 710 freeway, the heat would be on like Donkey Kong.

We went in through the back, and from what I could see, all of their furniture was heavy oak wood. Polished to sparkle. Comfortable country living. An old black-and-white TV was in the kitchen, a coat hanger for an antenna.

I followed Stephan to a sunken den and met his stepdaddy, two of his aunts, and an uncle. They were eating. His stepdad had a serious presence. Dark, bald, and sporting a goatee. He was on a big, plush sofa, an unlit cigar in his mouth.

Stephan spoke to everybody, introduced me to Aunt Edwonda, Uncle Glen, and Aunt Anabelle, then asked his stepdad, "Where's Momma?"

"Price Club down on Rosecran. You just missed her. She'll be back directly."

Stephan told his stepdad, "Tell Momma I came by."

"You gone already?"

"Yeah. Momma'll be shopping all day."

"You stop by the barber shops and holler at your brothers?"

"Too much traffic on Crenshaw. I'll hit 'em later."

His big-bellied Uncle Louie asked, "Where you off to?"

"I'm heading back to no man's land."

When we made it back to Diamond Bar, I invited him to come up for a few. I turned on the central air, set the ceiling fans on high to help speed up the cooling, then turned on my big-screen television and slid the remote to Stephan. He was on the rugged section of my parquet floor, craning his neck, looking around at my family pictures, at my parents' wedding picture, and my other art, most of which depicted African Americans in love. I was still an idealistic fool when I bought those paintings.

I smiled and said, "You can look around if you like."

He rose and meandered from room to room, stepped into my bedroom. Something about him being in that intimate space both made me uncomfortable and thrilled me at the same time. All day, little things he'd done, little things he'd said, had excited me.

He said, "You have a helluva lot of romance novels."

I said softly, "My Harlequin romance days are over."

"You do taxes?"

"Sometimes. Why?"

"Tax-prep and accounting books are on your headboard."

That set off another train of thought. "Stephan, I have a new laptop. Can you set it up?"

"Won't be much to do. Just plug and go."

"Can you make sure?"

"Yeah. When?"

"Not now, just whenever you have a moment."

Stephan came back into the living room and sat on the part of the floor the farthest away from me, like he thought I would bite him.

"I'm sweating," I said, and fanned my arms. "I'm going to take a quick bath before I melt."

"I'll leave." Stephan stood.

"Chill out. Watch the idiot box till I'm done. I like your company."

"Want me to wash your back?"

I smiled. "I'll think about it."

"I was just kidding."

"I wasn't."

I pulled back my golden shower curtains, ran my water, and dropped in strawberry- and champagne-scented beads. When I passed by to get a robe out of my walk-in closet, I saw that Stephan was glued to the television. I had to turn the light on to find my robe; that was when I realized it was dark. I wondered where the day had gone. I'd been in a daze, using Stephan as my guide.

I threw my robe over my shoulder, then headed into the kitchen and pulled a bottle of Asti Spumante out of the pantry.

"Thirsty?" I asked.

He shook his head. "I'm straight."

Back in the bathroom, I pinned my hair, slid down to my neck in the warm water. The bathroom door was halfway open. Music videos were playing. I sipped my Spumante, slipped into a mood, listened to the Queen of Soul chanting that a rose was still a rose. I closed my eyes, let her talk to me, sang along and kept affirming, kept telling myself that no matter what I'd been through, no matter what I'd go through, I was still a flower.

I ran some more hot water in the tub and heard comedians on BET doing their routines. Stephan was cracking up.

I thought, "Cute laugh. Kinda country, but cute."

Stephan said, "That D'Militant is funny as hell."

"Stephan!"

"Yeah?"

I hesitated. "I'm ready."

"For?"

"My back washing."

I hadn't expected to go there, but that boldness had popped out of me. I was daring him, waiting for him to back down.

A second later Stephan stood at the door. In the shadows. I smiled, covered my breasts with my palms, then quivered when I turned my back to him. The hall light was turned off, and the sensor for the automatic night light was activated, yielding a delicate light without stealing all of the charming darkness.

He asked, "Ready?"

"Only if I can trust you."

I closed my eyes. When he touched my flesh, rubbed my back, everything tingled. What was I getting myself into, inviting him into my bathroom while I sat booty naked in a tub of soapy water? Months ago this would've terrified me. Not now. My blood rushed. Underneath my coolness, I was nervous.

Stephan reached past me, moved his grubby paws like he was reaching to cop a feel on my 36Cs. I jumped a little. But he took the bar soap from the holder, soaped my wash cloth, then gently washed my back, circling clockwise, then counterclockwise. He scooped water into his hands and rinsed my skin. Slow and easy, taking his time. He moved into more personal territory and massaged my shoulders.

He hit a spot that made me *mmmm* and slightly arch my back.

He asked, "Why're you smiling so hard?"

"Why didn't you ask me for my number again, partner?"

"I asked once."

"Ask again."

"Once is asking, twice is begging."

"You're not going to beg?" I turned so he couldn't see, moved one hand from my bosom and sipped my hooch. If he saw, he couldn't see much anyway, only the round of my C-cups.

"If I begged, you'd never respect me."

"Some things are worth begging for."

"Some things are worth giving when asked for."

Stephan stopped massaging my back and sat on the floor. He filled my wineglass, took a sip, handed it back to me.

I slid down to my neck in the water, imagined I was a queen on the Nile, placed a heel of my foot on the rim by the wall.

I asked, "Where's your woman?"

"We broke up."

"Too bad."

He asked, "For who?"

I shrugged. "For whoever regrets it."

"I'll adjust. She'll get over it."

"Love her?"

"Infatuated beyond reason."

I'd never heard that response before. It sounded so real.

Infatuation, not love.

I asked, "Rub my shoulders again?"

This time I didn't cover my chest. I held my Spumante, pretended I was at Glen Ivy getting a rub down, and sipped my sin juice as he kneaded the kinks out. Moans came out of my body as he patted my skin, stimulated me.

"Better?" he asked.

"Mmmmmm. Yeah. You should do this for a living."

"Thought you were about to nod off."

"Could have." I had floated into another life. "You have strong hands, but they are so gentle at the same time."

"You have soft skin."

"Oil of Olay keeps me that way." I enjoyed the soft, kittenish tone of our conversation. I asked a silly question: "So, Stephan No Middle Name Mitchell, are you flirting with me?"

"I'm not your type."

I flicked wet fingers at him, splashed water on his face.

Stephan asked, "Where's your man?"

"You saw."

"You two going to get back together?"

"Fuck no."

"Getting a little hostile."

I responded. "Men make me the way I am."

"And how are you?"

I hunched my shoulders, asked, "Even when you have somebody, do you ever feel like you don't have anybody?"

"Yep."

"Like the relationship just ain't all that?"

"Yeah," Stephan said. "I can be with somebody, just finished, you know . . ."

I filled in the blank and said, "Getting your freak on."

"Yeah. And still feel alone."

I offered him my glass. "Want more?"

"No. I don't drink much."

"Neither do I. Mainly when I'm pissed or stressed."

He asked, "Which are you now?"

"I'm not sure."

I used my toes to grip the chain connected to the stopper and pulled it out of the tub. Listened to the sound of the water whirling out of the tub. Naked. Soap on my body, my eyes on Stephan. I stood, felt like Josephine Baker. Water and suds rained from me. I enjoyed watching him watch me.

I said, "Hand me my robe from behind the door."

I took my time about putting my robe on, and when I did, I let the belt hang loose. The fabric clung to my damp skin, outlined my body, gave the appearance of being nude.

Satin against soft and wet Nubian flesh.

I was exhilarated but kept my feelings in check.

Stephan asked, "What're you thinking?"

I hadn't had a decent lover in a while, and my body was starting to crave satisfaction the way a crack head craved crack.

"I'm thinking . . ." I took a breath and eased away. "It's getting late. Maybe I've had a bit too much to drink. And . . ."

Stephan waited. "And what?"

I dropped my head, took my eyes off his, blocked him out of the gateway to my soul. "C'mon, partner, you know the rest."

"Feeling's mutual."

Stephan invited me closer and kissed my forehead. He kissed me like he was kissing his little sister. I rose on tiptoe and kissed those thick brows, those curly lashes, then sprinkled light kisses on his lips, testing. Then I opened my mouth and invited him to relish my flavors. I'll have to admit, it was awkward at first, but the second kiss had a natural flow. I felt him adapting, slowing and tasting. I did the same, adjusted to his rhythm. I pulled him closer, felt him start to get hard, moved closer to feel what he had for me to feel, felt that bump growing. Then I eased away in the middle of the kiss. I hoped he'd resist me moving my body away from him, but he didn't.

He stared, mouth open like he was ready to whisper.

If only he knew, I wanted more, some more, and then some.

His passionate thoughts rose into his eyes.

He swallowed whatever he was thinking.

Stephan gave me another kiss on the forehead. "Good night."

"Thanks for everything."

"Welcome. I'll look at your computer some other time. I have a ton of software that you might want to check out."

"Okay. Sounds like a plan."

He headed out the front door.

A hurricane was swirling inside me.

I licked my lips, gazed at him through my living room blinds, watched him as he adjusted the stiffness in his pants and strolled toward his green car. I adjusted my robe over swollen nipples that were harder than what he had to offer.

"Stephan Mitchell," I whispered as delicate as a snowflake. "I know you're going to look back to see if I'm looking."

He kept moving away from my life.

I said, "I have power. You better recognize that, partner."

Then he glanced back and saw my silhouette pondering down on him. From where I stood, the way his face looked flushed under the streetlights, I felt him, his energy, his raging undercurrent, sensed that his breathing was just as disturbed as mine. He paused, stared like he couldn't decide which way to go.

All he could see was my dark shape, couldn't feel the mixed-up part of me that was wondering what kind of signal I'd just put out, couldn't see the tears that were in my swollen eyes.

He waved.

So did I.

With slow, heavy steps he moved to his car.

Stephan drove off.

I stood there, staring at the spot where he had parked.

I spoke over the lump in my throat. "Twice is begging."

# 18 Darnell

Ten p.m. Out in the Inland Empire it had been almost a hundred degrees all day, not a record high for the beginning of May, but hot enough to avoid any outdoor activity. It had calmed down to a warm night. All of the lights were off, except a black and golden lamp on my mahogany desk. I had been at the computer, writing. This was where I'd been since I made it home from the FAA at six, three hours and five pages ago.

The garage door whirred open, broke my stride. By my watch, Dawn was more than three hours late. Not that it mattered.

I tried to wrap up the paragraph, not lose my thought before Dawn made it inside. Keys jingled in the back door. I imagined her bringing in her briefcase, the negativity, the other things she dragged home from her office. The door that led from the garage to the kitchen opened and closed.

"Darnell, sweetheart?"

"I'm in the office."

"Doing what?"

"Working. You need help with something?"

"No." She paused. Paper was ripped, sounded like mail. Lights came on in the other part of the house. She asked, "What are you working on?"

I stopped typing and rubbed my temples. "Work."

"Legal work?"

I didn't reply.

She yelled, "Are you finishing up your unlawful detainers?"

I started to tell her what she wanted to hear, say I was using Dissomaster software and punching in info on a paternity action I had picked up from one of our neighbors, but I didn't lie. I said, "No. Working on my novel."

"Oh." Her tone changed. "So, you're playing."

"No, I'm working."

"You're playing."

Dawn's shoes click-clopped over the tiles in the kitchen, changed beats when she crossed the hardwood toward the bathroom. That door opened and closed. A minute later the toilet flushed. The door opened again, her heels click-clopped across the living room, then softened when she made it to the carpet. Her shadow eased down the hallway, crept into the office, stopped in the doorjamb. She had on green pants, cream-colored top. I was in plaid boxers and a plain white T-shirt. Her reflection was in my monitor. She was watching me, shaking her head.

I asked, "You worked this late?"

Her response was curt. "No."

She left it at that.

I asked, "Where have you been?"

She paused. "Sweetheart, you shouldn't stare at the screen so long. You might go blind."

"Thought masturbation did that."

"I'll let you know in a few weeks."

"What does that mean?"

"Means what it means."

"Which is?"

"If I have a baby that looks like my right hand, don't be surprised."

I let her snide remark go.

Again I asked, "Where have you been?"

She paused before she said, "I left work early."

"For what?"

"I rode up to San Fernando."

San Fernando was on the other side of Hollywood, a good ways from here in ruthless L.A. weekday traffic. "You skipped work and went all the way out to visit your mother?"

She clicked on the light, entered my world, destroyed my darkness. She didn't answer my last question.

I asked, "She all right?"

She tossed my mail on my desk, dropped her mail on hers. "What are you insinuating?"

"Nothing."

"If you have something to say, then say it. Don't try to use that backdoor tactic that lawyers use. Don't lawyer me."

"I wasn't *lawyering* you."

"I haven't been home five minutes and you're asking more questions than are on *Jeopardy!*"

"Well," I contrived a chuckle, "lately you've been doing a pretty good imitation of Alex Trebek yourself."

"You the one grilling me over where I've been."

I raised my palms in defeat. "I was hoping my mother-in-law wasn't sick and you weren't telling me, that's all."

Dawn backed off. She relaxed back in her chair, eyes pointed at the ceiling, stared deep into the overhead light.

I asked, "How is your mother?"

"She's my mother. I'll only have one. She doesn't have to be sick, it doesn't have to be a weekend for me to go see her."

"You didn't let me know where you were."

"I didn't know I had to check in whenever I left home."

"Just asking for the same courtesy you demand of me."

Her eyes came back to me. "Demand?"

I said, "Okay, ask—with an attitude."

She kicked her shoes off. "I see."

"I'll remember that the next time I walk out the door."

"You do that. But even when you're here, you're gone, so I don't think there will be much of a difference."

Dawn unloaded some papers from her briefcase. Unsnapped her bra, pulled it off, but left her blouse on. She never said exactly what she wanted, and I guess that made it my job to figure out what she was thinking. Mars and Venus were colliding.

She clicked on her computer. Whirs, clicks, the sounds of the machine and her separate printer coming to life. She went out into cyberworld and checked her e-mail. I went back to typing. Trying to, anyway. Dawn mumbled to herself while she read her messages, noises that wrecked my flow.

My thoughts were gone. Crushed.

She clicked off her PC and faced me. Her knee bumped against the paper tray on the printer when she spun around. I felt her watching me, but I pretended I didn't.

"Darnell, how long're you going to be up, sweetheart?"

"Don't know. Why?"

"I want to talk to you about something."

I didn't stop typing, feigned like I was deep into my work. But I wasn't. The moment that my wife said that she wanted to talk to me about something, Tammy came to mind. I wondered if someone had seen us together over the last two weeks while we sat and critiqued work, sipped cappuccinos, ate scones, laughed.

"Darnell, sweetheart. Did you hear me say we need to talk?"

"Yes, sweetheart."

She rolled her high-back chair across the tan carpet. "Can you stop with the hobby and give me your attention for a moment?"

I repeated, "Hobby?"

"Is what you're doing generating household income? Have you claimed what you're doing as an occupation with the IRS?"

"You know I haven't."

She emphasized, *"Hobby."*

I smiled, kept my blooming resentment for her feelings, or lack of feelings, for my *hobby* to myself.

She asked, "Think you can pull away from tip-tapping on your little computer long enough to give your wife a hug?"

I hugged her, spoke in a gentle way, "Hey."

She kissed me, then softly asked, "How was your day?"

Her kisses were sincere, but her speech was rote, so I sensed that moments of affection were what she wanted. I turned away from my computer and faced the beautiful creature who wore my wedding ring. She held on to me, rubbed my bare back underneath my T-shirt, ran her hands over my head, kissed my brow. I did the same to her.

She was creeping up on what was bothering her. I felt it.

Finally she said, "Darnell."

I waited. She made a sound like she was coming up for air.

She asked, "Do I satisfy you?"

"Yeah. Why?"

"What you did."

"What do you mean, what I did?"

"That evening in the garage. What you did to me."

"When we made love?"

"No, when you *fucked* me. You shoved me up against my truck like I was some dime-store hooker and *fucked* me."

We were eye to eye, treading in new bitterness.

"I felt degraded. Defiled. You just pushed yourself up inside of me like you were twisted and psychotic."

"Twisted and psychotic," I repeated.

I waited for her to take those words back, maybe rephrase what she'd accused me of, but she gazed at me with disdain.

I rocked in my swivel chair, smoothed my hands over my bare legs, gave up a primal grunt that signified that I felt confused. Perplexed because in that moment when we had been standing up, loving with so much fervor, she had let out back-to-back screams of passion. Now I was lost in my own house, lost in this marriage. Pain and animosity peppered my timbre. "You make it sound like I raped you."

Dawn ran her hand across her hair. "I wanted you to know how *I* felt."

"Are you saying that I raped you?"

"I'm simply trying to express to you how I felt about what happened. Don't turn this around and make it all about you."

"Yes or no, are you saying that I raped you?"

"You're the attorney, you tell me." Her tone was cruel and smooth. "What would you call it? You forced yourself on me in the broad of day, with the garage door wide the fuck open. I'm saying you treated me like I was less than what I am. As a woman, as your wife, I'm saying I felt degraded and humiliated."

Quiet and distance fell on us, asphyxiated us.

Sinking, sinking. My soul felt ill. Diseased.

She'd snatched the last twinkle of light from heaven.

I turned my computer off. Pulled on my khakis, Nikes, and changed into a gray T-shirt. Hopped in my car and went for a long ride.

# 19 Stephan

It was 10:20 P.M. and I was reading *Seize the Night* when the phone rang. Damn phone was always ringing. I'd called Samantha, then hung up when her answering machine kicked on, so I bet a week's pay that she was doing a *69. Either that or she saw my name on her caller-ID box and figured she'd better straighten things out right now.

I was wrong.

"I want my stuff," Toyomi said. "You ain't shit."

"That depends on who you ask."

Her voice was bitter. You'd definitely get more kindness from some old-school KKK at a Juneteenth celebration.

I hated when relationships dropped to that pitiful, juvenile, *I'm coming to get my stuff, you come and get all yours* point.

She said, "I want my television."

"You've lost your mind. That is not your television."

"That is *my* TV," she insisted. "I paid for it."

"You gave it to me for my birthday."

"I'll be damned if you and some other skank are going to be laying up watching my TV. And I want the comforter. I want my sunglasses that I left over there. I want my plants."

"What you did to my car wasn't necessary."

"What you did wasn't necessary."

"You gonna pay for my car?"

"Hell, no."

"Then I don't give a damn what you want."

I wanted to hang up, I should've, but she'd sucked me down to her level, made me so mad that spit was flying out my mouth, and I couldn't back off. God, I was glad that I got to see this side of her before it was too late.

Her remarks were scathing. "*You will.* Trust me, *you will.* You're going to regret this."

I snapped, "What about my suits you messed up?"

"I left your junk out by the trash. Shar did the rest. Call that no-good bitch."

"What did Shar do?"

"As far as your car is concerned, you knew better than to come out here after what you tried to pull."

"So," I asked, "you're not gonna reimburse me for anything?"

"I'm coming over to get my stuff after you leave."

"Oh, you're going to break in?"

"Don't have to. For all you know, I might have a key."

"How'd you get a key?"

She laughed.

Again I asked, "How did you get a key?"

"Never know. I could've had it duplicated."

I couldn't tell if she was real or gaming.

"Well," I paused and found me some calm, "I've already called the homeowners and told security about our situation. Rebecca's always at home, and I told her we broke up, so if you come inside without my permission, she'll be dialing 9-1-1 before you—"

"Stephan, go to hell. I have personal property inside your place, and I know my rights. I'll bring Five-O with me when I come. You've left a key out plenty of times. Droopy-titty Rebecca'll be more than happy to testify to that."

"Forget that. I didn't give you a key."

"You want to get me arrested? I've given you over a year of my life, wasted . . ." Her anger came on strong, and she choked on her words. "That's messed up. Both you and Shar are fucked up."

"What did she do?"

"I should've seen right through you and that bitch from the get-go."

I did feel bad. But I was more afraid of her than I ever realized. I tried to calm her down. "Toyomi—"

She howled like a bleeding canine. "I'm going to fuck you up fuck you up fuck you up fuck you up."

She slammed the phone so hard the vibrations rode the freeway, created a new fault from her heart to my front door.

Toyomi had played hardball, tried to rattle me.

It worked. Too well it worked.

As I licked my lips, Toyomi's threats echoed in my ears. There was only one door to my condo. One way in, one way out. I made sure the door was locked, put the chain on, made sure the patio was secure just in case she decided to climb up and surprise me, kept the inside dark so I could see her crazy ass first, waited for that lunatic to pull up.

I was so on edge that I'd be up half the night, pacing, jumping whenever a car hit the speed bump outside my window.

# 20 Darnell

It had been a while since I needed to escape.

Santa Ana winds roared in my windows. Disc one of R. Kelly's double CD rocked hard on my sound system. The CD lasted seventy-one minutes, long enough to give me the hard beats I needed on my sojourn to sanity.

Jake lived in the Playa Pacific town houses, a stone's throw from the never-ending traffic on the longest road in the state, Sepulveda Boulevard. The din of this area was too much for my liking. But I guess none of that constant rambunctious activity really mattered to Jake, because it matched his personality. Plus he was hardly ever at home. My catching him at home tonight was nothing but luck.

Pamela was walking around in a housecoat and slippers, moving from room to room like she lived there. She was brown-skinned; hair short, curly, and dyed the color of gold. Graceful neck, lissome torso, cool demeanor. Not beautiful, cute. Clever eyes that said every man in her life had underestimated her.

Pamela didn't smile, hardly said two words before she went into the bedroom and closed the door. The place smelled like baked fish. The scent of a fresh sweet potato pie was floating in the air too. Strawberry incense was slowly burning. Already, my sense of smell was overloaded.

I sat on the cream leather sofa, next to the shelves filled with jazz statuettes, and told Jake what had happened between me and Dawn. He still had on his fireman's blue and was on the love seat, facing a tri-matted photo of Nat King Cole and Ella Fitzgerald singing together somewhere back in time.

He stopped rubbing his fingers over his thick goatee, waved my words down, cut off my rampage. "I love you, and you my boy, but I've got to take her side on this one. And you know that's a stretch for me, because I know Dawn hates me."

"Can't deny that."

"How are you just gonna give up being a Perry Mason to write a stupid book? You ain't even had a book-writing class."

"It's called a leap of faith."

"You need to leap your ass toward some sense."

"You make it sound like I've lost my mind."

"You might need psychological evaluation."

"Stephan's read my work. He loved it."

"Stephan ain't shit," Jake said. "He let Toyomi punk him. Man, I'd've had my foot so far up her ass, she'd still be out there painting my door right now. Both her and Shar."

"They'd been together a long time."

"That was the problem. He should've hit that and quit that a long time ago. Her possessive and jealous ass."

"Think she was jealous and possessive without due cause?"

"You bust a nut, and before you can roll off and take a few Z's, women try to turn your ass into a mutherfuckin' ready teller."

I told him, "I'm going to meet Tammy."

Her rehearsal would be over in a few minutes. I was waiting for her to page me.

Jake went back to trailing his fingers up and down his goatee. First his face held contemplation, then he warned me, "Don't get in this game. Don't start lying. This is a game that's hard to get out of."

I let my wayward friend know, "Don't worry. I'm just going to get a cup of cappuccino and chitchat. I'm not from the Wilt Chamberlain school of romance."

He laughed. "Fuck you."

"I'm not cut out for infidelity."

"Let a woman tell it, every man is cut out for infidelity. And let me tell it, every woman is too."

"Not the kid. I'm not into drama for the sake of drama. I'm an old-fashioned fool that thrives on one-on-one love."

"You better write that corny shit in one of those books you call yourself writing." He mocked, "One-on-one love?"

"Yep."

"But you're on the way to Hollywood in the middle of the night to see a bitch you met in a bar."

I didn't say anything about the pejorative remark. If he did it again, I might hit him in the mouth, but for now, I didn't say anything.

He asked, "What's the real deal with you and Tammy?"

I admitted, "I like her. That's about all."

"Love, like, lust," Jake chuckled. "All of 'em start with the same letter, so there's not too much of a difference."

I said, "Not to you."

"At midnight, won't be much of a difference to you either. Tell me you don't want her to wrap her long yellow legs around your black neck and knock your boots from here to Tijuana."

I couldn't tell him that. "I'm not cut out for infidelity."

"Nigga, *puh-lease*. And the pope is having a sunrise service with Larry Flynt and Farrakhan at the Hugh Hefner mansion."

We laughed.

He peeped over his shoulder, then said, "You know what I like about Pamela?"

"She puts up with your idiocy."

"Besides that."

"Nope, but I'm sure you're going to tell me."

He shifted, got serious. "Let me tell you about Charlotte first. I love her. And I'm gonna get around to marrying her. She understands sex, the basic act and nothing extreme. Two positions of pleasure, and she likes to do both of those in the bed all the damn time. At least that's all she shows me."

"Uh-huh."

He massaged his face. "But I wonder if she understands sensuality."

"What you mean?"

"I mean, sensuality. What I get every few nights, after she's showered and scrubbed her face for what seems like an hour, is a woman in a beat-up T-shirt and worn-out underwear. Usually a pair of boxer-style shorts. Hair pinned up. Never a sister in some satin here, some silk there, some honey dust sprinkled here, some soft lights and jazz there. I guess loving me ain't the first thing on her mind. I guess I could *tell* her how to be a woman, how to become one of the most powerful creatures on this planet, ask her to put this on, to dab some perfume there, but my desires are, well, what I'm saying is that I need a woman who knows the art of being a woman, not somebody who needs to be taught how to paint by numbers. And getting her to the point of orgasm ain't a simple thing to do. Making her cum is about as easy as trying to catch a baby grand piano with a baseball glove."

All I could say was, "Wow."

"So, getting a ten-minute quickie ain't happening. It's all or none. After working four days in a row, twenty-four-seven, some nights I don't feel like giving my all."

"So you'd rather be with Pamela."

"Hell, no. Pamela is pinch-hitting. But still I'm crazy about her. What a woman does in bed makes a man feel alive."

"But it can't help him survive when the moans have died and the sweat between the sheets have dried."

"Put that shit in a book."

"I might."

"True, what you said." He sighed. "But as soon as a brother busts a nut, and that good feeling fades, all the other stuff comes back home. All the dreams come back."

I didn't say anything. He was back on those dreams again.

Jake said, "My advice to you is plain and simple. If you gonna keep kicking it with Tammy, you know what you have to do."

I wanted to know, "What do I *have* to do?"

"Hit it and quit. Don't get comfortable, and don't loiter in the pussy. Loitering has gotten many a brother in trouble."

"So, you loitering with Pamela or Charlotte?"

"Charlotte's my woman. You know that. When it comes down to it, everybody else is gonna have to hit the road. Ain't nobody better than Charlotte. That's where my heart is at." He had sincere words and a half smile. "But when a man ain't got no options, he has to put up with all kinds of shit to get laid. Charlotte'll put a nigga on a two-week dry spell."

I asked, "And Pamela? What about her?"

"She knows how to make a man feel like a man. She cooks, cleans up when she comes over, can find some of Charlotte's shit laying around and she won't sweat me over it. She's not as smart as Charlotte, won't ever have as much money because she thinks that her charge cards are free money."

I chuckled. "Free money?"

"The way Pamela can wreck a charge card, if I married somebody like her I'd be bankrupt in six months. But she has her pluses."

"She's a concubine."

He rubbed his goatee again, blinked like he was waking up, then asked, "What you mean, she's a damn porcupine?"

"Concubine, not porcupine."

"If that means what I think it means, I'm kicking your ass."

We laughed. His chortle told me he was offended; mine told him I didn't give a damn.

He lowered his voice, leaned in close. "I met this freak yesterday. Hispanic girl. Looks like Jennifer Lopez. Serious booty, tits for days. She was rolling out the lot by HomeBase, up at Slauson and Fairfax, right by the fire station."

"Uh-huh."

"She had just got her nails done at that Chinese manicure place, Mantrap. And man, she's fine. Hair down to her butt. She invited me to this party down in Orange County this weekend."

I said, "She must be into brothers."

"And it ain't even Black History Month."

We laughed.

He told me, "I mean, she pulled up in a brand-new convertible Jaguar, was all up in my face. Man, that fireman's uniform pulls more honeys than a little bit. She's called me three times today, wanted to make sure I was coming to the party."

I said, "Damn. Just like that?"

"Just like that. Miss Taco Bell has a thing for brothers."

I guess the real reason I came to see Jake was because I needed that kind of vile validation. Some wicked words to go with my blasphemous thoughts.

He confessed, "Man, I'm gonna miss all of this when I marry Charlotte. Vicki. Yolanda. Toni. Paulette. What's-her-face I met at Duet's in Westwood. What's-her-face I was with last night. All of 'em gonna have to get the boot."

"What about Pamela?"

"She's down for whatever. Knowing her, she'll be at my wedding throwing rice. Might even let her pop up on the honeymoon."

When I first got there, I had wanted to tell him what Dawn had accused me of. Pamela was floating around his space, so I didn't bring up the subject. Now I did. I ran that incident by him, told him what I did, and what she said I did, just to see if I was living in the right or existing in the wrong.

He responded, "Dawn's tripping. Every other woman would've loved that shit. A man can't rape his wife. That's bullshit."

"A man can, but I didn't."

"You know what I meant. Damn. You going back home tonight?"

My body was heavy, like I was made of cement. Eyes burned a little. I was getting sleepy. Part of me wanted to go home; another part needed to see Tammy, find out if there was some peace in the valley for me. To tell the truth, I felt like a rooster that didn't know which way to go, into the barn where I belonged, or back out into the yard with all the chickens.

He asked, "Want something to drink?"

"Water. Mouth is dry."

He yelled, "Pamela, get my homey a glass of water, please."

She did what he asked without hesitation or question. Then she went back across the room, moved like a cat, and went into the bathroom.

She came right back out and softly said, "Jake?"

"Yeah, babe."

"Our bath water is ready."

"Okay. I'll get with you in a minute."

"Want me to get the massager and hook up your back?"

"I'll be there in a minute. Keep it hot for me."

She sashayed away.

I felt sorry for that woman of low expectation. Felt sorry for Charlotte.

Jake was sitting underneath a photo of his parents that took up most of that wall. In the picture they were about Jake's age. Scrapbooks underneath his iron coffee table held page after page of his parents' pictures. I glanced at the monogamous love in the photo on the wall and felt pity for Jake.

Five minutes later, Jake was heading toward the steam that was waiting in his bathroom, toward Pamela, and I was driving up Slauson, passing by a sky-high billboard that depicted L.A. Laker Kobe Byrant flying in the air, his image mutating and implying that he was the next Michael Jordan.

Get real.

My radio was on 103.9. Al Green was singing about love and happiness. In my mind I changed the tune to loathe and unhappiness. Makes you wanna do wrong, makes you forget what's right.

# 21 Darnell

We sat outside in a tiled courtyard at the Atomic Café, across from Le Croissant Club. Atomic is a small, trendy digital Internet bistro that serves gourmet coffee and fattening desserts until the bewitching hour. Mike Camacho and Friends were playing jazz. People were out and about, but we had a wrought iron table in the corner of the courtyard to ourselves.

We were a few feet from Hollywood Boulevard, where homeless people slept in open doorways, used newspapers as their bed sheets and piss-smelling concrete as their pillows.

Hip-hugging jeans with wide legs, a beige T-shirt for "*Harriet's Return* starring Debbie Allen." Old, oversized, and faded Levi jacket. Light brown hair pulled back into a bun. A beige and brown Negro League baseball cap. That's what Tammy had on.

I sipped my tea, but staring at Tammy made me feel like I was on whiskey and cocaine. I felt guilty. Even if I never saw Tammy again, I'd feel guilty for the rest of my life.

She stopped singing in French, said, "You look sleepy."

"Getting there."

"It's after midnight. You sure you're going to be able to drive home without rolling off the 10 into a ditch?"

"Don't have a choice."

"Everyone has a choice."

I paused and gazed at her. "That they do."

She adjusted her jacket. "So, what did you think?"

I opened my attaché case and handed her the play she'd given me.

"It's damn good. You tackled the domestic-violence thing very well. Your characters, especially the wild and selfish sisters of the protagonist, were both tragic and funny."

She said, "Comedy is tragedy with a punch line."

"Your comedy keeps the story from being too heavy."

"It wasn't a hodgepodge?"

"A what?"

"Was too much going on at the same time?"

"Not at all."

She sipped. I watched the way her lips slowly parted, how I caught a glimpse of her tongue, the way she swallowed.

I nodded. "Your writing is very sensual."

"Not as erotic as yours."

She sipped, then casually gazed into my eyes.

Seconds passed before I moved my eyes from her charm.

She laughed.

I smiled. Felt like a silly teenager.

She said, "Shy?"

"Not really. Just being cautious."

"Don't worry." Again she sipped, gazed at me. This time I didn't turn away. My eyes asked her to tell me what was on her mind. Asked her to read and reject what was on mine. She said, "Darnell, I've had you on my mind a lot. Too much."

"Same here."

"Same there? So, you've had *you* on your mind too?"

I laughed. "You're so silly."

"When I need to be. I was kissing Bobby last night, and your face popped up in my head. I almost called him your name. It was strange as hell. I've known him for months, but all of a sudden I blanked out and couldn't remember who he was."

"I was with my wife." I paused. "I imagined she was you."

A long pause. Tammy shifted like she was very uncomfortable. Finally she said, "Well, I guess that's checkmate."

She moved her eyes away.

"Darnell, if you weren't married . . ." Her words trailed off.

"If I wasn't married and you weren't seeing Bobby, right?"

"No." Her hand drifted across the table and touched mine, rubbed like she was making a wish, her long fingers moving back and forth across my palm. "Just if you weren't married."

"If I wasn't married," I started as I held her hand, absorbed the softness in her damp palm, imagined each of her fingers inside my mouth, "I'd take that offer."

"Even if I was seeing Bobby?"

"Even if you were seeing Bobby."

"Then it's a good thing you have a wife."

"Yeah, it's a good thing."

She took her flesh back. Maybe I let it go. Don't know. Tammy sipped, put her questioning eyes back on mine, held her lips to the molds of her cup. Her scrutiny made me wish this was years ago. I watched the way her puffy lips moved, how they opened and closed, then caressed the edges of the cup, saw how the lines of contemplation flowered in her wheat complexion whenever she stopped laughing and had a serious moment. She gazed at me and those lines went away, made her seem five years younger, like a naive college graduate.

She said, "Still think I'm fantastic?"

"Yeah. I do."

She made a sound that could've been a laugh.

I asked, "What was that all about?"

"You tell me my story is sensual. Chanté read part of it and called me a freak. Karen thought I needed to address the masturbation issue for women too."

"What masturbation issue?"

"About how it's taboo, and how women aren't brought up and taught to enjoy sex, that women shouldn't be afraid to touch their own bodies, and women don't need men to be validated. She brought up the issue of how some cultures still practice clitoridectomy, you know, removal of a woman's clitoris and labia—"

"I get the point."

"Guess I went too far that time."

"Well, the clitori-whatchamacallit is a bit graphic."

She raised a brow. "And masturbation isn't?"

I shrugged. "Not at all."

"Karen wanted me to add a one-woman Water Pik sex scene to my play. That'd get me kicked out of the theatre. But then again, Water Pik sales might shoot through the roof."

As I laughed, I tried to put Dawn's face on Tammy's body. Anything to remove the crime of having an intimate conversation.

Her beeper went off. Her electronic leash let her know, let me know, that she was being summoned, being missed by somebody, somewhere else. It reminded me of the same reality in my life.

I asked, "That your boyfriend?"

"Told you, I don't have a boyfriend. I'm too old for that."

"That was Bobby?"

Her voiced rang with disheartenment. "Yeah."

"You have to go?"

She tapped her watch, spoke firmly. "And so do you."

"Yeah."

We were both parked on Hollywood Boulevard. Two minutes later we were saying good-bye at her car; I gave her a hug.

I told her, "What I feel for you isn't right."

"Who you telling. I think about you all day, Darnell. I'll have you on my mind the rest of the night."

"While you're with Bobby?"

Instead of answering, she kissed me. Not a tongue kiss, just leaned in and pressed her lips up against mine for a moment. She moaned; so did I. Neither one of us closed our eyes. I think closing our eyes would've been too symbolic for both of us.

I told her, "Something has happened since I met you."

"Don't tell me. I don't want to know."

"Why not?"

"I don't want to get too deep."

"You kiss me, then say you don't want to get deep?"

"I didn't *kiss* you."

"What was that?"

"That was a stage kiss."

"A stage kiss?"

"Right."

"What's the difference between a stage kiss and a real kiss?"

Her tongue slid in and out of her mouth, made circles in the air, tantalized and tortured the soft winds, teasing me.

She told me, "Do the same. Come closer. Do it with me."

I stood inches from her face. Mimicked her movements.

She sighed, winked, then whispered, "Now, if I had kissed you for real, that's what it would've been like."

"What happens if I kiss you for real?"

"You turn into a frog."

"I'll keep that in mind."

If you took away the urine stench of the gritty sidewalk, the rush of traffic blaring by on Hollywood Boulevard, the teenagers who were ready to exchange sex for their next meal, the homeless who kept moseying by like tattered zombies, it was the ideal moment to kiss.

The tingling, electrical sensation that was ruling my insides made me move toward her in a romantic way.

Tammy backed away, not right away, and not easily. Her face glowed with pain from resistance, breathing roughened, came in short bursts, like that subtle move had taken all of her energy.

I stopped my pursuit, adjusted my clothes, readjusted my mind, let my breathing slow. In a soft tone I said, "Let me know how far to let this go."

Her eyes went to the pavement. "I'm over here trying not to debauch my own morals, so I can't be strong for you, Darnell."

I nodded. What she was telling me was that she was feeling weak herself. Control was close to being lost. That she needed me to keep us from living in the wrong.

She sighed, then confessed, "I told my momma about you."

"Sounds like you're the one getting deep this time."

She massaged her right hand with her left. It made me feel good to know that I wasn't the only one who felt jittery.

She tilted her head, twisted her dark lips, licked them top and bottom. "I actually told her that I'd met somebody nice, but I didn't tell her you were married."

"What did she say?"

"She wanted to know if you were a white man."

She laughed.

I smiled.

She sounded nervous as she added, "If I drive out to Needles, since you really want to know who I am, I might take you. That's if you can get away for a day. It's a four-hour drive one-way."

"Thought you grew up in Laughlin?"

"Outside of Laughlin. In Needles. The middle of nowhere. It's the Arkansas of the desert. That's what my momma says. I haven't been out there in almost two years."

"Why haven't you been back home?"

She answered, forthright, "A woman ain't supposed to look back when she's running. Looking back slows a sister down."

I left that at that.

She slid into her car, blended with the bright lights of the big city, and headed up Highland. I followed her up the 101 as far as Lankersheim, took the 134 freeway to the 210, licked away the lipstick she had left behind, zipped through Pasadena feeling guilty, merged with 57 and found my way to the 60.

For the first time in my life I wondered if I'd become rigid in my life. Is that what my marriage had done? Had I given up my right to exhilaration and freedom?

Or was I becoming as primal as the fools I hung out with?

\* \* \*

An hour had passed. Once again I reached my hidden, sterile community that had one entrance, one exit. Whenever I came home I felt like Batman slipping away from the real world back inside the Batcave.

Batman. A man with two faces.

Longing made me pull over near the darkness and quiet of Lemon Creek Bicentennial Park. I pulled out my cellular phone, dialed Tammy's number.

She didn't answer. Inside, I felt some unwarranted heat.

Then I was back home, on the corner of Avenida Grulla and Avenida Deseo, staring at me and Dawn's two-story home with the tile roof and the perfectly manicured yard. At all the other two-story homes that maintained the same facade of happiness. The only way to know the truth of every household would be to go inside. But, like me, everyone kept their doors closed.

A click of my remote and my garage door whirred open, shattered silence, and announced that I had come back. I sat in the garage for five minutes wiping away anything that was left on my lips. I crept out and stood near the washer and dryer.

Tired. Sleepy. Body heavier than a boulder.

I touched the hood of Dawn's car. Warm.

The house alarm shrieked the moment the door opened; it took me a good five seconds to shut the wailing off. I'd made it deep into the hallway before I heard the television in the bedroom turn off. Sounded like soap operas. Dawn recorded those in the daytime, then played catch-up with that fake world at night.

Our bedroom door was closed. I turned the knob. Locked. Called her name. No answer. Tapped on the door. Covers rustled, but not a word.

I said, "What you think I'm going to do, rape you?"

No answer.

I wouldn't be surprised if she had a chair wedged against the doorknob to prove a point.

That was fine by me. I didn't want to see her anyway. Not right now. To tell the truth, I didn't want to see anybody. I wanted to cover up all the mirrors in the hallway because I didn't want to see myself for fear that I might not recognize me.

A moment later I was in our shared office, reading the last pages I had written on my novel, then switching sentiments and gazing at some of my professional books: *Civil Procedure Before Trial, Black's Law Dictionary, Community Property in California.* The title of the last one hit me hard, jarred me out of my mishmash of thoughts, pulled me away from my self-imposed fantasy. That fantasy was both writing, being what I desired, and wishing that I was desired by a wannabe star, someone I had no business yearning for from the first moment our eyes touched.

If that was what bad communication at home drove a person to do, then I was facing the on-ramp to the road of disaster.

Community property. That book was glowing, pulsating, humming. The toilet in the master bedroom flushed.

I called Dawn's name. No reply.

I'd done divorces for others, had to listen to them swear and squabble over nickel-and-dime material things, had witnessed them damning each other to eternity over community property.

I went into the guest room, undressed like a stranger inside my own house, and crawled into a cold bed.

# 22 Chanté

I worked a half day on Friday because I had to go to the dentist for a checkup and to get my pearly whites cleaned, waxed, and shined. Since my appointment was out east in Ontario, I got my nails and toes hooked up, then decided to call Karen and leave her a message before I headed back home. I wanted somebody to hang out with in the thick of tonight. Tammy would be busy doing her rehearsal thing, so I figured that me and the militant could play Dynamic Duo. Karen surprised me by answering her phone. I thought she'd be at work until the DMV closed down.

I chimed, "Miss you, too. I was worried."

"About what?"

I'd been scared for her ever since I witnessed all of that loot she had stashed in the trunk of her car. "It's the mother hen in me. I haven't seen you or Tammy, and I get worried when we're not face-to-face."

"Worried or lonely?"

I laughed. "Both."

She laughed but sounded distraught. "I really want to talk to you about something."

"I'm on the way over."

A coldness ran through me. That feeling a person gets when something's not right was all over my body.

Karen lived about twenty-five minutes away, off the 60 at the Blaine/3rd Street exit, the same freeway off-ramp where I'd met Stephan Mitchell. The Timbers were the two-story wood and stucco apartments that she'd been cooped up in for the last four years. The place was okay, I guess, but I wanted Karen to do better.

I walked in her first-floor crib, hugged her. She had on her ripped jeans and an orange sports bra. A Glen Ellen winery baseball cap was backward on her head, covering her new hairstyle.

I said, "You permed your hair?"

"Yep. I took off work today and bowed down to the chemicals. I'm conforming to the Anglo standards of beauty."

"And you put it in spirals?"

"Yeah."

"Damn. Let me see, let me see. Why are you hiding your do?"

She twisted her lips. " 'Cause I don't care for it. I should be wearing natural locks like Cassandra Wilson, or have my do did like Lauryn Hill, instead of this Barbie doll–looking mess."

She eased her cap off. Even though it reminded me of the good ship Lollypop, her hair was the boss. Looked good on her itty-bitty head and cute shape. And I knew that her do had to cost a pretty penny to get hooked up.

I picked up on the marijuana odor that permeated everything she owned, smiled my best smile, and asked, "You been getting high?"

"Don't start with your bitchcraft as soon as you come in the door. Bring me some positivity for a change."

I said, "I'm just asking. What's that smell?"

"Herbal incense."

I sniffed again. "What kind?"

"A scent of the sixties called patchouli. It awakes the desire for peace and love. With the kind of corruption that's going down, with it being open season on African American women that's what the world needs."

The way she said that jarred me. "What's wrong?"

She showed me her *Los Angeles Times*. Unbelievable. A nineteen-year-old sista had been gunned down while she sat in her car, shot twelve times by the police.

Karen glanced at her watch, then spoke in a chilled tone. "That happened right here in Riverside."

"Fuck."

"Another senseless killing. Racist police overreact every time they see a black face. Remember when some fools had robbed a fast-food store and they arrested the *first* black face they saw? Bishop Culmer. In broad daylight they handcuffed and Jim-Crowed the man in front of the children from his congregation. Can you imagine the psychological effect it has on a child to see his minister, his one true hero, shackled like a slave?"

"I remember, I remember. He was in front of his church, dressed in full vestment, and they still made him a suspect."

"Black means suspect whether you have your preacher's collar on or not."

"Same shit they did back in the sixties."

"Martin Luther King Jr. was a preacher."

"Malcolm X too."

"No respect."

"Nope."

"Ain't nothing changing but the clock on the wall."

I nodded. "True that a million times a million."

"Always something." Karen glanced at the gold-trimmed clock near the front door, peeped at her watch before she went on. "Seems like it was just yesterday when that brother in Jasper, Texas, was attacked by a pack of white supremacists."

"God, that was awful."

Karen said, "How can you justify chaining a man to a truck and dragging him until his body comes apart? That could've been any one of our relatives, our brothers, our daddies."

I shivered with the thought, felt anger and terror when I imagined that happening to my daddy. "That was jacked up."

"Royally. This is why I'm down with the death penalty."

I said, "I'd love to pull the switch on this one."

"Fuck the switch. You should do them in the same way. Drag 'em from a truck. Put them in a car and shoot 'em twelve times."

I read a little more about Tyisha Miller, the teenage sista who was assassinated. Twelve shots. And I know how police are trained to shoot. Always shoot 'em twice. Once to the head, once to the chest. Double-pop 'em. And that happened in a store parking lot, right before her relatives' eyes. Damn. In the photo she was in a sleeveless black dress, looking intelligent and spunky, arms over her head like she was ready to party her way into adulthood. Grinning like she was ready to live forever and a day.

Karen scooted next to me. "She was beautiful."

"Yeah."

"That could've been one of us. You. Me. Tammy."

"That's what I was thinking. Exactly what I was thinking."

A solemn feeling seized that slice of time.

"Well, she's an angel now," Karen whispered. I felt her rocking side to side, her warmth blending with my own. "No more dealing with the devils down here."

We sat side by side, shoulders touching, talking.

Moments like this were what I loved about Karen. What I missed the most. Over the years we've sat around, played dominoes, ranted and talked about everything from Clarence Thomas and his pubic hair on the Coke can, to the white girl from Newport Beach who was slaughtered in South Africa, to OJ's bloody glove, to prop 187, to whatever the hell was going on at the time.

All that passion, with a little more education, could take her a long way. I always looked in her brown eyes, listened to her speak with an unstoppable passion, and imagined her as a civil rights attorney, or an educator for our people. Not as a frustrated minimum wage cashier at the mall, or an underpaid and under-challenged, second-rate secretary at the DMV. I wanted my friend to make it through life.

I said, "People on the other side of the country watch television and think it's so safe in California."

"What a fool believes."

"I know I used to think that before I came out here from Chicago."

"Get real." She shook her head, peeped at her watch again. "The headquarters to the KKK is ten minutes away in Fontana."

"Too close for comfort."

"L.A. ain't no better. Interracial couples out that way wake up with crosses burning in their lawn, their pets executed and left on their front porch."

"Yep. I remember that too. That was by LAX in Westchester. They ended up on *Oprah* telling about that crap."

"They let you know where you don't belong."

Living in a multicultured area like Diamond Bar tended to suck the racism out of a sista's soul. Well, maybe more like made people pretend it didn't exist, or be politically correct and mask those feelings with a Cali smile. Racism existed. Karen was good at reminding me of what was real.

"You look good," I said after we'd pretty much exhausted that conversation. All of that talk about civil rights and what-ain't-right was weighty, kind of depressing, especially since we couldn't change it lickity split, so I put the newspaper to the side, said a silent prayer for those families, then eased the conversation in another direction, toward uncontroversial things, and tried to bring some good feeling and hope into the room. I held my buddy's hand and asked, "When did you get your nails done?"

"Yesterday."

Her fingernails had grown out to a half inch and were coated with clear polish. Well, all of them were that long except the middle one on her right hand, which I knew she kept short for lewd purposes. Her toes were pedicured. Her militant face looked softer.

I asked, "That's a new mascara?"

"Yeah. I used my discount and picked up some things."

"Nails done. New hairdo. New mascara. You're making yourself over head to toe."

She shifted, took her hand away like she was uneasy.

I glanced toward the counter and saw her stack of bills. A leaning tower of financial misery, some in pink envelopes.

A laundry basket was on the floor, and a few things had been put on hangers and were on her futon—mostly blouses, jeans, and T-shirts. Self-conscious about her new do, she put her cap back on, grabbed most of the things on hangers, and went to her closet, which was next to the front door. When she opened the closet, I saw a few manly things inside. Not shirts or things that she would wear, but pants that were too big and too long to be hers.

She closed the closet real quick, then gave me a tart smile.

Seemed like her mood had changed, just that quick.

I sat down next to her, chitchatted while I helped her fold up her panties, bras, workout clothes, sheets.

I asked her, "You still buying things on sale and reselling?"

She covered her mouth when she coughed. "Why?"

" 'Cause I might want that hook-up."

"You don't shop at Mervyn's."

"Damn. You trying to make me sound all bourgeois. I'm the queen of Kmart, I live for Ross or Marshall's, and don't get me to walking around either Pic-N-Save or a 99 cents store."

"Just repeating what you told me. If that makes you sound bourgeois, then who am I to say? How often do you come out here to Riverside and visit me?"

"You're never home."

"If you say so."

"Can I get the hook-up? They're having a sale on towels."

She sucked her jaw in. "Is that why you came out here?"

"No. I came to hang out. I thought I saw some more new stuff in your closet, and it crossed my mind, that's all."

She nodded, said, "You and Tammy can use my discount anytime, you know that."

I cleared my throat. "Tell me the truth. Is the money tight?"

She became very serene. "I'm managing."

"My offer still stands. You can come stay with me for a while. If you want to go back to RCC, I'll help with the tuition. Either that or I'll pay for your books, whichever costs the most. And you don't have to pay me back."

"I can handle it. I've been on my own since I was seventeen. If life has taught me anything, it's taught me that all I have to depend on is me."

That stung. Pierced like she'd twisted a rusty spear into one of my lungs. "I wasn't trying to offend you."

"I know." Her sarcastic laugh filled the silence. "You were just being you."

All of a sudden I felt cramped.

I let her know, "Tammy is bringing me her papers so I can do her taxes tomorrow."

"Is she?"

"Yeah. You want me to do yours?"

"Nah. I'm cool. Already got 'em done."

I paused. "Who did them for you?"

"H&R Block."

That jarred me. Quiet settled between us. I went to the potty to ease my bladder and get a moment to myself. Karen must've felt the awkwardness in the silence too, because she turned the radio on 99.1. Levert, Sweat & Gill were doing one of their freaky-deeky gimme-summa-your-coochie songs.

I went back and sat next to her. Looked around at her life.

Her studio apartment was smaller than a mouse trap. Everything in it came from IKEA: black and red futon, red end tables, black bookcase with five shelves of books, each shelf three-deep. Her walls had framed photos of Malcolm X, Coltrane, a sketch done by a street artist when she went to Times Square.

What was the most striking of everything in the place was the pure white wedding dress that was still hanging in Karen's hall, still protected by a sheath of cheap dry cleaner plastic.

I said, "Karen?"

"Yeah?"

"You've been engaged three times . . ."

"Unfortunately."

"I'm curious . . ."

"Uh-huh?"

"I've told you forty-eleven times, that dress is beautiful. If I ever get married, I'd love to have one just like that."

"Oh, I'm quite sure yours will be nicer."

When she said that, I hesitated. I went on, "But why do you keep that wedding gown hanging up in plain view?"

"Does it bother you?"

"No, it's just that, well, if a sista invited a brotha over and the first thing he saw was a wedding gown in her living room, well, that would be like walking into a man's place for the first time and seeing a big-ass box of Trojans on the coffee table."

Karen said, "Exactly."

We laughed at that.

She motioned at the dress. "Maybe you should hang one of those virgin gowns up in your front room too, huh?"

"Hell," I matched her chortle, "if I swing by the Pleasure Chest and get me a fat vibrator, maybe get a thick Victor like you got, I won't need the dress."

I held onto my laugh, but the pitch of my laughter had changed. Hers had changed too.

She was attacking my integrity, but I didn't care. She was my conscience, and I was hers. We'd always been like that. The opposite sides of the same coin.

I asked, "What you get Tammy for her birthday?"

"Silver necklace. Matching bracelet. What you get?"

"DKNY blouse. It's Lycra."

"Her chest ought to make it stand out."

Her phone rang. Karen glanced at the noise, then turned away.

I offered, "Want me to get it?"

"No."

She let it roll over to her answering service.

I didn't say anything. She always answered her phone between the first and second ring. Always.

I don't know if Karen had been doing it for a long time, but I finally noticed that she kept looking at the black triangular clock on her end table, then yawning.

I asked, "Wanna hang out tonight?"

"I feel run down."

"You work forty hours a week at the DMV, then you're on your feet all weekend at Mervyn's. I get tired thinking about it."

She dismissed what I was saying. "I skipped taking my herbs," she said. "Plus this monthly curse ain't making me feel no better."

"Want me to stay over? We can rent a video and catch up."

"Nah. I'm just gonna sleep this evening. Read *Riven Rock*, take a long bath, and sleep harder than Rip Van Winkle." She yawned, checked the clock again, and stretched. "I'll kick it with you and Tammy tomorrow. We'll party hearty."

She said that like she was ready for me to make my exodus.

So I did.

I was back on the freeway before I remembered that she had wanted to talk to me about something. I told myself that I'd call her the moment I made it home, but my phone was jumping off the hook when I walked in the door. It was Stephan.

He asked, "What're you doing tonight?"

"What did you have in mind?"

"I got a flier in the mail saying that it's Sarong Night at Shelly's. Is Tammy singing in the boondocks tonight?"

"Nope. You going out to Rancho?"

He said, "You want to?"

"On a date?"

He responded, "I'm not your type, but call it what you like."

"Sounds like carpooling."

"Drive up. You can ride with me."

I said, "You're not picking me up? Definitely not a date."

We laughed. Already I'd forgotten about Karen. Talking to him made me forget about a lot of things.

I said, "Remember, it's sarong night, so dress casual."

"You wearing a sarong?"

"Depends. What color are you wearing?"

"Why?"

"So we can *coordinate*."

He enlightened me: "This ain't no date; we don't have to *coordinate*. How am I supposed to booty watch and find my special perfect one if we walk up in the club looking like bookends?"

I warned him, "Don't be all up under me, 'cause I'm going to be doing some serious booty watching my-damn-self."

"As long as you don't interrupt my flow."

I asked, "Your posse going?"

His buddies wouldn't be tagging along. He hadn't talked to Darnell, and Jake had plans of his own. I told him that Karen was being a moody hermit, and that Tammy must be in rehearsal, because I hadn't heard from her.

"I'll be over soon."

# 23  Chanté

Stephan was on his stairs talking with Rebecca and a Hispanic man. At first I didn't recognize Rebecca because she was dressed in a pink short set and her hair was down. That made homegirl look younger, like she was in her late thirties. She had breasts for days. Made me feel flat-chested.

Stephan had on a blue linen shirt and khakis, a belt with alligator print. Shoes that matched his belt. Not bad, not bad at all. So with my light brown sarong wrapped around my body like it was a dress, the ties around my neck, both of us had on tones of Mother Earth, so we ended up being coordinated anyway.

He came toward me and said, "You're late."

"My parents called right as I was leaving."

"Everything okay?"

"Yeah. Those lovebirds are going to end up staying in Europe another month or so. Daddy's working on something major, and negotiations are dragging out. Why are you looking at me like that? I look funny or something?"

He said, "That Pam Grier Foxy Brown Black Momma Coffee Get Christi Love thang you did with your hair really works on you."

"Thank you. I think."

Stephan said, "No jacket?"

I pointed at my shoulder. "My butterfly has to breathe."

We walked up the stairs, and he re-introduced me to Rebecca. The middle-aged, potbellied, gray-haired Hispanic man in the plaid shirt and jeans was Juan, his downstairs neighbor. He had flirty eyes and seemed pretty cool.

"Did you eat?" Juan asked me.

"Lunch. Had some popcorn and a soda. Why?"

He beamed. "Rebecca cooked beef and pork ribs."

She said, "You're more than welcome to some of it."

"They're good, too." Juan grinned. *"Muy bueno."*

I replied, "I'd like to try some. I haven't had any decent barbecue since my daddy FedExd me some ribs from Chicago."

Rebecca actually smiled. "Some of my peoples are from Chicago. You know any Gauses that live on Polk and Independence?"

"Afraid not. I grew up in the 'burbs, but my parents sold the house last year and moved to a loft downtown."

Juan yawned, said good night and went back downstairs. Rebecca went into her apartment and made a plate of ribs; I asked Stephan to put them in his fridge until we made it back.

I folded my arms across my chest, walked behind Stephan.

"Rebecca always like that?" I asked.

Stephan waved her off. "She's just lonely."

Shelly's was sarong city. Blues, oranges, light greens—some of my sistas wore their material as mini skirts, others as long skirts, some as cover-ups. Men had on either jean or linen shorts and sandals.

Stephan parked and we went our separate ways, like we were

strangers. He strolled up the walkway between Shelly's and the Cuban restaurant; I followed the seafood aroma and the sweet sounds of the saxophones, sashayed around the side of the building and passed by Cucamonga Yogurt and Rose's Caffe Luna.

Too Saxy for You went on break, and I bumped through a crowd being consumed by the wall-to-wall body heat. I stopped under the neon Heineken sign to flirt with the band members. I asked the drummer, "When are you going to stop wearing those red leather pants and eighty-six the Scary Curl?"

He kissed my cheek. "The day after you marry me, Miss Thang."

"Buy me some sin juice."

He told the bartender to give me a glass of Cristal, gratis, then leaned into my space, gave up a crooked gotcha-now grin, and asked me for my phone number; I told him I'd take his; he asked if I'd call him; I told him he'd have to wait and see.

The rest of the band wanted to know where Tammy was, because they had an offer for her. A paid gig.

I asked, "A local gig?"

"Not really. She'd be on the road for a month."

I laughed. "You know Tammy ain't leaving Hollywood."

"That's what Karen said."

"When you talk to her?"

"She was—she was dancing, but I don't see her now."

"You sure it was her?"

He winked at me. "I bought her a glass of wine."

I looked around, went to the ladies' room, and came back to the same spot. No Karen. I did see Stephan. And he saw me.

The band went back to work. I dumped the drummer's number on the bar, and went to shake my moneymaker with a stranger.

Damn. Thaiheed swaggered his ass in the place. That's the problem with living in an area with very few black people and very few black clubs; we all ended up at the same watering holes.

He was in my face, standing in my space, before I knew it. The crowd kept bumping him closer than he needed to be.

"I've been thinking about you a lot." He smiled. "I hope this doesn't sound too strong or too sudden."

"And exactly what have you been thinking?" I asked him.

He was anxious. I stayed unemotional.

He said, "Wondering if me and you should be together."

Stephan was in the crowd talking, but he was watching me. I moved a few inches away from Thaiheed, let my body language be my signal. "Really, now?"

"You have a minute?"

"Sixty seconds." I looked at my watch. "Clock's ticking."

He fell into a song and dance, apologized for whatever happened between us. I listened but didn't care. He was trying to make an excuse for an inexcusable act.

He asked, "So, what's your status?"

My eyes went toward Stephan. Watched his every move as I answered, "Content and pending."

"Wanna dance?"

I smiled. "Yeah. But not with you."

He laughed nervously. Then his eyes darkened. At least I think they did. I was almost nervous, but his eyes went back to being soft and gray, radiating a warm, hypnotic gaze.

I laughed at my imagination and walked away.

Every few minutes me and Stephan ended up facing each other, or gazing from across the room, but still acting like we were strangers. In the ladies' room I'd changed the style of my sarong, funked it up and made it into a mini, and gave full view of my tanned legs, dark brown swim top, and the earring that sparkled in my belly button. Stephan laid his eyes on my body and held them there unrelentingly, like he was a voyeur.

My eyes dared him to follow up on what he was thinking.

He let out a short laugh, shook his head, turned away.

I held back a silly girlish giggle, shook my head too.

Stephan was dancing with a big-breasted beige sista, and I was trying to party with a lanky man who thought aerobics moves were en vogue. Stephan and I came back to back on the crowded dance floor, and for the entire song our butts grazed against each other. Our asses rubbed so much that it felt like I was doing a forbidden dance with him instead of the faceless man in front of me.

His ass on my ass. I liked that. I liked that a lot.

I turned around, danced on his ass, raked my fingernails across his arms, pressed my breasts against his back, stared at the sista he was dancing with while I blew a long stream of air into his ear. That jarred him, and he lost his rhythm and almost dropped his drink. *Gotcha*. I did that for shock value. Stephan turned around, real smooth and slow.

I winked at him.

The sista he was dancing with was ready to kick my ass.

Without a word I claimed my prize, took his hand, and pulled him along, abandoned both that sista and my lanky dance partner.

He said, "Why'd you do that?"

"She had skinny legs, lopsided breasts, and was shaped like a mailbox. You can do better."

He said, "Why're you playing jealous?"

"I'm protecting you, as a friend."

"Protecting me?"

"That's what buddies do."

I told him I was craving a cup of cappuccino, and we took the long route, through the tunnel between Shelly's and Havana Hut. But we never made it to Rose's Caffe Luna. Somewhere along the way we stopped in the darkness and he kissed my eyelids, licked around my butterfly, and we crept from putting soothing kisses on each other's face and neck into a closed-mouth kiss, then his tongue broke through my lips. I tried to keep his tongue out, but he slipped in the way I know he wanted to let his penis glide deep inside my abyss.

My hand came up, touched his face, outlined his square chin, admired the texture of his brown skin, his manly smell, his mystery, rubbed his hairline, caressed his earlobes.

I drew his face close to mine. My breath mixed with his; our lips were close enough to kiss, but we didn't. His hands grazed my breasts, then squeezed. *Ohhh, what are you trying to do.* My hands wandered down between his legs, massaged and measured and womanhandled that bump that was swelling in the name of Chanté.

My back was to the stucco wall. His hand went under my skirt, pulled my thong to the side, and traced the opening of my vagina, massaged the little slice of hair I had down there, drew small circles on my flowering lips, gently squeezed my slit between two fingers. He put his fingers inside his mouth, licked them, made them moist, then teased his way inside me.

The entire time we were eye to eye. Staring each other down.

Nobody was hiding the passion, but nobody was giving in.

Reality yanked me away from my forbidden thoughts. Made my heated body want to stiffen up and turn cold. I had to be real.

This wasn't the way to do the do.

Yet I was turned on. Extremely turned on.

He whispered, "What do you want me to do?"

"Do anything, just don't lose that rhythm."

"What do you like?"

"You. I like you."

That moment was coming on strong, the tingling was everywhere, surges of electricity raced through me, but the baggage that my soul carried started to get heavy, and my head was getting clearer. I took my hand away from his penis, pushed his moist hands from inside me. I kissed his fingers, one by one, put those damp fingers in his mouth, moved them in and out, deeper and deeper, broke his skin, became the ruler of this affair, made him taste the candy-coated juices of the soul that he had teased.

I stopped. Moved away.

I said, "We're friends, Stephan. So, back off."

He was panting, on fire. I headed back to the club first. I was on the floor, two couples over from Thaiheed—who couldn't keep his eyes off me—putting on my best smile and laughing, before Stephan came back inside. I guess it took him a while to get that hard-on to soften up.

This was unbelievable. I finished dancing, turned around, and ran right into Craig Bryant. He had on fresh khaki shorts and a bright yellow tank top. I could tell they were new because the creases were still in the material.

He frowned like he wanted to spit in my face. Some old feelings were still roosting inside me, but I was ready to spit in his too. Yep, he was mad. The lines in his forehead and the way he talked out of one side of his face told me that. He tried to sound cool. "That's messed up what you did."

"What on earth are you jabbering about, partner?"

"Play stupid. But that's cool. I'll get my revenge."

"What revenge?"

He almost smiled. "You'll be the last one to know."

My words were jittery. "What *revenge*?"

"I take pleasure in making somebody else uncomfortable."

"You know what, Craig,"—a rabid feeling was taking over me—"whenever I see you, my bullshit meter shoots off the scale."

I was face to face with that moron; the band was jamming a saxy version of Vanessa Williams's "Dreaming." I jumped when I felt warm lips on my butterfly, a strong hand gently caressing my butt.

Craig's eyes shot behind me. The floor was crowded, so no one could see what I felt, no one saw whatever Craig had seen.

I turned and faced Stephan Mitchell. Our gazes locked.

Stephan shot Craig a harsh look, then asked me, "You okay?"

I blinked a few times, then said an unconvincing "Yeah."

"He bothering you?"

"Yeah."

Stephan made eye contact with Craig. "What's up?"

Craig tilted his head back. " 'Sup?"

He walked away, bumped through the crowd.

And you know, I didn't care. Stephan made me feel safe. I stared at his brown eyes and felt nostalgic for something that I'd never had, for something that might never be a part of my life. Since the day we'd met, I'd longed for more than he was offering me, craved to get comfortable in a place where I felt connected.

Stephan strutted away without uttering a single word.

He was bold. And I was daring.

I followed Stephan to his car.

I glanced behind me once, saw Craig standing in the crowd, watching me with wicked eyes.

Stephan asked, "Who was that?"

"Nobody."

He bobbed his head. "Nobody with an attitude."

My hands drifted to my tummy, asked, "Did you see Karen?"

He nodded.

I asked, "Where'd she go?"

He shrugged.

"Was she with Tammy?"

Again he shrugged.

"What, you're not talking to me now?"

He didn't say a damn thing.

Stephan opened my door. I glanced around the parking lot, spied left and right to see if I saw Karen's buggy. Then I slid into Stephan's Mustang without a complaint.

He leaned over and kissed me. So much passion.

My insides tingled, my breasts were swelling. That stimulating feeling rushed back in and overwhelmed me just like that. Sensations that were aflame in the bottom of my belly stayed with me as we drove by the strawberry fields on Haven.

I'd left the memories behind.

Stephan put his hand on my leg, then slid his fingers down where my legs formed a V. My eyes closed. I shivered. He touched me there while he took a mellow drive up the 10 freeway. I reached over and massaged his hardness through his pants while he merged from the 10 to the 71 expressway.

Merge. That's what he wanted to do.

I make the choice. He can only do what I let him do.

Sweat was growing on my breasts as I told him, "I'm going home when we get back to my car. Don't get your hopes up."

Back at Phillips Ranch, he parked. I followed him up his stairs. He was still silent. Hadn't said a word.

Step by step I was giving in. Surrendering to kismet.

We went out on his patio. Touched and kissed. He turned me around, rubbed his hardness on my butt, moved in circles, up and down, kept putting his hands between my legs, stirring me.

"Why are you teasing me?" I moaned, tilted my head back and kissed him, sucked his lips in a hungry and easy kind of way.

He finally whispered, "Say you want me."

"Negative. I don't want you."

I stopped stroking him and turned back around.

"Good night, Stephan. I'm going home now."

He didn't say anything.

I mumbled out my true feelings: "Okay, I want you."

I put my hands on his shoulders, pushed him downtown. He eased to his knees; my back moved up against the door to his storage room. My sarong had loosened and risen, my damp thongs were pulled off in a move so smooth it felt illegal. My eyes went to the sky, gazed through the pine trees up into the stars. I felt so high that I'd have to take an escalator down a mile to get to heaven. Each one of those celestial bodies envied me.

My left leg rose, rested over Stephan's shoulder, and his face moved inside, that tongue leading the way, flicked in and out of me. My moan came on strong. He nibbled, sucked, teased, kissed, blew on a spot that was as hot as a thousand suns. I was afraid the temple he was tongue-praising might singe his face.

He told me I tasted good.

I floated into the living room, lay on his blue carpet, felt the firmness from being on the floor, on my back.

His tongue was on my knees, then on the back of my knees, waking up a few nerves I never knew I had.

My toes. Oh, God, he was sucking my toes. Felt like my whole foot was in his mouth, then one toe at a time.

I was as juicy as a pear apple and twice as sweet.

His fingers were around my breasts, made my nipples ache with pleasure, and it felt like they were the size of a silver dollar.

Let the clothes fall where they may.

He wanted to crawl on top of me, wanted to weigh me down with what he had to offer. But I wanted to go beyond the missionary.

I tongued him, let him know, "It's Sadie Hawkins Day."

"Okay."

"And one more thing."

"What?"

I said, "Wrap that pickle up."

"One sec."

My hand was all over him, and let me tell you, I was pleased with the girth. I hoped he knew how to work it. After he put the sheath on, I doubled-checked to make sure it was on tight. Had to have a good barrier between us. I raised my hips, eased down, allowed him to creep inside my love. He felt so good living inside me, sharing life, stretching my walls. My giggles stopped and changed into a stream of charming murmurs.

I was riding him, chanting out my pleasure, telling him how good he was making me feel, controlling the penetration, enjoying my own twinges and driving him crazy. Then we were rocking on one of his kitchen chairs, facing each other.

He jerked.

I said, "What's wrong?"

"Your nails. Not too deep, okay?"

"Sorry, partner."

"Dig any deeper, I'll need stitches."

I loved that kind of groove; he was in me deep, but his thrusting was limited because we were so close. That made him move slow and sensual, made him have to let me take over.

We moved the party back to the carpeted floor. Then took the fun and games to his bedroom.

I stopped loving and kissing him long enough to say, "Open the blinds so some moonlight can shine through."

"You like some light, huh?"

"I love light."

I hated loving in the dark where I couldn't see. When I was this turned on, I had to bathe myself in all of my senses.

His bed squeaked with our rhythm. Yes, yes, I loved a squeaky bed that echoed like a thousand mice. I loved to do my thing and make it sing a sultry song of sin and salvation.

A tri-fold mirror was on his dresser. I pulled his comforter back, turned sideways, reclined so I could watch him groove. He was watching me too. Watching and smiling. His body eased down on mine, but I slowed him down and reached for that divining rod of his. Had to make sure that condom was still on tight.

Then I held on, pulled him down, showed him the way.

My eyes went to the mirrors; I checked out my fluid movements that were making his fluids move. He massaged my butt, slapped it, made it sting so good. I saw him admiring me, and I gave up a devilish grin while I moved slow and easy. Stephan was so strong, so rigid, so powerful that I imagined that his orgasm would blow a big hole in my back.

I felt it. He was swelling. Growing. His eyes were shut tight. Breathing short. He was ready to burst like confetti. He was fighting it but losing the battle, about to spew his sweet and sourness inside the latex barrier between us. I had his wanna-be-cool ass going crazy. I wished he didn't have a condom on, so I could feel the rush when it entered my body.

I lost it, "Oh my God . . . oh shit . . . oh goddamn . . . oh Stephan . . ."

It snuck up on me that time. I was drunk with the feeling, on fire, walking through the door of that wonderful place. My vagina trembled, walls opened and closed, made sounds like it was gasping for air, sweet spasms making me feel as light as a feather.

I squealed, "Say my name."

His back was arching, forehead damp, face glowing with the same sweet pain I was releasing. Paralyzed by pleasure.

I demanded, "Say my name."

He held my hips and whispered, "Chanté."

"Now spell it."

He lit candles and we relaxed in the tub. Hot water and plenty of soap. He dipped his butt in the steam first, took up most of the room, and I sat between his legs, felt his penis sleeping on my back.

He was born in Mississippi. Came out here when he was in elementary school. Lived in South Central before moving to Baldwin Hills. Was teased about his accent, which has evolved into a smooth Calified tone. No middle name. Uncircumcised. Favorite color, blue. Hates coconut. Two brothers. A sister. Loves his mother. His daddy is dead. His stepdaddy owns three barber shops in L.A.: one on Crenshaw, one on Slauson, and one on La Brea. His other brothers went into the family's barber business. He didn't. His tone made me think that he refused to.

I said, "My momma gives my daddy baths every now and then."

"Sounds old-fashioned."

"Yep. She's from the old school. She believes in taking care of her man. Cooks dinner every day."

"Your mother submissive?"

"No. Extremely loving. Well organized. Momma handles all the money, so without her Daddy wouldn't have a dime. She runs the house."

I laughed. So did the naked man whose flesh was rubbing against mine. He was a little harder. I moved against him, felt him move, slip and slide against me.

I asked, "You have more condoms, or is that it?"

"I might be able to find another one. Maybe two."

"Two? Aren't we assumptive."

"Just ambitious."

"Ambition's good."

I wanted him inside me again. Needed to be moved back to that special place where nothing mattered but the feeling of contentment. A place of no resentment.

I jumped back a subject and asked, "Why, are you one of those men who think a woman is supposed to submit to a man?"

"Everybody has to be submissive in some kind of way. A man and a woman have to be submissive to each other."

He dropped water on my back, massaged my neck, made me moan.

I asked, "What does being submissive to each other mean?"

"Compromise. Team work."

I rubbed my back up against his penis, made it squish between us. Those fleshy things fascinate me. One minute it looked like a bloated worm, the next it was a gladiator's weapon. He was growing, then it softened again. He massaged my back, my neck. My hands were kneading his calves, his thighs, feeling every part of him I could feel. It felt so comfortable, so uninhibited, like we'd loved a million times before.

I leaned forward long enough to drain a few inches of water, then ran more hot water into the tub. "I heard that if a woman doesn't take care of her man, that if he has a hard penis, his heart will be hard. And if she keeps him soft, his heart will be soft. You think that's true?"

He paused. "Nope."

I thought about all the love I'd given Craig. All the days. All the nights. How I drove forty miles from Diamond Bar to Moreno Valley a zillion times, about how I had empathy for his economic plight and dug deep into my bank account to keep him satisfied. I just knew I was going to end up marrying him.

What a fool believes.

And still I wanted to feel like it was my fault.

In a disillusioned voice I said, "Me neither. I don't think it's true. Not in the real world. A woman can make love to a man until he's drier than Arizona, and it won't matter."

"Not if he don't love her."

I said, "People in love mess around."

"Okay, respect. If he don't respect her, or if he doesn't love her, it's just another piece of ass."

"Piece of ass. Ouch. That's cold-blooded and sexist."

"How?"

"A woman has a million qualities, and she's reduced to being a piece of ass."

"If you step into a man's locker room, don't expect the truth to be sugar-coated."

"Just another one of your sexist statements."

"You asked, I told you the truth."

"Is that what this is? Another piece of ass?"

"I could ask you the same thing."

"I could reach back and rip your penis off your body."

He kissed my neck, his tongue so warm, pulled my hair back and licked my ear, stilled that pissed-off feeling that was trying to rise up from my darkened soul.

I said, "So, all that matters is if a sista looks good."

"A woman looking good ain't never made a man stay."

"I know that."

"If he don't like you, he just don't like you."

"Why would he bother to hang around?"

"Sex. Money."

"That's fucked."

"Women do it all the time. It's called equal rights."

We laughed, playfully splashed water on each other.

Love. That thing that was like the wind. You could feel it, but you couldn't hold it, so you couldn't control it. It teased you, made you want it, made you hunger to be satisfied.

That was what Craig had stolen from me. My right to love. Had sipped my honey and moved on when the flavor of my sweetness no longer suited his taste. Had left this hollow feeling in that place. I hated him for allowing me to feel like that.

Stephan stopped sucking on my flesh, but kept rubbing his hot hands over me. "Where did you hear that?"

I snapped out of my trance. "Hear what?"

"Soft penis, soft heart."

"My momma told me that."

With every word it seemed like Stephan was filling that hollow space. Some of it at least. But I knew all of this was temporary. A dusk-to-dawn cure. We touched, talked, cleansed each other.

Stephan microwaved the barbecue that Rebecca had given me before we went to Shelly's. He put my treats on a portable table, and we crashed on his bed: windows open, ceiling fans on, Bobby Lyle jamming on his CD player. Stephan relaxed in front of me. I pigged out and wondered what he thought of me now.

I said, "Eating this late is gonna make me fat. I'll wake up in the morning with a Nell Carter booty."

He said, "Barbecue sauce is on your mouth."

"You sure you saw Karen tonight?" I licked my lips, traced my tongue around the edges. "I get it?"

"I could be wrong. And nope, you didn't get it."

He leaned over and licked the corners of my lips. Ran his tongue around my mouth, then let it linger inside. I put my food to the side, then straddled Stephan. If he hadn't had his sweats on, he would've slipped up inside me. Drops of barbecue were on my fingers, and I smeared that flavor on the side of his face, then licked it off.

I said, too serious, "Tell me that you're different."

"I can't. And you can't tell me you're different either."

"You and your girlfriend get back together?"

"Kind of late to be asking that."

"Never too late. You seeing somebody?"

He paused. "Nobody special."

I tried not to sound deflated. "I see. Mr. Evasive."

I took my tray into the kitchen and rinsed off the plate and silverware, then put the dishes inside the dishwasher. I put some space between us so I could think. While I was all to myself having a moment, Stephan walked through the living room and stepped out on his patio. He was staring at the sky like he was searching for answers.

I said, "Stephan?"

"Yeah?"

"I asked you if you had a girlfriend. You're supposed to ask me if I have a boyfriend. That's how it works."

"I know how it works. And I will."

"When?"

"When I want to know."

That meant he didn't give a fuck. That feeling we had a few minutes ago was already gone. I didn't know if I should feel insulted and squirt pepper spray in all of his underwear, or just remind myself that this was the norm in my life anyway.

I wrapped my arms around myself and watched him for a moment.

"What're you doing out there?" I asked.

"Thinking."

"You want me to leave now?"

He didn't answer. I went out and stood next to him. Leaned my body against his and asked, "You ever been in love?"

"Yeah. No. Maybe. Not sure."

"That's evasive."

"I know I've been in possession."

"In possession?"

"You know. You get so used to having somebody in your life, so comfortable with what they have to offer, that no matter how lacking, or how jacked up it is, you don't want to let it go."

We watched the stars in the sky for a few minutes.

Stephan pulled me close. "Do you have a boyfriend?"

I almost smiled. But that blush was crushed when images of Craig, Michael, Thaiheed, trampled through my mind.

I answered. "Negative."

Stephan said, "You hesitated."

"So did you."

"Who was the brotha who was all up on you at the club?"

It dawned on me why he was tight-lipped. I said, "Jealous?"

He moved a little, but didn't give me any real reply.

He was resentful. I smiled on the inside.

Then his phone rang. He rushed into the bedroom. I felt a lot more deflated. A little pissed off. That was why I followed him, stood right up under him, and kissed on his neck, got closer than close so I could hear what the hell was going on at midnight.

"I'm sorry, Momma," he said, then kissed my neck. "You had gone off way down the street when I was leaving. Momma, stop fussing. Go to bed."

Stephan laughed, told her he loved her, then said good-bye.

We crawled back into his bed.

I kissed his lips. "What're you thinking?"

He said, "Kismet."

"Good answer."

I kissed him again. Somewhere inside that kiss I decided that after I left here, whenever I left here, I wasn't going to call Stephan Mitchell anymore. That was my final decision as I teased my tongue down to his navel, then decided to take this moment to the highest and kissed around the tip of his penis. I made love to that part of him until my jaws ached and the corners of my mouth glistened with splendid traces of him.

I let him on top, gave him permission to take control. He let loose, and I was buck wild and free. Damn, it was so fucking good. I was moaning and cursing, delirious, crooning *oh Stephan*, chanting out irrational things. The more he gave, the more I wanted. Slivers of reality came and went, and in those moments I didn't want any of this, but at the same time I wanted it all.

I wanted to pull him inside my womb. With my fingers gripping his back, my nails digging, my coochie making sounds of its own, I pushed my face into his neck and muffled my sounds of satisfaction, and let his moans and groans flow in a coarse solo.

After that, he passed out like he was on anesthesia.

Which was good.

That way he couldn't see my tears.

# 24 Darnell

The last week of May felt like the longest week of the year. Monday and Tuesday found me in Phoenix at a hearing. Wednesday through Friday dragged because I couldn't wait for Saturday to come again. Electricity was running through my veins the way it does a six-year-old on Christmas Eve. I was living for the weekend, something I hadn't done in a long time. Waiting for the day I was going to get away and spend a few moments with Tammy.

By seven in the morning I was out cutting the yard. Which wasn't unusual because everybody had to get their yard work done before the heat moved in. Through the patio window I saw that Dawn had put on a golden skirt suit. I came back in and saw that she had packed up her open house signs. After that I heard her on the phone talking to Charlotte for about thirty minutes.

I watched the clock. Wondered why it was taking her so long to leave.

Finally she hung up and asked me, "What are you doing today?"

I told her that I had to drop off legal papers—three unlawful detainers and child-custody papers—with clients. One client was forty minutes east of us in Rialto, the other lived thirty minutes south of Rialto in Corona, down where the flies were the size of 747s and the smell of cows was stronger than Superman.

She said, "We're heading in opposite directions."

I agreed. Wholeheartedly, I agreed.

Dawn was gone before nine. She let me know that she'd be gone most of the day, that after she did breakfast with Charlotte she had an open house. After that she was driving out to San Fernando Valley.

I smiled a guilty smile.

Saturday afternoon. I was standing in the definition of heat. It had to be a hundred-twenty in the shade, and we weren't in the shade. I felt like an ant under a magnifying glass.

" 'Bout time Tammy brought you out here. I didn't imagine you to be this big. You's a big 'un. Thought she said you was a little man, like Purnell. Nice to meet you, Bobby."

Tammy cringed, held my hand, said, "This is Darnell, Momma."

"Oh, shit—" Tammy's mother blushed and dropped her head when she cursed. "Excuse my French. Nice to meet you, Darnell."

Tammy's mom was about five-four, with heavy breasts that hung to her waist. Thick legs, just like Tammy's. Lila sounded Cajun, so they might be part Creole. She didn't look directly at me, actually darted her eyes away when it looked like she might make eye contact.

Tammy let my hand go, shifted her stance, smiled like she was proud. "This is my talented friend who writes novels."

"Oh." Her mother looked me up and down, from my plain white T-shirt to my Levi's. "A book writer."

Tammy sounded nervous when she added, "He's a lawyer too, but he's an up-and-coming novelist."

We were outside, standing in the dirt lawn a few feet from the front porch of a yellow bungalow. Standing in a furnace called Needles, out on K Street.

I rubbed my eyes, then said, "Nice to meet you, Miss Lila."

"Just call me Lila."

Tammy said, "Darnell, you all right?"

The heat had sucked the moisture out of my eyes. They were aching. Dust swirled in the torrid breeze. The front yard had dried patches of green and light brown grass struggling to get out of the ground.

I told Tammy, "I need some Visine. The kind for allergies."

Tammy nodded, then said, "Where's everybody, Momma?"

Lila said, "They'll be here a little late."

"Momma, I begged you to make sure everybody was here on time for once. You know I have to get back to Los Angeles. Darnell has to work in the morning. I told you that."

Lila spoke like Tammy's wants, like my personal problems, were no big deal. "Margaux had to work. Beverly at home cleaning up. You heard about your little sister, Rhonda, didn't you?"

"Yeah, I heard she's pregnant. Don't bring it up in front of step-daddy because I don't want him acting stupid."

"He's at Margaux's house."

"What's he doing over there?"

"Drinking with her husband."

Tammy's brows furrowed, and she snapped, "Purnell's not supposed to drink because of his diabetes."

Lila fanned herself. "Can't tell him nothing."

A little black girl was a house down, wearing white shorts, no shoes, out in the shade near a broken-down Pinto, entertaining herself by raking circles in the dirt. Across the street a shirtless, sunburned, potbellied white man with a layer of dirt on his skin was sitting on his porch sipping on a tall one.

Tammy asked her mother, "You finished cooking?"

"Just started."

"What? It's already two-thirty. You said we were eating at three, right? Darnell has to get back home. I told you that."

Her mother said, "I worked the blackjack table this morning and I just got home. Turkey won't be ready for a little while."

Tammy frowned. "Why didn't Margaux or Beverly help you cook?"

"Your sisters are trifling."

Tammy checked her watch. "I need to be on the road by five."

I added, "No later than six."

Lila said, "Take Darnell out to Laughlin to the casino and let your friends see you with him."

"I don't have friends at the casino."

"They always ask about you."

Tammy said, "They *talk* about me, they don't *ask* about me."

We went inside the dusty white stucco house: a shotgun-style two-bedroomer where one of the bedrooms was used as a den. Wooden furniture. Wooden floors. Turquoise sofa that had a recliner attached to the end. Framed pictures of American Indians on every wall. Dust on everything. Which was understandable because every time the door opened a dust bowl blew inside.

Cakes and pies. I smelled them all. Felt the heat from when they were baked. The air conditioner wasn't on high; either that or it wasn't working too well. A turkey was still cooking in the oven, and that heat was spreading from wall to wall, sitting in the room and hugging me like we were old friends. It was almost as hot inside as it was out on the pavement.

An oscillating fan was on, so I sat near that. That way every ten seconds or so a breeze raked across my face.

Tammy and her mother talked, but they didn't touch. Didn't speak in a friendly tone. Tammy sounded defensive and rushed.

Twenty minutes later, her stepdaddy showed up. A fair-skinned man. A couple of young brothers helped him in the house. More like carried him and the Jack Daniel's funk with him.

He snapped, "I can walk my damn self."

"We gotcha, Purnell." That was the brother who had four top teeth knocked out at the gum line.

"I can walk by my-damn-self." Purnell tried to yank away, but damn near fell. "Don't need nigga hands on me."

Purnell was gray-haired, six feet tall, rail-thin. There wasn't enough space for them to get by, so I moved off the sofa and stepped to the side. Hot, dry air blew in from outside and sent me a whiff of his bull-dog scent.

There was a lot of commotion, everybody talking at the same time, trying to keep Purnell from knocking over everything he staggered past. The small rectangular room had lots of furniture, plenty of Indian-style knickknacks, not much room to maneuver.

Tammy's teeth were gnawing her top lip. She didn't look at me. I had a hard time acting like this was normal.

But I did my best.

Nobody looked surprised but me.

I stood up. Purnell saw me, rocked side to side, tried to focus his eyes. "Who the hell this nigga?"

Before I could open my mouth, Tammy moved near me and said, "This is Darnell. My friend I told Momma about."

Lila said, "He's a lawyer. And he writes books."

Purnell snapped, *"Who gives a fuck?"*

One of the brothers said, "Where you want us to put him?"

The other brother was staring me down, like he was the sheriff and I was a drifter in the wrong town.

Lila said, "Pookie, you know better than to be letting Purnell drink like that."

The brothers laughed. "Can't tell a grown man what to do."

I was looking at Purnell's crotch. Not on purpose. His green work pants had a dark wet spot. A spot that was getting rounder, bigger, and wider. And a whole lot wetter.

He went limp and fell forward. Right at me. Face first. Scared me. I jumped and caught him before he slammed head first on the wooden and glass coffee table. Held him by the shoulders, kept him at arm's length so his urine wouldn't splatter my way.

He screamed, "Y'all get me to the bathroom."

The brothers laughed, then they turned around and left, just like that. Didn't take Purnell out of my hands, didn't say good-bye. They leaped off the porch, headed up K Street, and left me breath to breath with Purnell. I had to let him lean all of his funk on me and take him and his dead weight through the kitchen, walk his aroma past the food, to get to the bathroom. He grabbed part of the wall. I pointed him toward the toilet, and left him on his own. Lila went inside and helped him unzip his pants. He started to pee, and all but two drops hit the floor.

Lila cursed nonstop. "Let me let the damn toilet seat up first! I just mopped in here yesterday!"

I went in the living room with Tammy. Had no idea what the hell I was supposed to do in a situation like this. Her eyes had watered up, but she wasn't crying. I said, "You okay?"

"That's why I don't like coming out here."

Purnell screamed, "I need some pants. Get me some pants."

Lila screamed back, "You see Tammy got her friend here with her for her birthday dinner and you acting up."

"*Who gives a fuck?* This my house. My fucking house."

They spent five minutes cursing each other out. Tammy ended up in the kitchen stirring her own birthday food. I plopped down on the sofa, pretended I was mute, watched a news report about brush fires. I couldn't hear the reporters because of all the shouting and cursing and things getting knocked over. Lila and Purnell were trying to out-vulgar each other.

Lila walked by with Purnell leaning on her shoulders, grabbing what he could to stay upright. He was butt naked. Lila scowled at Purnell. Both of them were swapping insults. Purnell glanced my way when he tottered by. Dropped his head. Started back cursing.

They had made it around the corner to the bedroom when Lila shouted, "I should let your ass fall down and learn you a lesson."

"Get me some fucking pants," Purnell said. Then there was a thud; he grunted and screamed. "You let me fall."

"Damn right. Now do as I say. Stop acting up."

"All right, we gonna see about this shit."

"Purnell, you need to lay your ass down and go to sleep."

Tammy was standing to the side, arms folded tight against her breasts. Her face was on fire, eyes swelling up like golf balls.

I asked, "You okay?"

Tammy shook her head, wiped her eyes and motioned for me to follow her. Then she yelled to her folks, said, "I'll be back."

"Where y'all going?" That was her momma yelling back.

"Outside."

"You going 'round to Margaux's house?"

"No." Then she lowered her voice to a whisper, "Hell, no. I don't even know why you asked that."

Her momma screamed, "The food'll be ready in a little bit."

Tammy put her fingers between mine and led me out of the madness and into the heat.

Out on the porch, I slowed her down a bit. Gave her a hug, tried to smooth whatever anger was mushrooming within her. I didn't hug her long because, good or bad, right or wrong, it was too hot to share any kind of body heat.

She exhaled and said, "Thanks."

"Why didn't you tell me it was your birthday?"

"No big deal. Just another day."

"It is a big deal."

"Tell them that."

To the left was a train overpass. On the other side of the tracks, where the street snaked uphill, a green Holiday Inn sign poked up and waved me down. Tammy's irritated sigh said the same thing that I was feeling. After a four-hour drive, I could use a quiet, cool place to kick back and relax.

Two long hours later, the food wasn't done. Tammy's sisters showed up later than late, walked in within ten minutes of each other. Nobody had a present for the birthday girl. Nobody offered to help do a thing.

Beverly drove a cheap Monte Carlo with four-thousand-dollar rims on it, and wore denim shorts with flaps across the front, an outfit that barely covered her butt and showed off long legs with about a mile of cellulite dangling from thigh to ankle. Her belly hung over the top of her shorts. Gold lipstick and gold shoes. She was twenty-one, wore two pagers, one green, one pink.

When she came in the front door, the first thing she did was scream into the kitchen, "The food ready?"

Lila screamed back, "Almost."

"Damn. Then why y'all have me come over if the food not ready? I was watching *Martin*."

Tammy was in the kitchen, washing dishes, while her momma hustled and sweated. Tammy peeped into the front room, saw her sister, then stepped in and said, "Beverly?"

"What?"

"Why didn't you help momma coo—" Tammy did a double-take and said, "That wouldn't happen to be my gold necklace you have on?"

"Don't start nothing, your uppity ass." Beverly had one hand on her hip, rotating her neck. "I don't see why nobody cooking for you. You act like you don't know where you come from."

"I know where I come from." Tammy had a look in her eye that said, *I know. And that's why I don't come here anymore.*

Beverly countered, "Don't mess with me because I'm tired and hungry. I didn't get much sleep. My damn neck is hurting."

"Stop, Tammy," Lila said. "You work last night, Beverly?"

"Naw. I got my hair did and I slept in a chair so I wouldn't mess it up. I went to visit Mookie and I wanted it to look good. He likes it when my hair looks good."

Her hair was in a hard-freeze style, shaped like a crown, all kinds of glue and glitter and arts-and-crafts crap in it.

Tammy said, "I'm not through with my conversation."

They fell into an argument about Beverly always stealing from people. Beverly had been to Tammy's place and helped herself to Tammy's herringbone slacks a few months back. A blouse before that.

Beverly's eyes tightened, her scowl went to me. She said, "You must be Tammy's friend Momma was telling us about."

I said, "Yeah."

Beverly smirked. "You met J.J.?"

Tammy said, "Don't go there, Beverly."

Beverly's scowl turned into some sort of smile. She said, "Oh, so your funky little friend don't know about J.J.?"

"His name is Darnell," Tammy said. "What did Momma tell you about bringing that up? My business isn't everybody's business."

"This necklace wasn't nobody's business, but you brought it up in front of every-damn-body. Who you trying to impress? Why don't you take your friend around to Purnell's old house so he can meet J.J.? All of y'all can drink and have a good time."

Tammy growled, "Give me my necklace."

"I ain't giving you nothing until I'm ready."

"Take it off or I'll snatch it off."

"That'll be the last thing you snatch."

"Don't you girls start to fighting," Lila said. "Beverly?"

"What?"

"When your boyfriend getting out of jail?"

"Mookie should be out this month. He only doing six months this time because it got reduced to a misdemeanor and the place is so crowded they're letting some of them out early. Actually four months because of good behavior."

Beverly went into the den, got on the phone, turned on another television. Martin's voice boomed from the tube.

The pregnant sister, Rhonda, was sixteen. She wobbled inside with her thirty-year-old boyfriend trailing behind her with nervous baby steps. She was five-seven. Leon was at least two inches shorter. I knew his name because he had a golden overlay in his mouth that spelled his moniker in crooked letters.

Seven conversations were going on, everybody was trying to out-loud each other, the radio had been turned on, so that no matter how much volume I gave the television it wasn't enough.

"Who gives a fuck?" That was Purnell. Every three minutes he'd scream that, then say, "Somebody get me some goddamn pants."

Tammy sat by me. She looked wounded, ashamed, glanced at her watch about ten times a minute. We knew I had to get back home to my wife. We both had different kinds of frustration.

She closed her eyes for a moment, massaged her temples, opened her eyes, said, "I'm sorry."

"It's not your fault."

"I thought for once they'd give it a rest and act civilized."

It went on for a while, all the noise, all the bickering.

Tammy stopped bouncing her leg and said, "Let's step outside for a minute. We can sit in the car and listen to the radio."

By the time we got in the car, Tammy was crying and blowing her nose, but no hard weeping noises.

She asked, "Still think I'm fantastic?"

"Yeah. I do."

"Well, you wanted to know me. Now you know me. This is the mess that I come from. This is the mess that I run from. One day I'm going to Europe, like Nina Simone, and leave all of this behind. My kids won't ever know that any of these people exist."

I didn't say anything for a while.

I asked her, "Who's J.J.?"

"When I was fifteen"—she blew out a long stream of air, her tone almost faded—"I messed around and was pregnant by J.J. I'm not down with abortions, so I put the baby up for adoption."

"Boy or girl?"

"I never saw the baby. Just heard the baby cry when they wrapped it up and took it away. Some nights I can still hear that cry." Her voice deepened with the sadness. She continued, "When I'm acting, whenever I have to do an emotional scene, I use all of *this*. It's called sense memory."

I repeated, "Sense memory?"

"It's a technique. You think of something or somebody in your life to get you to the emotional state you need to be in."

"Uh-huh."

"When I have to be angry, I think about my family. When I have to be sad, I think about my baby, thinking about the pain I felt and how I was all alone when I gave birth, then how happy I was when I heard it crying, remember how that cry faded when the nurse disappeared through that door, and the tears come just like that."

"What about when you have to be happy?"

"I think about being in Europe, singing with Nina Simone. Most of the time. When I had an audition the other day, for the first time I thought about something else to get my joy."

"What?"

"You. Having you hold me. Feeling you kiss me. Making love to you in the rain." She sighed. "But you're married, so my imagining I'm on stage with Nina Simone is more realistic."

"Is it?"

Her eyes drifted toward mine. "You tell me."

"I don't need to say what's obvious."

"I'm not weak, but at the same time I feel myself getting weak for you, Darnell. You're the most positive thing in my life. Right now anything can happen." She laughed. "I've actually considered cutting Bobby loose and being your mistress."

I patted her hand. Rubbed my fingers across her skin.

She told me, "Problems in relationships don't come out of thin air."

"What do you mean?"

"When did you realize that you and your wife were having problems?"

I thought a moment, then said, "In the receiving line when I tried to get a hug. She brushed me off so she could go to her buddy Charlotte and the rest of her bridesmaids. And I was her husband. I'll never forget that. I think she was more in love with the idea of being married than she was in love with me."

I waited for Tammy to ask me if I loved my wife, was ready to tell her I did, ready to confess that sometimes love wasn't enough, but the question never came.

She said, "I never should've come back."

"Why? These are your people."

"Sometimes leaving town is a polite way of breaking up."

"Breaking up with who?"

"Everybody in that house. Maybe I'll move on from here. Get married and have some sane babies."

I said, "Marriage isn't always a happy ending; sometimes it's a troubled beginning."

"You speaking on your marriage, or marriage in general?"

"Shhh. Sing one of those Nina Simone songs for me."

I was in my car in the desert holding another woman's hand, wondering what my wife was doing at this moment. And I wondered if Tammy cared where her man was.

Lila stuck her head out the door, interrupted Tammy's soft flow of the theme song from *Porgy and Bess*. I loves ya Porgy. Her mother yelled to let us know that the food was done.

Tammy moved slowly, took short, reluctant steps toward the house.

The scene inside the house was unbelievable.

The vegetables, salad, pies, everything was on the counter. Lila was pulling the turkey out of the oven.

Purnell screamed for his pants.

Then everybody attacked the food, elbowed and pushed each other so they could get to it first. No one had a chance to bless the birthday meal that Lila had slaved over before Tammy's sisters—who already had knives in hand—started cutting, cursing, and arguing while they snatched legs off the turkey, pulled off pieces of meat before Lila could put it down on the counter. They were grabbing vegetables, bowls of salad, whole pies.

My face was rigid, eyes wide open; I couldn't move.

Tammy mumbled, "A bunch of fucking vultures."

Nobody heard her. Too many arguments were going on.

Beverly made four plates of food, three plates of dessert, bitched about there not being any soda in the house, and rushed out the door. Rhonda's round belly bumped her momma out of the way. She piled food on two plates, for her and her old man with the graffiti on his teeth, grabbing all the best parts of the bird, acting like this was the last meal she'd ever eat.

Tammy took my hand, pulled me back toward my car. This time she was practically running, dragging me along. She opened the door and got in on the passenger side, told me to get in.

She asked me to start the engine.

I asked, "Where we going?"

"Back to civilization."

"You're not going to eat your birthday dinner?"

"Please, Darnell, just get me away from here."

"Okay."

"Every time I come out here and try to show them love, I always leave with tears rolling down my face."

I cranked the car up.

She adjusted the vent so the air could blow in her face. "Well, now you know more about me than Karen and Chanté do. They've never been out here. And they never will be out here. And don't let word get back to them that you were out here. They wouldn't understand."

I rubbed her hand. "Don't worry, it's between us."

"Seems like we can't tell anybody about anything we do."

I felt her pain when I whispered, "Seems like."

Tammy was silent for a few moments. Then she said harshly, "J.J. is Purnell's oldest son."

That chilled me.

She blew her nose again. "J.J. was the fool who carried Purnell in the house and left him with you. Eleven years later, and he still has the nerve to act jealous. Me and J.J. used to date before Purnell married my momma. Momma met Purnell because of my troubles. Purnell left his wife to get with Momma. His ex's in Vegas, and I think he still sees her from time to time. It's a mess."

Four years of law school and all I could say was, "Wow."

"I was knocked up by my stepbrother before he was my step-brother. But people around here just say I was pregnant by my brother. Some reputation, huh? I always think I'm going to make it one day, maybe get a Grammy for singing the soundtrack to a movie, or an Emmy for *my* television show, or that Oscar for that movie I'll do with Denzel, and one day when I'm on *Oprah*, sitting on that soft sofa, laughing and girl-chatting about whoever I'm seeing at the time, fans everywhere, somebody in the audience will be from around here, will stand up at the microphone, give that knowing smile, and ask me the million-dollar question I don't ever want to hear, and all of this, all of this fucking past will come out, and I'll be humiliated and chastised and booed out of my own life."

Without saying good-bye to her people, we headed up K Street.

She never looked back.

She cleared her throat, shifted, put her seat belt on, swallowed whatever she was thinking, said, "Small town, huh?"

"Yeah. Small town."

"Small town, small minds."

Her face had turned scarlet from her forehead down to her neck. Tammy closed her eyes and blew out five octaves of passion. I don't know what the song was, but it was in French. *Ne Me Quitte Pas.* She dove into her own world and chanted that emotional chorus over and over.

We grabbed sodas from a laundromat. Shared a honey bun from 7-Eleven. Headed toward the freeway. Toward the L.A. County line.

She took my wedding ring out of the ashtray, handed it to me.

I put it back on.


# 25   Stephan

Saturday. Six p.m. I was at Pops' shop on Crenshaw, across the street from Crenshaw Car Wash. The sky was gray out this way, so not many people were getting their hoopties flossed, but the barber shop was crowded, all kinds of conversations going on. Every other minute one of the boulevard's career hustlers stopped by trying to sell every-thing from Disney T-shirts to XXX videos.

Jeremiah Junior, my baby brother, was cutting my hair. I wanted my top short, sideburns long. I kept my face clean-shaven, sort of like the models in *EM*. Posters of Mo Thugs, The Fugees, Rappin' 4-Tay, Snoop Dogg, and others were on the mirrors at Junior's stand. The largest poster was of a caramel sister in a two-piece bikini, with inviting lips. The caption read "NOTHIN' LIKE A BARBER'S TRIM."

We were arguing sports.

I said, "Sacramento is a graveyard for NBA players. It's the elephant's graveyard of the NBA."

"That's cold."

"That's the truth. *Damn.*"

"Be still before I mess your wop-sided head up."

A *Best of Jerry Springer* tape was playing on the television facing Crenshaw. About five barbers had customers lined up along the wall; all were watching the tube and talking. On the show, a heavyset sister wearing a ton of gold sucker-punched a skinny sister who'd been in her face talking crap. Everybody in the shop cracked up and pumped it up, "Jerry, Jerry, Jerry."

Pops walked in looking like a short, aging Michael Jordan. Junior looked just like his daddy, only with hair.

I said, "Evening, Pops. Momma up at the house?"

"She's up there." He wiped something off his jeans and polo shirt. "Come see me when Junior gets done with your head."

He didn't look too happy. But he never did look too happy to see me.

Junior said, "What you do this time?"

"Hell if I know. Knowing him, he'll blame the rain on me."

Junior said, "It's overcast. It ain't raining."

"He'll blame me for that too."

Five minutes later, I went into his office.

He was behind his chipped wooden desk. I stopped in front of a poster of Ali, Frazier, Foreman, Holmes, and Norton, all in tuxedos. Champions Forever.

Pops motioned for me to sit. I did. I always did what he told me to do. Always had to. Everybody had to.

He said, "What you do to that pretty girl with the ugly name?"

He was talking about Toyomi. I said, "Nothing."

Pops told me that she'd been calling up to the house all day, ranting and raging.

He asked, "You thank a television and a few other thangs worth all this trouble?"

"Those were gifts."

"If she bought 'em, then give 'em back."

I shook my head. "It's the principle of the thing."

He shook his too. "I talk, but you never listen."

"I'm listening."

"Son, if she paid for it and she want it back, give it to her. You working, get another one. If you done fall on hard times, I'll buy you one and you can pay me back when you can."

"I can afford a television. Like I said, this is about principle. What about what she did to my car, to my clothes—"

"That's not the point, son. As long as you got what she want, you ain't gonna have no rest. And stop jingling that change in your pocket."

"Yes, sir."

"You've seen this before. You've seen it happen to other people. You have to learn from others' mistakes, 'cause you ain't gonna live long enough to make 'em all yourself."

Days like this reminded me why I didn't like him. I knew his attitude wasn't because I wasn't his blood child, because he treated my older brother, Nathan, more favorable.

I asked him, "Have you ever liked me?"

Pops leaned back in his chair, stared at me. At last he responded, "I don't have to like no man, nigger, white, or otherwise."

"Didn't say you did."

He leaned forward and asked, "Have I ever mistreated you?"

"Not *mistreated*."

"If it weren't for me, ain't no telling where you would be. I tell you, men like me, men who step in and pick up where other men leave off, and don't ask for no more than a thank-you every now and again, don't get nothing but bullshit and grief."

"You always treated me different."

"Raise your head up, son. If you want to talk man to man, look at me when you talk to me."

I did.

The chairman of the board said, "Now state your case."

I did.

At the end he rocked in his seat, said, "If I did treat you a little different, it's not directly because of you. You're the spitting image of your pappy, and it's hard for me to see past that."

"I'm not my daddy, Pops. I'm me."

"You're your pappy in more ways than you realize."

I shifted.

He added, "That's why me and your pappy fell out. One of us was still trying to be a boy, one of us was trying to be a man."

"You never did like my daddy, did you?"

"He was my best friend. We played together as children. But even the best of friends might not stay that way forever. That's the fork in every man's road."

"You ever think about him?"

He nodded. "I raised his children like they were my own. I did what he didn't do. I did more for you than I did my own. That's why I expect more from you than I do my own."

My reflection was in the mirror over Pops' desk. My ears were with his words, but my eyes stayed on my image. After all those years he still held a grudge for my daddy.

Junior stuck his head in the door. "Steph, phone."

I turned around. "Who?"

"Brittany. You've been tracked down, bro."

Brittany had paged me damn near a hundred times since sunrise, putting in 9-1-1 each time. In the past she had ignored so many of my pages, so I didn't break my neck calling her back.

I headed for the phone that was outside the office.

Brittany said that we needed to talk, face to face. Her voice had an edge of impatience, strained, up an octave.

I got ready to go see what was up. Before I could get to the door, Pops called me to the side.

He grunted. "Stephan?"

"Yeah, Pops?"

"I'm telling you just like I told your brothers. The same thang I told your sister. The same thing my daddy told me when I was a fool. So don't think I'm aiming at mistreating you."

"Uh-huh."

"Common sense ain't *common* sense. Everybody ain't got it."

An hour and a half later I was back at the Phillips Meadows condominiums, facing Brittany, a jittery woman with a snarl of agony spreading over her flushed face.

"Do you have the claps?" Brittany asked.

"Do I have the which-a-what?"

"Claps."

"Hell naw," I said defiantly. "Why would you ask me that?"

She maintained eye contact, showed me eyes haunted by inner pain. "Tony said I gave him the claps."

"You serious?"

She folded her arms. "Would I lie about something like this?"

I asked, "You been to the doctor?"

"Yes."

"And?"

"Gonorrhea."

A tremor ran through me, clutched my neck.

I hadn't slept with Brittany since I'd been with Chanté. Hadn't felt the slightest hint of anything clogging up my plumbing. It's funny, but the moment Brittany gave me her grief, that was who I thought of. Chanté. My relationship with her.

It was late Saturday evening. I'd parked, then walked over to my uncovered spot where Brittany had parked, right underneath the noise from the freeway. Cow smells, carbon monoxide odors masked the pleasant scents from the evergreen trees nearby and the fruit trees in the distance.

She said, "You sure you don't have the claps?"

"Positive. I'd know. As soon as I pissed, it'd burn like I was being jabbed with a hot needle."

"So, you've had it before?"

"Back in high school. Been there, done that. You?"

She nodded. "Freshman year in college."

I said, "Tony could be playing you."

"Meaning?"

"Maybe he caught the claps, and now he's trying to make you think you gave it to him. Reverse clap-ology."

"I thought about that." She paused, then said, "I took an AIDS test."

"AIDS?"

I stopped breathing. Shudders came. Gripped me the way I imagined the Grim Reaper took hold of its next customer.

She added, "Took two, actually."

My breath caught. "Why two?"

"Because I didn't trust the first one."

I swallowed, licked my lips. "And?"

"Negative. Both of them."

I released my wind. Cleared my throat. Shudders went.

The fleshy part under her red eyes looked puffy, heavy, made her look elderly, worn out. I wasn't used to seeing her without her smile. Not used to this mood she had.

I said, "This is scary."

"Don't I know it."

"We've been skydiving without a parachute."

She sighed. "Don't I know it."

She rubbed her nose, sniffled, cleared her throat.

I asked, "You seeing somebody else besides me and Tony?"

"That's irrelevant."

I didn't press her any more because I didn't want my questions to boomerang back to me.

She was too intense for me to feel comfortable. She pressed on.

"You sure that you didn't give me the claps, then somehow forget to tell me?"

"Britt, we go way back."

She sighed. "I know. You were my dream man back then."

"And you know me."

"For an eternity I've known you. You practically lived at my apartment for a year. Until you met Michelle."

"And she dogged me out."

"Well, Stephan, what goes around . . ." She sounded bitter for a moment. Like old feelings that she'd been hiding all of these years were rising to the surface.

I leaned against her car. She did the same.

Cars went over speed bumps. Up Town and Country some white kids had their portable goal out, shooting hoops on the blacktop. A few families were strolling here and there, walking rat-sized animals that were passed off as dogs.

She said, "What happened between us?"

I shrugged. "We met too young."

"I wasn't too young. It was you who couldn't slow down."

For a few minutes we talked about who we were then.

Then who we were now.

I told Brittany, "We need to back off."

In so many words I said we needed to stop acting like high schoolers and grow up and be responsible.

She smiled. "Oh, boy. Here we go again."

"What?"

"I've heard this speech before. You've met somebody."

"Yeah. No. Hell, I don't know."

"Six months from now you'll be back to your same old ways."

That assessment of my character hurt. That summed up what she thought of me. I blinked a few times and wondered about me. I put my hand in my pocket, jingled loose change, heard my daddy's wisdom in the winds, and wondered about me.

"You crying?" I asked her.

She wiped her eyes. "Just thinking about a sad song I heard today. Thinking about a sad movie. Anything but crying."

In the middle of her denial, she pulled a Kleenex out of her pocket. The way the tissue was nearby let me know she'd been shedding tears awhile. She dabbed her eyes, finger-combed her golden hair as she shook her head and chewed the corner of her bottom lip.

"Maybe you should work it out with Tony. Neither of us are getting any younger."

"Uh-oh. Sounds like your sensitive side has come back."

"I'm serious."

She blew her nose. "I know."

Brittany shows up and tells me that she's more radioactive than Chernobyl. All of this shit catches up with you, sooner or later. You play, you pay. Then you forget the price, ignore the lesson, get that immortal and invincible feeling, move on.

Brittany said, "I'll call you in a couple of months, just in case you've toggled back to your senses. That's if she hasn't dogged you out, like Michelle did, and you've already called."

"I'm serious."

"You say that now, but with tomorrow you'll get restless."

We hugged. Kissed. She'd never kissed me that good. I didn't want to kiss her, but I didn't know how to not let her kiss me. Didn't know how to close this meeting in a civil and comfortable way. Either way, it's a damn shame when a beautiful woman kisses a man with that much passion and it does nothing for him.

Her eyes said she felt the nothing that I gave her.

I wanted to tell her that we needed to stop being a hit-and-run thing. We were creeping up on thirty. And these years have flown by. That means all of us will be forty before we know it.

This ain't the lifestyle I want to be trapped inside when my pubic hairs start to gray.

She sighed. "I used to love your stanky drawers."

"Used to?"

"You know why I keep coming back?"

" 'Cause you still love my stanky drawers."

"Because I care about you and it's hard to let go. Plain and simple. What I feel for you has made it impossible to completely give myself to anyone else. It's not easy knowing that you'd do anything for a man who wouldn't do half of that for you."

My heart felt so heavy.

She hopped in her car and gave me that bright-eyed smile that was so much a part of her. Her mask. She said, "And you know why you keep coming back to me?"

Nobody answered that question. It hung in the winds that blew from the south.

She said she had a couple more stops to make.

Probably to have the same conversation, I thought.

She zoomed away, bounced over the speed bumps.

I mumbled, "Sky diving without a parachute."

My dwindling desire to waste my time and money on a woman who already had a man had left Brittany more undesirable than I'd ever imagined. Even if we gave a relationship another shot, I'd never trust her. Especially if she was following me on the freeway. She'd never trust me either.

As I started up my stairs, Rebecca opened her door. Smelled like she was frying fish.

She said, "That girl from Palm Springs was out here."

"When?"

"Little while ago."

"You sure it wasn't Chanté?"

"It was that chile from Palm Springs. I'd just come back from buying a new VCR, and the next thing I knew she was stomping up the stairs like she was about to blow the place up. I opened the door and saw her wiggling a key in your lock."

A familiar voice came from behind Rebecca: "Key did not work. She kicked the door a few times, and she left cursing."

Juan was behind her, sitting on her sofa. He was taking Rebecca's new VCR out of the box, getting ready to hook it up to her big-screen television.

I spoke to him.

He said, "*Señorita* was very angry. Very, very angry *mujer*."

At midnight, Chanté was in my bed, in the spoon position, naked and just as sweaty as I was. My fears became the passion that I loved her with, loved her strong. I kissed her on the back of her neck. The sweet and sour taste of her love was still in my mouth. Her breath held the scent of me.

I needed to slow down. With her was where I wanted to rest.

I sat up for a moment. Her hand rubbed up and down my back while I loosened the satin scarfs from around her wrists. I had tied her up, did things to her that made her crazy. Her breasts, thighs, and a few more spots were sticky because of the honey.

She purred. Kittenish eyes. Right now I'd feel guilty if I ever tasted any other tongue. Every subtle gesture from her came from the heart. The same feeling echoed from me.

She's educated. Ambitious. Gives her all. And like I said, she has life skills, so she wouldn't be a burden, financial or otherwise.

Infatuation, love, whatever I felt for Chanté Marie Ellis was rolling in so fast that stopping it would be like trying to halt a freight train. I wanted to take a scalpel and dissect my emotions, try and understand what about her made me feel this way, but there was no one thing I was drawn to. It was just the things that added up to her being her.

And that scared me.

This was one reason men saw other women. To thin out this feeling.

Spread it around and keep it impure before it fucked you up beyond recognition.

She whispered, "Thirsty, partner?"

"A little."

"I'll get you some water."

She took a couple of steps, then looked back.

I was eye-massaging her bare brown booty.

She said, "What I tell you about gawking at my ass?"

"Stop walking like that."

She drifted away with rhythm, hips stirring the air and enticing every creature in a five-mile radius, laughing, left me squirming. That nighttime persona she had was large and in charge. It left me feeling aggressive and hungry. Empowered.

But I wanted more than sex.

Even with the good feelings I had, what saddened me were the words that Brittany had left behind. What she really thought of me. That's what hit home.

I lost my virginity at fifteen and hadn't looked back since. Men aren't supposed to look back. That's what my daddy had told me. Find 'em. Forget 'em. For a moment I closed my eyes and I was back in a high school locker room, listening to the stories of weekend unfaithfulness, tales that rang with such tremendous clarity that they were as tangible as this morning's *Daily Bulletin*. Mexicans. Brothers. Asians. White boys. Everybody had a tale to tell. Lockers slamming. The smell of sweat. Musk. I heard shoes screeching, all of our voices echoing in locker rooms. Being men. Sharing stories about how we found 'em. How we'd fooled 'em. How we'd fucked 'em. How we'd already forgot 'em. High-fiving as we passed on tricks of the trade.

That was years ago. I've been with so many women that I'm not sure I know how to be by myself. Some days I've felt like I was the Man of Tomorrow. Right now I felt like less than a man.

*"You say that now, but with tomorrow you'll get restless."*

Brittany might be right. She might know me better than I know myself. I've met a lot of beautiful and intelligent sisters who pushed my buttons, if only for a while.

Chanté ran her tongue slowly over her lips, gazed at me with eyes that were dark and smoldering. We stared at each other admiringly, gave each other roughish and predatory smiles, kisses on top of kisses.

One day Chanté might be in that line of sisters who used to be a special part of my life and wasn't anymore. But not today.

# 26 Chanté

Stephan's phone rang and scared me awake. It was dark.

When he took his arm from around me, I woke up, but kept my eyes shut, pretended I was knocked out.

Stephan cleared his throat, answered, "Morning."

Yep. I imagined the way he rubbed his eyes, the slow way he moved was what he had done whenever I had called and woke him.

He talked on the down low, so I had to strain to hear. Left me wondering if he'd take me for granted and be rude enough to engage in intimate conversation with me coochie-naked in his bed.

Stephan whispered, "Nothing."

Anger made me stir. *Nothing.* That single word sounded like the answer to the question "What are you doing?" That quick I'd been reduced to one word. *Nothing.*

I made a bogus waking-up noise before I eased to my elbows. No attitude. Well, no 'tude that I was going to let show. The fat lady was singing, so that meant it was time for me to get dressed and go. I knew this situation was my choice, and I'd said I could handle it, but I felt foolish.

I threw the comforter back and began to rise to my feet.

Stephan turned and smiled at me. "Hey, cutie."

I let my voice be heard. "Don't even go there. You're not supposed to see me looking like this."

My eyes felt swollen. Breath was kicking like Bruce Lee. Hair was flat on one side. I bet I looked like a booger in search of a nose.

He reached out to me, ran his fingers through my wild hair.

"Cold?" He asked me that without covering the receiver.

I lied when I nodded. I didn't whisper. "A little. The temperature dropped big-time."

He pointed to the wall. "Turn the ceiling fan off."

"I'm cool."

Stephan went back to the phone, sounded frustrated. "Did you call Darnell? Dawn told you to go to hell? Shit, man. All right. Brookhurst and Broadway. Past Lincoln. Third light pole. Damn."

I whispered, "Everything okay?"

Stephan put the phone to his chest. "I have to make a run."

"This time of night?"

"I won't be long. You can go back to sleep."

This scenario brought back unpleasant memories of Thaiheed doing a hit-and-run, then leaving to go see Peaches.

I said, "I'll go with you. Give me something to put on."

He paused, then finally said, "Okay."

Stephan gave me some heavy green sweats that swallowed me, just like his bathrobe had done. He grabbed a pair of blue sweats and threw them over his shoulder. That confused me because he'd dressed in jeans and a white sweatshirt.

I stood with my arms folded, eyes half-opened. Underneath the sweats, parts of my body felt gooey, mucky because of the leftover honey. Stephan yawned and headed into the kitchen, took some items out of his pantry and stuffed them in a Lucky's grocery sack. When he turned around, white powder was on his hand. That made me unnerved. Bothered me enough to wake up.

"Stephan," I said, "I hope that's not some kind of drugs on your hand."

Stephan looked at his hand, told me, "Flour."

He held the bag open; I peeped inside. A sack of flour. A carton of eggs. A huge container of Crisco oil.

"Where are we going this time of the morning?"

"To make a cake."

My head lay on Stephan's shoulder. Oldies on KACE was on as he cruised. At first I held his hand and hummed, him rubbing my fingers, but I had to let it go when he shifted gears. Before he made it to the on-ramp to the 57 freeway, I had given in to my heavy eyelids and was snoozing, slobbering, wondering who in the hell this Stephan Mitchell was. And why I was drawn to him.

I woke up when Stephan exited the freeway. That was when his weight shifted and my head slid off his shoulder.

I wiped my mouth and stretched, tried to figure out where the hell he'd taken me. I asked, "Where are we?"

"Anaheim."

"By Disneyland?"

"Other side of town. Off the 91 freeway."

"Oh," I said. A street sign said we were on Brookhurst. I asked, "Where're we going?"

"Few blocks down to Broadway. Across Lincoln Boulevard."

It was warm and stuffy. I let my window down a bit. The clock on the dash said that it was 3:25. Stephan cruised in the right lane as traffic whizzed by in the other two.

We passed by hundreds of single-level family homes, then blocks of businesses, everything from Chinese fast food to Blockbuster Video, then came up on Lincoln Boulevard. A bowling alley was on the corner. A bowling alley that had a hundred-foot-tall blue fluoresent bowling pin anchored high out front, spinning like a ballerina and brightening the desert night.

Stephan slowed down in front of the gigantic apartment complex that was next to the bowling alley.

Stephan counted to himself, "One, two, three."

"What are you doing?"

"Counting light poles."

"Why?"

"Just following directions."

Stephan made a slow U-turn and stopped across the street right in front of a row of waist-high evergreen bushes that separated the sidewalk from a few houses. Just as Stephan put his car in neutral, a huge man in a black trench coat and jean shorts stomped around the corner toward us. God, this felt like the middle of a drug deal. The strange man dipped his hand under his jacket, peeped down into our car. His face was close enough for me to see he had a swollen eye; blood ran from his head and down over his nose. I yelped. He glowered at Stephan, did the same at me, grimaced left and right, furrowed his brows, then marched away.

I damn near shouted, "You see his face?"

"I saw it. That wound was fresh. He needs stitches."

"He's getting ready to jack us."

He said, "You're trembling."

"You're shaking too. You're scared and that's scaring me."

"Kiss me."

"What?"

Before I could ask another question, he pulled me close and stuck his tongue in my mouth. My stomach muscles tightened, and I clung to him like a wild creature. When we finished, the man in the trench coat had crossed the street and was peeping in bushes. He stopped moving right underneath the fluoresent bowling pin that was twirling high in the air. Homeboy stood still long enough to fire up a cigarette. Then he started kicking the bushes down that way. Searching and kicking, over and over.

Stephan rubbed my leg with his sweaty palm. His hand was trembling. A couple of seconds later the white wrought-iron gate opened when a car headed into the complex; the moment the gate was wide enough to squeeze through, a raving Hispanic-looking lady ran out of the complex and dashed toward the bowling alley.

I stared at her, asked Stephan, "Is that Jennifer Lopez?"

"Looks like her, but I doubt it."

"How would you know?"

"Lopez has a better ass. A tight fly-girl booty that's out of sight."

"You're sickening."

"You asked, I told you."

The light brown woman dashed up to the bloody-faced guy in the trench coat, and they started arguing very loud in Spanish. He staggered and titter-tottered like a night of alcohol had the best of him. The short lady wore a dark housecoat, no shoes, and kept her distance from him, especially after he swung at her.

I said, "Damn. Some domestic crap is going down."

The Hispanic man screamed some vulgar names at her. Then she dropped her head and raced back into the complex. People were hanging over their balconies, traffic on Brookhurst was slowing down—everybody in Mickey Mouse land was watching the whole scene.

"Stephan, this isn't a drug deal?"

"No. Stop asking me that."

"Why can't they meet you in a house or an apartment instead of on a dark street at three-forty in the morning?"

The guy in the trench coat flipped his cigarette out into the street and peacocked back into the complex. He disappeared.

Something hit my window and scared the shit out of me. I grabbed Stephan's arm and screamed, "Ahhhhhhhhh!"

Stephan jumped, then took a breath. "Open the door."

"Start the car and go!"

"Open the door."

"What?"

*"Quick, open the door."*

The moment I did, the bushes rustled with life. Like something out of a horror movie, a shadow rose up out of the dirt and bushes and dashed toward the car. Before I could get a grip on the handle and close the door again, the menacing silhouette squeezed its way into the backseat. I jerked around and saw a dark and sweaty man in his BVDs holding something that looked like a gun.

I jumped out and ran so fast I left my scream behind.

My arms were pumping, breasts bouncing, and I ran as hard as I could.

*"Chanté!"*

I caught my breath, slowed down just enough to look back and see if Stephan was catching up, but he had got out on his side and was motioning for me to come back.

He yelled, "Chanté, it's cool."

I hurried back, reluctantly crawled back inside.

The damn near naked guy in the back was breathing hard and struggling to put on the clothes Stephan had left on the backseat. He'd brought in the smell of terror and alcohol. His face let me know that he was twice as scared as I was.

My voice cracked, "Who in the hell is that?"

"Chanté," Stephan said, "you remember Jake?"

His friend panted, said, "This ain't the time for no damn intro-fucking-ductions. Get me the fuck out of here. Wait, drive around the block. They ain't getting away with this shit."

I grimaced at the terrified man's sweaty face, at his thin goatee, then saw Jake's pinkie ring, and my memory clicked. I frowned. "Aw, yeah. I remember you from the club. I danced with you. You had on the Kente suit. You asked me for my number. You asked my best friend Karen for her number. And then you tried to get my other friend Tammy's number too."

The man in the trench coat staggered back out onto the street.

Jake ducked and knotted up. "Shit. That motherfucker crazy!"

As the man turned around, his trench coat flew open. A gun was tucked in his belt.

"Excuse me." Jake's voice trembled. "If you don't mind, my life is on the line, a'right!"

Stephan pulled away from the curb, slow and easy.

He asked his funky friend, "What the hell was that about?"

Jake sat up and started rambling. "Man, I met this Mexican babe—"

Stephan quizzed, "That's who you were with last night?"

"Yeah. Last night I hooked up with her at a birthday party. She was coming on strong and we were damn near getting busy in the bathroom, but people kept knocking on the door. We had a few drinks, asked me if I wanted to go for a ride, so I left my car at the hotel and she drove me back over here to her place. We had just finished knockin' boots and dozed off when I felt somebody grabbing and shaking my goddamn feet. At first I thought it was her trying to wake me up.

"Man, I looked down and this big nasty-looking motherfucker was in the dark at the foot of the bed. Damn near shitted on myself. I hoped it was her brother or cousin or something, right, because she's Mexican, he's yakking in Spanish, they could've been related, right?

"Man, she woke up, saw him, she screamed, and her eyes damn near bugged out of her head. Then they started going off on each other in Spanish, and I politely interrupted and asked who the hell he was, she says, 'Me loco husband,' like he was in the wrong for coming home. I said, 'When you get married!' 'Cause she was single when she was up in the party, right? I said, 'You brought me up in your house and you a married woman?' I mean, I said it real loud so he could hear and know that I didn't have the 4-1-1, right? Right. Letting him know she played us . . ."

I was shaking my head.

Jake wiped his face and kept on rambling. "I tried to tell him what was up. I did sign language and pointed at her, but either he didn't understand or he didn't give a shit."

I mumbled, "This is a damn shame."

Jake kept on talking. "Then that idiot was screaming and pointing at me, had his fat finger all up in my face, so I knocked his hand down, and he ran into the closet, said a lot of stuff in Spanish I didn't know, but I definitely understood the word *nigga*, 'cause that word's international. So I jumped out of the bed and grabbed my drawers, tried to find my pants, but he Rambo'd out of the closet, stumbling and struggling to load the nine, right? He was so drunk, he was putting the clip in upside down, right?

"I didn't know who he was getting ready to cap, and I wasn't about to wait for a interpreter, 'cause by then his woman was hysterical and bouncing around. She ran over and started trying to wrestle the gun away from him, and when he turned his back, I cold-cocked him with a lamp. Then the bitch flipped the script, started cussing me out, and tried to jump on me. She was mad 'cause I hit him. I shoved her to the side, and I had to fumble around in the dark, 'cause when I broke that lamp, the lights went out. I managed to grab my c-phone and my wallet before he got up, but everything else is still in there."

After we circled a few minutes, Jake directed Stephan to the parking lot that was in front of the tennis courts and had him stop.

Jake asked Stephan, "This the bag?"

"Yeah."

Jake grabbed the grocery sack and jumped out. He raced into the underground part of the parking lot, ran real low like he was a soldier in a war movie.

I asked, "What in the hell is he doing now? He's running like he's trying to save Private Ryan."

"Making a cake." Stephan frowned. "Making a stupid cake."

My eyes widened. That fool had lost his mind. Jake was vicious, slamming all the eggs into a green Jaguar. He splattered eggs into the paint, used the sack to spread the gunk around, then opened the jug of Crisco and poured it all over the car.

I gasped. "Men do shit like that?"

Stephan replied, "In college he caught this girl he was seeing mess-ing around. He used acid on the guy's car."

"Damn. Like in *Fatal Attraction*?"

Stephan nodded. "Broke all his windows out."

"Damn. You do shit like that?"

Stephan shook his head.

This was pathetic. My hands were over my mouth, all the time I shook my head. Jake dashed back to Stephan's car.

Jake shouted, "Bitch'll trip tomorrow."

Stephan sped away, sighed. "That was jacked up, Jake."

Jake snapped, "Damn. I left my keys in my pants."

Stephan shook his head. "I know you don't think I'm driving an hour to L.A. this time of morning, then drive another hour all the way back down to Orange County."

Jake was slapping himself in the forehead, smacking himself silly. "I'll crash at your crib and regroup. Get my head straight. You can take me by Charlotte's and get my extra set in the morning, then you can take me to my ride."

Stephan shook his head. "Chanté's staying over."

"What that mean?"

"That means Chanté is staying over."

The way Stephan said that made me feel good. Important.

Jake paused, wiped the dampness from his forehead, and made a pissed-off noise that was aimed at me.

Again Stephan asked, "So, what you gonna do?"

"Hold on." Jake yanked out the antenna on his cellular phone and jabbed in a number. His tone changed; he began sweet-talking somebody, asking if she was asleep, said he was still kicking it with Stephan, too bad she had to work and he missed her being with him all day, that he had lost his car keys in the club, he thought some Mexicans stole them off his table and Stephan was going to drop him off, then he hung up.

Jake said, "Drop me off at my fiancée's house."

"Fiancée?" I repeated. "This is messed up."

"Chanté," Stephan said, probably to slow me down.

"I'm learning, boy, am I learning. Men are easily lured away," I chastised. "And, Stephan, don't you say a damn thing because you're a coconspirator."

"Shut your mouth," Jake spat out. "Nobody was talking to you."

"Don't get stupid with me," I snapped, then turned around. "I'll make Stephan go back and drop your foul mouth off right in front of that psycho Richard Ramirez."

I let my window all the way down. Cold air rushed in.

"Chanté," Stephan said softly and took my hand.

I moved away from him. "Get your hand off me."

Jake snarled, "Stephan, don't let her punk you. If a woman punked me like that in *my* car, she'd be walking."

I frowned at Jake. "If you were so bad, partner, you wouldn't have been butt naked in the bushes. So who's the punk?"

That shut him up.

"You should've left his butt in the bushes," I huffed. "He ain't got a damn thing to say as long as I'm in this car."

Jake rustled around and groaned, *"No, no, no."*

Stephan slowed down. "What's wrong?"

"This ain't my wallet. This ain't my goddamn wallet."

Stephan's face froze with concern. "What?"

"I grabbed the wrong wallet. This is that Mexican's wallet."

I shook my head and laughed quietly. "You left your keys *and* your wallet. Well, good for you, funky man with the foul mouth."

Stephan asked, "How much money was in your wallet?"

It sounded like Jake fell back into his seat. "I ain't worried about the money. Now that fool has my address."

I mumbled, "That's what your black ass gets."

Stephan squeezed my hand, ran his hot fingers over my cool and sweaty palm. I knew that was his polite way of telling me to leave it alone. His touch subdued me. Five minutes later, I was in a safe place, relaxed with my head on his shoulder.

Then I was asleep.

I'm not sure if their words were creeping into my dreams, or if I was imagining things, but I thought I heard somebody whispering about nightmares that had a bunch of furious rugrats chasing somebody all round in a hospital and trying to shove a vacuum cleaner up his butt.

I jerked awake when Stephan ran over a speed bump at the entrance of his complex. We were back on Town and Country Road. 4:20 A.M. I stretched and glanced in the backseat. No Jake. Damn. I didn't know when we had stopped.

After I mustered the energy to get out, Stephan bent over and let me hop on him piggy-back style. My arms went around his neck, and he held my legs and carried me the way my daddy used to. Only this was different. I liked the way my legs molded around Stephan's back. He felt so strong. So much like a man.

But that rendezvous we'd just gone on had left him smelling like a dog. They run in packs.

When we were at the bottom of the stairs, I asked, "Can you carry me all the way up or you want me to get down?"

"I'll carry you."

"I'm not too heavy?"

"Not at all."

"Good answer." I held on tighter. "Don't drop me."

He said, "I found out something about you."

"What?"

"You get grumpy as hell when you're sleepy."

"Like you don't."

Rebecca's door made an abbreviated creak, then opened all the way. Juan backed out of the darkness inside her condo. Rebecca was all over Juan, kissing and groping him like you wouldn't believe. Juan had on the same clothes he was wearing when I saw him earlier. Only now that plaid shirt was wrinkled. Rebecca peeped out and saw us. Homegirl pulled her housecoat tight—part of her gigantic boobs were showing big-time. She gasped and shoved Juan outside. She closed her door.

Juan stared down at us, a nervous grin on his face, his shoes in his hand, shifting from bare foot to bare foot.

"Oooo-weee," I snickered in Stephan's ear. "Looks like she got more than her VCR hooked up."

Stephan waited for Juan to come down so there would be enough room for us to walk up. With each step Juan grinned a little more and gave away his secret. As Stephan piggy-backed me up the stairs, I whispered, "Rebecca'll have a better 'tude tomorrow."

"I hope that makes two of you."

I tightened my legs around him and bit at his ear.

Once inside I crawled into bed. Started kissing on Stephan Mitchell. He helped me pull my clothes off, but before Stephan could strip to his skin, I was sound asleep.

Then his phone rang again.

# 27 Stephan

It wasn't over. Not yet.

Charlotte had kicked Jake out of her house. He was sitting on the front steps, slouching, barefoot, rubbing his fist into the side of his leg while he stared off into the golden skies brought on by the impending sunrise. Watching yesterday turn into a day of repentance. He turned in my direction when I cruised down Garden Court toward Charlotte's driveway.

This was one of those neighborhoods with strict community planning. You paid all that money and you couldn't paint your house the color you wanted, just what they allowed. And the choices were between beige and beige. So, with very slight variations, every house was a clone of the one next to it.

Dawn's truck was parked across the street. If she was awake and on this side of town before the sun met the sky, something was definitely wrong.

I didn't want to get out of my car.

When I'd dropped him off earlier, the yellow porch light had been on, as well as a couple of the inside lights. Charlotte had been up and waiting. I hadn't wanted to wake up Chanté, so Jake kept his lips tight and slid out on my side. I was back on Chino Hills Parkway speeding home before he made it to the front porch.

My stomach was in knots, insides bubbling like they were coated with acid. I parked behind Charlotte's Saturn. I killed my engine and called Jake's name. Jake stood up.

Before he could take a step, the locks on the wrought-iron front door clicked open and Charlotte came out with a serious stride. Her five-foot-five frame rushed across the morning-dewed grass. She was dressed in house shoes and pink sweats with a green sorority insignia on the front.

"Hello, Stephan," Charlotte said, her face strict.

I stepped out of my car and replied, "Morning."

"Sorry that I had to disturb you at the crack of dawn."

"No problem." I exaggerated a yawn, and let my nervous eyes go to my buddy. "Jake, ready to go get your car?"

She cut me off, stepped up to my face in a determined way. "What club did you and Jake go to last night?"

I went blank. Her sharp words caught me off guard. I'd never seen her incensed.

In the same adamant tone she added, "Tell the truth. I've feasted on enough falsehoods to last a lifetime. It would hurt me so much if you stood out here and lied to me, Stephan."

I blinked twice because I couldn't remember if we'd discussed a club, so I backed off a foot or two.

Jake hurried over. "Charlotte, I already told you what—"

"I thought you said if I didn't believe you, to just ask Stephan." Charlotte turned back to me. "Stephan?"

My expression told Jake that I didn't appreciate him yanking me out at this time of the morning, for the second time, to cover his back when I didn't know what the hell was up.

Charlotte looked at me for an answer.

My mouth opened, but not a word could be found.

Jake jumped in, "I told you we were in Newport."

She glared at her fiancé and shook her head. Her eyes broadcast a level of knowing. Charlotte took my hand and led me past Jake toward the house. That was her divide-and-conquer move, I suppose.

"Charlotte . . ." Jake's voice was crammed with desperation.

I should've worn my boots 'cause it was getting deep. It was a good thing I didn't drag Chanté out here for this.

"Excuse us for a couple of minutes." Charlotte said that to Jake, then motioned for me to follow. "I need to have a word with you, Stephan."

"Wait, hold on, now." Jake tried to slow her stroll.

"Please refrain from touching me, Jake."

He backed away. "This ain't that serious, a'right?"

"Jake," Charlotte said, "we'll be back in a minute. At least Stephan will. Feel free to leave or make yourself comfortable on the porch until he comes to get you. Do not disturb my neighbors, or I will have you removed."

"Removed?"

"Did I stutter?"

Charlotte gently closed the wrought-iron outer door, then double-locked the wooden front door. She locked me in with the aroma of coffee and confections. Women were walking around. I heard them moving. Heard them chattering in low, hostile tones. Buzzing like bees and ready to sting.

A voice called out, "Charlotte?"

"Yeah, Dawn. Stephan is with me."

Dawn walked into the room from the kitchen, dressed in jeans, a yellow and red scarf around her head. Valerie, Charlotte's next-door neighbor, came into the room. So did Valerie's dark-skinned sister. They stormed across the floor like a SWAT team. All quieted down when they laid their eyes on me. None of the women had on makeup; all of them, except Valerie, looked like they'd been dragged out of bed.

I was scared. I was on a simple recon mission. I didn't come prepared for battle. My mouth dried up.

Charlotte spoke to them. "Let me have a few moments with Stephan. Valerie, you go ahead and get your morning run in."

Her support group gave her hugs. They went out the front door and ignored Jake in unison.

"Coffee?" Charlotte asked me. She walked past, motioning for me to follow her into the kitchen.

"Yeah."

She put a fresh box of miniature powdered doughnuts on the table. I ate one, hoping she wouldn't expect me to talk with my mouth full. Two cups of coffee were on the table. The red and white cup had Jake's name engraved in the side. It rested next to his cellular phone.

Her engagement ring rested next to her cup.

I couldn't help staring at the ring.

Charlotte moved both cups, rinsed her cup out before she dropped the red and white one into the trash.

She said, "You know, Jake is going to be in serious trouble for what he did to that man. And for what he did to that car. Did he think he could get away with something like that?"

I didn't say anything. I felt like a second-grader who was sitting in the principal's office.

Charlotte shook her head. "I wouldn't be surprised if he lost his job behind this. I pray that you didn't have any part of that. The ripples of this will reach far and wide."

A tall stack of unlabeled audio cassette tapes were on my side of the table, next to a cassette player and some other hardware, so I pushed them away to make room for whatever.

"Cream and sugar?" she asked.

"Sure."

Then she was so quiet. I didn't know what was worse, somebody who got mad and flew off the handle like Toyomi, or someone like Charlotte who kept all of her inner voices to herself.

She sent out a shallow smile and put her hand on top of mine and patted it a few times.

Charlotte said, "Jake left his billfold and his clothes at that married woman's house. Her husband called here and asked if I knew him. He couldn't read English, but he could read the phone numbers. He described Jake. Told me what happened. About Jake and his wife. Told me that Jake violated his wife, then attacked him. He thought I was Jake's wife."

I didn't say anything.

She added, "For a while I thought I was going to be."

Unfortunately, Charlotte spoke fluent Spanish.

She maintained her hurtful smile and held my hand. She came across as more tired than hurt.

"Before Jake called and lied, Dawn had already called here and told me he was up to something. He was stranded in Orange County somewhere at a friend's house. She wanted to know why his friend couldn't take him home, or why he couldn't just spend the night or wait until a decent hour to call her house. She hung up on him and called me."

I nodded and listened. That was all I could do.

"After that, I was up walking the floor and worried, peeping out the window every other minute, waiting for him to call me to pick him up from wherever."

She paused.

I waited.

Charlotte said, "Jake walked in half-dressed, barefoot, stress sweating, and smelling like some other woman's vagina."

All I could do was lend an active ear.

"You know," she went on, "the real reason Jake asked me to marry him was because I found out about him and Pamela. You know that, don't you?"

I didn't know that. My eyes told her that.

"I've seen her. I drove out to Venice, went to Ralph's grocery store, watched her, and stood in her line. Stared dead in her face. She knew who I was."

I wanted to feign ignorance, but her narrowed eyes weakened me. The words slipped from my mouth: "How do you know?"

Her eyes darkened.

"She knew who I was. She looked right here"— Charlotte used two fingers, motioned at her own eyes— "and she smiled."

Silence. The absence of sound frosted the room.

"He cares about you." I knew my words were contrived, but I guess true homies always try to stick up for each other. At least this way I could walk out and tell him I tried.

She lost her smile. "I care about me more than he ever will."

"He's sorry."

"He's sorry he got caught."

"C'mon, you know he loves you, Charlotte."

She ran her hands over her hair. "If this is his idea of love and caring, it's time for him to start hating me and go away."

I couldn't give up. "You want to try to work it out?"

"You're joking, right? Don't insult me in my own home."

"I want you to think about it, that's all."

She pointed at the engagement ring. "I've thought about it for a long time."

I massaged my neck, hard. No hope lived in this room.

She said, "You want to know why I stuck it out this long?"

"Why?"

"Like a fool, I thought he would change. I thought the power of the right kind of love would make him change. But that was *worldly* thinking. Spiritual changes have to come from within." Charlotte slid the stack of tapes over to me. "Take these."

"What are these?"

"I put a recorder on my line."

"A recorder?"

"I tapped my own phone."

My breath caught in my throat.

She nodded. "Bought it at Radio Shack. Over the counter. Thirty dollars. Best investment I ever made."

She held her eyes on me, gauged my reaction.

My raised eyebrows, the way my jaw had dropped, told her I was surprised. "That's why your phone line was clicking."

Her eyes looked weary, but her lips curved up at the ends. Underneath her innocent eyes was a canny woman. Educated, underestimated, and as shrewd as the 'raptors in *Jurassic Park*.

I asked, "All of these tapes, you recorded all of these?"

Charlotte rat-tat-tapped her short nails on her cup. "I turned it on when he came over. Clever, huh?"

I sipped my coffee, tasted nothing but treachery.

"I know it was wrong, invading his privacy, but since I wasn't getting any straight answers for his unaccounted-for hours, I did what I had to do to find out what I needed to know. Listen and you'll see what I did was justified. Wrong, but justified."

She handed me the tapes, the engagement ring, a sack of clothes, but kept the cellular phone.

"You know what hurts the most, Stephan? I compromised myself. I went against everything I believed in and compromised myself. That's what I'll have to pay for."

I felt her heart aching, and I looked up at her. Then my eyes drifted away, and my head became too heavy to keep up.

"One more thing, Stephan."

"Yeah."

"Those dreams he has, he knows what they're all about. He's been cursed with the nightmares of the damned."

My brows knitted as I echoed, "Cursed?"

"The being chased by evil spirits. The dead coming out of the ground in droves, the familiar faces that won't stop hounding him, making him toss and turn all night. *He knows.* Some of them look like his parents, that means they look like *him. He knows.*"

The cold-blooded way she said *he knows* chilled me.

Charlotte led the way and clicked her front door open. I went out first. Jake blinked out of his stupor, launched to his feet and looked to me. I didn't return the eye contact. The clothes in my hand told him there was nothing I could do for him. He looked past me at Charlotte. His face was pleading like a criminal begging the parole board for clemency. So much remorse.

Jake's voice was humble. "I love you, Charlotte."

She snorted disgustedly. "It's over."

She was angry but still not cruel. Never cruel.

Jake was damn near on his knees. Tears popped up in his red-rimmed eyes, his face contorting. "I need you. No other woman on this planet, in this universe, means a damn thing to me. I love you more than anything. We can get married right now. We can pack up and go to Vegas, or make plans to get married in Cancun, get married at sunrise on Maui, anything you want, just say it."

The world paused.

"If you felt that way in the beginning," Charlotte said, and without a drop of harshness or bitterness in her voice, "we wouldn't be standing where we are now. Take care of yourself."

Jake begged a little more.

Charlotte's face changed to something gruesome. "Why would you want to be with a bad-performing, nonfulfilling woman?"

Confusion flooded Jake's watery eyes.

Charlotte calmed herself, said, "Play the tapes."

I got in my car. Jake eventually followed.

I maneuvered the surface streets, then drove south on the 71. All the way I fought the heaviness in my sleep-deprived body and headed into the new sun to shuttle Jake to pick up his car.

For a moment I wondered what was up with Darnell.

I asked Jake what he thought about that.

His words rode on a wave of anger. "Tammy. He's been tipping out to see Tammy."

"Tammy who?"

"That bitch you was with tonight, her friend Tammy."

"Her name is Chanté," I snapped in irritation. "Chill with that *bitch* crap, all right?"

"Nigga," he wheezed like air was fleeing his lungs, "what's your problem?"

"Just because your program was one-hundred-percent jacked up last night, and you got *me* smack dab in the middle of this bullshit, don't mean that you have to blame every-damn-body."

I was pissed, tired, sleep deprived, constipated. I'd left a woman in my bed and come out to be faced with this crap. All of this told me that I should value Chanté a lot more. It's not every day a man meets a strong, beautiful woman. That's as rare as a million-dollar bill.

I said, "Charlotte said you know what the dreams are. She said something about your being cursed with the nightmares of the damned. Some spooky crap like that."

All of a sudden he leaned forward and let out a hard breath, panted like a dog on a hot summer day. Vulgarities poured from his mouth.

I ignored his temper tantrum and thought about Darnell. Tipping out to see Tammy. Dawn was a good woman. Another strong sister who had life skills.

The world was coming apart at the seams.

Maybe not the world. Just our world.

Jake stopped cursing out the universe and put in one of the tapes. That stole my attention away from every other thought.

Shocking.

First Jake's voice came out of nowhere.

Then Darnell's voice came out of nowhere.

Uncut words that made me swerve a time or two. Jake jerked around like a man in an electric chair. His voice was low. "What the— I don't believe she did this."

The tapes were crisp and clear, loaded with conversations of Jake and woman after woman. Explicit phone-sex conversations with Pamela. Mocking, laughing, and making plans with other babes while he was at Charlotte's house. Women accepted his invitations to come by the fire station, to his condo for dinner. One call was to my number, and when he got my answering machine, he pretended he was having a conversation with me, then used me as an alibi to get away. It recorded when he called home and checked his messages, picked up the phone numbers they left behind on the trails of their sweet voices of surrender.

"*I got me some of that, and she rolled over and went to sleep. She's getting better, but still, a bad-performing and a non-fulfilling woman drives a man to stray. . . . If I hadn't stayed at Shelly's so long, I would've went to see Pamela. She does some booty-licking shit that drives a nigga crazy.*"

I nearly rear-ended the car in front of me. I shouted, "Damn."

"*I'm going to hook up with Pamela. Now, she always answers the door in satin and silk, runs a brotha's bath water, rubs him down, ain't got no hang-ups, tries to turn a brotha out every time she sees him. I try to do some real shit with Charlotte, and she gets all tense.*"

"*Work with Charlotte.*" That was Darnell's voice. "*Buy some kama sutra books, check out some erotic movies and watch 'em together. Maybe try some nude yoga, give each other oil massages.*"

"*Man, Charlotte is almost thirty years old. What am I going to look like trying to teach her what she should already know?*"

That was just the tip of the iceberg.

Jake wilted in his seat, grabbed at his goatee, tugged like he was trying to yank out one hair at a time.

# 28 Darnell

Dawn came into the house, making all kinds of noise, talking to herself. I was on the service porch, taking a load of white clothes out of the washing machine and putting them in the dryer.

I asked, "What happened?"

Dawn stopped in the doorway and stared me down. "Did you know about the other women Jake was seeing?"

Her cross-examining tone made me feel like I was on the witness stand. "What do you mean, other women?"

She told me what had happened in Chino. Repeated what Charlotte had recorded on tape. At the end she shook her head. "I'm just going through what every woman goes through when her friend goes through something like this."

I supplied the mental state: "Doubt."

"Yeah, doubt."

I said, "Our marriage must be on shaky ground if some outside party can inject doubt."

I didn't know if I was talking to her or talking to myself about the way I'd been feeling since I met Tammy.

Then I confessed, "Well, I've been having doubts too."

She hesitated before she spoke. "What about?"

I said, "Us."

She looked jarred. "Okay . . ."

"Something's changed."

She thought this over a moment, then responded. "True."

"There's a lot of stress under this roof. Stress that we're not coping with very well."

She said, "Nobody asked you to sleep in the other bedroom."

"You called me a rapist."

"Those were your words, Darnell. I was asking for tenderness. I attempted to communicate my unhappiness with you about that incident, and you turned it around."

"Do you enjoy making love to me?"

"Yes. For the most part, yes, I do."

"For the most part? What does that mean?"

"Well," she shifted, chuckled a little bit, "sweetheart, you've put on a little weight."

"So, I turn you off."

"There you go doing it again. That's not what I was saying."

This time I paused. "Do we still value each other?"

She spoke in a mechanical way: "I love you, Darnell."

"Maybe you love me the way you want to love me, not the way I want to be loved."

"How do you want to be loved?"

"Unconditionally."

She made a face that was supposed to slow me down.

I kept rolling. "But that wasn't the question."

"If you have something to say, then say it." She was getting defensive. "I've been up half the night dealing with idiocy—"

"Nobody asked you to run out when she called over here."

"—and I'm tired. And I didn't do anything for her that you wouldn't've broke your neck to do for Jake. Damn. Look at the time. I've been up all damn night."

I said, "Don't walk away."

"I have an open house, so I'll have to be up all damn day. I need to sleep a few minutes."

"I'm trying to make a point here."

"Then make your point and stop beating around the bush."

I paused. "Why so hostile?"

"What's your point?"

I said, "We used to laugh together."

"That's it? That's your point?"

"Most of the time it feels like we're jockeying for control."

"You're the one trying to control our destiny."

"See, that's what I mean. Whenever I try to talk to you about what's going on inside me, a lot of resentment sprouts up between us. It's like this wedge that's shoving us in two different directions."

"Sweetheart," she folded her arms, rigidified her tone, "my only *resentment* is that I thought that somewhere down the road, after you finished law school, that we would be striving for us to grow and eventually go into some sort of business together. What you're doing, this hobby, that fantasy that's taking up *my* quality time, wasn't the plan. I don't want to be an old-ass woman having my first baby. Or no babies. I don't have time to see you start over. If you start over, that means I'm starting over, and dammit, I'm through starting over. Hell, I paid my be-patient-while-I-get-my-career-together dues while you were in law school. Feels like my whole life has been on hold for you."

"I worked and paid my way through law school."

"And that nonstop studying and working made you an absentee husband. For the last two or three years I've wanted to spend more time together and strengthen this marriage, but you always have something else to do. And when you should have free time, it seems like you *create* something to do."

"Why do you get hostile whenever I try to talk to you about what's going on between us?"

She walked away from me and my concerns. That made me doubt her commitment to a lifelong marriage. I felt our vows cracking under pressure.

I went into the office, pulled out some paperwork on a child-custody case I was working on the side.

I heard Dawn on the phone talking to Charlotte. She was on the cordless and passed by the office twice, consoling and complaining, no doubt trying to see what I was doing. That went on for a few minutes. She hung up. Her footsteps made a slow stride back toward the part of the house I was in.

Dawn appeared in the door. "Sweetheart, I'm just tired. And this thing that Charlotte went through, well, I found it traumatizing. I kept looking at Jake, realizing how trifling he really is, and wondering about you. Right before my eyes I saw their relationship shatter, I saw how devastated Charlotte was, how she had to fight to maintain her dignity in front of us, and I became afraid. Afraid of that happening to me. To us. All you're hearing me broadcast is my fear. The deception she had to put out to keep from being deceived was a bit much for me."

I turned away from my PC, faced her. "I understand."

"You know what that fool had the nerve to say to me when I walked outside? This was when Charlotte was talking to Stephan. On the way out I told Jake to get a clue, that it was over. Tried to bring some reality to the front lines. Know what that smug bastard said? 'It ain't over until I say it's over.' "

"Wow."

Dawn paused, leaned against the doorjamb. "Am I losing you?"

I matched her pause. "Resentment makes anything possible."

She left the room, but came back a few minutes later.

Dawn said, "Why don't you come lie down with me?"

I watched her, tried to read her new mood.

Her voice was tender, bending like a willow in the wind. "I think we're both stressed. Maybe we can *unstress* each other. Maybe what we need from each other is beyond words."

I shook my head.

"Darnell . . ."

"I can't touch you right now."

She said, "Please? Let's make this right."

"You don't like the way I make love to you, I'm fat, so what's the point? You want to put a Band-Aid on something that needs stitches."

"You'll make up any excuse to get back to that book."

"I'm not working on my *hobby*. This is legal work."

The ringing of the phone interrupted us.

Dawn said, "Put that work aside for a while. I'm feeling insecure right now."

"Why?"

"Because." Her voice dropped. "I think you know why."

"What happened between Charlotte and Jake is between Charlotte and Jake. Don't bring that into this house."

Dawn's mother's voice came through the answering machine in the bedroom.

My wife said, "Darnell."

"Yeah?"

"Who is Tammy?"

My insides jumped; my eyes went to her.

She said, "Before you say anything, a friend of ours told me she saw you all the way out at Venice Beach eating lunch with her. Her name is Tammy, right? She's an actress, true?"

The answering machine clicked off. The voice of Dawn's mother faded.

"She's a friend," I answered.

"Why don't I know this friend, and why didn't you inform me of this lunch date?"

"The same reason you never inform me when you're working late. Same reason you didn't inform me the day you took off work to go to the valley."

"That's different."

"Of course it is."

She wanted to know, "How long have you known her?"

"Not long. She's a writer."

"I know. A few days ago I saw papers, some sort of book on your desk that had her name on it."

"What were you doing on my desk?"

"Now who's defensive?" She sighed. "This is scary."

"What's scary?"

"How your body language changed when I mentioned her name."

I sighed too. "She understands what I'm doing."

"Understands you?"

"Yep."

A lot of nothingness came into the room, hovered over my heated words like an unseen vulture over our dying relationship.

Dawn said, barely above a whisper, "That hurts."

The stillness was interrupted when the phone rang twice, then stopped before the machine picked up.

The emptiness lingered, the kind of nothingness that made my gut echo like an empty barrel when a rock was tossed inside.

Dawn said, "These are the arms that held you when you thought you weren't going to pass the bar. These are the knees that I fell on in church and prayed and cried for you when you thought all of that was too much. And now you tell me you won't make love to me because some other *bitch* understands you better than I do?"

"I never said that. Now you're putting words in my mouth."

Stares of pain held us in a vise grip. Walls were closing in.

Dawn spoke up. "When you wake up in the morning, and the morning after that with nobody beside you, remember who was your rock, who helped you get to this point." Dawn's lip was trembling. "Sweetheart," she said, "you don't have time for me, but you can drive across the state to meet with some strange woman."

"It was business."

"How would I know?"

"Don't make something out of nothing."

She fumed, "I find out that you're having a secret rendezvous, and I'm making something out of nothing?"

"It wasn't a secret rendezvous."

"Then, when can I meet your new friend?"

No reply, just a lot of shifting.

Abruptly Dawn asked, "Are you sleeping with anybody else?"

I cleared my throat. "No."

So much paranoia was in her words. "Since we been married?"

"No. Since I put that ring on your finger, no."

"Would you tell me?"

"Would you want to know?"

Her tears weren't falling because she had too much pride.

"So tell me, my husband, do we still value each other?" With a sigh of discontent she turned, left my space.

A minute or so later I heard her pick up the phone, listened to the echo of digital beeps when she dialed. Then she was marching from room to room, pacing and complaining to her mother. I made out the words when she mentioned my name in an angered way, venting out the last few minutes of our personal conversation, sharing our personal business.

She sounded so pained.

So weakened by love.

My heart reminded me how much I loved my wife.

Loved her and loathed her in the same breath.

Loathed because even with her in the same house I was feeling lonely. I understood what was swirling inside me. Dawn was so wonderful in certain ways, but she owned a side I couldn't fulfill. With her I don't feel like I'll ever be able to be my whole self. Six years of compromising, of living in reservation and expectation, felt like a lead weight on my heart.

I stood, opened the closet door, and appraised myself in the full-length mirror on the back of the door.

Pushed my love handles. Felt the softness. Touched my belly. Missed the hardness it used to possess. My six-pack had turned into a forty-ounce, pretty much. Law school, more time studying than working out, and Dawn's fried chicken had done that.

My wife told me that she didn't desire me like she used to.

She knew about Tammy.

I closed my eyes, let my mind take me back to the night I'd been at the Atomic Café, facing Tammy, both of us tongue-stirring the gentle breeze.

One moment paranoia had me shaking.

The next moment I didn't care.

# 29  Chanté

*Beep—Chanté. Stephan. I tried to get back before you left. Mmm, let's see. I want to see you. Soon. Real soon. Real, real soon. Today if possible. Did I say this was Stephan?*

That message made me feel sweet sixteen. I was on my bed, wearing Stephan's jean shirt over my Levi's and white T-shirt.

Tammy lingered in the doorway, smiling and eavesdropping. I'd played his message on the speaker phone, so she heard every sweet word.

"What?" I said.

"You're glowing like a firefly."

I laughed and touched my face.

I'd told Tammy about my sexcapades with Stephan. It was so good that I couldn't keep it to myself. Over two bottles of Snapple, I had blushed and jabbered the two hours I was filling out her delinquent tax papers, gave her the nitty-gritty details from my last sundown to sunup.

Tammy gave a devilish grin. "He have a buck-fifty wee-wee?"

We laughed.

Karen wasn't here yet, but I heard her voice inside my head. *Shit, my sister, sometimes I wonder how many dicks have been inside you.* I shrugged away my discomfort.

Tammy asked, "How much do I owe you for hooking up my taxes?"

"You know I don't charge you and Karen."

"Chanté, you are a blessing. I bow at your feet, oh ye queen of itemized deductions. The slayer of a Caucasoid uncle named Sam. Oh, mighty Chanté, conqueror of the 1040."

"Make sure you pay me what you owe me when you get paid."

My other messages were from jerks.

I dialed Stephan's number, got his answering machine, left a sweet message and told him that we were going to Shelly's. As I hung up, a tremble came over me in waves. A fear that made my silver bracelets rattle. I liked him too much. Had done too much. I knew better, but I'd done it anyway. I wasn't in any condition to even think about being with somebody. Not on the level that I was thinking about. I'm a wounded bird.

Tammy yelled, "Oh, ye queen Chanté. Karen of Riverside just pulled into the kingdom of Allegro from Diamond Bar Boulevard."

"About time."

Tammy had wandered into the front room, but rushed back in and stuck her head in the door. "One more thing. It's *very* important."

"Okay."

"It's my birthday. Don't start nothing with Karen. If she says something to piss you off, let it go. For me. Okay?"

I felt bad that she felt she had to say that, but I held on to my smile and said a cheery "Okay."

Her tone was soft, serious. "I love both of you, but when you fight, it forces me to choose sides, even when I don't want to."

Before she left the doorway, I called out, "Tammy?"

"Yeah."

I tried to make her understand what I thought she already understood. "Just because two people argue don't mean they don't love each other."

She smiled. "I know."

\*   \*   \*

We were at my dining room table. The lights were off and twenty-eight candles brightened up a lemon cake. Glasses of Muscat Canelli were under our noses. Karen and I had slapped on dark shades, were rocking side to side and wailing out a seriously off-key, hand-clapping, foot-stomping version of Stevie Wonder's *Happy Birthday to Ya* song.

The birthday girl beamed. "Help me blow out some of these candles. If I was any older, the sprinklers would come on and drown all of us."

We blew and we blew. And we cracked up. Especially because the more we blew, the more the candles lit up.

Tammy cackled, "Trick candles!"

We were having so much fun, hugging and being the best of friends while Tammy opened her presents. The silver necklace and matching bracelet that Karen had bought her were the bomb. Tammy put on the silk blouse that I'd given her and modeled it all.

Tammy was so teary-eyed and sentimental. "You know what's a shame? That people you aren't kin to take care of you and love you better than your family ever will."

All of us were blowing snot bubbles after she said that.

Karen slid a bag toward Tammy, one toward me, and said, "I bought you another present, Tammy. I bought you a gift too, Chanté."

Silver jewelry. And not to mention that Karen had on a new brown skirt and beige rayon blouse. She'd outdone me in the present department. I wanted to ask her where all of this spare money was coming from, but I remembered what Tammy said to me about not starting anything. Instead I slapped on a gracious smile and said, "For me?"

She smiled. "For all of us. I bought me one too."

Tammy had suspicious, questioning eyes over her grin.

Karen had also bought us T-shirts. The front of it said:

*SINGLE BLACK FEMALE: attractive, gifted and independent, seeking a mature, honest, supportive, God-fearing, financially stable, physically and mentally fit black man*

The backside read:

*. . . if you are a non-supportive, no-good, lying, jealous, nagging, broke, unemployed, uneducated, jive, two-timing two-minute brother, PLEASE DON'T CALL*

We laughed and high-fived and read that message to each other like it was a scripture from our hearts.

Tammy said, "I want y'all to throw up a prayer for me."

Karen leaned toward her. "Everything all right?"

"I auditioned for a commercial. Mickey Dee's. A national."

I beamed. "How'd it go?"

Tammy smiled from ear to ear. "Very, very well."

I remembered the message I was supposed to give Tammy. "The band at Shelly's wanted to get in contact with you. Sounds like some work. A road gig."

Tammy said, "You're lying."

Karen didn't say anything.

I asked Karen, "Weren't you at Shelly's that Friday night?"

She flat-out said, "No."

"Pee Wee said he bought you a drink. It was when they had sarong night."

"Oh. Yeah. I went by there, but I didn't see you guys, so I only stayed but a hot minute. It's not like I hung out."

Tammy asked her, "Who'd you go with?"

"Nobody."

I asked, "You see me?"

"Nope. Walked in, walked right back out." She sipped her Muscat Canelli. "Who did you go up there with, Chanté?"

I paused, saw Tammy's tense expression, then confessed, "Stephan Mitchell sorta asked me out."

Karen laughed. "So much for you hooking him up with me, huh?"

"Karen, I'm sorry. It wasn't planned. Well, he called, it sorta just—"

"Chanté, it's *okay*. I'm happy for you."

Karen leaned over and hugged me. Her warmth was so nice.

Tammy interrupted, "Since we're talking about us and men, and we're always open and honest, I need to talk to y'all. I'm in conflict, so I need somebody to talk some sense into me."

We waited for Tammy to say what she had to say.

Tammy tunneled her fingers through her hair, over and over, sighed, "I've slipped, tripped, and fallen in love."

Karen perked up. "With Bobby?"

"Nope. Somebody else. And it's different."

Karen said, "How is it different?"

Tammy thought a second before she answered, "What I feel for Bobby is like getting pricked by a doctor's needle, like when you get a tetanus shot. The other man is more intense, like getting an arm cut off with a rusty ax."

Karen cringed. "Damn. That's intense."

I said softly, "It's wretched."

Tammy was troubled. "Feels like I finally met my soul mate."

"So what's the problem?" I wanted to know.

She held up her black T-shirt, showed us the backside, then said, "They should've added *married* to this list."

I was speechless. Karen was too.

Gently I asked, "Do we know him?"

Tammy nodded.

Karen asked, "What does he do?"

"He's an aspiring writer."

I echoed, "Aspiring? Oh, Lord."

Karen frowned. "He's broke *and* married?"

Tammy said defensively, "He's not published yet, but I know he will be. He's passionate, sensitive. I've never met a man so mature. He thinks I'm fantastic."

Karen groaned. "Who is this pronoun called *he*? And please tell me you haven't had sex with him."

Tammy said, "We haven't kissed. Just talked."

My arched eyebrows met in the middle of my forehead. "How can you fall in love with somebody you ain't slept with?"

Karen quipped, "Don't be shallow, Chanté."

I matched her sarcasm: "Don't be unreal, Karen."

That was where our rapid-paced conversation went, surged onward to the topic of falling in love with a man that you hadn't seen butt naked yet. We were all talking, voices overlapping, cutting each other off.

Tammy said, "I'm with Chanté on this one. First you get your freak on, and if the man can work it, then you try and see what kind of a relationship you can make out of what's left."

Me and Tammy high-fived.

Karen waved us down, said, "But the problem with that way of life is when a sista finally gives in—"

"*Gives in?*" I frowned and shook my head. "Why does it have to be *giving in?*"

Tammy backed me up. "That sounds like we're victims."

Karen waved, talked louder. "Let me finish. When a woman succumbs to the dick and gets her freak on—"

I wailed out my protest, "*Succumbs.* That's even worse."

"*Chanté!*" Karen said, then pushed me. "That's when a sista's just starting the relationship. After sex, men are done. Mission accomplished, they move on. Like locusts."

I raised my voice in offense. "Chill with that locust mess. My coochie ain't no crop."

Tammy threw in, "Yeah, but you sho' be rotating it."

Karen and Tammy gave each other finger snaps.

I flipped both of them off and said, "Shut up."

Karen waved me away. "But that's besides the point. Tammy, who is this invisible man?"

Tammy hesitated. "I shouldn't've brought this up. Let's just skip it." She chuckled. "I don't want to be the one to mess up my own birthday celebration."

We tried to pry the info out of Tammy, but that was all she would say. We backed off. After all, it was her birthday.

Our laughter went on and on, until I turned to Karen. "Well, don't tell me you're sneaking behind my back and seeing somebody too?"

Karen's eyes bucked at my out-of-nowhere question. Then she shook her head, made her Shirley Temple curls sway, and let out a stream of contrived laughs. "My coochie is a vegetarian, and no meat will get between these lips."

I winked at her. "Nobody but Victor."

She winked. "Nobody but Victor."

# 30 Stephan

The first two weeks of May had been nice, nothing but sunshine, but I should've checked my Farmers Almanac because during the third week, without warning, El Niño paid Southern Cali another visit. The temperature dropped twenty degrees as rain came down and the non-drivers clogged freeways. Mud slides. It had been that way Sunday through Wednesday. Each day rain fell and the winds blew hard enough to break leaves off a few palms. Thursday morning the sun was still MIA, but the drizzle had gone away.

I had just walked Chanté down to visitors parking. She threw her jacket, umbrella, and soft leather attaché case in the backseat, then grabbed a handful of my butt. I did the same.

"What's wrong?" I asked her.

"Nothing." She wiped a piece of lint off my chin.

"You seem a little distant."

I helped Chanté adjust her lime skirt, made sure the zipper lined up in the back, checked to see if her white blouse with the big buttons was tucked in and wasn't bunched up in the rear.

Juan came out of Rebecca's apartment, barefoot in jeans and a

T-shirt. Rebecca followed him. She had on a long skirt, slippers, and a soccer sweatshirt with Spanish writing. That was the soccer shirt that Juan had worn up to her house last night.

Rebecca saw us and waved. "Don't y'all look nice."

Juan yelled my name, then came over. He asked me to help him move some of his furniture and a few boxes to a storage facility a few miles over on Fairplex, near the fairgrounds.

I said, "You're not moving out, are you?"

"No. I am moving in with Rebecca."

I grinned. "A lateral move."

"No, an upward move."

We laughed. Juan slapped my back in fun.

"*Si,*" he smiled. "We can save money. I will rent my condo."

Chanté had gone silent. Juan and I looked at her. Her eyes were disturbed, but her lips suddenly curved up into a smile. She said a weak "Congratulations."

Juan left, went back to Rebecca.

Watching them, Chanté said, "That's sweet. They're gonna work on that relationship." I didn't say a word. She whispered, "They really have something."

Her radio was on KJLH. Cliff and Janine were playing "Making Love in the Rain." Chanté sang a few bars, had that seductive, tight-eyed look. Then all of that sensuality went away, became unreadable.

Her voice lost its softness, became deep: "Stephan?"

"What?"

"Maybe we should talk."

"What do you mean?"

"I mean, I've been staying over here every night."

She'd gotten in her car, so I kneeled so we could be eye to eye. "Chanté, you make it sound like you've been kicking it over here for months."

"I haven't been home in three days."

I asked, "So what are you saying?"

"I'm saying, well, I'm an obsessive compulsive."

"So, you're trying to tell me that you're crazy?"

She laughed. "Okay, maybe obsessive compulsive is the wrong way of putting it."

"I hope so. That's what Robin Givens said Mike Tyson was."

"That was manic depressive, silly."

I said, "Sounds just as scary."

"I'm intense." She chilled with the smile and turned on the serious voice. "I'm the type of person that if I have one cookie, I have to eat the whole box."

"And I'm the cookie."

"I've had the cookie. Now I'm starting to want the box."

I swallowed. Felt pressure on my temples. She reached and held my hand. Her hands had turned as dank as the morning air.

She confessed, "I've already had a rough time at this shit."

"You saying that you're falling in love?"

"I don't do *love* anymore. No more fairy tales."

"Then what do you have to look forward to?"

"Sanity. Love ain't nothing but a .38 aimed at a sista's temple."

She ran her hand over my face, touched my lips. Her every movement contradicted her words.

Chanté said, "I don't want a boyfriend. I don't want you to think that you have to be my boyfriend."

She curled her bottom lip in, bit it with her top and smudged her berry-colored lipstick, ran her hand over her wild and wavy hair, then smoothed the lines out of her forehead.

I asked, "You're seeing somebody?"

She looked offended. "I really like you. I like what you do when you do the do. I like what you do when you're not doing the do."

"If you didn't like the way I do the do?"

"I'd school you, work with you on doing the do, turn you out, have you wanting me so bad you'd wash my car in a hurricane."

"And if you didn't like me, but the sex was good?"

"I'd freak you once," she said with a joking smile, "maybe twice just so it wouldn't be a one-night stand, then bounce you like a basketball."

"So, this is all about spanking that booty, then?"

"Shut up." She playfully hit me. "The emotional relationship is what makes the sex good. I hope you can see beyond that. We don't always have to go there. I love being with you and doing nothing, because that's the way I am. But I loved it just as much when we didn't go all the way, like when we sat around day before yesterday, watched cable, and read steamy parts of Darnell's novel to each other."

Silence.

She left it at that. She kissed my forehead, said, "Don't be a Big Foot."

"What does that mean?"

"Don't disappear."

With a smooth smile I said, "You want me to not disappear, but you don't want a boyfriend?"

"Stephan Mitchell, I don't know what I want." She chuckled, ran her fingers over her bushy mane again. "I wish I could just go on like this, be with you just for the pleasure of experiencing pleasure, but eventually the strings will start to show up."

Her voice had caring, positive emotion. The way she talked and smiled made me want to run and snatch her oh, so sweet ass up and take her away. Her heart was in her voice, in her eyes.

Maybe it was just my imagination brought on by infatuation.

I licked my lips. "Are you seeing other people?"

"It's kind of late to be asking that, ain't it, partner?"

"Are you?"

Her response was quick: "Would it matter?"

I patted her leg and sighed.

"Stephan, relax, I'm not trying to be your girlfriend."

"You threw that wall up real quick."

She admitted, "The real problem, outside of what's in me, is that night we went to rescue your foul-mouthed, funky friend."

"What does that have to do with me?"

"Those who associate, assimilate."

"Meaning?"

"Dogs run in packs."

I paused and thought of my argument. "In other words, since you and your girls run in a pack, that means you, Karen, and Tammy are exactly the same."

She turned her windshield wipers on. The first swipe raked dirt and a few fallen leaves from her window.

Chanté frowned. "I shouldn't't've brought this up."

I replied coolly, "You said what was on your mind."

Her stiff tongue made her jaw protrude.

"Stephan?"

"I'm listening."

"Let's back off. Maybe we shouldn't talk for a few days."

I clucked my tongue, said, "If that's what you want."

"It's starting to rain again. A bad sign. I'd better make it over Kellogg Hill before traffic gets too bad."

She closed her door, cranked her car up.

I held onto my bland face and headed toward my Mustang. I knew what that was all about. Women talked about men being flaky, but they were just as bad. Just as ready to fuck us and forget us.

Samantha called me right before lunchtime. I was in the clean room with about twenty people from the Air Force, working with metrology, running diagnostics on a device that measured inertia on flight hardware.

I found some space on an extension and tried to find out what was up.

She wanted to know why I hadn't called her in eons.

I said, "I called."

"Guess my answering machine took every message but yours."

"A brother answered your phone in the middle of the night."

She didn't say anything.

I said, "You hear me?"

"What's with the 'tude, sweetheart? You're not going to get stupid, are you? You don't even call me on a regular basis."

"You know my schedule's tight."

"It wasn't so tight when we first started going out."

"I call."

"Not like you used to. But you brothers are always like that with us in the beginning. All nice and considerate. Right?"

I stayed on point. "Who answered your phone?"

"My cousin's husband. I told you my cousin Gretchen and her husband were coming down for a few days."

"I don't remember."

"I gave them the bedroom. The phone was in there. It rang, they answered it. Anything else?"

We talked a few moments. Then she got to the bottom line.

"I miss you. Come see me."

"Not in the rain."

"What if I made it worth the drive?"

Another outside line lit up and buzzed. A technician answered, put the caller on standby, then motioned at me. I put Samantha's promises on hold.

But the next voice chilled my blood.

Stiff and cold, she said, "Hello, Stephan."

I gritted my teeth. "Hey."

"This is Toyomi."

"I know. What do you want?"

"I want what belongs to me."

"Toyomi, I'm not down for no bull."

"Don't make me drive down to your job and act a fool."

I said, "You wouldn't be acting."

"Bastard."

The phone line Samantha was on stopped blinking.

"Toyomi, stop calling me, stop calling my job. Stop calling my parents' house. Just stop calling and go away."

"Fuck you."

"Been there done that."

"You know I'll fuck you up, don't you? What I did to you when you came out here wasn't nothing compared to what—"

I hung up on her.

# 31 Darnell

Tammy adjusted her peach satin robe and said, "Dag. What did you do, Darnell, swing rope to rope or hitchhike on a 747?"

"Took Highland, waved my Uzi, threw up a gang sign, yelled 'Westside,' and people moved out of my way."

She laughed and her breasts bounced.

I laughed too. It was right before noon. She'd called me at my job this morning, told me that she had some news to share with me. Without a second thought I took off from work and drove through the flooded streets and freeways toward Hollywood.

I asked, "Did I get here too quick?"

"You got here a lot sooner than I expected. I just stepped out of the shower. This place is atrocious. I was at rehearsal half the night and didn't have time to clean up."

I closed her front door behind me. Stepped from the mists of North Hollywood into a rectangular room with off-white walls, plenty of furniture, lots of pictures. African sculptures here and there. A kitchen table draped in bright yellow. Dramatic but not overbearing. Lots of candles. The incense aroma in the air was circulated by a slow-moving ceiling fan.

She asked, "You have a hard time finding Chandler Boulevard?"

"Directions were good. All I had to do was follow your fragrance to the peaceful-colored two-story stucco building right next to North Hollywood High."

"You look good. I love men in wet suits."

We hugged. Caressed a little longer than was necessary.

I said, "Your music is jamming. CD or radio?"

"CD. Sista named Smooth. Hip-hop soul on the true R&B tip."

Her damp hair was wavy, smelled like strawberries. Her robe, short and clinging. A million fantasies raced through my mind.

I asked her, "So, what did you have to tell me?"

"Be patient. I'll tell you while we share our writing."

"Good news or bad news?"

"Depends. Could be neither, could be both."

"You're a tease."

She winked. "When I need to be. A woman's prerogative."

I smiled. She pressed her lips against mine. A stage kiss.

"Get comfy," she said with a hungry sigh as she eased away from me. "I'll be back in a sec."

"Where are you going?"

"I'm a mess." She pouted. "Hair's wet. Oh, I've let you see me without my face on. Plus I don't even have drawers on yet."

That last sentence startled me, aroused me.

She adjusted her gown to show less of her breasts, but most of her legs showed at the split, and her nipples stood high and mighty underneath her robe. Awake and staring. I watched her thickness sway across her gray carpet, a barefoot stroll that had a rhythmic flow, eyed her as she kept her flirty eyes on me.

She grinned, eased her tongue out, stirred the air.

I did the same.

She asked, "You feel me?"

"I feel you. See you. Taste you. Smell you."

"Me too. And I hear your thoughts, Darnell."

"Read my mind to me."

She leaned against the doorjamb and baptized me with a smile. "In some strange way, I want to be completely yours too. Can't get you off my mind, no matter what. I was so nervous waiting for you. Scared of what might happen when you got here. That's why I'm not ready. I bathed longer than I usually do, couldn't figure out what to do with my hair. Felt fat. Looked in the mirror and hated my thighs."

"You're fine. I'm the one who should be running to find a tofu sandwich."

As her subtle smile disappeared into the bedroom, her voice flowed from her den of sin. "Make yourself at home. Juice in the fridge. My new headshots are on the table. Tell me what you think."

She eased the bedroom door up, but I didn't hear it click.

I'd expected to see a shrine of Nina Simone photos, but there was only one photo of Nina, a framed picture that shared a wall with Dorothy Dandridge and Sarah Vaughan. In the picture Nina was young, dark-skinned, hair in a bob.

I put my attaché case down on her kitchen table. Behind a vase of fresh-cut flowers were a stack of black-and-white headshots. A flyer for the play *Who Will Be There for Us* was on the table, next to six tickets, all stamped with the word COMP. I stared out the window at the rain that was leaving lake-sized puddles in the tennis and basketball courts at North Hollywood High. Then I moved her *Dramalogue* and *JAZZIZ* magazines to the side.

Smooth's music grooved me while I twiddled my thumbs.

Pictures of jazz greats Charlie Parker, Ella Fitzgerald, Louis Armstrong, Billie Holiday, Astrud Gilberto, and Antonio Carlos Jobim were on another wall. Movies from Spike Lee to Hitchcock. CDs from BeBe Winans to Missy Elliott to Bonnie Raitt.

What I was looking for, I didn't see. No family pictures.

Photographs of her, Chanté, and Karen, smiling and hugging, were in one of the cubbyholes on her entertainment center.

A sweet smell came in and pulled my attention toward the bedroom. Tammy must have been putting on perfume, dabbing drops on her pulse points, between her thighs, the same woman thing that Dawn did every morning.

Anything that happened today, I wondered if I could leave it between me and God. Or if I would break down and throw myself at the feet of my wife-for-life.

I called out, "Where's the bathroom?"

"This way. To the left."

Tammy's bedroom door wasn't closed, open wide enough for me to see her on her four-post bed, on top of her green and gold comforter, wearing jeans, still barefoot. Her hair pinned up in a French roll. Sitting still. Wearing no bra. Breasts not hidden. Dark nipples on cream-colored flesh. An awesome contrast. I stared. She wore red lipstick, eyes on me, her mouth open wide enough for me to see the pink of her tongue.

Fresh-cut flowers were on her pearl-colored dresser.

I pushed her door part of the way open.

She didn't jump, or reach for something to cover herself.

Tammy swallowed, licked her lips before she asked, "How was work today?"

My eyes stayed on hers, my mouth so watery I thought I was about to drown in my own saliva. "I'm working on a settlement offer to Circus Circus. They shipped ammunition, another hidden shipment of explosives that they neglected to tell FedEx about."

"Seems like everybody has to hide something."

I nodded. "Last week I sent a notice out for one hundred thousand. They offered twenty thousand."

"Big difference in what you want and what they want to give you." Her hands touched her breasts, squeezed them, then she let them go. She said, "Sometimes you have to take what you can get."

"There's always a middle ground."

"Not always."

"I'm going to reject it and send a letter out for fifty thousand. I want thirty-five, but that's how you play the game."

Her eyes were soft, so agreeable.

She spoke airily. "Yes. That is how you play the game. When you can't get what you want, maybe not as much as you want, I guess you drop your standards and accept a lower offer."

With care, I replied, "Just because you accepted a different offer, that doesn't mean you've lowered your standards."

Tammy patted the bed next to her. That was where I sat.

She loosened my tie, slowly, like she wanted to make sure what she was doing was okay by me. She unbuttoned my shirt. Folded both, lay them to the side, then pulled my T-shirt off.

For a moment I was topless, uncomfortable. Body conscious and uneasy with my physical faults. Until she touched me softly, told me she appreciated what she saw. Even with the flaws, her eyes spoke of desire that went way beyond the physical.

Then we lay back and I held her. The only sounds were the Smooth CD playing an up-tempo tune. Which was good. The sound of that rain and the dark skies had already created a dangerous mood. Anything slow, anything too sensual would have added to the temperament in the air and made this moment explosive.

I had been feeling really unloved. And somebody had come along and made that feeling go away. I didn't want to leave this moment. I was feeling as though I'd never be desirable again.

Consequences. Everything has a consequence.

I kissed Tammy. Soft tongues and heavy breathing. I held her breasts to my chest and savored her softness. That single kiss seemed to last for the better part of an hour.

She moaned, "Darnell, baby, your kisses are like lilac wine."

"So are yours."

I stopped swimming upstream against my emotions.

My hand drifted down, tried to find her zipper.

Her fingers caught mine, gently stopped my journey.

She whispered, "Darnell."

"Yeah."

She groaned. "I'm on my period."

We laughed.

Within two hours the rain stopped. The sky was still gray. We were fully dressed, had finished critiquing each other's work. Tammy had put on a white button-down blouse, lacy black bra.

For a while we had lounged across her bed, engaged in verbal intercourse about the art of writing, discussed character motivation. Talked about our ambitions.

Now we were at her table eating a chopped fruit salad topped with raspberry sauce. It tasted like cuisine for the gods.

I covered my mouth to keep from spitting out my food, laughed with Tammy, and said, "The band wants you to go to Perris with them? That's no big deal. That's on the other side of Mo Val."

She sipped guava juice. "Not *Perris*, California. *Paris*."

"France?"

"*Oui, oui monsieur.* That is where *Paris* is located."

I was impressed. "Your French accent was great."

"They're going to Europe. All expenses paid. The two Nina Simone songs I did blew them away."

I smiled, then felt an immediate emptiness when she added that she'd be gone for a month. Thirty days without water was forever. Already I felt the drought coming on.

I asked, "You tell your family?"

"Oh, please. Outside of my mother, those fools wouldn't care one way or another. If I danced naked on top of the Eiffel Tower, they wouldn't telegram me to get my yellow ass down."

I cleared a lump from my throat, tried not to make my words sound too heavy when I said, chuckling, "Are you coming back?"

"Would you miss me if I didn't?"

My answer was a vulnerable smile. But that numbness was still growing in the pit of my stomach. "What about Chanté and Karen? You tell them?"

"Not yet. And no, in case you're wondering, I didn't tell Bobby. Actually, I might not tell him at all."

"How's he treating you?"

"Well, the relationship has definitely reached a plateau. It's kinda like working out. You reach a level, get comfortable, then you either have to work out harder, or get a new program."

That reminded me of the Peter Principle. The rule that said every man eventually rises to his own level of incompetence. I wondered if the same applied to relationships. To marriages.

"Nope, he don't know." Her voice softened. "You're the first to hear it from my lips. I wanted to tell you first."

I reached across the table and took her hand. Her red fingernails matched her lipstick and the paint on her toes.

"What about the play?"

"I'll do a few performances. Then an understudy will be glad to kick my butt out on Santa Monica Boulevard at curtain call. She'll be happy as hell. It's Hollywood. The show goes on."

"So you're going to go with the band."

"Only a fool would turn down a free trip to Paris."

She took a few bites of her salad; I did the same.

She swallowed, washed her food down with her juice, then asked me, "You think I shouldn't go?"

"Only a fool would expect you not to go."

We held hands a little longer. Our palms were sweaty.

A thousand years of wanting were in her voice when she asked, "Will you be able to come to opening night?"

I remembered the date on her flier. I said, "Your play opens mid-week."

"On a Wednesday night. I'd love to see your face in the place."

"I saw the date." It hurt to do, but I shook my head, released truthful words that were hard to say. "Dawn has already made plans. We're going to dinner and a movie."

"That's your first time saying her name."

Cars passed by under her window, tires squelching on the wet pavement. Another skidded out on Chandler. Somebody who wouldn't let their dreams be deferred by a day of rain was at the high school shooting hoops.

Tammy asked, "Can you come by Shelly's tomorrow night?"

"I'll try."

"Even if you can only come for a quick minute, hang out in the back and at least wave at me. I'm working on a different Nina Simone song. My wink'll mean it's dedicated to us."

Her words gave me a blissful feeling. "What song?"

"It's in French, *Ne Me Quitte Pas,* and I'm really scared to sing it in front of a crowd of black people."

"Why?"

"They might not appreciate it."

"Don't underestimate our people. Half of them hadn't heard of Nina Simone, myself included. You've opened a lot of us up to a whole new world. New music. A new way of thinking."

She smiled. "Be there for me, if you can."

"I'll try."

We held hands a little tighter. Talked awhile. I must've drifted, or maybe a look was on my face, or something in my eyes.

She said, "Penny for your thoughts."

I put what we had on the line, stayed honest, and took the chance of offending her. "Do you ever dream about your child?"

"All the time. Think about it every day. When I see a baby that's close to my complexion, I look and wonder if it's mine."

*It.* Not him or her. *It.* She really didn't know, hadn't seen her own child. Would never see that child. That made me sad. Made my problems insignificant.

Tammy closed her eyes and hummed a melody that could soothe

the world. One that could rock a baby to sleep. I closed my eyes, tried to latch on and travel to that same peaceful place.

She trembled a little. "I want to experience you before I go. Some of that love I see when you look at me, I want to take some of that kindness across the Atlantic with me."

My voice was of surrender. "I want to experience you too."

Tammy asked, "Will we make love before I go to France?"

I nodded, a simple and silent yes.

"Penny for thoughts," I said, smiling. "Nickel for a kiss?"

Tammy smiled. "Only if you gimme a dollar's worth."

# 32   Stephan

Around midnight my doorbell sang. Keys were jingling.

Rapid, angry knocks. At first I hurried toward the door; then I recoiled in horror, was almost overwhelmed by the fear that Toyomi had shown up to create *Fatal Attraction II*.

Whoever it was had put their finger up to the peephole so I couldn't see much more than a fingerprint.

I asked, "Who is it?"

No answer. Whoever it was tapped on the door, but didn't move their finger from the peephole. I stepped to the side. I'd seen movies where people put a gun up to the peephole and blew out a fool's brains. I wasn't about to go out like that.

With a rougher, no-nonsense tone I asked, "Who is it?"

"Opportunity."

I put the chain on and cracked my front door.

Chanté.

I took the chain off, opened the door just wide enough so she could see me standing in my plaid boxers. As she stood under the yellow light, the night behind her was a deep blue shadow being punctuated with the sounds of freeway traffic. The rain had stopped, but the streets were still wet. I could smell the wet earth and damp pine trees in the cool, humid air.

Her hair was wild as the wind that was scattering debris across the complex. Intelligent eyes as tender as a willow in a gale. Brown skin under a tan trench coat that was buttoned up to her slender neck.

Eloquent, odd, unique, beautiful, and unforgettable. A smart woman with life skills. She was all those things. Men should carve her likeness in every mountain.

But I'd never be weak enough to tell her that.

She said, "I called Karen and talked to her on lunch."

"About?"

"You."

"And?"

"I told her that I told you I didn't want a boyfriend."

"And?"

"She surprised me."

"How?"

"She said I messed up, in a major kind of way."

"Okay. So, what are you saying?"

"I'm saying that I messed up."

"And?"

"Be my boyfriend. That's if you think you can hang."

"I'll have to think about that."

"Don't think too long."

"Why?"

She eased open her trench coat, let it fall like a leaf, tossed it at my feet. With red pouty lips she whined, "I might catch cold."

I said, "You're naked."

"Negative. It's called a negligee. I'm wearing pumps."

"My eyes didn't make it down that far."

"Freshly showered Nubian skin. Just for you. If you want to be my boyfriend. I've never done this for anyone else."

"Chanté," I groaned. "Chanté Marie Ellis."

She smiled. "My butterfly is getting cold."

"Is it?"

"May I bring it inside and warm it up? If you don't want me to, I'll go back home."

"My foot's holding your coat down. So, unless you have your car keys hidden in one of your orifices, you're gonna be walking back down the hill to Diamond Bar butt naked."

I kissed Chanté. Daring. Add daring to that list of things.

She led me into my bedroom, then went over to the television.

She asked, "Where's your camcorder?"

"In the closet. How did you know I had one?"

"I didn't."

She wanted me to connect it to the television, then point it at us, use the TV as a monitor and we could watch ourselves.

Chanté took candles and matches out of her pocket.

"Karen gave me these aromatherapy candles on my last birthday. Lemon is supposed to cast off the chains of confusion and set your mind free."

"What's the other one?"

"Ylang ylang. It's supposed to let you open up to a world of possibilities and leave boundaries behind."

Chanté sat on my bed, and I adjusted the camera.

She said, "Can I tell you something, and you don't think bad of me?"

"Go ahead."

"Today," she said in a sweet, alluring tone, "I was driving to work in the rain and trying not to think about you, but I did. The rhythm of the windshield wipers moving back and forth in slow motion, well, that made me fantasize about the way you move in and out of me. I've been dreaming about having you inside me all day. I got wet thinking about being with you. I want you in me so I can squeeze you with my inner walls. I love the way you hold me tight and say *ugh* when you're coming."

Her words turned me on. I was growing.

I said, "Smile."

She did. Shifted around and smiled.

"Stephan, go ahead and put a blank tape in it."

"You sure?"

"I've never done this before. Yeah. I want to see what I look like when you do the do. Let's see how long you can hang."

"Who gets to keep the tape?"

"Nobody. After we look at it, we'll record over it."

Glowing candles, just enough light. Scent just right.

"Stephan?"

"Yeah?"

"Wrap that pickle up."

I dressed my penis in the latex tuxedo and got ready for the party. She slipped her red lace panties off and stretched naked across my white sheets.

"Stephan, can I ask you something else?"

"Go ahead."

"Does a man feel anything when a woman comes?"

I winked at her. "It's like finding another part of the pussy way in the back. A whole new room in the house."

"C'mon. Come find a new room."

"You're horny."

"Completely. I want to feel your hands under my butt. Explore me. Make it so good that tears come down my face."

My fingers walked over the silver earring in her belly. I stroked her neck. Her eyes told me that she got a rush from my touch. I slipped two fingers inside, felt what was already humid.

I said, "You're hot."

"As hot as Chicago on the Fourth of July."

She pulled me on top of her. Opened her thighs, wrapped her legs around me. Sucked my tongue while we talked. Then she took a hand and massaged my penis near her sex. Stroked it back and forth across her slit. Her lips made a wet, insatiable sound. First the humidity of her vagina drew me in; then her muscles contracted around me with the firmness of a handshake.

Chanté sucked in, let out hot breath.

Her back arched, my bed squeaked and shifted under our weight, sang when her hips rocked against mine. I lowered my mouth to her breast so I could let my tongue massage her nipple.

"*Shit*. That feels so good, Stephan."

I bit a little harder. "Does it?"

"You keep doing that, I'm going to come."

She shuddered, intense and sweet.

I turned her over and her eyes stayed on the TV screen. I made her get on her knees, watched her backside spread wide.

"All right now, Stephan, what you plan on doing back there?"

"Hold on, let me get my gerbil."

"*Your what?*"

"I was joking."

"What are you going to do to me?"

"Depends on you."

"There are certain things I want to try, but not today."

"Relax."

Her breathing changed, like she was afraid of what I might do. Her fists held the sheets like they were her only salvation.

I smelled her sex. She growled like a hungry woman.

A car bounced over the speed bumps outside my window.

I sank deep inside her. Slipped inside her secret place with the ease of a murmur. Went so deep I almost fell inside her. She hissed, then her eyes closed in pleasure.

Her eyes were back on the TV. Watching and participating.

She moaned, "Fuck me."

Then she giggled, ran her hand over her breast.

"What's funny?"

"That was so dramatic. But I've always wanted to say that."

Part of me wanted to make love to her slowly and sweetly.

The animal part of me didn't.

She growled, "Harder. Give it to me."

I did. .

She turned her head, made a guttural sound, "That . . . oh God . . . the best, mmm . . . you can, ahhhh . . . best you can do?"

I smirked. At least I tried to. Moved mercilessly.

"Ooo . . . slow down . . . baby . . . shit . . ."

She buried her face in the mattress, grunted and shrilled that she was about to come. And when I hoped that she'd had enough, she reached back, pulled me in.

I gripped her hair like it was a horse's rein, got ready to ride, turned her face up so I could see her expression on the television. I wanted to see her face; witness her vulnerability cast all over.

Her vagina radiated. My penis felt her every throb, sent her sensations through me; her mouth was open, gasping for a spoonful of air. Heat made me swell more than I could stand. I fought the feeling, teased, but everything was swimming out of focus.

It was pain. And pain was good.

The room went black, my eyes rolled inside my head.

She reached back, slapped my flesh, scratched me. I heard her vagina take on its own life, make noises, hiccup, open wider, vibrate. She put her face in a pillow, muffled her screams and grunts, then yelped for me to *come for me baby come for me.*

My toes curled, legs locked. Orgasm rippled along my skin, numbed me, made me feel like I was tumbling and spinning, weakened me to the point that I couldn't keep my balance. Chanté did a bump and grind, swerved her butt against me and rushed me into that place of peace and tranquility.

Sheets were still clasped in her hands, almost yanked off the bed, when my eyes finally rolled back to where they belong.

I floated away, drifted into a feeling I wanted to embrace as long as I could. Felt absolutely ethereal. I pushed deeper, like I was trying to get back into the womb of a woman, and she moved in invitation, maybe she was daring for me to try.

She was whimpering. Making noises like a cat. A lioness. Her body quivering, sensual eyes viewing me on the tube.

Chanté lay flat. Sweat was all up and down her spine, puddled in the curve right above her butt. I eased my dank body down on her damp and insatiable wiggles, angled her head so we could tongue each other down. Her lips trembled when mine smothered hers with hot, sloppy kisses.

I choked on our saliva, then panted, "God, that was intense."

Chanté winced, contracted her muscles around me, made sexy noises, wiggled slow and easy. "I've *never* come that hard."

"Tell me anything."

"Stop trying to get your ego stroked."

She held her groove. I tried to keep from getting soft. But my body was already starting to feel heavy.

"Stephan, I wish you could be a woman for a moment."

"What, you trying to tell me you go both ways?"

"*No.* So you could feel how good our orgasms are. It seems like a man comes in this quick spurt, *spoosh*, then you're done, but our orgasms come in waves. Beautiful waves that make me feel like I'm drowning. Mine keep coming and tingling and rousing, feels like they could go on all night."

I slipped out of her a bit, she made sure the condom was still on, then jiggled me back inside. I held her hips, pushed.

She moaned, "You ever wish you were a woman?"

I was keeping an eye on the TV, enjoying and envying the ecstasy that was gleaming in her face: "Nope."

"Boy, you said that real quick," she said, rubbing her nose, then went back to arching her back and rolling her butt. "Sometimes I wish I was a man."

"Why?"

"Men can sleep with as many women as they want and still get respect. A sister is—mmmm, I think I'm coming again—expected to hibernate until Mr. Right—mmmm, hold it right there right there, ahhhh, oh God, don't move—comes along."

"Is that what you want to do?"

"Nope." She sounded intoxicated and exhilarated. "I was just saying. Let me be quiet. I have a habit of chattering after good sex."

"You chatter during sex."

"Do I yadda yadda yadda?"

"You yadda yadda yadda all the time."

She laughed. Her muscles tightened around me when she did.

She said, "I feel like running outside and yodeling."

"Please don't." I asked, "Thirsty?"

"Yeah. I could use some water."

"Me too. Yodel your way into the kitchen and get some."

She slapped back at my arm. "Sexist."

She reached and made sure the condom was intact, eased me out of her refuge, pulled the latex off me, staggered into a wall, dropped the condom in the trash, collapsed on the carpet.

"Stephan, partner, I feel drunk as hell."

"I'm too dizzy to move."

She panted, "Is it stuffy in here?"

My heart was beating in my neck. "I'm about to suffocate."

"Open a window."

I tried to stand. It had been a helluva day, part fantasy, part atrocity, and my eyes were too tired. The last of my energy had been drained from me. I took a step, then crumbled on the carpet near her. The room smelled like musk, sweat, satisfaction, and scented candles. She wiggled my way and put her bushy head on my chest.

She rubbed her fingers across the sweat on my belly. "My hair is gonna be a mofo in the morning."

"You bring clothes?"

"Negative." She shook her head. "This was impulsive."

She was crying. Smiling and crying.

I hate it when women do that shit.

Soft tears dripped onto the hair on my chest.

"So, you going to be my boyfriend or not?"

I thought about Jake. Those dreams that were driving him crazy. I thought about Brittany's woes. How Samantha had had some other brotha answering her phone in the middle of the night. About Toyomi and her psychosis. Pops rambling about common sense, and other things.

Darnell was searching for peace, and I had peace right here in my arms. And rain, just like snow, was God's way of telling a man he needed to slow down.

I responded, "Yeah. We can give it a shot."

"Well, you don't have to sound enthusiastic about it."

I trailed my fingers over her tears, licked my fingers. Then I helped her up, and we crawled back on the bed.

She pointed at the screen. "Big brother's watching."

A red light was still winking at both of us.

Both of us waved, then let out exhausted laughs.

I leaned over and grabbed the edge of the comforter—it had fallen to the floor during our love dance—gripped the rumpled covers, and pulled them over us.

I told her, "Darnell has been seeing Tammy."

"I already figured that out."

"When?"

"The night when we read his novel. I remembered how she was all over him at Shelly's. She said she'd fallen in love with a married man. A writer. I'm no Sherlock, but I'm no nincompoop."

A beat later I said, "He went to see her today."

Her jaws tightened. I felt heat rush over her body. She swallowed. Sighed.

I answered what she was thinking, "I hope not."

Sleep eased into the room, covered us both with serenity.

# 33 Chanté

I'd had a great week with Stephan No Middle Name Mitchell. Monday evening he invited me up the hill, and he made me a seafood pasta. Linguini with smoked salmon and shrimp. The brother can cook, so that gave him some serious brownie points. He'd bought me a Tina McElroy Ansa book as a gift too. Just because. The next night he was at my place eating spaghetti. The next we were at L.A. Fitness gym playing racquetball, again being physical to the point of exhaustion. Outside the club, in the darkness, we became as devious as high schoolers. We kissed out in the parking lot, rubbed our sweaty bodies on each other for over an hour, but we didn't keep each other company that night. Which was cool, because I wanted him to want me for more than *that*, no matter how bad I wanted *that* from him. The next day we talked on the phone from work; talked for over two hours. That was so nice. When Friday rolled around, I said that I wasn't going to see him, that I was going to take some time to myself and read the book he'd given me, just because.

I had bathed, put candles all around the house at sunset, and was relaxing, lying across my goose down comforter in my birthday suit—my favorite way to be when I'm at home—reading *The Hand I Fan With*. And every time the main characters made love, I thought of Stephan. Damn words in the book were so strong my stupid nipples were erect, and it had gotten so hot in here that I had to turn the air on. The physical love they shared was so powerful. It was more than the act of penetration. The desire of wanting to give one's all was so romantic. I'd always given my all. Too much of me. The next thing I knew, I'd folded the pages, closed my eyes, whispered Stephan's name as I hoped he could feel my energy, and made love to him in my mind.

He has made me smile for days.

Everything about him was so casual, yet so intense.

I wanted him to come put this fire out, but I didn't want my flames smoldered with his passion. I had to hear his voice. He wasn't home so after I savored his outgoing message, I left a nice yadda yadda yadda message.

Then I went back to my book. To nurturing my fire.

Damn. The love I was reading about was so good, I felt like I was suffering some serious envy. I loved pleasure. I loved love, making it and being overwhelmed by the passion. Especially making it when I was deep-deep-deep in it.

But that mental pleasure was all I'd get all weekend.

This is where the shit hit the hand I'd been fanning with.

Saturday, the schizophrenic weather was overcast one moment, then had breaks of sunshine the next. I spent all morning paying my bills, doing laundry, cleaning the cobwebs from the corners of my loft, mopping, vacuuming, cleaning the stove, being more domestic than Hazel. By sundown I'd gotten my nails done, picked up my laundry, called my folks in Europe, had my nap, and was ready to get away with the girls and do some female bonding.

Big mistake. I should've kept on reading my novel. Then I would've avoided a wretched catfight. More like a real fight.

It ended up being one of the most atrocious nights in my life.

It was really stupid the way the argument started. I mean, really stupid. It happened so fast that I'm not really sure what happened. But I know why it happened. It was inevitable.

We were all at my condo getting ready to go out. My stereo was turned down low, on KACE, letting DJ Shaina Looks play some slamming oldies and get us in the mood. All of us were laughing, doing our nails, doing the girl talk thing, snacking on low-fat chips, sipping on a little wine. At first we were just going to get diva'd-up and hit Shelly's, but we decided to break the routine and do something different for a change. Tammy, Karen, and myself, well, all of us were in a hip-hop kinda mood and wanted to get out of the San Gabriel Valley and escape to some place that didn't have the same old faces, the same old music, some place where the brothers didn't recognize us before we sashayed in the room.

Tammy suggested, "The peeps from the play are hanging out at the Hollywood Athletic Club. That's on and popping."

"Let's leave early and get a bite to eat first."

I asked, "Where?"

Karen said, "Anywhere that will have a bunch of good-looking brothers. The melanin-sufficient homo sapiens out this way are tired."

I agreed. "Ain't they, though?"

Karen added, "They'd rather go watch pigs race at the county fair than do something meaningful, spiritual, and cultural."

I said, "Shark Bar always has a room filled with sharks."

We laughed and got dressed to kill. All of us wore all black. Karen had on a one-button top and long skirt, all silk, shiny, and sexy. Tammy had on dark leggings and a *bad-ass* strapless black corset that pimped out her mega-boobs. She wore a light black jacket on top of the sexy lingerie. Her hair was pulled back, and the diamonds in her ear sparkled like the sun.

I asked her, "Where did you get the new earrings?"

She smiled nervously. "Darnell gave them to me for my birthday."

Just like me, Karen *tsked* and shook her head. She looked heated, but she didn't go there. Neither did I.

Anyway, I had on dark hose and a cute-cute Ally McBeal–ish short skirt that hugged the round of my butt.

I looked in my mirror and smiled at what I saw. Loved the sweet and sensuous smell that was coming from my body. I said, "God, I wish Stephan could see me before I went out."

Tammy adjusted her boobs. "I wish Darnell could see me."

Karen said, "I wish both of you would shut up and come on."

We walked out of my crib looking like En Vogue, ready to hit the highway and have a bona fide L.A. night. An evening of hanging out with the plastic and the pretentious bottom feeders.

First we ended up on La Cienega, waiting in a line longer than the ones at Disneyland trying to get into the Shark Bar.

These three brothers in dark suits who looked about as attractive as the Pep Boys came up and tried to get their flirt on. They recognized Tammy from her commercial, but after that I guess they were trying to size us up, see what kind of demigoddesses Karen and I were.

Anyway, by the time we made it inside the maître d' told us it would take damn near half the night to get a table so we could grub on the seafood and pasta, food we could smell from outside, so we just let the men treat us to a couple of glasses of chablis, and before they could ask for our numbers, we pretended we were going to the ladies' room to powder our noses and did an exit stage right, headed to the Hollywood Athletic Club.

When we got there, Tammy hung out with her Hollywood friends, so me and Karen made the rounds, strolled by the pool tables, then flounced upstairs to the dance hall.

Ten minutes later, this bourgeois bucktooth brother from Birmingham was following us and trying his best to get his mack on. Karen started being friendly with him. He offered her a glass of wine, she accepted. I turned down the offer because I had to drive the crew back over forty miles of freeway.

This is where it got blurry.

One second he was talking to Karen; the next he was in my face, in a casual sort of way. At some point he leaned over and asked us where we went to college—which is very unusual for a Hollywood conversation—and without a second thought I told him that I graduated from Cal Poly Pomona.

He took off the jacket to his pinstripe suit and told us that he'd gone to college back at Morehouse, came out here to work on his master's at UCLA, was in radio, but after that I wasn't paying attention. If Stephan wasn't talking to me, then I wasn't listening. Besides, I was watching Tammy. Her actor friends had her shooting pool while they played drinking games. I thought we partied hard, but that was a wild bunch. She was nursing another glass of wine, looking tipsy as W. C. Fields, getting sillier by the sip.

Anyway, the brother who went to Morehouse smiled toward me and asked, "So, what's your degree in?"

"Accounting." I yawned. "I work for Moss Adams."

"What's that?"

I proudly said, "One of the largest accounting and consulting firms in the U.S. of A. I'm their double minority."

We laughed. Mine was that bogus Hollywood chortle.

After that I sort of shifted my body the way a sister does when she's taking herself out of the conversation.

He turned to Karen. "Let me guess. You're a double minority at one of the largest accounting firms in the U.S.A. too?"

"Nope. Afraid not. I'm in sales."

"Ah, marketing."

She corrected him, "No, sales."

"Oh, so you must have a B.A. or an M.B.A. from Poly?"

I said, "Karen didn't go to Poly. She's in sales."

He asked Karen, "Where did you go to college?"

She sipped her wine. Swallowed. Finally said, "Riverside."

He said, "UC at Riverside?"

Her voice changed. "No. Riverside Community College."

He echoed, "Community college?"

Karen held on to her smile and nodded.

His voice lost its enthusiasm. "Oh, so you have an A.A."

"If you must know, I don't have a degree."

Without thinking, I smiled and threw in, "And Karen's a secretary too."

Karen laughed and playfully elbowed me. "I'm an administrative assistant, not a secretary."

He perked up a bit and asked, "For what company?"

Karen looked at me, then at him, and asked, "Okay, Birmingham, why are you marching all up in my Kool-Aid?"

That pretty much sucked the wind out of his sails. Like a puppy who knew he was about to get kicked, he left.

We stayed at the bar with the shoulder-to-shoulder crowd.

I checked my watch and thought about Stephan. With him was where I'd rather be.

Karen downed a glass of wine like it was tap water before she turned and faced me. She had that look that let me know a monsoon was brewing behind her eyes. She spoke over the noise in the room. "You always have to have the spotlight, don't you?"

I blinked out of my trance. "What?"

"You heard me."

"What did I do?"

"The same thing you did the night you met Craig. The same thing you did with Stephan. The same thing you always do."

"What did I do?"

"Always coochie blocking."

"I do not coochie block."

"Why is it every time a brother starts talking to me, you ease your way into the conversation?" She shook her head and chuckled. "You just have to step in and steal my thunder every chance you get."

"What did I do?"

"First you scream that you work for Moss Adams, like somebody really gives a rat's turd. Then you had to give me a smug look and throw in 'She's a secretary' like my job ain't nothing."

"I didn't mean it like that. I was bragging on how hard you work."

"Bragging? Why did you have to say it like that?"

"What, did I lie?"

"Nobody asked you to be my damn spokesperson."

I said forget the dumb stuff, left her at the bar, and went to get my dance on. Karen got her boogie on too. I saw her throwing down the alcohol and dancing record after record.

But she wasn't the only one sipping a little too much of the brew. I'd turned my back, and by the time I found her, Tammy had sipped on one glass of wine too many and was tore up. She was in the ladies' room in a stall, tossing her cookies.

Tammy choked out, "Damn. I should've ate something first."

"You gonna be okay?"

"Hell no. I'm getting sick. Get me out of here before I embarrass myself."

So, for us, the party was over. Karen wasn't ready to go because she'd met some brother, but I told her that we needed to get Tammy out of here. That was why I ended up driving back home with Tammy hanging her head out of the window like a sick puppy.

On the way back home, of course, Karen's liquor was talking loud and clear, so we did get back into a heated discussion.

"Whew!" Tammy said, and patted her sweaty forehead. "I need some fresh air. Karen, let your window down some more."

The best I could figure, Karen was still mad because I told the brother she was a secretary, because I'd said I'd graduated from Cal Poly.

Irritated, I demanded to know, "Karen, what exactly is your job title at the DMV?"

"Administrative assistant. I'm not a damn *secretary*."

"And if you told the truth, with the nonsense work you say they give you, your job is a rung below a real secretary."

"I'm an administrative assistant."

Tammy mumbled, "What y'all yelling about?"

I said, "You make it sound like I lied to the bucktoothed brother. You didn't graduate from RCC, you dropped out—"

"I didn't drop out. I stopped going."

"Are we going to Denny's?" Tammy tried to adjust her body in the back and get comfortable. "I'm too sick to eat."

"Okay, my bad, you stopped going. Which isn't the same as dropping out. Fine. But your job isn't a degreed position."

"No, I don't have a degree, but when I feel like it, I'm going back and get my B.S. or B.A. or whatever I want to get."

I didn't believe a word. "What does your job position lead to?"

"There's nothing to get promoted to, unless I leave the DMV."

"So you have a dead-end job."

"Why are you so concerned about my damn life?"

"Oh boy," Tammy said. In the rearview I saw her patting her forehead. Then she started taking the bobby pins out of her hair. "I got a hangover and I ain't even went to sleep yet. Lawd. I know better than to drink on an empty stomach."

Miles of freeway passed in minutes.

Tammy was passing out, but me and Karen kept going at it.

I let the bad things that had been floating around in my mind run free. "Karen, I wasn't going to say anything, but the last time I was at your place, I saw a stack of bills sitting on your kitchen counter. And they were in pink envelopes, so that meant they were late. A stack of debt that looked like a leaning tower of misery."

"I pay my own bills," Karen said. She sucked in one side of her cheek, pursed her lips. "Nobody helps me."

"You buy weed before you pay your bills. Help me to understand that."

Her tongue clucked; her face stretched out at the chin.

"Karen, don't get me wrong." I was on a roll. "All of this is love and concern. I did your taxes for you the last couple of years, and to be honest, you didn't have any financial growth. Over and over I've told you that I'm just worried about your future. Where you're going to be five years from now."

That's when Karen took control of the conversation, reached back into the past, dug down into her bag of insults and started bringing up all kinds of old mess. And, of course, I had to do the same.

By the time we were zooming up the 60 and passing by the Hop and Puente Hills Mall, Karen had her finger in my face and was spewing out, "Just like when Michael fucked you over and you had to attack me to get your self-esteem back."

"This ain't about that."

"Well, I might not have a job at Moss Adams, but at least I'm not waking up in the middle of the night because somebody's *wife* and *three* kids are at my door yelling for their *daaaadeeeee*—"

I scowled. "That's over and done with, so don't go there please."

"Maybe the people at Moss Adams should teach their employees to be intelligent enough to at least see where a man lives before she bends over and drops her drawers down to her ankles. That's common sense."

With wide eyes and a fiery tongue, I echoed, "Common sense."

"If that's what you heard, then that's what I said," she said with power. "I remember all the crap you've said. *Friend*. All of your little digs. Yeah, why would Craig ask somebody like me out? I don't have a boring white-collar job or an overpriced condo or parents that have kept me so sheltered from the real world that I don't have a *clue*."

All I could say was, "Ouch."

Karen added, "When Stephan walks over you, call one of your friends who has a career to save your ass."

"What makes you think Stephan is gonna walk over anybody?"

"Because they all do."

I gripped the steering wheel. Felt my throat tighten. My eyes were hot. Tears were on the way, but I used all of my energy to make them go back. I lost that battle.

Karen continued, "And you make it easy for them, because you're so quick to get butt naked and horizontal."

"I hope you choke on Victor."

She chuckled. "Is that the best you can do?"

Tammy woke up long enough to shout out, "Damn, I'm sick!"

"Tammy, don't holler in my damn ear," I said.

I wiped my eyes with the back of my hand.

Karen didn't say anything else.

I didn't say anything. By the time I got off the freeway at Grand, my throat was so tight I could hardly breathe.

My insides felt heavy, and I knew I was two seconds from the first drop in a bucket of tears. She'd hurt me, but I felt bad for hurting her back. We'd both been stabbed with the truth.

"Karen, you know I didn't mean it like that. I'm high, and the Spumante has me yakking out of the side of my face."

Karen wiped her eyes. "Funny how alcohol makes people address what's in their hearts."

"You should know."

I rat-tat-tapped my nails on the steering wheel as I drove the last stretch to Diamond Bar Boulevard. Since I didn't have a passenger-side air bag, I wanted to ram Karen's side of the car into a light pole, make her fly out the window like a crash-test dummy, but I didn't want to hurt Tammy. Or my red car.

Tammy was knocked out, so deep in the backseat that I couldn't see her. She'd slept through most of the bickering.

It was after two in the morning when we made it back to my haven. Karen grabbed their overnight bags, and I went to help Tammy's inebriated butt.

Tammy said, "Are we at—we at, hell, where were we going?"

I told her, "We're at my house."

"Somebody help me," Tammy slurred as she stumbled out of my buggy. She leaned against the car and ran her hands across her messed-up mane. "Where we at? Denny's or Coco's?"

I told her, "Take my hand before you fall over. You gonna help me or what, Karen?"

"Let her fall and bust her head wide open," she said. "That'll stop her from drinking so much."

I said, "I hope my neighbors ain't watching."

"Who cares about all of these white people?" Karen said. " 'Cause they sure don't care about you."

Tammy took a baby step and moaned. "We there yet?"

Karen went up the few stairs, opened the door, and went inside. Left me to drag Tammy's oversized butt by myself. It wasn't easy, 'cause she wasn't cooperating too much.

I took Tammy straight to the bathroom. And I did it in the dark. Except for where the night light outside the bathroom shone, the house was pitch black. Well, some illumination stole in from the porch light, but not enough to make a difference.

Before I got to the living room, I heard these awful choking, gagging sounds. I dashed into the hallway and turned on the light so I could see.

Tammy had her face in the toilet bowl, sweating like she had the fever of death, crying, drooling, and slurring, "Lawd, I need me some

Pepto-Bismol. I promise, if you make this stop, I'll never drink again. I promise. I know I said that the last time, but I mean it this time."

Karen had stopped in the living room and stood in the darkness. I heard her voice, "Both of you bitches are pathetic."

"Who are you calling a bitch?"

"Who answered?" She'd jumped too bold for her own good. "She's chasing a married nigga, and you're ready to ho with every nigga that lays his eyes on you."

"I'm going to pretend I didn't hear that."

"Oh, you heard it. Pretend all you want, you heard it." Karen shook her head. "Look at her, acting like a lush. Everything that both of you do is so degrading to black women."

"Stop it, Karen."

"No, you need to stop it. You might have a middle-class life, but you have ghetto values."

I grabbed a towel and wiped Tammy's face. Her face had turned red in some spots, ashy in others. Her eyeliner had melted and made her look like a sick raccoon. After she had regurgitated as much as she could, I cleaned her and lay her on the bed in the guest bedroom, under the ceiling fan, and put a cold towel across her neck, a remedy my momma had shown me when I came staggering home on prom night.

I moved her hair from her eyes, said, "Let me know when the towel gets warm, okay, sweetheart?"

Tammy squinted her face and almost nodded. She mumbled, "What y'all yelling about?"

I asked, "The fan too high?"

Tammy slightly shook her head.

"Y'all stop yelling. My head can't take no noise . . ."

A trail of Tammy's sins were in my carpet, but it wasn't too bad and didn't smell. Even if it was splattered wall to wall, that would be the least of my problems. I soaped a towel and wiped over the mess. I'd get the carpet cleaner later.

I raised my eyes. Karen was standing over me. Silent. I stepped into the bathroom and closed the door.

"Chanté?" Karen called.

I didn't answer.

The doorknob turned, slow, and the door eased open.

We looked at each other through the darkness.

She spoke up. "I've answered your questions, now answer mine."

"What question?"

"How many dicks have been inside you? Or have you had more buck-fifty lovers than you can count?"

I jumped up to Karen's face.

She didn't flinch.

The heifer stuck her finger into the middle of my forehead and pushed, snapped my head back so hard I thought she'd broken my spine. I lost my footing and fell down on the bathroom floor.

Karen gritted her teeth, stood over me. "I wish you would."

"*Bitch*, get out," I said. "Get your ignorant ass out of my mother-fucking house."

"Ignorant?"

"Your no-ambition ass."

Karen paused, then turned around and walked away.

The front door opened.

Karen's voice came back, "It's time for me to go back to my little box in Riverside. My dead-end job is waiting for me."

Silence.

Karen emphasized, "Don't call me anymore."

The door clicked closed.

I sat on the floor in the darkness for a minute. I tried to wipe the sweat from my face, the tears away from my eyes. Tried to hold it all back but I cried.

# 34  Stephan

Darnell called me early Sunday morning. A very stressed, angry Darnell.

He said, "Jake has been acting up."

"How bad?"

"He's going to end up behind bars."

"That bad?"

"That bad."

Rain was tapping on my windows. Draining from the roof, falling through the evergreen trees outside my window. Phase two of the storm had blown in yesterday afternoon, and it was raining like crazy. Out west in Malibu, million-dollar homes were slipping off the hills.

I said, "Damn. Where he is?"

"At his condo. But he's not answering."

"Then how do you know he's home?"

"Pamela called."

I was shocked. "Pamela called you?"

" 'Those dreams are fucking him up.' That's a quote. She made him sound like a crackhead wandering around skid row."

Jake sat up, coughed for a while before he got his words out. "As soon as I fall asleep I start suffocating . . ."

He was wide-eyed and shaking, unshaven, in a wrinkled LAFD T-shirt, dark blue firefighter pants, reeking like he'd slept in a pasture of cows. Eyes beet red.

As I eased off my damp trench coat, I said the only thing I could think of, "It was only a dream."

Darnell was sitting at the dining room table, dressed in jeans and a short leather jacket. We'd driven in separate cars, and he'd been here about ten minutes. I'd wanted to carpool, but for some reason Darnell didn't want to. Which didn't make any sense.

Darnell's voice boomed, "Deal with it or stop bringing it up."

Pamela walked into the room, stopped underneath the picture of Jake's parents. She had on blue pants and a white polo shirt, her work clothes.

She said, "He choked me. See these marks on my throat?"

Our eyes went to the bruises that looked like elongated passion marks on her neck.

"He was screaming, and when I woke him up"—her saliva looked as thick as clam chowder—"he started choking me like he was trying to kill me. I almost passed out."

Jake said, "Stop exaggerating. That was an accident."

*"Accident?"* With that, Pamela walked out of the room, muttering, "You strangle me till I turn blue and that's an *accident?"*

That was as much as I'd ever heard her say.

I asked Jake, "Pamela called the police on you?"

"Naw. Charlotte flipped out and dialed nine-eleven."

My mouth was wide open. "Serious?"

Darnell asked, "What the hell did you do?"

"Nothing."

Darnell barked, *"Nothing?"*

I said, "Darnell, calm down. We're here now, so calm down."

Outside, the rain was coming down. While I'd struggled up the 60 west and crept past downtown to the 405 north, rain had come down so fast my windshield wipers could barely knock the water away. It took two hours to drive a forty-mile stretch.

Jake sounded baffled. "Hell, she can't be serious. I've sent her flowers almost every day. Long-stem roses. Last night when she got home, I was waiting for her with roses in both hands. I put them in a nice vase and left them in her living room."

I asked, "She let you in?"

"I used my key."

Darnell dropped his head, rubbed his lips. I did the same.

Jake snapped, "She ran next door to Valerie's house and called the sheriff. When I went over, she pointed a damn .380 in my face."

Incredulous, I said, "Charlotte pointed a gun at you?"

"Right between my goddamn eyes."

I said, "You know she's scared of you."

Darnell responded, "If he didn't then, he knows it now."

Jake shook his head. "Then Charlotte called the chief at the fire station, called my damn job and tried to file a complaint."

I said an unimpressed "No shit?"

"*Get a clue,*" Darnell shouted.

Jake raised both of his middle fingers at us.

A pause.

Darnell said, "She said you'd been following her."

Jake shook his head, "I ain't *followed* no-damn-body."

Silence.

Visions of my daddy, begging my momma. Tears of diplomacy. All of that popped in my head. As clear now as it was then.

I blinked that remembrance away.

That was when I saw Pamela had come back. She was standing in the door frame between the bedroom and the kitchen. Arms folded. Tears rippling down her face. She scowled at Darnell, glowered at me.

She said, "That cow sent me some tapes. Sent them to my job. Stuff she had recorded off the telephone."

I had no idea what I had said, or what Darnell had said, but her dark eyes said that we would never be her friends.

Jake chuckled, "Charlotte's crazy. Man, she duplicated those tapes and sent copies to my family, with a note telling them that 'The wedding that was never planned has been called off.' "

Some silence, not much. Rain made all the noise.

I asked, "How much sleep have you had?"

"Few minutes. Every time I nod off, those dreams come back."

Darnell looked irritated. I felt the same way.

From behind me Pamela said in a scathing voice, "His babies."

Jake jumped and shot a serious frown her way.

Darnell said, "What was that?"

She said, "He's dreaming about his babies."

Pamela marched away again. Hard, even steps. She went into the kitchen. Opened cabinets. Sacks ruffled.

I asked Jake, "What baby?"

Pamela's agitated voice came back, "*Babies*, not *baby*."

"You have kids?" That was Darnell.

"I ain't got no kids." His voice was heavy.

Pamela said bitterly, "Not the babies he had, but the babies he didn't have."

I was confused. Darnell's brow rose too.

Jake summed it up in a word: "Abortions."

I swallowed at the icy way he uttered that.

Jake slumped on the bed. "I'm haunted by the babies that I had women put to sleep. That's why all of 'em look familiar. They resemble women I used to kick it with because they're the babies of those women. All of 'em are women that I slept with."

Darnell said, "Every one of them had terminations?"

Jake massaged his goatee. Lines appeared in his forehead. Veins in his neck. His six-foot-one frame shivered.

Darnell swallowed, looked like he wanted to puke.

Jake stuttered, then found his rhythm. "It's their faces on those babies, on those teenagers that keep chasing me down."

I mumbled, "That's why they resemble your folks."

" 'Cause some of 'em look like *me*."

I said, "Your own children are after you?"

Darnell's voice echoed, "Your babies are hunting you down, trying to kill you, just like you did them. That's what you're telling us?"

Tears ran down Jake's face, flowed like the rain that was sliding off the windowpanes. But he still played the part he'd grown used to, wiped the useless water away from his face with the back of his hand, then masked it with an insincere chortle.

Darnell was standing stiff, mouth wide open. Speechless.

I was Darnell's mirror to Jake's horror.

"Damn, bro." I asked Jake, "How many times?"

He knew what I meant. We all did.

He shrugged. "A nigga don't count crap like that."

Darnell said, "Just hit it, quit it, forget it."

Jake jeered, "*Fuck you.* I ain't done shit that neither one of you ain't done."

Darnell said nothing. Neither did I.

Jake stared at the photo of his parents for a moment, stroked his goatee over and over, dropped his eyes. "We're men. That ain't supposed to bother us, right?"

Darnell said, "Consequence. Everything has a consequence."

*"What's that shit got to do with me?"*

"What about the women?" Darnell said. "You carrying this shit, you don't think they're carrying that shit too?"

I'd read about women who marked the day an unborn child

would've been born, women who secluded themselves and lit candles on birthday cakes, but they did it unseen and unheard.

This shit was too eerie. I said to Darnell, "Lighten up."

But he thundered, "You owe some people some apologies."

Jake's voice boomed back, "And neither of you don't?"

Darnell nodded. "Dreams are the X ray of the soul."

Dreams. I thought about mine.

I shook off that memory, said, "Charlotte said you knew."

"Hell, she ain't no damn psychologist. She might not be right."

Darnell said, "Just like you don't want to believe she's not coming back."

Jake whispered, "Don't let her attitude deceive you."

"Want to put some money on it?"

No answer from Jake.

No words from me. I was too busy thinking about my own past.

Straight up with no chaser, Darnell stated, "You're a fool. Every man kills the thing that he loves. Some with a look, some with flattery, the *coward* with a kiss."

Jake stood up, grimaced at Darnell like he wanted to drag him over the hill and kick his ass all up and down Crenshaw. Darnell's chest stood out. A dare.

Then Jake backed off, said, "Think about that when you're with Tammy. Everything has a conse-fucking-quence."

His woman friend came back into the living room holding a yellow gym bag that was stuffed to burst. She grabbed an umbrella from behind the door and lugged her baggage out the door, bumping side to side, her mood as dark as the sky.

Jake asked her, "Where you going?"

"Call me when you stop crying over that bitch."

She paused long enough to massage her neck, then opened the door. Didn't look back. Winds sent a burst of cold air into the room. Pamela went into the storm without opening up her umbrella, no coat, no hat on her head.

Jake went to the door, looked down where she must've been, then gestured like she had a problem. "She's tripping."

We talked a few minutes, pretty much staying on the same topics, still getting nowhere. All I'd eaten was a blueberry muffin and a banana, and my stomach was growling like a bear. I tried to talk Jake into washing his ass and riding over to Inglewood to Coley's for the Jamaican buffet, my treat, but he didn't want to leave his space. Depression was on his shoulders.

Darnell went into the kitchen and used the phone. He paged Dawn.

She called back in less than a minute. He told her that he was with me, that we were at Jake's.

He hung up, then made another phone call. His voice was too low to hear, but I heard him laughing, saw him check his watch.

I thought that we were going to stay awhile, but when Darnell hung up the phone, he said he was leaving.

I said, "We might as well wait for traffic to thin out."

"It's raining," Darnell said, again looking at his watch. "Traffic won't thin out until damn near nine tonight."

Jake grabbed our coats, handed us our black umbrellas.

Even then I tried to talk to Jake some more, but right now there was no talking to him.

Jake said sullenly, "I'm not crazy. Both of you can leave me alone."

We left.

My Mustang was next to Darnell's BMW. We stood there for a few seconds, under our umbrellas, the rain rat-tat-tat-ting down in soft baby thumps. Sky so glum it felt like I was in a black-and-white movie.

I put my fears out in the open. "You don't think he'll do anything to himself, do you?"

"I'm worried more about him doing something to Charlotte."

Horns blared. A crash came from over near the Fox Hills Mall. Fiberglass mating with fiberglass at forty miles per hour. That grabbed our attention for a second. Just a second.

I asked, "You said dreams are the X ray of the soul."

"They are."

"What do you dream about?"

"Getting published."

Darnell got into his car. I tapped the window. He unlocked the passenger side. I got in and closed the door.

I asked him, "Dawn in your dreams?"

"She used to be all I ever dreamed about."

He checked his watch again. I was still rattled about Jake dreaming about abortions, about his children coming back for retribution, but I didn't want to talk about no shit like that.

I asked, "You're going home or back to work?"

He shook his head. "Heading to North Hollywood."

It took a moment for me to understand what he was saying. That was when I realized why he'd paged Dawn from Jake's, to give the illusion that here was where he would be for a long while.

"That's not cool, Darnell. Not at all."

"Why not?" He leaned toward me. "I've been covering for you and Jake for years."

"You're not me. And you ain't as stupid as Jake."

"You think you're better than me?"

"I know you're better than us."

He was more forceful: "Would you do the same for me that you've done for Jake?"

"Jake ain't married."

He argued, "He's engaged. Well, *was* engaged."

"I wouldn't do that to your wife."

"But you'd do it to Charlotte. You did it to Charlotte."

Our eyes met for a moment. Man to man. Friend to friend. We'd had years of friendship, years of him covering for me.

Now the tables had turned, and he was testing the waters.

Oh, what a tangled web we had weaved.

He said, "Let me rephrase the question then: would you do the same for *me* that I've been doing for *you*?"

It felt like there was no right answer to his request. I felt lost. Either way I'd feel like I was less than a true friend, betraying somebody. That wasn't cool. That was what a man felt when the shoe was shoved on the other foot.

I hesitated, rubbed my eyes, said regretfully, "Sure."

Then I felt bad. My soul was lined with guilt.

A burst of hard rain came down, thumped the pavement, beaded up on Darnell's car, reminded me that I needed to wax mine. The whine of a police siren interrupted my superficial thoughts, headed toward where we'd heard the crash.

I said, "Didn't you just give a speech on consequences?"

His voice was removed from my reality. "Nothing on the freeway but tension. Nothing at home but tension."

"Let me quote you: 'Deal with it.' "

He shook his head. "It's bad enough that I have to deal with Dawn's pressure, but now Jake's fucked-up anxiety is inside my four walls too. I need to find a few minutes of peace."

There was nothing I could do to sway him.

"I need peace. Something just for me."

I saw it in his eyes. He was on the verge of a change.

His last words were, "Dawn thinks I'm with you."

That was his way of telling me not to dial his home number, not to return any calls from his wife, until he heard from me.

I got out. He drove away before I could open my car door.

# part three

---

# Long Way Home

# 35 Stephan

By Sunday the grounds were dry again. L.A. had sun to bring in the month of June, and after church service at FAME we all changed and were dressed in jeans. I was holding hands with a lovely woman, walking around my folks' home, going from den to foyer to all four bedrooms.

Chanté said, "This is a boss crib."

I said, "It's all right."

"Learn to take a compliment."

"Thanks."

We were talking, looking around, when one of the kids found us and said, "Uncle Step, Big Momma said it's time to eat."

It was Soul Food Sunday. A lot of the neighbors had come by, and between the kids and adults, it was crowded over here.

Momma, Pops, my two stepaunts, my maternal uncle, Chanté and myself sat down to eat in the formal dining room. I let Chanté's chair out for her, got ready to grub and relax a bit.

All the children were in the den. Momma called out, "Children. Stop fighting over the TV."

At the same time all the kids said, "Yes, ma'am."

The doorbell rang, and Momma hurried to the door. A second later, Momma was laughing and talking while Dawn and Darnell followed her through the living room, back down through the den, and into the dining room. Dawn was wearing a green shorts set. Darnell had on jeans and a lime polo shirt.

I told them, "You got here just in time to eat."

Dawn spoke to everybody; so did Darnell.

Darnell had an unnatural smile. "How are you doing, Chanté?"

"Fine." Her words were knowing. "How've you been, Darnell?"

Dawn said, "Oh. You know each other?"

I said, "They've met. Dawn, this is Chanté."

Dawn raised a brow. "And you are Stephan's . . . ?"

Chanté evaluated Dawn, then looked at me.

I said, "We're dating."

Pops said, "Everybody get settled so we can bless the food."

We did. The TV was turned down, all the kids came in, stood still and held hands, while Pops almost prayed the food cold.

When he was done, Dawn asked, "Jake coming?"

I shook my head. "Haven't heard from him."

Darnell said, "No news is good news."

I asked, "Charlotte coming?"

Dawn shrugged. "She wanted to pop in and say hi, but she didn't want to create any drama."

We had started eating when the doorbell rang again. One of the kids ran-jumped-stumbled down the stairs in the direction of the door.

Chanté scooted her chair closer to mine and fed me one of the ribs off her plate.

Debra DuBois came in, carrying a couple of sweet potato pies. We moved the ribs, corn on the cob, turkey links, greens, and other food to the side so Debra could put the pies down on the table.

Across the table, I saw Darnell tense up a bit.

Debra smiled at Chanté. "Aren't you Tammy's friend?"

Chanté smiled. "Yeah. I met you a long time ago."

Dawn looked at Debra, then at Chanté. Darnell shifted enough for me to notice.

Dawn asked, "Debra, are you talking about the same Tammy that you saw down on Venice Beach having lunch with Darnell?"

"Yeah."

A few more clumsy words were said before Debra left.

The moment we heard the front door close, Dawn said to Chanté, "So, you know Darnell through Tammy?"

"No," Chanté said. "Not exactly. I met Stephan a while back, when he fixed my car for me."

"Then Stephan introduced Tammy to Darnell?"

Darnell interjected, "Dawn."

She stopped the showdown and went back to eating.

The old folks were in the middle of their own conversation, talking about their own issues, not really paying attention.

All except Pops. His eyes were in one direction, but his ears were like surround sound, picked up everything.

The doorbell rang again.

Momma called out, "Somebody get that. That's probably Debra coming back for something."

Kids stumbled and ran to the front of the house.

I heard her talking before I saw her.

I cringed. Felt my throat tighten.

It couldn't be her. No way.

But it was.

Toyomi tramped into the dining room, tight jean shorts smothering the firmness of her backside. Peach blouse, serious attitude. The driver's side of her body was tanned from the long haul from Palm Springs.

Everybody saw something brewing in Toyomi's eyes, then looked my way. Then they did something they never did, not even in the middle of an earthquake.

They stopped eating.

Toyomi smiled.

That bothered the fuck out of me.

Momma, Pops, and everybody else braced for the confrontation they knew was about to jump off. I didn't realize I was sitting there with a mouth full of ribs until I tried to say something and damn near choked to death.

My Bible-toting Aunt Anabella shifted her double wide ass and laughed so hard her cubby cheeks danced like jello. "You a'right, boy?"

Uncle Glen smiled like an idiot. "Leave him alone, Ana."

Momma cleared her throat, then cut her eyes at me. "Don't be rude to your company, Stephan."

She went back to pretending she was more interested in her food than the situation. Everybody followed her lead and stuck their forks back in their food. Momma would let things flow so long as they didn't get too nasty.

"Afternoon, Toyomi." I clucked my tongue on the roof of my mouth. "Long time no see."

My leg started to shake. In my peripheral, Chanté was checking out Toyomi, gazing up and down. Chanté eased away from me.

My heart crept up to my throat when I realized how many sharp knives were on the table. My mind told me Toyomi wasn't that crazy. My heart told me I'd never know until I screamed.

Toyomi slid her purse off her right shoulder and caught it with her left hand as she walked around the table.

Again she and Chanté made eye contact.

"Hello, Momma Faye." Toyomi leaned over and kissed Momma's face. Momma kissed Toyomi back. That pissed me off.

Toyomi spoke to Dawn, Darnell. Dawn didn't hesitate to hop up and hug Toyomi like they were long-lost sisters.

"Nice to see you again, Papa Jerry!" Toyomi sounded so excited. She kissed him. He chuckled and blushed like a elementary-school boy. She rubbed the top of his bald head.

She gave individual greetings to Aunt Edwonda, Aunt Anabelle, and Uncle Glen, then had the nerve to lean forward and put her elbows on the table, damn near stuck her buttocks in Chanté's face, while she got all into my family's business.

"How's your diabetes, Aunt Edwonda? Still thinking about buying that boat, Uncle Glen? You bring one of your slamming sweet potato pies with the homemade crust, Aunt Ana?"

Chanté had chewed her ribs so much she had a mouth full of rib soup by now.

Toyomi shot Chanté a curt "Hi."

"And 'Hi' to you, too."

"I don't believe we've met," Toyomi said. "Are you a relative?"

"No, I'm not."

"A friend of the family?"

Dawn interjected, "That's Stephan's *date*, Soror."

I had to jump in. "Toyomi, what, you stopped by to say hi?"

"Stephan," Momma said. "Offer Toyomi something to eat."

"Thank you, no," Toyomi said with enough sweetness to overdose a honey bee. "I'm not hungry. Not at this moment."

Dawn said, "Pull up a chair next to Stephan."

"I'm only going to be here a couple of minutes."

I asked Chanté, "Could you excuse me for a moment?"

Chanté had a crooked smile. "Go right ahead."

Toyomi gazed over at Chanté, all comfortable and welcome. Stared for a second before we headed toward the front door.

I went through the dining room first, but when I reached the living room, she jostled past me. I followed, felt everybody glaring at the back of my head.

Little Akeem and Nathan Junior rushed in just before we could get out the front door. Nathan Junior's mouth dropped open.

"Toy," Nathan Junior said. "What the heck are you doing here?"

Toyomi tsked. "Well, ain't that rude."

Akeem's eyes bucked.

"Ooooo!" Akeem blurted out, "Uncle Step got two girlfriends up in the house! Ooooooo-weeeeee! Mack daddy, daddy mack!"

Nathan Junior clamped his hands over Akeem's mouth. He said, "Pay him no mind. He got dropped on his head when he was born. He's crazy."

Toyomi hissed through her teeth, "Akeem, was that necessary?"

He responded, "Don't hate the player, hate the game!"

Toyomi didn't see the humor. She slapped on her shades, rushed out the door. She stopped by Chanté's car. Her arms folded, raised her breasts a good five inches.

I took my time getting to her.

"What's up?" I asked.

She snatched her shades off so hard one of the lenses popped out. "Who is she?"

I stayed calm. "Who is who?"

"You know who."

"A friend."

"Is she the best you could do?"

The point was, and I knew it, no matter what the other woman looked like, fault would be found. Too short, too tall, too black, too light, hair too long, hair too short, too fat, too skinny.

"Toyomi," I said. "Get your finger out of my face."

"Why did you bring her over here? Everybody stared at me like I was a damn joke, and you had that need-a-perm-looking bush bitch sitting all up under you—"

"You don't know her, how are you going to pass judgment?"

"Hos attract each other."

"And since you went out with me, what does that make you?"

I thought she was going to jump out of her skin and bite me. She took a few steps toward her car, then charged back with a kamikaze glower in her Asian eyes.

"Toyomi, what do you want, huh?"

While she stared evilly at me, the front door opened. Chanté came out, putting her shades on. She had her purse over her shoulder.

Toyomi muttered, "I ought to kick her ass."

Chanté followed the cobblestone walkway to the driveway. Her slow stride brought her to me. She said, "Hello."

"What's up?" I asked.

"Nothing," she said. "I'm leaving."

Toyomi said, "You're not finished eating, are you?"

"Lost my appetite. Drama upsets my tummy."

Chanté looked at me, waited for me to say something. Then her eyes wandered back to Toyomi's warlike glare. She smiled, extended her hand. "My name is Chanté Ellis."

Toyomi hiked her purse back on her shoulder, mimicked Chanté's posture, said a profound "Toyomi Wilkins."

When they touched, Toyomi's nostrils flared.

Chanté asked, "And you're Stephan's, what?"

"Girlfriend."

I said, "Ex-girlfriend."

"Okay," Chanté sang, "slight difference of opinion."

Toyomi asked Chanté, "And you are Stephan's what?"

I interjected, "She's my date."

Chanté tilted her head. "Date? *Okay*. My bad."

"Chanté, let me finish with Toyomi and I'll be right back—"

Chanté said coolly, "Stephan, can I have a word or two with you? That is, if Toyomi doesn't mind."

"Go right ahead." Toyomi headed back toward the house, some sort of indication of squatter's rights, I supposed.

Momma was in the door and held it open for Toyomi.

"Stephan," Chanté ran her hands over her hair, then machine-gunned, "I don't appreciate this situation. You left me sitting at the dinner table while you ran outside behind a hooch who has her pants stuck all up the crack of her butt."

"Look, it's not all that."

"If she drove from Palm Springs, it must be *all that*. She knew everybody in your family. Walked in, everybody hugging and kissing on her. Looks like she's already part of the family."

"Don't trip."

"You hear all of your relatives laughing?"

"No."

"You need your hearing checked. They laughed so loud, people in China turned around. That humiliated me."

"They're country. They watch reruns of *Hee Haw*, so they'll laugh at anything."

"What about 'Don't hate the player, hate the game'?"

"Akeem is just a child. He watches too much MTV and BET."

"Maybe you should go play with him, partner."

Somebody was spying out the window; the curtains were moving side to side. The front door opened, and a stream of children in cutoff shorts and bathing suits dashed out and headed next door.

Akeem stopped and pointed. "Oooooo!"

Nathan Junior slapped his hand and dragged him away.

Akeem screamed, "Player, player!"

They ran away like roaches when the lights come on.

Chanté said, "I guess you train 'em when they start walking."

"I apologize for this scene," I said.

She didn't say anything. Her look was distant, face going through subtle changes that let me know she was thinking a thousand thoughts a second.

I asked, "What're you thinking?"

"Locusts. Just like locusts."

"What?"

Chanté snapped out of her thoughts and firmed her stance. "Stephan, lose my number. Forget my address. Have a nice life. And if you see me at Shelly's, act like you don't know me, and I'll do the same."

"You're going to leave me here?"

"Yep."

"I rode with you."

"You can make it back to Pomona, partner. If Darnell and *his wife* won't take you home, get somebody with shorts riding up the crack of her booty to drop you off between here and Palm Springs."

"Are you serious?"

Chanté's tone was hard. "I'm just your *date*, partner. Nothing more, nothing less."

Chanté got into her car and drove off, left me curbside. Before her car disappeared, Toyomi's immature butt came out the house carrying two paper plates with foil wrapped around the tops. She goose-stepped right up to me.

I snapped at her, "You want your stuff?"

"I drove all the way out here, so I must want my stuff."

"Toyomi, you came in a Saab. How do you expect to fit all of that in that car?"

She backed off a bit, shook her head.

She asked, "Your friend left?"

"What do you think?"

She set free a contrived laugh to match her devilish smirk.

I asked, "Why are you doing this?"

"Doing what?"

*"Fucking with me. Why do you keep fucking with me?"*

She answered my question with a question. "Was it that easy for you to just walk away?"

"What? You broke it off. Remember, I came back to you and you ran me out of Palm Springs. You messed up my car, tore up my suits, left that foul message on my door."

"So what? You wasted over a year of my life, and it didn't mean a damn thing to you, did it? It's only been fifty-seven days. If I meant anything to you, at least you could've called."

I massaged my temples, closed my eyes, wishing that she had never been born. When I opened them, she was still there.

Toyomi let out a sad, nervous laugh. "I was looking through the pictures we took skiing, hiking—"

I threw in, "The ones you didn't destroy."

"I kept a few. We took more pictures than I realized. Guess we did all kinds of things I'd taken for granted. I didn't mean to pressure you like I did. What we had was good."

I sighed.

Toyomi asked, "Is there any chance that we can get back together, Stephan?"

Before she finished that sentence, I was already shaking my head. "Too much has happened. Let's move forward."

She switched gears, tensed and snapped, "Bastard."

"What I do?"

"I just told you the most shameful part of my life, and that's all you can say? I just poured my heart out to you."

"You asked, I told you."

"Fuck you fuck you fuck you fuck you fuck you," she sang as she marched to her car. Toyomi slapped the plates of food on top of her Saab, bumbled for her keys, opened the car, got in, slammed the door. Engine started. She drove off. The paper plates were still on the top of her ride. They slid off like Humpty-Dumpty. Crashed. Food spread all over the streets.

Pops strolled out a second later, his hands jingling the loose change in his pockets. He whistled, checked his lawn sprinklers, lit up a King Edward's cigar, and meandered over next to me. As I stood there with my hands deep inside my pockets, looking in the direction both women had driven, he put his wide and heavy hand up on my shoulder.

I thought, here comes the lecture. He always had to lecture.

"I done told you about trying to be a Jody, ain't I, son? Don't brang you nothing but hurt and trouble."

"Yes, sir."

"And you know I love you like you was my own."

I asked him, "Do you?"

He sighed, blew cigar smoke away from me. "When you was coming up, every single night, who helped you with your homework?"

"You did."

"Who taught you how to fix cars?"

"You did. Pops, you don't have to do the whole list—"

"Who ran out in the middle of the night when you was down with the flu and got you something to ease your suffering? Who did more for you than you done for yourself?"

Humbly I answered him, "You did."

"I didn't do it because I like you, and I didn't do it because I love you. I did it because somebody had to."

"Yes, sir."

"Now, I took you to Disneyland because I cared about you. Me and your momma wanted all'a y'all to do thangs that were never possible for us to do down in Miss'sippi. And I'm gonna tell you the truth, the truth as I know it. Duke, your own daddy, never would'a done none of that for you. He wasn't that kinda man."

We stood there for a moment.

He asked, "You thank I'm lying?"

It pained me to answer. "No, sir."

"Now, I ain't never asked you for nothing, have I?"

"No, sir."

"Now, I'm gonna ask one favor of you."

"Yes, sir."

"Man to man, so raise your head and look me in the eye."

I did. We did.

"Your daddy dead," Pops said. "You can carry him with you all you want. You can take him with you everywhere you go from now until your bones turn to dust. That's your right. But when we're up here, let's leave him out of this house."

A moment or two passed before I nodded.

We stopped the man-to-man, eye-to-eye ritual.

He said, "Yes, sir. When a man steps in and fills another man's shoes, it's a thankless job. Doing right is a thankless job. You can work your fingers to the bone trying to do right, and you never get so much as a thank-you."

I cleared my throat, shifted. I asked, "Anything else?"

"One more thang. And this ain't a request. This is me telling you what I won't tolerate," Pops said. "Don't be branging trouble around here. Women do some unpredictable thangs when they get riled, you hear me? I've seen many a man put in the ground for less than what you've done. Me and your momma don't want it, not on our property, don't need it."

"I invited Chanté over. Toyomi just popped up."

"That's not the point, son." He gripped my shoulders. "Stephan, my son. If I done told you once, I done told you a hundred times. Don't go dabbling in ho soup, because you might choke on the bone. Today you choked."

He turned and headed back toward the house.

I called out, "Pops?"

"Yeah, son? What you need?"

"Nothing. I just wanted to say thanks."

He nodded, then pointed at the street, toward the scattered food and paper plates that had fallen off Toyomi's car. "Now go clean up that mess. We ain't down on Crenshaw."

"Yes, sir."

# 36 Darnell

At first the ride from Baldwin Hills was pretty quiet. For Dawn, quiet meant anger. Stephan was in the backseat. I had no idea what his quiet meant. Mine meant Tammy was on my mind.

I asked, "Stephan, you all right?"

"I'm cool. Just listening to the music."

"Radio's not on."

"The music inside my head."

"What you hear?"

"Teddy singing that the whole town's laughing at me."

I chuckled a little bit at his self-deprecating humor.

So did he.

Stephan said, "I was just feeling good about me and Chanté, then Toyomi showed up."

"You sow it," Dawn said stiffly. "You reap it."

We crossed the 605 and approached the City of Industry. The freeway sign said that we were eighteen miles from Pomona.

Dawn said, "When I asked, no one ever told me about Tammy. Chanté ran out the house before she answered my question."

My response was, "Nothing to tell."

In the rearview, my eyes met Stephan's. I saw it in his face—that scene had left him distraught. The last time I saw him come close to looking like that was years ago, when a girl he was living with left him high and dry. He was uncomfortable, shifting around like a fugitive who was shackled and being driven on the gray goose to Chino Hills Correctional.

Dawn broke the silence. "Darnell and I have been together as man and wife for years."

I asked, "Who are you talking to?"

"Myself," she said. She continued staring out the window at the rolling hills, speaking right above a whisper. "It hasn't been easy, but we've survived. The hardest part was when Darnell was in law school. Law school was probably harder on me than it was on him. He was never home, and when he was he had his nose in a book until the crack of dawn. It was to the point where we had no communication. He'd do his thing. I'd have to find something to do.

"Yeah. I was lonely. And I still am. Guess you can say I've been lonely for a while. Now that things are settled, when we should be coming together and rekindling our marriage, Darnell wants to go do something else. Something else that would change the dynamics of our marriage.

"Something else that would leave me on the sidelines playing cheerleader on a losing team.

"And after all I've done, he corners me in the garage and violates me in the broad of day. Didn't care what kind of mood I was in, or if I had to pee, just didn't care. That really made me feel like a woman. Sure in the fuck did. Is that the way you treat the women you date, Stephan?"

I jumped in, "Don't take my business to Stephan."

"Why not? You took it to Jake. Lie and say you didn't. I know you did, because Jake told Charlotte, and Charlotte told me. I didn't appreciate that. Not at all."

Stephan said, "Watch your speed, Darnell."

Dawn kept staring out the window. "Then my husband says he's met somebody who understands him better than me. Hell, maybe we don't know each other."

I asked her, "How many pages of my work have you read?"

A moment passed.

I said, "Okay, Dawn, how many paragraphs? Sentences?"

Another moment.

I said, "When you've decided you want me to be someone I'm not, you've decided I'm not the one you want."

"Someone you're not? Darnell, you don't know who you are."

"No, you want me to be this image of the black man you want."

"No, you don't want to be responsible."

"I'm responsible. You're not supportive."

"I'm tired of this shit."

"Well, that makes two of us."

"I love you, but I'm not afraid to hate you, Darnell."

Stephan raised his voice. "Darnell, you're drifting into the other lane. Watch out for that—"

A horn blared. The car in the next lane swerved to the right; I swerved to the left.

I gripped the wheel and stopped riding back and forth on the bubbles in the lanes, shouted, "Stop screaming in my ear. Damn. I saw that car."

Dawn snapped, "He saw you too. That's why he flipped you off."

Stephan suggested, "Why don't y'all talk about this when you're by yourself? When we're not going ninety miles an hour."

Dawn rampaged, "Between him working, writing, and as much as he runs the streets with you and Jake, I have to get my words in when I can."

Ten minutes later, I pulled off the freeway at Fairway Drive.

Dawn stared straight ahead. "You're taking me home first?"

"Yeah."

"Why?"

"I'm dropping you off, then I'm taking Stephan home."

"Why can't I go with you?"

"Why would you want to?"

"Why wouldn't you want me to?"

"I'll be back. We're going to talk."

"Why do you have to go talk to Stephan?"

"Same reason you run out to talk to Charlotte every time she breaks a nail."

Stephan said, "Darnell, I'm cool. Drop me off first. Better yet, I'm only six or seven miles from home, so if you would please slow down to about fifty and pull over to the right, I could dive out, break a few bones, and limp to Phillips Ranch from here."

I said, "Stephan, don't worry about it."

Dawn faced her window as we bounced over two sets of railroad tracks, stared at nothing until I pulled up in our driveway. She opened her door and got out without saying good-bye.

Stephan crawled into the front seat.

I called to Dawn, "Need me to bring anything back?"

She didn't answer.

On the way to Pomona, I told Stephan what Dawn had done when Toyomi had dragged him away from the dinner table.

Dawn had been chewing her corn on the cob when Stephan made his exodus. His aunts had wobbled to the front window, were laughing and peeping outside to see what was going on.

When he was out of the house, Dawn smirked and asked Chanté, "Had you met Toyomi before today?"

Chanté answered, "Nope. Afraid I haven't had the pleasure."

"Isn't she beautiful? She's extremely intelligent as well."

Chanté didn't say anything.

Dawn continued, "Her and Stephan have been together for years."

I corrected, "Not years. Just a little over a year."

"Seems like years. We've gone on ski trips to Big Bear, hiking up at Griffith Park, went to the Maui Jazz Festival—no, wait, he didn't take Toyomi to Hawaii. That was Samantha, the other girl he was seeing at the same time. He took Toyomi to Cabo. Or was that Brittany? No, he never takes Brittany anywhere. I don't know, I've lost track. Could've been what's-her-face or what's-her-face or what's-her-face."

Dawn went back to eating.

Chanté addressed Dawn, "You finished drilling me?"

Dawn smiled. "I'm not the one drilling you. Ask Stephan that question. He's the king of the drill. One way or another, I'm sure he'll be drilling you later."

They locked eyes briefly.

Chanté excused herself and never came back.

Stephan had me get off the 57 at Diamond Bar Boulevard. I was on my car phone, talking to Tammy. Stealing a few moments to hear her voice, making plans to rendezvous before she went to Paris. Between rehearsals and practicing with the band, her schedule was tight. I'd miss her opening night at the play, but the night before she left for Paris, we'd be together. We decided that. I felt like a kid waiting for Christmas.

Or a prisoner waiting for his final hour.

I hung up. Stephan didn't say anything, but he shifted like ants were feeding in his crotch. He wanted to release his thoughts, but he didn't. He knew it wouldn't do any good.

Stephan had me ride into Allegro, the condos across from the post office. That strip held miles of condominiums.

I went up Montefino Drive. He didn't see Chanté's car.

He borrowed a pen, a slip of paper, and wrote a note. He opened my car door but didn't get out.

I asked, "You leaving the message or what?"

He shook his head and asked me to take him home.

Toyomi had been by his place. She'd made a stop after she had left L.A. I'd never seen the f-word carved in a door so many times in my life. In all sizes and shapes. On top of that, in large red letters, she said that she wanted her shit.

I told him, "Looks like it's time for a new door."

Hell would be living between my walls when I made it back to my castle. I knew that. I expected my queen to be on a rampage, packing up my clothes and throwing them out on the lawn.

Instead Dawn was in her peach satin slip, lying on our California king-size bed. She'd changed the bedding, put on sheets, comforters, bedskirt, shams. All in a soft, romantic floral print. Next to her were our white photo albums. Pictures of our wedding. When I was thinner. A glass of wine was in her left hand, in a crystal goblet that we had received as a wedding gift. She flipped through the pictures with her right hand.

Fresh strawberries were in a crystal bowl, another one of our wedding gifts, sitting on a TV tray, within reach. Candles were in wrought iron holders, but they weren't lit. A Will Downing CD was playing. Music of bewitchment. She'd showered and put on perfume. Her scent was all over. Her hair down, loose and free.

She looked and smiled like nothing bad had ever happened between us. "Come here. Let me show you what you've been missing when you're not next to me."

"Looks like you have an agenda."

"Everyone does."

I agreed with a nod.

She said, "Sometimes when the road you're on gets bumpy, instead of changing roads, you just have to take the time to smooth out the one you're on. Bumps or potholes, I love the one I've been traveling with you."

"So, this is supposed to make it all better."

"Darnell, I'm not perfect. You're not perfect."

I told her, "That was a non sequitur."

"My thoughts, just my thoughts."

I touched my belly, felt heavy. Felt as imperfect as they come. I asked, "What does that 'not perfect' speech mean?"

"It means that no matter how much we go to church, pray, whatever, we'll never be perfect. You'll fall short. I'll fall short. We will always have problems. No matter who you're with, Darnell, you're going to have problems."

She smiled down on the pictures we'd taken over the years. Memories were just that, memories.

Dawn patted the bed where she wanted me to sit. She'd patted a spot the same way Tammy had done when I was at her side

She rubbed my arm, pulled me down on her. "You're hard to get along with because you're going through one of those middle-age crisis things. I'm a young woman, and I know how to rub your back, make you feel like a man and bring back your youth."

She bit a strawberry, fed me the rest. Bit another, rubbed it on my skin, sucked the juices off my flesh.

Then she was undressing me. Kissing my nipples, slipping her hand inside my pants, moving my hands and making me touch her in her hollow—a place that was already hot, swollen, and moist.

I couldn't get up off that bed.

Not without another fight that would last through the night.

I settled for peace.

But not before I made the room too dark to see or be seen, took the Will Downing CD off, and put a Nina Simone CD on.

# 37 Chanté

Male or female, friend or foe, at this point I was through with every-body. I wasn't returning any phone calls, and I'd turned my pager off.

Before I made it to Moss Adams on Monday, Tammy had jingled my company voice mail and left a message that she had an early rehearsal for the play, then in the afternoon had to go over a few numbers with the band. The band rehearsal was in Montclair, out in my neck of the woods. Since the fiasco with Karen, Tammy had paged me forty-eleven times, but I never called her back. So she came over and banged on my door as soon as she had wailed her last note. That was around eight p.m. She surprised me, caught me feeling so ashamed to be me.

"I want to know two thangs," Tammy said as she marched through my front door and made her way into the kitchen. She dropped her French book on the coffee table. It landed with a thud. " 'Cause I'm about to get pissed off right about now."

I felt it coming. Already my stomach had knotted in defense.

Tammy planted her hands on her hips. "Okay, what's up with you and Karen?"

"What do you mean?"

"What do you think I mean? Nobody has called me in over a week. And don't get me started talking about little Miss Karen."

She took two plastic bowls out of the cabinet.

"I called her this morning, and she had a 'tude with me. She practically hung up on me. I paged you, and you didn't hit me back. And you're acting all funny toward me now. Y'all mad at me because I got too drunk and puked a little?"

"Are you serious?"

She was being real.

All Tammy remembered about that night was getting sick at the Hollywood Athletic Club, saying good-bye to her friends, walking out to the car, getting dizzy, then waking up with a hangover and a nasty taste in her mouth. That morning I'd pretended I was asleep until she left for her rehearsal, so we never talked.

I said, "Well, you missed it all."

"What did I miss?"

"Me and Karen had a fight."

"You're always arguing."

"No. A fight. A real fight."

I dropped down the details.

Of course, I played it all down like it was no big deal.

Tammy cracked up. She thought it was funny as hell.

She said, "Get real. I don't believe you had a fight over a buck-toothed brother from Birmingham."

"You think I was wrong, don't you?"

She waited a moment, then said, "You've changed a lot, Chanté."

I sighed.

She added, "I'm really worried about you."

"About?"

"Well, just like a lot of the things you try to tell Karen to help her out, about thinking about her future, I think that maybe you should listen to some of the things she tells you. In some ways, you need to think about your future too."

Criticism sounded so much softer coming from Tammy. She had a skill, she knew how to talk to people. "I see. Well, thanks for being honest with me."

"Me too," she added, her voice so sensitive. "I have to think about my future too. That's another reason why going to Paris is so important to me."

"Well, partner, life has dragged all of us up some strange roads," I said. "I've done things that I never thought I'd do."

"That's life, baby. All you're doing is living. One thing about life, you never know which way the winds are gonna blow. Hollywood or Paris, You never know where you're gonna end up."

I gave a warm smile, patted her hand. "I'm okay."

"I don't think so. And you don't think you are."

Then she fell silent. I was quiet too. I stopped concentrating on self, and wondered if she was okay.

I said, "Karen made me so mad."

"She has that talent. And you have that talent too."

"Don't you ever want to get back at somebody?"

"Sweetheart, I live in Hollywood. The home of the backstabbers. I want to get back at somebody twenty-four-seven."

"Why don't you?"

"Baby, in Hollywood, today's secretary is tomorrow's movie producer. You have to keep your past from biting your ass."

We laughed.

Somehow we started talking about men. I told her what had gone down at Stephan's during the Sunday dinner. I told her about that half-breed hoochie from Palm Springs who came storming up in there and claimed Stephan as her man. I let her know that Darnell was there with his wife. I did that because I wanted her to back off from making herself available to Darnell. In my mind, I could still see the look in Michael's wife's eye when she caught him in my bed. I remembered how I felt when I realized I'd been fucked over by a married man. And that feeling didn't rest well with me. I described Dawn from head to toe, told Tammy every word of what she had said to me.

I asked my girlfriend, "If Darnell wanted to leave his wife and get with you, what would you do?"

"Give him a key. He already has the map to my heart. He's already stimulated my mind. Now, right or wrong, this body has become an instrument I'd love him to play."

"Damn."

"I'm serious. I love him. But love ain't nothing new to me. To be honest, I don't know why he has my heart."

"Tammy, baby, there are a million men out there you could be compatible with, why a married man?"

She shrugged. "The love stopped here for some reason."

I thought about Stephan. I was mad as hell at him, but I missed him more than I wanted to admit, when I said, "Kismet."

"Nothing more, nothing less."

"Me. You. Stephan. Darnell. You wonder why all of us ended up in the same place on the same night?"

"Every damn day. If we had've gone to another club that night, everything would be different."

"Definitely kismet."

She repeated, "Nothing more, nothing less."

"So, where does that leave you?"

"I wouldn't try to take him from his wife, because I wouldn't want anybody to take him from me. I just plain old love him."

"What about Bobby? Don't you care about him?"

"I kicked Bobby to the curb."

"For Darnell?"

"Nah." She waved like I was silly. "Some girl called me at three in the morning begging me not to take him from her."

"When?"

"A while back. She was cool about it. She didn't clown. She found my number and wanted to know if Bobby was playing her. I told her he was playing her like a game of dominoes."

She laughed like it was no big deal. I laughed along, not because it was funny, but just so she wouldn't be laughing alone.

Behind my fake ha-has, my feelings were hurt. I wondered why she hadn't called me when it happened. That was what I would've done, called her and called Karen. I would've rushed to lean on them because I would've wanted somebody here with me to share and help thin out my misery.

Tammy said, "So, Paris for a month will do me some good. I can put space between me and a lot of things, past and present."

"What things in the past?"

She patted my hands. "Things I never been able to talk about. A part of my past that's going to come back and bite me one day. There's a lot about me you don't know. I'll tell you one day."

I knew there was a lot about her I didn't know. She kept her woes and secrets on her hip; I wore mine on my lips. Since day one, Tammy has brought only good news, friendship, and comfort to my doorstep, never the bad. If I hadn't asked now, I probably never would have known she'd broken up with her beau.

Her words relaxed me, and a lot of tension fled my used and abused body. I grabbed a bowl of ice cream, and we sat at the dining room table with a plate full of Chips Ahoy cookies between us. Dipping, eating, and putting on the calories.

Tammy moaned, "This will go right to my thighs."

"All four of 'em."

"Forget you. May your ass spread like butter."

I put the sweetness between two cookies, made a too rich sandwich. Even though we were talking about other things, between every breath I was contrasting my old lovers to Stephan.

I asked, "What're you thinking about?"

She hummed a bit. "What do you dream about, Chanté?"

"I used to dream about being married, me and my husband and my children taking vacations to places abroad, living comfortably, sorta like the Cosbys. Yep, I used to dream about me, Craig, and a bunch of kids that looked like him."

She sighed. "If we don't get a move on, or a decent sperm donor, our ovaries are gonna shut down"

"We could always freeze our eggs."

"And have a baby that looks like a Popsicle? I think not."

We laughed so hard ice cream drooled out of our mouths.

I told her, "I can't imagine you with a baby."

Tammy looked kind of solemn for a quick sec.

She asked, "What do you dream about now?"

I shook my head. "I stopped dreaming."

"When did you stop dreaming?"

"I should've stopped when *The Cosby Show* went off the air."

We talked some more. About different things. Mostly about how foolish me and Karen had acted over a brother who needed a dental plan. We'd had arguments, but we'd never gone that far.

I confessed, "I already miss talking to Karen."

"Forget Karen. She'll calm down. What you got left to eat?"

"Look and see."

I went into the bedroom, checked my answering machine. Thaiheed had called to say hi. I fast-forwarded past that one. One was from Stephan. I listened to it twice.

> BEEP
> *Hello, Chanté. This is Stephan.*

That was all he said. He struggled to get those words out, paused before he hung up, almost like he couldn't put together the thoughts that were in his head.

I erased his voice. Romance was over. Time to move on.

Tammy yelled, "Karen call?"

"Nope," I answered. My thoughts returned to that stupid fight. On true friendship. It's not like I have a lot of friends. I really felt bad, like I'd messed up big time. We were a threesome, had been a threesome so long. I felt so sensitive, like a little girl, when I called out, "Tammy?"

"What?"

"I want to resolve things with Karen."

"Call her."

"No. Face to face. Now. The sooner the better."

Traffic wasn't bad on a Monday evening, so we decided to drive the twenty-something miles out to Riverside. I felt derailed, and I had to get some of my emotions back on track.

I could've gone alone, but I needed Tammy there for balance.

It was ten-thirty, so after working all day at the DMV, Karen should be home, hair in rollers, getting ready to hit the sack.

I had Tammy stop by the Lucky's grocery store across the street, and I bought another pint of ice cream, a bona fide peace offering. With that detour, it was close to eleven-thirty when we got off the 60 freeway, drove up Blaine to the Timber Apartments. Karen's Altima was parked in her stall.

Delicate contemporary jazz flowed from inside the first-floor apartment. I stayed back, held the ice cream, reluctant because I felt unwelcome.

Tammy rang the doorbell.

I swallowed deep. Karen was going to read me up and down.

Tammy did her usual foolery by sticking her hand over the peephole to black it out.

"Think she has company?" I whispered.

"Her coochie's a vegetarian."

"True."

"She's probably humming and coming with Victor. She can put that artificial weenie on pause for a few minutes."

"Does a vibrator have a pause?"

Tammy shrugged. "Hell if I know. I think it has a fast forward."

"Maybe I should talk to her first—"

"Stop looking for an excuse to leave."

"What if she—"

Tammy shouted, "Karen, open up!"

Tammy rang the doorbell several times before Karen's sleep-ridden voice finally responded: "What?"

"It's Tammy."

"Tammy?"

"Is there an echo in Riverside?"

"What are you doing all the way out here?"

"Open the door and find out. Don't worry, I'm through throwing up. At least I think I am."

The door opened a little, just enough for her illegal herbal aroma to creep out in the night breeze.

Karen was tying the wrap on a satin robe I'd given her when we exchanged gifts last Christmas. We'd given each other presents while we sat underneath my Christmas tree and sipped hot apple cider. If she was wearing something I'd given her, maybe all hope wasn't lost. I smiled at the memory, then at Karen.

She had some serious cleavage going on. Legs bare. Sweat on her brow. Hair pinned up.

Tammy joked, "Damn, that smoke is thick as San Francisco fog. What the hell is your sweaty ass doing in there this time of night? Getting high and working out to a Donna Richard tape?"

I thought Karen would either come out, or let us inside. When she'd opened the door, she didn't crack it but a touch. The yellow porch light was in my face. The door was wide enough to reveal Karen's surprise to see me.

She exhaled my name, "Chanté."

I inhaled, then did the same, "Karen."

Tammy playfully pushed the door open a little wider. Karen frowned at me like I was the last person she wanted in her life, gripped the edge of the door, and stopped Tammy in her tracks.

I was jarred by her rudeness, and so was Tammy.

"What's up?" Tammy asked. "Why're you going off on me?"

"Nothing is up," Karen responded softly. She glanced at me, at

Tammy, then her face shifted to a sideways glare that screamed out her sentiments.

Tammy's hands were on her hips. "You going to invite us in?"

Karen shook her head. "Can't."

"Busy?"

"Kind of."

"Masturbating?"

"No."

"Alone?"

"That's not important."

Karen and I looked at each other for a moment. She was acting all hard, but I knew her, so I recognized the look in her eyes. We mirrored the same hurt, were both waiting for the other to say something first.

I took the melting ice cream out of the bag, held it up, and gave her my wavering smile. "Butter pecan. Our favorite."

I thought she would laugh a little, but Karen's facial expression didn't change. That nullified the only magic I had.

I moved up. "I'm sorry. I apologize for whatever I said at the club that night. I apologize for jumping in your face and putting you out. Can we still be friends?"

Karen was belligerent. "I don't know."

"What you mean, you don't know?" Tammy interjected.

"I mean," Karen reinforced, "I don't know."

"Just say yes or no," I said.

Karen drummed her fingernails against the rim of the door frame, looked at my uneasiness, then shot a scowl back at Tammy.

Karen said stiffly, "Let's get together and discuss this later in the week."

"Hell, no!" Tammy said. "We need to resolve this. Now. You know I'll be in rehearsal all week, and I'm leaving for Paris next weekend."

Karen made a who-gives-a-shit expression, said, "We'll talk when you get back from your funky little trip."

Tammy said, "You dogging me like that?"

"Please, Karen?" I begged. "I'm losing sleep over this, all right?"

Tammy grabbed my wrist, pulled me behind her, then pushed her way through Karen's door. Just like she had done me, Tammy's bull-headed charge had caught Karen off guard. The base of the wooden door jammed Karen's toes. Cursing, she let go of the door so she could grab her foot. She lost her balance and did a one-foot hop with the pain.

We were in the box-sized candlelit room. Tammy stumbled over a stack of Mervyn's bags filled with clothes that were on the floor. What caught my eye was the clothing that was viciously scattered all across the floor. Pumps, men's shoes, boxer shorts, panties.

Tammy said, "What the hell is going on here?"

A stale sexual odor stood out from the herbal funk, became more prevalent when we were inside.

A whole lot of mess happened after that. A whole lot.

Tammy's face lost its eagerness. Mine lost its old anxiety, and found some new distress. We were facing Karen's daybed. Gawking at a man who was lounging in his birthday suit.

Tammy said, "Oh, boy. Must be Victor's night off."

Karen moaned with wide eyes, limped toward her daybed.

The brother who was sitting up underneath the framed Malcolm X poster, BY ANY MEANS NECESSARY, pulled the sheets up.

We—me and him—stared hard at each other.

He pushed back on his elbows, took a deep breath and sat up.

I looked at Karen, then at him.

I had to accept the obvious.

Dizzy. I'd been holding my breath, and I was getting dizzy.

"Oh, my God!" Tammy said when she finally caught on. "Craig Bryant? Is that you?"

I went numb. My brain had turned to slush.

I said, "Craig? What are you and Karen doing . . ."

My words evaporated, drained away to the place where all stupid questions went at the end of the day.

The flickering candlelight showed his moist face. A condom box on the floor. One of the economy packs. A glass of wine on the night-stand, next to Victor the Vibrator, oils and jelly.

A wrathful lump grew in my belly and boiled. My eyes went back to Karen's bloodshot and arrogant expression, then back to my ex-boyfriend's wannabe Maxwell sneer.

He cleared his throat. "And how've you been, Chanté?"

I shrieked and threw the ice cream at him. He ducked; Karen covered her face and screamed. The ice cream hit the wall right over his head, but it splattered all over her face.

I sneered at Karen, waiting for an explanation, something that would justify what was going on.

Karen wiped her face and held on to her righteous scowl.

My voice broke loose. "Karen, you ain't shit."

"Look who's talking," Karen shot back.

My hostility turned to Tammy. "Did you know about this?"

Tammy finally closed her mouth, shook her head, slow and loathsome. She said, "Baby, you know I didn't."

I raised my heavy eyes to Karen. I wanted to say a lot of things, but only one word found its freedom: "Traitor."

That pure white wedding dress was still hanging in her hall, protected by a sheath of cheap dry-cleaner plastic.

My legs wanted to run, but I held on to a corner of my sanity and
walked out the door. It was a strut of dignity, but I was crumbling
with each step. Behind me, I heard Tammy say a few unkind things to
Karen and Craig before she followed.

The door slammed hard behind us.

# 38 Stephan

I said one word: "Brakes."

"Well, do you have time to fix them for me?"

"I'm at work. I hadn't planned on coming into L.A. until the
weekend."

"In other words, you're telling me that it's Tuesday, and I'll have to
wait all week to get you to come out and look at my brakes?"

I sighed. People always call when they want something.

I asked, "Where you at?"

It was after lunch and I was in my cubicle, on the phone talking to
Samantha. She was at work and had called me in panic mode. Told me
that for the last day or so she'd heard a faint squealing, a scrubbing
sound coming from the back of her car. The faster she went, the louder
and faster the noise. When the car stopped, the noise stopped.

She said, "I'm still at work. Should I drive it home or have it towed
to a mechanic?"

"You can drive it."

"It's overcast. What if it starts back raining?"

"It'll be good enough to drive home. That noise is just your brake
sensors letting you know you need to replace your pads."

"Pads?"

"Brake pads."

"Come over and fix them for me."

"I might can swing by tomorrow. Maybe the next day."

"Why not this evening?"

"By the time I get off work it'll be too dark."

She paused. "Come over anyway."

"For what?"

Tenderness peppered her tone. "I've missed you, Stephan."

I let some quiet fill the line before I spoke again.

I said, "That sounds cool. I could take a half day and fix your car in the morning, if it's not raining too bad."

"Or we could take the day off and hang out if it is."

Samantha had called me and started talking like there had never been a break, no kind of lapse between us.

When it came to women, it was a season of confusion, heading toward famine. Chanté hadn't returned my phone calls, and from the dirty expression on her face the last time I saw her, that was history. I wasn't in the mood to go out and meet somebody new because I didn't feel like starting from ground zero. So that made Samantha's offer look damn good.

But I should've listened to the howling winds. They were predicting a storm.

Samantha opened her door, stood there in her jeans pants and shirt, wearing a diabolical grin. She smelled sweet. I ran my hand across her dark skin, over her short, curly hair. Smiled.

She said, "It's raining."

"Yeah. Not as hard as it was earlier, but it's raining."

"Guess you'll have to fix my brakes in the morning."

"What we gonna do until then?"

"I'll think of something."

She closed the door and gave me one of those serious I've-missed-you kisses and rubbed herself against me. And I'd be lying if I said I wasn't happy to see her. I missed her positive spirits. One glance at her and I was ready to kick myself for not being with her from jump street.

She asked, "Like the changes?"

"Wow. Guess I haven't seen you in a while."

She'd painted one of her walls in the living room from off-white to a hunter green; one wall in the hall was a heartfelt blue; one in the bedroom a mysterious shade of red.

It was too much for my eyes.

I said, "Looks nice."

A table with small cans of paints and brushes and other things she'd been working on was in the dining area, surrounded by books, mostly political science and Anne Rice.

Everything was fine until her phone started jumping off the hook. It wasn't her phone's ringing that bothered me. It was her attitude. She acted as if she didn't hear the phone, and her body language said that she thought her playing the deaf role would make me hearing impaired. I didn't question what was up. I didn't have to because she was all over me.

The sounds of the falling rain faded to a light drizzle.

In the middle of the loving, she leaned over and turned the ringer off. Bad news. When a woman stopped in the middle of sex to do a chore, that was bad news. She ain't with you.

She was distracted and uneasy. And I wasn't really into it because thoughts of Chanté had clogged my mind. I missed her. Actually, if the truth be told, this drive to L.A. in the rain was just a distraction, something to make meaningless hours go by. Chanté was who I really wanted to be with.

But I was here.

And something wasn't right.

Samantha wasn't right.

The lovemaking was perfunctory. It felt more like she was doing me a favor. Her distraught eyes gazed past me, like she was miles away. She had an orgasm. At least she made sounds like she was coming. Just so I wouldn't be confused, she was even kind enough to announce that she was coming. But her face didn't have that glow. Her body jerked, but that didn't come from deep within. It was forced. Faked. Her flesh didn't have the heat that it usually had when she was getting off. After that, it was like she was barely moving her hips, waiting for me to finish. She caught me looking at her, then pushed her face deep into my neck and held on tighter than tight.

I stopped moving. I asked her what the problem was.

She said, "I'm hungry. Haven't eaten all day."

She wiggled until I slipped out of her. Grunted until she got my weight off her. She said, "Let's go to Baja Grill."

"All the way to Marina Del Rey?"

"Yeah. Let's go before the rain starts again."

I pointed at my hard-on.

She insisted, "We can finish later."

"You serious?"

She nudged me out of her bed. Her voice was rushed. "Let's get to Baja before it closes."

"You okay?"

"Hungry. Head hurts because I haven't eaten. Get dressed."

"Can I shower first?"

"Shower?"

"Can I at least wash up?"

"Go ahead, get showered."

"What about you?"

"Hurry, hurry. I'll catch up."

We usually showered together, but this time she pushed me toward the bathroom. After I turned on the water and pulled back the curtains, I noticed there weren't any extra towels in the cabinet or on the towel rack. Looked like she'd cleaned the bathroom up before I got here. I had to step out to get one from the hall closet. She was sitting on the bed, naked, in profile, on the phone, having a whisper-fight. A sneer was carved in her face.

"No!" she whispered. "Well, too bad. Don't. That's your problem. None of your damn business. I can hardly hear you. Why are you on a cellular phone? *What?* I won't be here. I'm on the way out the door right now. I'll be gone all night. Why?"

I stepped back into the bathroom before she eased the phone back into its cradle. She stuck her head in the bathroom door and smiled. "Hurry up. I'm ready to get out of here."

Her composure had dissolved. She kept watching the clock. Chewing her tongue. Waiting for me to finish. I took my time. When I stepped out again, she was hanging up the phone. I didn't hear it ring, so she must've made a fast phone call.

She rushed by me and hurried into the shower.

Somebody banged on the door.

I was naked, rubbing lotion on my skin.

Something was going down. That was anger's kick-ass cadence.

She rushed out with a towel around her, sopping wet, soap sliding down her back, stormed past me and peeped out the peephole. Which was stupid.

A brother yelled, "Samantha, I see your eye in the peephole. It went dark. Open up. It's me."

She didn't answer. She tipped away from the door.

Our eyes met. She lowered her head.

I followed her and kept my voice low, "Who's that?"

He knocked a few times.

She didn't answer. The knocking stopped. Keys jingled. One was put in the lock. Turned. It clicked open. My heart triple-timed. Her eyes bucked, her mouth opened like she was ready to scream, but when whoever was on the other side pushed on the door, the dead bolt kept it from opening.

I was taut, head to toe.

Samantha sighed, sounded like air slipping out the pinhole of a balloon. Sweat was on my nose. The keys jingled like they were being put away. Whoever it was walked away.

"Damn." Samantha rubbed her temples and cursed real low, "Bastard."

"What's up, Samantha?"

Both of us jumped at the same time.

Pebbles were being tossed against the bedroom window. Three or four hit every ten seconds or so. Not hard enough to break the glass, just hard enough to announce that somebody needed some attention before they lost their mind.

She marched in circles. I said her name a dozen times, but she didn't answer. She was in deep thought.

She tippy-toed by me, slid the curtain to the side enough to peep out, bit her lip, and her face contorted. Finally she looked at me, slow and remorseful. She gave some don't-ask-me-any-questions eyes.

"Stephan," her voice was rattled, "can I meet you at Baja?"

"You want me to leave?"

"I need to take care of something."

Samantha peeped out the window again, saw the coast was clear, then speed-walked to the front door. She wanted me to hike up the stairs, stay to the wall, and slip down on the other side farthest away from her apartment.

She wrung her hands. "If you don't mind."

"I do mind."

"Okay, you want me to beg, then I'm begging."

"Who's banging on your door?"

"Stephan, *please*."

"Not leaving until you tell me."

She trembled. More pebbles danced against her window.

She said, "This guy who wants me to marry him."

"Marry?"

"Yeah. Marry."

"So, you've been seeing him?"

Her eyes shifted. "Kinda."

"What the hell is kinda?" I said.

"Well, yes. I did let him spend the night, before—"

"Sleeping with him?"

"Don't do this, Stephan, okay?"

"I'm laying up in bed with you and somebody's banging on your door, has a key, is waiting for you outside. For all I know, the fool could have a gun—"

"He does have a gun."

"What? Call the police."

"Can't."

"Why?"

"He's a police officer. LAPD."

"Great. A legal gang-banger with a gun and radio."

"He gets hostile sometimes."

"Well, that makes me feel a lot more at ease. How long have you known him?"

"Eight years."

"Eight years?"

"We used to live together."

"You used to live together?"

"Stop repeating after me."

"I'm not repeating after you."

"You are."

"I'm not."

"Don't do this."

"Somebody might be outside ready to blow my brains out and all you can say is, 'Don't do this'?"

A series of thumps came from above. On the roof.

Samantha said, "Rain. It's only the rain."

Sweat was on her forehead. She ran her hand over her hair.

I said, "That's who answered the phone when I called?"

She blinked hard, answered with a soft sigh, "The only reason I started seeing him again is because you haven't been around. You're hot and cold. Either you're my man or you're not. I'm human. Shit, I get lonely sometimes, waiting for you to call or to call me back."

"I get lonely, too."

"Give me a break," she snapped. "I don't think so."

"What does that mean?"

"Stephan, I'm not stupid. I still remember when your friend Dawn said that it was nice to see me again, and we'd never met. How do you think that made me feel?"

I massaged my forehead. "Dawn made a mistake."

"You better believe she did. A mistake that changed everything between me and you."

"You act like you're the only person who gets lonely."

"Yeah, but you only call when you get lonely. You aren't concerned about me. If I call you when I'm bored or just want to spend some time, you can't make it for one reason or another."

"A madman is outside your door, with a cannon strapped on his hip, waiting for you, and you're trying to trip on me?"

Samantha looked me in the eye and said, *"Dog ass nigga."*

"What?"

"Does that ring a bell?"

She knew. My eyes said that I knew what she meant.

She explained. "I took off work that Friday and ended up out your way at Ontario Mills. On the way back, I stopped by your place, thought maybe we could do something, and saw that message on your door. I saw it. Bold red letters. Straightforward. Easy to read. And that hurt. It told me a lot more than you'd ever tell me. That's why I ended up with Keith that night."

Pebbles hit her window. Thumped like an irregular heartbeat.

She asked, "Why so quiet?"

I shook my head.

She said, "I've been dogging him out because of you. And you've been dogging me out. Vicious cycle, huh?"

I was numb. "What do you want to do?"

She stood and held herself.

I asked, "Want me to meet you at Baja? Go ahead and shake him, then we can hook up later."

"No."

"What do you mean, no?"

Her voice softened, trembled. "I want you to get the fuck out of my life. Don't come back, not even if I call you crying."

I gathered my things, packed up my remorse without arguing.

Samantha locked her door behind me.

My thoughts were still on Chanté, on that door that she'd locked behind me as well.

With my gym bag over my shoulders, I dodged the rain that was coming down, walked upstairs. When I crossed to the other side, an apartment door opened. Two sistas stepped out. Both had to be in their twenties, dressed in heels, jeans, iridescent tops.

I gave a friendly smile and said, "How're you ladies doing?"

"Fine, and you?" That was the short sister. She was shaped like the Liberty Bell, had healthy breasts and a southern accent so thick I thought she had a speech impediment.

The tall sister with the butt-length blond spaghetti braids looked as happy-go-lucky as Forrest Gump.

Before I could stray two steps they told me their names. The short one was Andrea, the tall sister was Neandra.

I complimented them both, then asked where they were heading. They were going to Aunt Kizzie's for a book club meeting.

A middle-aged yella fella with wavy hair was on the trunk of Samantha's car. Rain was falling on his red-turning-gray hair. His short multicolored rayon shirt was unbuttoned with the tail halfway out. Soaked. He wiped water from his eyes and threw a pebble and hit the glass just as we turned the corner. Then he saw us and jumped up like he thought one of us was the woman he was searching for. Then he went back to tossing pebbles.

I was shoulder to shoulder with the women. As we passed by, he glanced at us, then turned his attention back to the window.

"Keith," Andrea said. "Didn't recognize you out of uniform."

"What's up?" He nodded. His eyes landed on me.

I nodded.

It was the same voice on the answering machine.

He had a leather pouch around his waist. The kind that off-duty officers keep their loaded firearms in. His hand touched the belt, like he was about to go for it. But all he did was drop his head and look at his nails.

I kept on walking with the Liberty Bell–shaped woman at my side. She was the biggest, so she'd be the best shield.

Out of earshot, Neandra smirked. "They're at it again."

Andrea said, "That fool's gonna catch pneumonia."

I asked, "Who's at it?"

"That asshole," Andrea growled. "They were out here two or three times last week arguing. They fight all the time."

Samantha stepped into the lot. She had thrown on yellow sweats, her blue and white sorority umbrella held high. Keith hopped off the car and headed toward her. Samantha looked around, saw me near Andrea and Neandra.

Our eyes met for a moment.

I was pissed off, but I felt sad at the same time. Sad for her, and sad for me.

She stormed back to her place. Keith followed.

I wondered what he would think when he walked inside. Her sheets were tossed. Sex spiced the air. Condom wrapper was in the trash next to her bed.

The kindhearted southern sisters walked me to my car.

Neandra reached into her purse and took out a bone-colored business card. She handed it to me, "Call me."

I responded, "Sure."

I tossed her card before I made it out of the lot.

# 39  Chanté

I ran into Thaiheed at the 24 Hour Fitness in Chino. The gym was nicknamed The Dungeon because there aren't any windows, so except for the front doors, no sunlight could get inside. I was on the front row of Ed's high-impact aerobic class, working to sweat a poison named Stephan out my system, grunting out some of the stress caused by a backstabber named Karen and her cohort Craig, when I looked over and saw Thai standing in the window by the Stairmaster.

He waved. Those gray eyes sparkled when he saw me.

In between doing squats and lunges, I waved back.

He smiled and walked away, headed toward the free weights.

After I finished working my abs in Ed's class, I wiped some of the sweat off my neck and arms, put on my gloves, then headed for the weights too. Worked on my biceps, did a little with my triceps. Thai-heed stared me down in the mirror.

He came on over, and we ended up working out together.

We laughed. Had a good time pumping iron for about thirty minutes or so.

Since I was boyfriendless, damn near friendless, pretty much spirit-less, I needed something positive right about now. One thing I did feel bad about was only seeing one brother at a time. Traditional dating had always been my downfall. Then I wouldn't despise Craig so hard. Then I wouldn't be thinking about Stephan so much. I should've al-ways kept somebody on the back burner.

After the workout, I showered, changed into a Fila sweatsuit. When we met out front, he asked if I felt like hanging out. It wasn't like I had anything special to do. We walked across the lot to Kelly McQue's pool hall.

He took a couple of easy shots, said, "I'm thinking about riding down to Temecula for some wine tasting this weekend."

"Really?"

"I might drive through Old Temecula and eat at that Mexican restaurant that used to be a bank."

"Yeah. We had a good time down there. They have excellent crab enchiladas. You should bring me some back."

"I can do better than that. You want to tag along?"

I shrugged, then surprised myself when I said, "I'll let you know by Friday. If you go Sunday, I might go."

He asked, "Want to catch a movie tomorrow night."

"No can do. Tammy's play is opening tomorrow night, so I'll be on the front row cheering."

He asked, "How're your girls doing?"

A chill ran through me. I wanted to say one of them was getting ready to commit adultery, and the other has been tipping behind my back and sleeping with the brother who shattered my heart, but I said, "Fine. Both of them are happy."

In that breath, I didn't feel too good about my friends.

Or myself.

Or much of anything.

I said, "Let's go somewhere and have a drink."

He smiled. "Sure. Follow me up to Shelly's. We can grab some grub. Have some drinks."

And drink we did.

An hour later, both of us were eating seafood pasta and tipsy. Sipping wine, eating seafood. Talking. Flirting.

Thaiheed had moved to another apartment off the 210 in Duarte. He wanted to show it to me, because he said there were some houses on the market up his way. So I left my car at the restaurant and rode home with him. His excuse was lame, but I didn't feel like being alone.

Thaiheed's place wasn't too far from Raging Waters. He had it fixed up like a romantic home, a peaceful chateau. Hand-carved African statues made of ebony and soft woods. Busts from Haiti and Kenya.

I told him about Stephan.

He said, "So, he's your man?"

"Nope. Just a friend. Even less than that now."

I told him what had happened at Stephan's parents' house.

Thaiheed said, "He played you."

He said what I was already feeling inside.

Thaiheed was playing me close too, telling me how much he'd missed me. Apologizing for that ordeal with Peaches.

We started kissing. Not because I believed him, I just wanted to be kissed. I didn't necessarily want to kiss *him* though, so I closed my eyes, let the buzz from the alcohol take over, and pretended he was somebody I wanted to kiss.

We lay down on the leather sofa.

I wanted to just be held until I went to sleep. He wouldn't go to sleep. He wouldn't stop kissing me.

One thing was leading to another.

Tammy was leaving, so I wouldn't have her in my corner for a long time. Karen's backstabbing ass wasn't my friend anymore.

I felt so alone. So sad.

Thaiheed didn't waste a moment getting naked.

I was stripped to the bone, bare, except for my panties.

I didn't feel comfortable. It didn't feel right. I told him to grab a condom and wrap up that pickle.

All of a sudden, I wasn't tipsy anymore.

I don't know what I was thinking about, but I tried to push him off me before anything could really happen. I couldn't go through shit like this over and over again. He wouldn't move, so I stuck my nails in his back, whapped him upside his head. He fell off me cursing and plopped on the floor.

He yelled at me, "What's your damn problem?"

I focused, tried to explain to him how I felt about Stephan, how I felt about what I was doing to myself, let him know that sex wasn't why I came over, explained to him how I *didn't* feel about him. When I was putting my clothes back on, he started roughhousing me. He grabbed my bra and threw it across the room; took a strong hold on my wrists; pushed me around.

"Thaiheed, I'm not playing with you."

"You gonna let me waste a condom?"

I wrenched my wrists free and shoved him. I yelled, "Stop."

He snapped, "Why you change your mind?"

"Because," I told him while I grabbed my sweatsuit. "I'm just trying to get back at Stephan."

"Then get back at him, then."

"It don't work like that, partner." I yanked on my sweat pants, my T-shirt, my jacket, grabbed my cross trainers. I demanded, "Take me back to my car."

He flipped out and tried to tear my clothes back off me.

I yelled at him, "What's wrong with you?"

"What's wrong with you? You owe me."

"I owe you?"

"All that damn money I spent on you. Loaning you money to get this done to your condo, to pay for that, all the gifts I gave you, the drinks I've bought for you and your friends—"

"Let me go."

I broke free and started throwing stuff at him. Knickknacks from Africa. The lamp. He growled, came at me like he was Jack the Ripper. His gray eyes had darkened. Lines popped up in his forehead. I was scared as fuck of that wild animal expression, but I told myself to get out of this jungle and be scared later. He grabbed me, and before I could get loose, we were wrestling and he ripped my Fila jacket. I grabbed between his legs, squeezed and twisted like I was trying to make orange juice.

He begged me to let him go.

I squeezed harder, growled, "You let me go, I'll let you go."

"Okay, okay, all right. Don't twist 'em, don't—"

The short bastard let me loose.

And I took my time about letting go of his family jewels.

The moment I let go, the maniac lost his damn mind and attacked me again, ripped my jacket some more.

I was screaming and scratching. I got loose and made it to the phone on the wall in the kitchen. I picked it up and dialed 9-1, and dared his ass to make a move toward me, or I'd dial the last -1. He backed off, then I put the phone down. I was huffing and cursing. Sweating like I was back in aerobics. He apologized a thousand times. But as soon as I smashed the phone in the receiver and raced for the door, he cut me off and hit me in my face with his fist.

I screamed, "Oh, no. *Hell*, no!"

I raced for the phone, but he beat me to it that time.

I ran into the kitchen and grabbed some of his cutlery knives. The big ones. By the time he caught up with me, I had two blades in one hand and one in the other. He got bad and dared me to cut him. That was all I needed to hear. I swung and he tried to block me with the cordless phone he had in his hand. But my knife cut into his flesh. When he felt that blood squirting out his hand, he dropped the phone and backed off.

"You cut me!"

"Damn right."

"Get away from me."

"Negative," I shouted. "In five minutes one of us will be dead as hell, and it ain't gonna be me."

I chased him all through that apartment, had him diving over counters, throwing pillows, yelling like a punk. Blood was dripping everywhere, getting on the carpet and everything he touched. He yanked the venetian blinds down, then tried to open the window and jump out.

I yelled, "Go ahead. Jump out from the third floor."

"Chanté, back off. Leave me alone. Okay, okay, you win."

"Oh, no, partner, this party ain't over."

I went after him.

He turned over furniture and tried to get away. Wherever he darted off to, I was there, knife first. He ran into the bathroom and tried to slam the door before I could catch up, but I managed to get one of the blades between the lock and the door jamb, slid it up and down, poked it at him, and tried to slice and dice his hand off.

He screamed, "You're crazy."

"You think I'm crazy? Step back out, I'll show you crazy."

"I'm bleeding. I need an ambulance. Chanté, please."

"Nobody hits me. Fool, don't you know I'm from Chicago?"

Finally he managed to wrestle the door closed.

I went into his kitchen, shaking like a leaf in a windstorm, poured a glass of bottled water, pulled a chair up to the hall that faced his bathroom, sat down and thought of how in the hell I was going to get out of his place.

He cracked the bathroom door.

I slung a knife at him.

He ducked and slammed the door. "C'mon now, I'm bleeding."

Knifes were stacked at my feet, one in my hand. My hair was all over the place. Eyes darker than a quarter past midnight. Every time he opened the bathroom door, I charged and did a Zorro move, made the air *swoosh* and *swish*. He slammed the door, whined and begged for me to let him come out.

That was where I left his punk ass.

By four a.m., we were leaving the emergency room at Queen of Angels. I'd paged Tammy 9-1-1 and she'd come down from Hollywood and rescued me from the streets of San Dimas. She'd just gotten out of rehearsal, still had on a pair of black nylon sweats. Now, thanks to me, both of us were up all night. Before she carted me to the hospital, I had gone home and taken off my ripped-up sweatsuit, put on something decent, changed to jeans and a light blue blouse.

I apologized to Tammy forty-eleven times. Tonight would be the opening of her play, and I was giving her grief and stress, the kind that could steal all of her creative energy.

She patted my hand. "Shush. You're going to be fine."

"Does my eye look bad?"

"It doesn't look as bad as you make it sound. A little Fashion Fair will make you look good as new."

My black beeper was vibrating nonstop.

I said, "That jerk is still calling me."

We stopped by a pay phone after I picked up my prescription at Sav-On. Thaiheed cursed me out. I told him that I had talked to an attorney, had my ripped-up clothes bagged and tagged, taken pictures of my face, and had been to the hospital. So far the only true part was the hospital. Other than being pissed off to my highest degree of pisstivity, nothing was wrong with me.

"I'm standing outside the police station getting ready to file assault and attempted rape charges."

"What?"

" 'What' ain't what I said."

"Things got out of hand. I'd been drinking, you'd been drinking."

"No, you got out of hand. Who gave you the right to grab on me like you owned me? What part of *no* didn't you understand?"

"I apologize. You right, you right. I shouldn't have—"

"Now, that's a better attitude." I touched my face. "I'm going to show the police what you did. Nobody touches my face."

"Why're you going to the police?" he said. The nervousness in his voice let me know who was in charge. "This is between me and you, right?"

"You hit me. I'm filing charges."

"Why you want to do that? We can sit down—"

"Keep away from me," I warned. "I want you to pay me for my clothes. Today. Right now. I went to the emergency room and they looked at my face. I could've lost my eye. How am I supposed to go to work looking like this, like a damned raccoon and have everybody asking me questions? I want the five hundred for the doctor's bill too. I want it now."

"What about my hand? I had to wrap my hand up and drive myself over to Pomona Medical Center and get seven stitches. You broke half of my African statues."

"Go to the swap meet and get some more."

"Blood's all in my carpet and on my furniture."

"Whoopty-doo."

"Who's going to pay for that?"

"*You.*"

"Chanté." He groaned. "Come on. Be reasonable."

"That's more reasonable than going to jail, don't you think?"

"All right, all right."

"I'm coming to get it now. Have it ready."

We drove to his place. Tammy went to his front door while I waited in the car. He wrote a check for fifteen hundred dollars, just like that. He begged Tammy to convince me that it wouldn't be necessary to go to the police.

"Bastard," I said.

Tammy hadn't said too much since she'd picked me up. She whispered, "Keep your hand off your eye."

"How did he look?"

"Scared as hell. You messed him up *real* bad. His place looks like a tornado came through holding hands with an earthquake. But he'll survive."

"If he's still breathing, it wasn't bad enough."


# 40  Darnell

When I made it home from the FAA on Wednesday evening, Dawn had on ragged socks and her housecoat. A shower cap was on her head, and she was in the kitchen rubbing ice on her face. She'd called me at work and told me that our weekday plans had been modified. A couple of her friends were coming along as well.

I asked Dawn, "What are we doing tonight?"

"We're hanging out with my friends. Is that a problem?"

"No, I just want to know how to dress."

"Jeans and a nice shirt."

"California casual."

"Dress like we're going to a movie. Be comfortable in case we decide to go to Santa Monica and walk the promenade."

"Santa Monica on a weeknight?"

"It's not against the law, is it?"

"Not at all. It's just a long drive."

"Hurry and get ready."

"Where are my—"

"Your jean shirts are in the walk-in closet."

"When did you—"

"I picked them up from the laundry yesterday."

"How—"

"Thirty-eight dollars for all of your clothes."

"Thanks."

"Hurry, Darnell. My friends'll be here by seven. I want you ready then."

"What friends?"

"Just be ready."

The surprise friend was Charlotte. She showed up right at seven with a date. A doctor. Tall, nerdy-looking. Smiling like he was happy to be with her.

Everybody was in jeans. Charlotte had on a nice, colorful blouse. Charlotte's date had on a plain-wrapped, pink polo shirt. I had on a jean button-down collar.

Dawn came out in a dress, the colors of sunrise and sunset in the material. It was tight, showed her figure. Her dark hair was down, thick and long, in a straight style. Makeup done perfectly.

Charlotte playfully remarked, "Miss Thang, I didn't know that you were going to outdress us."

I said, "Thought you were wearing jeans."

"I never said that."

We were all in the living room. Laughter bubbled up. Jovial sounds that echoed with the facade of happiness. Two different brands of perfume. Two fragrances of cologne. The odor was so thick a match could set the air on fire. Dawn put on her real estate hat, that proud homeowner smile, and gave our guests a tour of the house. I tagged along and tried not to yawn.

When Charlotte's date stepped into the bathroom, she separated from the pack and asked me, "Have you heard from him?"

*Him* meant Jake. Her eyes misted when she spoke of him. She didn't want to say his name. I shook my head. "Have you?"

"Flowers and phone calls."

We said nothing for a moment. She looked sad, confused.

I asked, "Are you going to see him?"

She shook her head. "The good thing about this is that everybody knows. That forces me to be accountable for my actions. He has to be accountable for his."

"Yeah, everybody does know."

She had a hard time saying it, but she did. "Dawn turned me on to an attorney. One of the guys you went to law school with. I didn't want to come to you because—"

"I understand."

"I had him served papers. They served him at the fire department."

"Wow."

"I didn't want to do it that way, but he was never at home when the process server went by."

"Everybody's going to know."

"Everybody needs to know. I've filed a restraining order."

Dawn and the date walked up. Charlotte threw on a Miss America smile, and we changed the conversation. Her nerdy friend saw my degrees on the wall, and we talked about what schools we had "matriculated" from. We'd surpassed the level of graduation and were in the realm of matriculation. Word by word, we drifted back into the land of the superficial.

Charlotte perked up and said, "Nice crib-ola, peeps, but we better get on the road or we're going to miss the beginning."

I asked, "What time does the movie start?"

The nerd said, "What movie?"

I said, "We're going to a movie, right?"

Charlotte smiled. "We're going to opening night at a play."

My heart sped up. "Really? What play?"

Charlotte held onto the nerd's arm and laughed. "Don't tell me that Dawn changed the plans and didn't tell you?"

Dawn joked, "He never asks anything. Darnell walks around with a blindfold on, seeing what he wants to see."

I asked, "What's the name of the play?"

Dawn smiled. "*Who Will Be There for Us*. It's at the Hudson. On

Santa Monica near Highland. It's the one that the sista who's in the orange juice commercial is in."

Silence.

She held on to her false grin and came to my side, spoke with bogus cheer. "Didn't I tell you?"

I shook my head. "No, sweetheart, you didn't."

Dawn added, "She's a friend of Darnell's. What's her name, sweetheart?"

Our eyes locked.

I pushed my lips up into a smile. "Tammy."

She asked, "Do you already know the way to the theater, or will you need a Thomas Guide?"

"I'm quite sure you have the directions."

She kissed me in front of everybody. I smiled in front of everybody. Once again we were the happy buppies. But when we made it to the car, we'd talk with tongues of fire.

Outside, Charlotte and her nerd were heading for their Mercedes when Dawn said, "Charlotte, why don't you and your friend ride in my Range Rover with me and Darnell?"

Charlotte said they didn't mind driving, but Dawn insisted they ride with us. Charlotte gave in without a word. That way I couldn't say anything, at least she hoped I wouldn't. And I wouldn't. She knew me too well. With Charlotte's date being there, they couldn't talk about Jake, either.

Somewhere between here and there, Dawn said, "Why're you so quiet all of a sudden, sweetheart?"

"Just listening to the music."

"Radio's not on."

"Music inside my head."

Charlotte and her friend laughed.

My insides were hot, but Hollywood was much cooler, following the typical pattern of the desert climate. Thong bikini days and light jacket nights.

We parked on a side street in a three-dollar lot. At least fifty people were in line to get tickets. Some were dressed up, some were dressed down, some were hardly dressed at all.

As we passed by the crowd and made our way to Will Call, I saw Chanté walking into the theater. Her casual suit set looked so tame: a white sheer silk blouse and matching wide-leg drawstring pants. She gave a quick wave, lowered her face, checked her watch, and moved on. The way she checked her watch made me think she did that just to break eye contact.

It felt like I was in the middle of a conspiracy.

We reached the marquee with the pictures of actors and actresses in the play. Dawn's eyes went straight to Tammy Barrett's head shot. My wife made some unidentifiable noise. Like something a creature made right before it attacked.

She said, "Her initials are TB. Like the disease."

"Don't be tacky."

She took my hand. "Damn, it was just a joke. Her bio says she just finished a McDonald's commercial. She's done a lot."

"Yeah, it says she has."

"And she's still struggling, I bet. This place is nice, quaint, but it's not exactly Broadway. Not even close."

Dawn wouldn't let go of her criticism. She added, "Most people in this profession aren't realistic. They look for a lump sum instead of working on a true career."

"Sort of like writers, huh?"

The house lights flicked on and off, letting everybody know the show was about to start. We filed into an L-shaped theater that was big enough to hold ninety-nine people. It was intimate. So small that everyone could see everyone. No way to hide. Not from anybody in the audience. Not from anyone on the stage.

Dawn said, "The stage is bare. What, no budget?"

"You have to use your imagination."

"This will be interesting."

"Just like I do when I'm writing. You have to open your mind and imagine something that's not there."

"Like some people do in a marriage."

"Yeah. Like in a marriage."

"I was hoping you would disagree."

A spotlight hit the center stage, and a comedian came out and opened the show. Jokes about entertainers, weaves, Jheri curls.

Ten minutes later, the comic had loosened up the crowd, and he left to a huge applause.

It was dark. A total eclipse of the sun.

Then a light, like a single star shining down.

Her voice came first. Then others blended in. Melodic, chanting out some spiritual chords, asking for help from above.

Laughter, street sounds, subtle changes in the lights.

Tammy was the first person to enter the stage, dressed as a homeless character. Gloves with the fingers cut out, ripped polyester pants under a tattered dress, one three-inch high heel and one tennis shoe.

The audience fell under her spell, her magic.

Dawn held my hand tighter, leaned her body into mine.

Tammy's ridiculous walk and belligerent attitude had the audience rolling already. She hadn't said a word. She rushed to the edge of the stage and broke the fourth wall by getting in a woman's face and asking, "What y'all laughing at?"

It took the laughter a couple of minutes to die, because whenever it would diminish, Tammy spiced up the sarcasm by cutting her eyes at somebody else. She got in Chanté's face, was nose to nose with her friend, and did the same.

The laughter was reborn.

The place was small. The lights weren't that low. I know Tammy saw me. Dawn had made sure we had front-row seats, center stage.

Intermission came an hour later. Chanté glanced our way, saw me, but stayed in her seat, almost as if she didn't want to cross paths with anyone who knew Stephan. Dawn led the group back out to the lobby, where people were standing around, chattering about the play, reading the actors' bios.

During the last act, Tammy strutted across the stage in a risqué red dress. She brought her dress to life with her wicked walk. Her homeless character had become rich and she'd come back to the ghetto to help some of her downfallen people. A bit contrived, but a well-meant message.

Tammy did a spiritual up-tempo solo during the closing number. She lived inside the music. The spotlight followed her as she sang her way through the audience, touching and shaking hands.

Everyone was good, but in my eyes Tammy was the show. The way she moved. One moment she'd had the crowd laughing so hard they could hardly breathe, then next on the verge of tears. Dawn felt that power. I could tell by the way she held on to me. Even if she denied it, she couldn't ignore the way her friends had laughed uncontrollably, how people had popped out Kleenex and dabbed their eyes when it was crying time.

Tammy went down the row, smiled and sang right in Dawn's face. Dawn had to shake her hand. Had to smile when she did.

The cast joined in, held hands, sang along, took their bows.

When the lights went up, the applause was strong. Dawn's unblinking eyes, her halfhearted smile lived on Tammy. They drifted across the other actors, but Tammy had her attention.

Most of the crowd started leaving, but quite a few people were hanging around. I tried to lead our pack out of the theater, but Dawn didn't let us get two feet from our seats.

Dawn told our group, "Let's wait."

I asked, "For what?"

"So we can meet the people in the play." Dawn became group

leader and said, "Don't you guys want to hang for a few and meet the people in the play? At twenty dollars a ticket, they should be happy to sign our programs for us."

Dawn playfully nudged me. "Don't be rude and leave. Don't you want to tell your friend how good she was? You were tee-heeing and ha-haing, smiling and falling over laughing at every joke, so I know you want to thank her."

One of the actors came out. People applauded. He went to his friends. Actresses came out. More applause. Then Tammy appeared. She'd changed into a pear brown skirt, a tan blouse.

Everyone applauded, except Dawn.

She'd created this situation, now I was willing to play it through. Chanté was the first one to take her smiles and hugs to Tammy. That was when I noticed Chanté's eye was bruised.

Tammy's eyes drifted our way, her eyes smiled, then went right back to her friends.

Dawn held my hand and we all filed that way, weaved through the crowd, went straight to Tammy and her group.

Tammy was being silly, accepting compliments and flowers from her friends. "Tank you berry mucho grande taco bell."

Dawn chiseled her way into the conversation. "Chanté, I'm surprised to see you again. What in the world happened to your eye?"

Chanté said simply, "I bet you are. I slipped and bumped it, that's all. Hey, Darnell."

Dawn was watching without looking, waiting to see how we reacted to each other. I wanted to take Tammy's hand. Wanted to hug her. Wanted to kiss her and make her vagina shudder with desire to feel me living deep within.

Tammy smiled. "Darnell, hey, buddy. Surprise, surprise. I'm so glad you could make it out here to the 'Wood."

I told her, "You were great."

"Hush. How's the writing coming along?"

"It's coming."

She hugged me, told everybody else who was in our space, "Everybody, listen up, this is Darnell, the guy I was telling you about who is writing a novel."

One of the actresses said, "Oh. The *brilliant* writer."

A few people laughed, shook my hand like I was the man.

When Tammy let me go, Dawn took my hand again, pulled herself up so close I couldn't tell where my face ended and hers began.

I shifted, told Tammy, "This is Dawn."

She shook Dawn's hand and said, "So nice to meet you."

"Likewise," Dawn said. Her handshake was brief, all business, then she took her hand back and hooked it around my arm. "I've heard a lot about you, Tammy."

"Your husband is so very talented. Have you read his book?"

Dawn's plastic smile was there. "Not yet."

I said, "Dawn skips over me to get to Sue Grafton."

Everybody laughed.

Dawn slipped in a question, "Where did you and Darnell meet?"

"I was singing at a club . . ." Tammy made a subtle face of thinking. "Oh, yeah. His friend Jake was trying to get my phone number, and somehow all of us started talking about writing. Well, not all of us. Anyway, Darnell knew what he was talking about."

I had cut my eyes toward Charlotte when Tammy made that comment regarding Jake. At the mention of his name, Charlotte grimaced. Her face couldn't hide what she felt. Then she gestured for her date to follow her outside. No matter where she went, something to do with Jake was there.

I asked, "Where's your friend Karen?"

No reply.

Tammy stood in my wife's face and said, "Dawn, listen, me and Chanté are going to pop in the coffee house and chitchat with the cast for a moment. Why don't you hardworking people come hang out with us starving artists?"

Their smiles were sturdy, eye contact was strong. Reading.

Dawn declined, said she needed to get Charlotte and her friend back to our home.

Chanté touched the bruised side of her face, said some things. The conversation changed, other people took over, more laughter came and went. Then we were leaving. Tammy was in front of me. I kept my eyes to the ground to keep Dawn from being able to accuse me of any wrongdoing.

Dawn went with me to get the Range Rover. I was going to circle the block, then pick Charlotte and her friend up out front on Santa Monica.

Inside the Rover, Dawn told me, "She's pretty."

"There's more to her than a face."

"What do you think about when you're with her?"

"What do you mean?"

"Just the writing? Other things? Tell me. Be honest."

"Dawn, don't start."

"Trust is like sex. Both are best when it's a little painful."

"Dawn, let's not go there."

"Feels like I'm building a sand castle, and you're going to let someone else stomp on my dreams."

"Didn't Tammy answer all of your questions?"

"Tammy's a good pretender, and so are you. But Chanté's as transparent as water."

"Tap water or bottled water?"

"Fuck you."

"Dawn, don't."

"Don't patronize me." Her words came slowly, but with the authority of King Solomon. "I saw it all there. Chanté *knows*. She was too uncomfortable."

"Knows what? There's nothing to know. She was uncomfortable because of what happened at Stephan's parents' house."

"Have you put your hands on Tammy's hips?"

"What do you mean?"

"You know what I mean."

"I'm fat, remember? Why would someone as pretty as she is find a Chubby Checker like me attractive?"

She growled, "Have you fucked her?"

"What's your definition of *fuck*?"

"Okay, Mr. Lawyer. Since you want to play it like that, have you made love to her? Gone down on her? Has she pretended she was Monica Lewinsky and gone down on you? Has she touched your dick? Has she seen your dick? Have you put your fingers inside her?"

I answered all of that with a simple "No."

"If you have, Darnell," she sighed, closed her eyes, sounded desperate, a tone I rarely heard come from her, "we can get past this. I can understand if you're feeling disconnected from me, me not being there when you needed me, that you need something and don't know how to handle the neglect I've been giving you."

I asked, "Why so paranoid?"

"Because I love you. It takes two to make a relationship."

"But only one to mess it up."

"Yes. Only one."

She didn't say a word for almost two seconds. That felt like ten years of peace.

"Pull over, Darnell."

"They're waiting for us."

"Please?"

I did.

"You know what a tort is, Darnell?"

"Of course I do."

"What is it?"

"It's a legal term that mean offenses against people."

"Wrongful acts."

"Yeah, wrongful acts."

"Such as negligence. Emotional distress. No, even better, *intentional* infliction of emotional distress."

I patted the steering wheel. "Just like false imprisonment."

"So is trespassing." She was looking at her wedding ring. "Which is when your ass is on somebody's else's property when you should have your ass at home."

"So, what are you saying?"

Dawn asked, "Have you kissed her?"

"You sure you want me to answer that?"

"Oh, God." Her eyes stared straight ahead for a second. Then she mumbled, "You can't be married and be a Lothario at the same time."

I nodded. "You finished preaching yet, or should I take up a collection and sing 'Amazing Grace'?"

"Jake was the catalyst for this. Jake's foolishness caused this. Well, I'm not having it."

With that, I pulled away from the curb. I was passing all the single-story family homes, getting ready to make two rights and head back toward the din on Santa Monica Boulevard.

Dawn said, "I'm going to tell you something you don't know."

"Which is?"

"I almost left this marriage. When you were in law school, and this didn't feel like a marriage was supposed to feel, I was going to leave you. All you ever needed was for me to help you memorize something, or dub a tape."

"That's what friends do."

Dawn asked, "Does she kiss better than me?"

"I'm not answering that."

"Do you want to lick the honey between her thighs?"

"What's wrong with you?"

"In the game of sex, a kiss is only the first step. I *know* that for a fact. You don't kiss people unless you want to fuck them. They don't kiss you unless they want to fuck you."

I was tense, but I didn't release my anger.

Dawn hit the dash, snapped, "Talk to me, dammit. I'm fighting for my happiness. At least I'm trying. Dammit, I don't know how to fight, not when it comes to shit like this."

"Dawn—"

"I know you're unhappy. You know I'm not happy."

I let it alone.

But Dawn didn't. "I bet you've fucked her and hurt her and made her come and rocked your hips against her ass and banged your balls against her—"

She stopped, shook her head. She gasped, "I don't believe I just said that."

I'd made it around the block and was pulling up in front of the theater. Dawn smiled at the people we were approaching.

Charlotte and the nerd got in, both holding cups of cappuccino. There was no passion in their date. Before the door closed, they were laughing and chattering about the play.

Charlotte glimpsed at me, then turned away.

She knew. Before she came to my home, she'd known what the entire evening was all about. She'd known that she was going to be riding with me.

Right inside the door to the theater, Tammy was standing, talking to others. She looked at me, sending her thoughts toward me, asking if she did okay with Dawn, if everything would be all right for me.

I winked at her.

She winked back.

I talked to Tammy the next morning, bright and early. She told me that she had almost lost it when she walked out and saw me and Dawn in the front row. That was why it took her so long to get to her first line. She went blank and had to improvise.

Tammy said, "Your wife is a very pretty woman."

I didn't respond to that compliment.

She said, "I want to see you."

"Me, too."

"Next weekend will be my last weekend before I go to Paris."

"This weekend?"

"No, the weekend after this one. I'm ten days from Europe."

My insides sank. It felt like part of me was being yanked away. My heart was heavy. I stared at my ring and told myself that I didn't have the right to feel what I did, but I did.

Softly she told me, "My schedule will be hectic. I'll be busy with the play. I'll be packing when I can, selling most of my furniture to friends and neighbors, and that Saturday night will be my last performance with the band at Shelly's."

She paused, let me think that over.

She said, "I'll be near you. Sunday, I'll be on a Concorde flying over the ocean to a new world."

I understood what she was telling me. Our clock was ticking.

With so much feeling, enough to last me for two millennia, she said, "I have to see you the night before I go. If I can't take you with me, I have to say good-bye to you the right way."

I asked, "You want me to come by your place afterward?"

"I'll rent a room nearby the club. Up by restaurant row. There's a Hilton right up the street at the 10 freeway. We're going to be partying, so I know nobody'll be driving too far."

"You're going to get tipsy?"

"No. With you I want to be sober. If your kisses affect me like champagne, then the rest of you will be more than enough to get me super-duper high. I want you straight, no chaser."

"Two Saturdays away, then," I said. "Straight, no chaser."

"Ten more days without you. I don't know if I can take it."

"Seems like a lifetime away."

"Two lifetimes, baby. Two lifetimes."

# 41 Chanté

Tammy hopped to her feet before I did. Maybe because she cared more than I did. She got up so fast, she stumbled. The cheap plastic Kmart chair she was in turned over and bounced on the dark tile floor.

My own chair bumped into the beige wall hard enough to chip the cracked paint. Both of us were startled when we heard the old white man yell out my name. He was flipping through the paperwork I'd filled out as he hurried over toward us.

He looked up at Tammy's statuesqueness, extended his leathery hand upward, said, "Miss Chanté Ellis?"

Tammy shook her head and moved to the side.

He turned to me, said, "Miss Ellis?"

I cleared my throat. "Yes."

"Harold Levis. How are you doing this morning?"

I responded to the mechanical question with a programmed answer, "Fine."

"Come with me."

He wore a single-breasted blue blazer over brown polyester pants and beat-down insurance man shoes. The surviving hair on the top of his head was slicker than the look on his face.

We followed him past a lot of wooden desks, beyond everybody else's stress and depression, and shuffled by other employees who were performing at a snail's pace, talking to their frantic Monday morning clients.

Tammy said, "Damn. This place is crowded."

"The weekend must have been busy," I mumbled.

"Every weekend is a busy weekend for criminals," the man said, then chuckled. "That's why the jails are overcrowded."

I said, "I don't think that's funny."

He responded, "Nobody does."

Tammy sat down in the brown chair in front of his scarred-up wooden desk, which had names and phone numbers inked into the faded wood. I was the actual client, so I had to sit closer to Marlboro breath, in the pleather high-back chair on his left side. He moved a stack of paperwork to the side before he took the final sip of coffee out of a dirty styrofoam cup. He crumpled the cup and dropped it into an overfilled trash can.

"Coffee?" he asked.

I shook my head.

Tammy didn't answer.

"You look young," he said, and sounded like he was getting his flirt on. "Are you an attorney or a paralegal?"

I know he asked me that because of my no-bullshit demeanor and the olive business suit I had on. I was the picture of bitching authority. Tammy's ripped jeans, oversized jacket, and frantic face made us look like lawyer and outpatient.

I answered, cut and dried, "No."

He smiled, exposed his stained teeth. "You look like one."

I cut him off, "Will this take long?"

"I have to explain a few things to ya."

Bozo cleared his throat and explained more about the bailing process than I ever wanted to know. How they charged a ten-percent fee, how the collateral went to the insurance company, how if the bailee skipped bail, a bounty hunter would hunt their ass down.

He said, "If the bailee is exonerated, you'll get your money back in fifteen days."

Tammy spoke up. "Exonerated?"

I supplied the definition. "Innocent."

Tammy sulked. "So much for that."

I asked Bozo, "You talking weekdays or working days?"

"Working days. Now, if you're using personal items as collateral, they will be appraised by street value, as opposed to market value."

I said, "You don't have to keep babbling. I got the point five minutes ago."

Tammy touched me, simply said, "Chanté."

I cleared my throat and said, "If I have a little bit of an attitude, Mr. Levis, don't take it personal."

He laughed. "I won't. Everybody who walks through that door is stressed as hell. I try to make it a little lighter by adding some humor. Sometimes it works, sometimes it—"

"I have the money." I exhaled. "Your recording said you accept cash."

"We sure do."

With mixed emotions I put fifty crisp twenty-dollar bills on the desk. My money. The last bill left my hand, and I regretfully pulled my hand away. I knew I'd never see my money again.

Bozo peeped over the top of his wire-rimmed glasses, pulled the money to his side of the desk, opened a desk file cabinet and took out some forms. The fool blew his nose on a handkerchief and had the nerve to put the refuse back in his suit pocket.

I gagged, felt disgusted and squeamish.

I sat back in my stiff chair and looked at Tammy. Her face was puffy, with mascara-smeared, bloodshot eyes. She'd cried half the night and paced the floor the other half. I know, because she was at my condo and I was blowing snot bubbles and pacing with her, waiting for morning to get here so we could go to Wells Fargo and withdraw the money from *my* bank account.

I had to maintain composure. Both of us falling apart wouldn't do anybody any damn good.

I stared out the window at the Riverside police station.

Tammy was doing the same.

Bozo asked, "First time to a bail-bond office?"

I answered, "And hopefully my last."

I hated being here, hated everybody I saw, just because. And the more I thought about why I was here, the more I wanted to snatch my money back from Bozo and bolt out of the door.

Karen was in jail. Locked up like Manson.

And even though I was doing it, I still didn't know if I should bail the two-faced off-the-rack ho out.

Late last night, Tammy had knocked on my door with the sob story. After being locked up at the free hotel for the whole weekend, Karen had broken down and called Tammy. At first Tammy thought the holier-than-thou heifer was joking. But after a couple of words Karen's hysteria rang through loud and clear. Tammy turned into a wimp and felt sorry for Karen, because Tammy was like that.

I didn't feel sorry for her.

"So what?" I snapped. "I hope she rots."

"We can't just leave her down there."

"*We* didn't put her in there."

Tammy had a head full of rollers and was almost in tears. "She doesn't have any family besides us. You know she doesn't have that kind of money."

"What kind of money?"

"Thousand."

"A *thousand*?" I threw my hands in the air. "How much of it do you have?"

Tammy wrung her hands. "Chanté, you know I'm still waiting for my residual check from the—"

"How much?"

"—commercial. Well, and the play. You know how black folks are when it comes to money. They still haven't paid me, and I'm going to need that money when I go to Paris—"

"Oh, so I'm supposed to just hop up and give that bitch a thousand dollars? She ain't my friend. Evidently she's your friend, so you take up a collection and run and get her."

"You didn't hear her. God, I've never heard her sound like that before. She sounded like she was in bad shape."

"Tammy, you already owe me a few hundred dollars."

"I know, I know," Tammy cried. "Do it for me, please? Just loan me the stupid money, and as soon as I get my check, I'll just sign it over to you, all right?"

"I don't believe you came over here with this noise."

Tammy continued pleading.

I was tired of hearing it. I stormed into the bathroom and slammed the door. I shook my head. "What goes around, comes around."

Tammy's voice said, "Chanté?"

*"How could she let a dog come between us?"*

"Please?"

"She mutilated our friendship."

"Do it for me?"

"She let a man come between us."

"I'll give you my Paris money. I won't go."

"A no-good man at that."

So many other thoughts weighed me down. I wanted to hate Karen, wanted to hate her so much that I didn't care what happened to her.

Tammy was sobbing. "You and Karen are the closest things to family I have."

"She's a Judas."

"Say what you want to say, but Karen has been there for you when you were at your lowest."

"Just like Judas."

"She was always the first one to show up for you. She always stayed, no matter how long it took, and nursed your crazy ass back to sanity."

"Judas, Judas, Judas."

I rubbed the bridge of my nose and fought back confused tears. Damn. Now I was mad at myself because I couldn't stay as angry as I wanted to, or be as cold-blooded as Karen. I rolled off a pound of toilet tissue and dabbed my face. Just like my resistance, my eyeliner was melting.

"I can't let myself cry for a closet ho."

"Chanté?" Tammy tapped on the door. "Please?"

"A dog gets what a dog gets," I reminded myself. "Dogged."

"Pretty please?"

I dropped my head between my legs and tugged at my hair, twisting and stomping my feet as I screamed to be left alone.

"Please, Chanté?" Tammy said real soft.

*"Damn, Tammy will you leave me alone!"*

When I snatched the door open, Tammy's pitiful and wet face greeted my pitiful and wet face.

We hugged.

I said, "You make me sick."

"Then you'll do it?"

"Bank doesn't open till morning. So she'll have to wait in the free hotel till then."

"Thanks. I knew you wouldn't do that to her."

"All right. What did she do?"

Tammy told me what she knew.

Craig had been using the hell out of Karen, had turned her broke ass into a ready teller and was getting her to under-ring all kinds of stuff at Mervyn's. Craig would primp his butt from aisle to aisle and take merchandise from other departments, then drag it to Karen and get her to under-charge it on her register.

The first time it was simple stuff. A shirt for him, a blouse for Karen. Then greed grew.

"Security was watching," Tammy said. "That's the kind of stupid stuff they expect us to do."

Tammy told me more of what Karen had said.

Two days ago, first thing that Friday morning, Craig brought his sister Jamala to meet Karen. They went to her register with Nintendo games, two suits, blouses. Craig told Karen that it was for Jamala, her struggling husband, and two children. The merchandise totaled over a thousand dollars. Karen rang it up for thirty bucks.

Before Craig and his sister could get out of the store, security had cut them off and detained them in an upstairs office. The store manager moved Karen to the side and pulled her cash register tape. Karen said she played naive by looking confused and being too accommodating before she excused herself to the ladies' room and slipped out the back door during the investigation.

A couple of hours later, Craig called Karen from jail. They had arrested him, took him downtown, and he needed her to come bail him out. He promised her he would give her the money back as soon as he got out. She went by her bank, withdrew her rent money from her checking and the little money she'd stashed in her savings account, got a cash advance on a charge card, and made his bail.

Craig walked through the jailhouse doors and checked out. As soon as they set him free, they handcuffed Karen. Arrested Little Miss Felon on the spot. The same grand-theft charges.

They took Karen to the holding cell and handed her change to make three phone calls.

Tammy told me the first call went out to Craig. He said he was on the way out the door to the bank, and wanted her to sit tight for about an hour.

Seven hours later, no Craig.

I interrupted Tammy's flow. "He pulled a no-call, no show."

"That's not funny, Chanté."

"That's a familiar story. At least I know it wasn't just me."

Tammy said that Karen called again. This time loud rap music and a female voice was giggling in the background when he answered the phone. He laughed, cursed Karen out, and hung up.

The third call was to Tammy.

Karen had choked on her words, told Tammy what had happened, where she was, who to call.

Tammy said, "I called the DMV and told them she was sick and wouldn't be in today."

I stormed ahead of Karen and Tammy.

We boned out of the police station and headed to the parking lot. Karen hadn't slept, bathed, or used the bathroom in almost two days, and she reeked like the middle of last week. She smelled so bad that flies were buzzing around her head.

I heard Tammy asking her, "Why didn't you bathe?"

Karen said, "I was afraid of the filth and the germs. There are some perverted, sickening people in there. Prostitutes. Druggies."

I mumbled, "Traitors. Let's not forget traitors."

Her used-to-be-curly-like-Shirley hair was tangled. Makeup was mixed with sweat and tears, and had dried into her face.

Tammy called after me, "Her car was impounded, so we have to give her a ride."

I marched on.

Tammy called Karen, "Come on."

Tammy crawled in the backseat.

Karen stayed silent in the front, leaned close to her window. "I *really* appreciate this," she said. "I can't thank you enough."

"Shut up," I snapped, and threw my car in reverse. My buggy screeched. Tammy flew forward and bumped into the back of Karen's seat. Karen lurched forward and her head almost hit the dash. Once again I wished that she'd flown through the windshield like a crash-test dummy.

I went against the grain of traffic and drove west.

Karen said, "I live the other way."

I snapped, "You think I don't know where you live?"

At my place, Karen made a beeline for the bathroom.

I lurked outside the door, waiting for Karen. The moment she came out, I threw her a fresh towel, pointed toward the shower.

I paced and ran my hand across my bushy hair while I waited, while I listened to the sounds of the running water.

"Chanté?" That was Tammy.

I snapped. "Stay out of this, okay?"

Karen called out, "Where's the toilet paper?"

"Under the sink."

"You have air freshener?"

"Strike a match and open a window."

Tammy let out a worried sigh, then nodded her head. "Don't go ballistic, okay?"

"Stay out of it."

Twenty minutes later, the shower stopped. Ten minutes passed before the bathroom door opened.

Karen stepped into the living room with the towel wrapped around her. I took a slow stroll over to Karen, asked her, "Feel better?"

She shifted, looked away, said a dry "Yeah."

"*I don't.*" I slapped that convict so hard the towel popped away. I slapped her again, then she staggered backward like she couldn't figure out what the hell was going on. I followed and kept on swinging. Every last drop of my anger and hate and hurt that had happened over the last year had moved from my heart and lived in my hands. I hit her again.

Karen found her balance and threw her hands up.

I yelled, *"Put your hands down."*

Karen said a soft, "Sorry, Chanté. I'm sorry, okay?"

*"Move your hands."*

Karen shook, eased her fingers from her face. I drew my hand back as far as I could, got ready to slap her again on the reddest spot I saw, a smack that would echo from here to the Magnificent Mile, but Tammy grabbed my arm and screamed, "You're going too far, Chanté!"

I pushed Tammy back, made that Amazon stumble, and whatever evil she saw in my face made her run to the far side of the room.

Karen was naked in front of me.

Scared of me.

I put my finger in the middle of her forehead and pushed hard enough for Karen to fall back into the wall.

I yelled, "Do something."

"I'm sorry." Karen covered her face. "I fucked up, okay?"

"Don't go soft on me. Come on, Karen, come on."

"That's enough," Tammy whimpered from across the room. "Please stop."

All of us were breathing hard, chests rising and falling.

"I want you to know something." My voice trembled, but it had lowered enough where each of my words didn't bounce off the walls. "Craig doesn't have a sister."

Karen's eyes met mine.

"He's an only child, just like me. He went out with a girl named Ja-mala before I met him. He played you."

Karen picked up the towel, covered herself and her slumping shoulders, turned her head, made some woe-is-me sounds.

I could tell the knowledge I'd dropped on her had hurt more than all the slaps combined.

I massaged my hand and spoke low. "A dog gets."

Karen was trying to pull herself together.

Tammy ran across the room, ran to Karen.

I grabbed my purse and walked out the door.

Thirty minutes later, I was back. Karen was sitting on the floor in front of the patio's sliding glass door, with an ice pack in her hand, rubbing her face on the spots I'd hit her.

She was barefoot, wearing my gray sweats and a NO PROBLEM T-shirt.

Karen said, "I hope you don't mind. I borrowed this because my clothes were, you know . . ."

I nodded.

Tammy was on the sofa, looking all worry-eyed. No music was on. I had come back with a vegetarian pizza and sodas.

I set the food on the dining room table. "Convicts, entertainers, let's get ready to grub. Drama makes me hungry, so everybody wash your hands. I hate eating alone."

I put the food on the dining table, pulled out some silverware, paper plates, cups and ice, and then put both of my hands out to my sides. I cleared my throat, blew air before I said in a raspy, tired voice, "Ladies?"

Tammy crept over and reached for my left hand, but I gave her the right. I gestured, said, "Other side."

Tammy said, "I'm always on this side."

"Other side. Take my right hand."

Tammy hesitated, then changed sides.

I said, "Karen, you coming?"

Karen dragged her fingers through her hair, then came over and held my left hand. I heard Karen's stomach growl.

We bowed our heads in silence. We ate in utter calm.

When the sun started going down and the eastbound traffic thinned out, I hopped on the 60 and drove Karen out to the police impound. She was broke as a joke, so I had to loan her almost three hundred dollars to get her car, then I followed her home.

Tammy had to go to rehearsal.

So it was just us and our tension.

I walked into Karen's place and stood in the doorway. I turned up my nose and fanned. The air in the apartment was spoiled. Foul. Karen had left the bloody wrappings from a package of chicken in the plastic trash. With the desert heat and the closed windows, it had spoiled beyond belief. Ants were all over her counter, crawling the walls.

She grabbed a can of Raid and sprayed them until they drowned.

I stayed glued in the doorway. First my eyes were stuck on that wedding dress that was hanging like a Negro at a lynch party—yes, my thoughts were still vile and violent—then my numb gaze aimed at the daybed I'd witnessed our breach of friendship on.

Bad emotions lived inside me. Too many wicked and intense feelings that when combined could make me snap and go psycho on her ass. God, earlier I'd wanted to do some serious damage to Karen. Had wanted Karen to hit me back, match anger, so I'd have an excuse to go all out, for us to fight until one of us couldn't breathe enough to fight anymore.

Karen said, "I want to talk about it."

"I don't want to hear any of it."

I already knew too much and didn't need to know the details. Something that I'd been trying to get over had resurfaced. The anguish from way back when had returned.

I told her, "Get your phone."

"For what?"

"What's Craig's number at work?"

"He never gave it to me."

"Karen. Don't play me."

"Serious."

"Well, we're going to take care of Craig."

I called March AFB information, got the number for the base information, who in turn gave me the number for the base locator, who, without question or a thought, passed on Craig's work number. It didn't take but a hot minute to find out what squadron Craig was with. A minute after that I had the squadron's orderly room number. The orderly hooked me up with Craig's commanding officer. That was the HNIC—Head Negro in Charge—I was trying to find.

I primed him, gave him the 4-1-1 on what one of Uncle Sam's recruits had been up to, then handed Karen the phone. "Tell him everything."

She did. Karen reported what had happened, in detail.

That sent Craig up the military creek.

This was supposed to be sweet, but it had a bitter taste.

I didn't know if I was getting revenge from what Craig had done to Karen, or what he had done to me, or if I was intentionally putting a rift between them, or getting Karen for what she had done to me.

It didn't matter. 'Cause I was doing it all.

A dog was a dog was a dog.

"Keep away from the base," I advised Karen after she hung up.

"I will."

"Don't talk to Craig."

"I won't."

"He'll fuck you over. But that's up to you."

"Okay."

"Don't talk to anybody but his commanding officer."

Karen nodded. "Chanté?"

"What?"

"That girl Jamala. She was locked up with me. She was bailed out two days ago."

"I rest my case. In the land of the expendables."

Karen asked, "Will you accept my apology?"

"The only thing I'm accepting from you is cash. Outside of all the money I just spent, I had to take a vacation day from work. That's a full day's pay you owe me, sweetheart."

Karen lowered her head. "I'll pay you as soon as I can."

"Did you sleep with him while we were going out?"

"No."

"Do you have the money to pay me back?"

Karen shook her head. "I'll get a check on Friday."

"And your rent is due and you have to eat."

Karen wiped her eyes.

"And you're going to need some time to get back on your feet." I looked around, eyed the black lacquer entertainment center, the Panasonic stereo, the wall filled with pictures of Malcolm X and others. The daybed. I said, "Until I get my money back, you're going to have to give me some collateral. You've already stabbed me in the back, and I'll be damned if I let you twist it. I don't trust you any further than I can spit."

"Okay. Whatever."

"Yeah. *Whatever.*"

"I didn't mean it like that."

"I want your stereo, television, the VCR. Jewelry. CD's. And I want you to carry all of it out to my car. I'll help. If I don't hear from you soon, don't expect to get any of it back."

"Chanté, I'm sorry. Let me explain what happened."

"I don't want to know. It ain't going to change nothing. I don't respect you anymore, and you don't respect me."

"I respect you."

"Karen, I love you and I hate you at the same time." My voice splintered. My saliva felt like quicksand. I barely got my words out. "That bothers me. I'm not gonna let you make me crazy. If you need anything else, don't call me."

# 42  Stephan

Momma asked me, "How was your week, Stephan?"

"Calm. Not too eventful."

"You didn't get that many phone calls here this week."

With a smile to mask my empty feeling, I said, "Good."

"That made Jeremiah happy."

Momma was spending her Saturday feeding the family, boiling a large pot of red-hot smoked sausages for Nathan, his too-cool son Nathan Junior, and big-mouth Akeem. I'd just left the gym, so after I shot the breeze with them, I went into the house. I took off my gym clothes, showered, put on my jean shorts, tennis shoes, and a white ribbed T-shirt, then hung out with my family for a few. I'd done the same thing last weekend. Came up to the house, hung out with my brothers, did some work on Momma's car.

Akeem was running around screaming, "Westside!"

Momma yelled at him, "What I tell you about doing that?"

I grabbed an extra sausage and threw it in a hot dog bun and covered it with relish, mustard, and ketchup. Momma had chopped and cooked some onions, but I passed on those. Pops was asleep in the den, his empty plate on a tray while the television watched him. I went and rubbed him on his head.

He jerked awake with his fist balled up and saw me smiling.

He said, "What I tell you about waking me up? Mess around and get shot like that."

I rubbed his head again.

He said, "Unass me, boy. I get mad, it's all over but the crying."

I rubbed his head one more time, then took his empty plate, and left him to his sleep. I wanted to talk to him. The way a son talked to a father, I wanted to talk to him. Wanted to ask him at what point wisdom moved into a man's life.

Some other time.

Everybody else sat out back on lawn chairs and enjoyed the L.A. sunshine. I was so distracted by my own thoughts I didn't hear much of the conversation that Momma and Nathan were having. Both of them liked to yak it up. I noticed every now and then they'd get quiet and look at me, because one of them had just asked me a question I didn't hear.

"What?" I looked back and forth to find out who had just said something to me.

"For the third time, I said"—Nathan chuckled—"I saw Jake when I passed by the fire station. He told me to tell you hi."

"When?"

"Hour ago." Nathan chomped the last bite. "He was standing out front."

"Doing what?"

"Staring at the sky."

"How's that boy doing?" Momma asked. "I ain't seen him. He usually stops by to say hi. How's he been?"

I answered, "Same as me."

I stopped by the fire station and checked on Jake. After the things he had told me and Darnell about his dreams, I didn't know what to say. But I didn't want to avoid him when his life had become too thick. I saw him before I got to Slauson and Fairfax—he was standing outside shooting basketball in solitude. Seeing him doing something made me feel a little better. Seeing him doing it alone, carving out his space, had me worried. I didn't know how he felt about what had happened to him that night. If he was going to blame me for part of it, even though none of it was my fault.

I parked across from the fire station, in the lot between Mail Boxes Etc. and LA Hot Wings. He saw me coming and threw me the ball. I went in for a slam dunk. It bounced off the rim. He caught the ball before it bounced into the fire house.

"You giving real brothers a bad name," Jake said.

"Legs are dead from working out this morning."

"What you do?"

"I went to the 24 Hour Fitness in the Hilton. Pushed some weights with Dwayne, worked on my abs with Stomach Man, then hit Evelyn Orange's aerobic class.

"A lot of honeys up in Evelyn's class."

"Yeah. It was packed."

He charged at me Michael Jordan style, his tongue dragging the ground and making sparks on the concrete. I tried to cut off his layup, but he made it by me too quick. I got the ball. He guarded me as I tried to drive in, but his defense was too good. I backed off to the edge for a three-pointer.

"How come you ain't called nobody?" I asked, then missed my shot, again hitting the rim. The ball bounced back into the fire house. Nobody went after it.

"Don't know." Jake wasn't sweating, but he fanned his shirt and strolled over to a bench. "I didn't want to weigh everybody down, I guess."

We sat in silence, stared south and watched MD-80s, DC-10s, 747s flying into LAX. A series of police sirens and a helicopter cranked up in the distance.

I asked, "You been sleeping?"

"Some."

"You look rested."

"As rested as I can be, considering."

I asked him, "Dreams not bothering you?"

"Some. But they're different."

"How so?"

"I don't run from them anymore."

A couple of Jake's co-workers came out for a minute and talked some business with him about doing this-and-that in the station. When they saw he wasn't enthused, they walked off.

I asked, "What do you mean, you don't run?"

"I talk to them. We talk. All of us talk."

"You talk?"

He told me that all of his dreams had him cornered, and he stopped being afraid. He sat down and waited for them to do something. They didn't. That was when he started talking to them. First he apologized. Begged for forgiveness. Then started asking them their names. Talking about sports with some of the boys, other things with the girls.

He said, "These voices inside my head, they won't turn off, but they've turned down. Changed from screams to whispers."

I didn't question the sanity of what he was saying.

A sista drove up and parked across the street. A beat later, a brotha came out from the fire station. She unbuckled a car seat and helped a little girl with pink ribbons in her hair cross the street. They made their way over by a shade tree. First he squeezed and kissed his wife, then did the same with his giggling daughter. Then they all hugged and kissed and tickled each other.

Jake's eyes said that that should've been him and Charlotte.

The sista had a package of Chinese food, and they sat across from us on the grass and ate together. They waved at us, then went back to their pocket universe. Fed each other and laughed.

He asked me, "What's on your mind?"

"What makes you think something's on my mind?"

"You look uneasy. Am I wrong?"

"Nah, you're right."

"What going on?"

"Darnell is hooking with Tammy tonight. At a hotel."

Jake chuckled. "Thought he wasn't cut out for infidelity."

I picked my cuticles, sighed. "He's using me as a cover."

"Uh-huh."

"Tonight's the band's last night before they go to Paris."

"So he's gonna get one last ride on the roller coaster before the park closes."

I answered, "Uh-huh."

"Wish I could be up in there. It's gonna be live."

Silence. Chanté Marie Ellis. I was thinking about Chanté.

Jake said, "He's gonna fuck up a good thing. Dawn has her head on straight, works hard, looks good. That book shit he's tripping off on is just an excuse. He'll be sitting with his head low, realizing that it wasn't nothing but a fuck."

I softened my words with a joking tone, "Like you."

"Like me. Yeah, being selfish won't do him no good. All he's doing is digging his own grave. Yeah, we always think the other woman is better than our own."

He appraised me with a glance.

I patted his shoulder, said, "Why don't you give Darnell a call before tonight? Tell him that."

"Nope."

"Why not?"

"Let'm fuck up. You know misery loves company."

We laughed.

Jake said, "I'll give him a jingle. Yeah, wish I could be up in Shelly's tonight. It's gonna be wall-to-wall honeys."

"What's up with you and Pamela?" I asked. "She still on?"

"We still kick it every now and then. But you know how that is. She ain't it. Man, I don't know what I was thinking. Messing with her when I had Charlotte right in my hands."

He started talking about women, his flaws, why he always had to have so many. Through all the years of us hanging out, he'd never been this vulnerable. He opened his heart and wondered. Why no matter how good one seemed, another had to be tested. Each new woman had something to offer that the others didn't. Always trying to trade up to a better woman, even when you had the best one holding on to your arm. Looking for somebody perfect to make you feel complete. He said he wished he could melt them all together and mold the perfect woman he wanted.

I told him, "That wouldn't make any difference."

"Why you say that?"

"She'd be too perfect."

We laughed. It was good to hear him laugh.

He said, "Yeah, you right. She'd be too boring."

"Too predictable. A special perfect woman would be too predictable."

"I have to have a challenge."

"Me too."

"Somebody who can control my ass."

We were fools who didn't mind looking through windows but hated to look in a mirror. We'd both been looking for something new and didn't want to give up nothing old. Minimal investment with maximum payoff.

I wanted to talk to Jake awhile, tell him that my daddy had died all alone. With all of the women he ran, all of the men like him, like us, that my old man shared stories with, when he died there was no one to buy him a grave, or throw a spoonful of dirt on his city-furnished pine box as a token of friendship and remembrance. I wished I could've been there to say good-bye. To jingle the change in my pocket as he was being given back to the earth. Then maybe his leaving me wouldn't have hurt so much.

I never got around to it. After all the years I've known Jake, I still didn't know how to talk to him like that.

He said, "Charlotte is beautiful and intelligent. A brotha's dream. She was a little frigid. Passive. She wanted me to do all the initiating. Made me feel like some kind of freak. Like I wanted her too bad. Or she didn't want like I wanted her."

"She might've been holding back because she knew."

"Guess so. Damn. One bad day changed everything."

I shook my head. "Man, ain't no love for a brother out there on them corners. You have to stay home for that."

He sighed like his life would never be the same.

He said, "The other women were just something to do. Something to make time go by. I was looking, trying to find something better than what I had at home. Than what I used to have at home."

"Always looking for a better offer."

"Always."

"Same shit I've been doing. Toyomi. Brittany. Samantha."

"Hell, don't name every-damn-body." A beat later he asked, "Who you kicking it with these days?"

I shook my head. "Nobody. Just chillin'."

"I tried that once."

"What happened."

"It lasted two days. My dick started talking to me."

We listened to the sounds of the streets. Watched a flock of cute sisters walking into the Cienega Apartments across the street.

Jake flashed his smile, waved at them, then said to me, "I love Charlotte. Not seeing her ain't easy for me. I'd rather have twice the number of dreams than to lose her for a day."

"I know you would. But you can't keep following her around. You can't keep calling her."

With a burdened tone he mumbled, "I know. But I love her. I realize now how much I did. That I do. Damn shame, ain't it?"

"You need to let her be. Set her free."

"Don't do a Jesse Jackson and start rhyming." He sighed, massaged his goatee, and nodded in agreement. He said back when they went to court, Charlotte refused to glance his way. When he called her name, she passed right by him in the hallway, moved by him like he was Casper the Pining Ghost, and hurried into the courtroom. Charlotte stood next to some African guy Jake didn't know—he didn't think he was a boyfriend or nothing like that, more like an adviser—and talked to the judge. A couple of people from Charlotte's job showed up as witnesses. Others signed a notarized statement.

They told the judge about Jake calling all the time, about his coming by the hospital making unwanted visits, upsetting Charlotte and leaving her unable to work. One of Charlotte's friends was dramatic, said distractions like that could leave Charlotte unfocused and cause her to give a patient the wrong medication and have them go flatline.

He said the judge nodded in agreement. People who used to smile at Jake when he'd take Charlotte to lunch had turned their backs on him.

"Man, Judge Son-of-a-Bitch asked me why I was doing this. I told her, and I said it to Charlotte, stood up straight and proud, looked everybody in the eye and said that I loved her, acknowledged I'd fucked up a time or two, and would do *whatever* it took to get back on track. I said it real loud in front of everybody. All Charlotte did was shake her head."

"What did the court say?"

"Told me I can't come within one hundred yards of her for three damn years. Every time I violate the order, I'll get five days at the Sherman Block Inn. Told me if I come back to bring a good lawyer and a toothbrush 'cause that's all I'll need."

"Three years."

Jake told me he had to go back to court next week. The Mexicans were suing him. They'd had a new car and no insurance. A doctor's bill that they wanted him to pay.

I said, "Damn."

"If I don't pay, those bastards might garnishee my wages. Maybe put a lien against my condo."

Again I said, "Damn."

"All of this because of five minutes of pleasure with a big-booty heifer who looks like Jennifer Lopez."

In the middle of his catharsis, the alarm went off. Jake jetted back into the station to suit up.

Before I crossed Fairfax to my car, the fire trucks whipped out, made a quick right, turned left and whizzed down Slauson. They were headed back in the direction that Jake grew up. That scared me. Made me think deadly thoughts. He was heading back toward the area where a fire had made both of his parents angels. Another day, another unforeseen moment that had changed everything in Jake's life.

The truck disappeared. I stared in Jake's direction and mumbled, "Find 'em. Find yourself. I'll try and find me."

On the way home I stopped at Darnell's. He wanted me to help him set up his master plan so he could get away. Dawn was walking the floors, and I was in their office, looking at Darnell's broken scanner. I told him one of the leads was broken.

He asked, "What does that mean?"

"The board is defective."

"Damn."

"I'm joking. All I'll have to do is resolder a new inductor and it'll be good as new. Won't take but a few hours."

Actually, it was a five-minute job, if that. We were loud talking the techno stuff. Doing that for Dawn's benefit.

Darnell was in jeans, a plain T-shirt. I already knew that his clothes for tonight were hidden in his car. He grabbed his keys, the scanner, and I followed him into the garage.

Dawn was right behind us, moving slowly, like she had a lot on her mind, so much that it had weighed her down.

"Darnell?" she said.

"Yeah."

"Leaving?"

"Yeah."

"Coming home soon?"

"I'll be with Stephan for a while."

She asked me, "What are you guys planning, Stephan?"

I paused, then said, "I'm gonna stop by Radio Shack, get the part to fix his scanner, then we'll sit around and talk about Jake."

Nobody laughed but me.

She asked her husband, "How long do you plan to be gone?"

Darnell replied, "Awhile."

She made a sound that said she didn't like his answer. She said, "Can you come here a minute?"

He passed the scanner to me and went to her. They stepped inside the house. I couldn't hear her voice, had no idea what she said. Darnell's face was different when he came back. Anger. Confusion. I don't know what it was. Something that Dawn said had disturbed him to the point of silence.

The garage door was up and I was parked behind his BMW. I'd put the scanner on my backseat before he came back out.

I asked, "You okay?"

"Let's go." He said that abrupt and quick, like he had to leave before he exploded.

Dawn called out, "Stephan?"

"Yeah, Dawn."

"Make sure your friend has condoms. I don't want him bringing nothing home."

She closed the door.

The mailman was walking up as we drove away. Darnell was in front of me. I saw the mailman wave, but Darnell didn't respond.

I followed him up the 60 freeway as far as the Phillips Branch Road exit. I went home to get ready for tonight.

He went to rent a suite and get ready for his downfall.

# 43 Stephan

Nine p.m. came faster than I wanted it to.

There was going to be a lot of trouble tonight.

Heartbreak and embarrassment. But mostly trouble.

I did the three S's. Flossed while anxiety had my insides tossing and turning. Brushed my teeth while my nerves cranked into overdrive. Lotioned up and felt a chill of discontent. No suit tonight. I threw on my olive linen slacks and alabaster white cotton shirt, dark brown belt, dark brown Italian shoes. Headed toward a powder keg ready to blow. All the way my sound system pumped out some sweet jazz by Najee. But not even Najee could mask the sound of discontent crackling in the air.

People were on the walls outside the restaurant, dancing everywhere. The parking lot was packed, trees decorated with ribbons and balloons. Shelly's was more festive than a backwoods juke joint on New Year's Eve.

Darnell's car was parked near the law offices that faced Foothill Boulevard. I parked by his ride, and as I got out, the music jumped into a familiar and dangerous Afro-Cuban groove.

The air crackled with passion, thundered with Tammy's voice.

> See-line woman, dressed in purple,
> watch out man, that woman'll hurt 'cha

Cheers. Laughter. Oooos. Ahhhs.

I saw Chanté as soon as I walked under the ivy-covered pathway. Black skirt, dark blue sleeveless blouse with a wide collar. Wild hair jutting out like she was the Queen of Trend. Silver bracelets. She was at a circular high-topped table, her backside on a black bar stool. Several glasses—some half empty, others half full—were under her nose. There she was, laughing, smiling, touching the shoulders and elbows of the brothers who were at her table, cheesing like life was the best.

The seven days since I've seen her have felt like seven years. And now each moment that I watch her next to someone else feels like twenty-four hours of the blues.

Sistas always looked better, always looked so damn happy after the love was gone. Yep. Absence had definitely made her look better.

She saw me, stopped laughing for a second, turned away, then went back to whooping it up with the men at her table. One of the vertically impaired brothers took Chanté's hand with too much familiarity. She held on and freely bounced up to join in with the crowd's sexy moves, tugging her form-fitting skirt down to decency as she followed.

I stood in the door glaring like a chicken hawk working overtime at Foster Farm.

> See-line woman, wearing a weave
> make a man fall down to his knees

More cheers, a lot of laughter.

Tammy sang to Chanté as she came up front, "*See-line woman, with wild hair, shake that ass, make the brothers stare.*"

Darnell was off to the side. Watching. Smiling. Waiting.

Chanté wiggled close to Tammy and threw down some moves. I watched her break a sweat trying to keep up with Tammy's groove, hoofing it up with a big-ass grin plastered all over her face.

In between finger pops and improvised lyrics, Tammy saw me and waved. Darnell found the time to stop admiring Tammy and waved at me too. My attention was elsewhere. Chanté and her partner were on the floor, his crotch creeping up on her butt, dancing like it was a ritual to a Cucamonga mating call.

She cut her eyes at me, made sure I was watching.

That was all I needed to know.

My grim expression showed my feelings.

Two sisters who were sitting on the wall near the fountain saw me. They sipped wine and mouthed something to one another when my hunt sent me their way. One of the sisters had artificial blue eyes to go with her blonde hair. A wannabe. The other chocolate-flavored sista held onto a c-phone as well as her liquor. I did like Jake always did and sent them an ice-breaking smile. They waved. It was on.

They both spoke. The girl with the phone spoke a little louder. I guessed that was her way of saying she saw me first.

"You from around here?" the one with the blue eyes asked. She smiled and showed a gap between her front teeth.

I glanced back. Chanté's eyes were still on me. I moved closer to the girls and answered, "Phillips Ranch."

The one holding the phone livened up. "Where's that?"

"Part of Pomona. Unincorporated."

"Sounds like a black woman with no money. *Po Mona.*"

They laughed. I didn't. My humor was on hiatus.

"Wyoming, Ohio, is where we're from," Blue Eyes said. She looked me up and down. "We're out for a hair show."

Phone added, "We're beauticians. Staying at the Red Lion."

We talked about that for a few minutes. Laughed. Shared never-ending smiles. Light touches.

Now Chanté was frowning at me like she was the chicken hawk.

Phone said, "Stop by for a drink. Call us. Room 803."

Both had on domineering wedding rings. Each sparkled like a candle. The one with the blue eyes was about twenty-five; the sista gripping the phone looked thirty-something. They were flirty, out of town and out on the town.

The music had changed. The band was playing an instrumental, something for people to cha-cha to.

Blue said, "Somebody is watching you."

Chanté was at her table, glaring. Drink in hand. Legs crossed tight enough to asphyxiate her love. The guy she had danced with was talking to her, but Chanté's attention was with me. She gave a trifling half smile.

I nodded with the same lack of desire.

Chanté hopped off her bar stool, pulled her skirt down, bumped, pushed, and zigzagged through the thick crowd, headed my way. She was moving fast, her sexy stroll fierce.

The women I was talking to stood and adjusted their clothes.

"Don't forget. Room eight-zero-three, if you can make it."

They swayed away, moved past the coffee house and candy store with the rhythms of black cats stalking.

Chanté's shoes click-clopped up to me. She wanted to know, "Who were they?"

"And I'm doing fine" was my stubborn reply. "How are you?"

"I'm okay."

"Your hair looks good."

She touched her mane. "Thank you. Now answer my question."

"Problem?"

"There you go, trying to be suave and debonair. Good thing they left. Now you don't have to introduce me as your friend."

"Whoa. Where did that come from?"

"Like you did when Tsunami stepped up in your folks' house."

"Toyomi."

"She was acting like a tsunami."

"And oh, thanks for leaving me stranded in L.A."

"Anytime, partner."

"That was foul."

"I'll tell you what was *foul*. You know, it really hurt me that *first* you introduced me to Dawn as your date, whatever that means, *then* you told your ex that I was your friend."

"What was I supposed to say?"

"I thought we were trying to be more than just friends. What was all of the nights and days and what-have-you all about?"

I sighed but didn't say anything. The guy that she had danced with was staring us down.

I said, "Who's your admirer?"

Chanté said, "He's buying all of us drinks. It's nothing. He's trying to front like he's a high-roller."

"Weren't you just dancing all up on him?"

"*Negative.* The floor was packed. I was bumped back into him."

A girl passed by, spoke and smiled.

Chanté asked, "Who was that?"

"Girl I went out with a few times."

"She have a name?"

"Gina. Maybe Gloria. I don't remember."

"Damn, partner. Seems like everywhere we go, we run into your ex'es. How many women did you used to go out with?"

"I grew up out here."

"You grew up in Mississippi and Los Angeles."

"You know what I meant."

"The way Dawn talked about you, I hope your reputation didn't get you banished to Pomona."

"No more than yours got you exiled from the Midwest."

"What is that supposed to mean?"

"If we were in Chi-town, I'd run into a lot of your ex'es."

"I doubt that. Did you sleep with all of these women?"

"They were my girlfriends."

"Good thing I only made it to the rank of *friend*. Actually, I think I was referred to as your *date*, whatever that means."

"Well, since you went there. Forget Chicago. How many brothers up in here did you used to date? Seems like I'm the last one in the whole damn club to get a date with you."

Chanté shook her head and grumbled, "Fuck you."

"That's what you did whenever you found it convenient for you, so what's the difference?"

Her mouth dropped open. She started to say something, but instead she flipped me off and stormed back to her table. The moment she sat down, she frowned and popped right back up like she'd been shot out of a cannon, and marched back to me.

"Thaiheed," she snapped, "I don't want to fight with you—"

"My name is Stephan. Or should I wear a name tag?"

Her eyes woke up and her lips crept open. She slowly covered her mouth, shifted her weight from one leg to the other.

She said, "You don't care about anything, do you?"

I spoke soft and definite. "Enjoy the night."

"No, why don't you enjoy the rest of your life?"

"I intend to."

"Fine."

"Fine."

She growled, "Men."

"Women."

"*Niggas.*"

"*Bitches.*"

"Queen Bitch to you."

"Mister Nigga to you."

"Take twelve steps off a f'n cliff, *partner.*"

"Lead the way."

"Not this time. I'm going back inside where a real man who knows how to respect a black queen will be more than happy to ease this misery you've dropped on me."

"You wouldn't know a real man if you saw one."

"True. But he'll know me. A real woman."

With her last word, she turned so fast it took her two feet of wavy hair a few seconds to catch up. Her high heels clicked a pissed-off pace back toward the club and her friends.

She went to the brother at her table, pulled him to the floor so fast it surprised him, started dancing all up on him while she frowned at me. That stung. The blood from my slaughtered heart was dripping down my chest.

I kept my cool, smiled, sent her a shallow "that's cool" nod, turned and decided to walk toward my car. An even-paced stroll that, for the people who were watching, didn't look like a retreat. That didn't look like my constitution was mangled.

But when the music changed to a soft bump-and-grind melody, I did take a chance on turning to stone; I glanced back.

By my watch it was ten-thirty p.m.

Close to showtime. The real show that would light the skies like the Fourth of July.

Darnell was on the floor, holding Tammy, living cheek to cheek inside a fantasy that was about to erupt like Mount St. Helens. I nodded to myself, about-faced, and strolled out into the cool air. With each step, old feelings, old ways that I had tried to suffocate had a jealous heartbeat driven by spite, were coming alive inside me.

This made me take hold of what I wanted to put to the side.

Show no mercy for those who menstruate.

The best way to forget a woman was with another woman. The poison was the remedy. Just like Chanté knew the best way to forget a man was by falling in the arms of another man.

"Stephan."

My insides twinged; I jumped a bit.

That voice was in front of me. Off to the side. I'd been walking with my eyes on the ground so I hadn't seen her.

I was surprised, but then again I wasn't. I said, "Dawn."

She was in the parking lot, lurking between two dark high-profile vehicles, watching the party. A imminent massacre was in her voice, written on her tight lips, stirring to life in the darkness of eyes. She was dressed. Mini skirt. High heels. Sleeveless blouse. Hair down. Perfume tickling the winds. Looking like a queen, but her back was straight like a proud warrior's. She was ready for battle.

She whispered like she was in a trance, "He's with her."

I didn't say anything.

The music was sultry. As I felt the heat and humidity from the lust in the room, I imagined everybody holding whoever they were dancing with a little tighter. Sisters with their heads deep into the necks and shoulders of the brothers. Holding on tight. Eyes closed. Fingers running up and down their backs. Strong hands walking down the curves of satin dresses.

Dawn's distressed expression told me that was what she saw.

"Stephan, I brought all of this on myself."

"How are you gonna blame yourself?"

"Neglect always catches up with you."

I let her words drift into the land of the rhetorical. My eyes didn't look back because I didn't want to see what she saw. A sexy song was humming in the air; the sounds of the sax were seducing the city. Darnell had to be all over Tammy. That would explain the pain in her eyes.

My friend's wife was standing, arms folded. Watching without blinking. As far as I could tell, she wasn't breathing.

Silence breeds a thousand thoughts.

She knew Darnell was here because I'd told her what was up. That wasn't easy for me to do, but I did it. Jake had fucked up part of our friendships, I'd done my share, and I didn't want Darnell to destroy what little was left. I'd told Dawn about the opening night of Tammy's show. It was my suggestion that she crash the party. That's why I didn't go, or show up. I didn't want Darnell to look in my eyes and see the sparkle of betrayal.

"What are you gonna do?"

She said, "It's my problem from here on out. It's Darnell's problem. I'm going to make it Tammy's problem, too."

I headed toward the Red Lion. Angry. Scared. Feeling out of place in my own life. Not feeling too tight about myself. Having that internal battle with integrity. That inner turmoil, that mental struggle was good and bad. Good, because I hadn't had that battle in a long time. Bad, because I wasn't in a fighting mood.

I knew what had to be going on at the club right about now. I saw it all in my mind. My second sight was bombarded with images of Dawn storming through the doors at Shelly's, calling Darnell out in a voice so demanding that everyone would freeze in place, the music would screech to a halt.

In the next moment, pure pandemonium.

I was trying to do the right thing, trying to keep that marriage together, but it left me running low on character. Which made it so easy for me to transfer all of my hostility toward Chanté. Thinking about the way I'd gone off on Chanté didn't help my low spirits either.

Another one bites the dust. Back to ground zero.

Room 803. A place of temporary solace.

I didn't want to go home. Didn't feel like escaping into the city of Lost Angels, either. Maybe I'd hang out in the lobby of the Red Lion with some sophisticated and upbeat women from Wyoming, Ohio, for a few minutes, try to clear my head, then head home and wait for the results from the brawl.

The wannabe diva who had the fake blue eyes answered the phone and knew who I was by name before I'd identified myself. She reminded me her name was Natalie, and her friend's name was Perri. I couldn't remember if they had told me their names at the club, didn't care. From my first hello she was excited to hear my voice.

I asked, "You ladies coming back down to the bar?"

"Come on up, Stephan."

"You sure?"

She laughed. "We were hoping you'd come see us."

Back inside my mind, more images flashed before me. I could see Darnell trying to get in between Tammy and Dawn. Hair being pulled from two different directions while he was getting scratched and slapped and kicked like a piñata on Cinco de Mayo.

Natalie, the dark and radiant full-figured sister, was still dressed when she opened the door. A beautiful, warm smile. She hugged, pulled me deep into her healthy bosom like we were old friends.

I'd never been with a big woman.

The suite was huge. Presidential. All the curtains were opened, and moonlight gave the place some serious atmosphere. Still, my mind was at Shelly's.

Natalie told me, "Perri just got out of the Jacuzzi."

"Downstairs?"

"There's one in the bathroom."

"Must be nice."

"You can get in, if you want."

"I don't have any trunks."

"We don't wear clothes."

"Skinny dip?"

"Is there any other way?"

I laughed.

She asked, "You shy?"

"Nope."

"Want to dip in the water?"

"I'll think about it."

"Let me know."

A half-full, iced bottle of champagne was on the table, next to two glasses, both with lipstick on the rims. The television was the cable show *Cochran & Co.* The sound was muted, but I recognized Johnny and Montel. The caption on the screen read "Montel Williams Harassment Suit Dropped."

Montel. A man of character and integrity. Principles.

Perri swayed out wearing a short housecoat. Its split showed her legs up to the peak of her thighs. They offered me some champagne. I told them I didn't drink. Perri went down the hall and came back with three sodas and a small bucket of ice. All three sodas were for me, so I took that to mean Perri intended for me to stay awhile.

I glanced out the window, stared toward Foothill and Haven. I didn't see flames, no smoke, heard no sirens, but I knew the aftermath of what Dawn had done had to have left Shelly's looking like Florence and Normandie the morning after the last uprising in L.A. And that would be my fault.

Natalie interrupted my fears, told me about how they were thinking about moving to California.

Perri made herself comfortable in a chair and began flipping channels. Natalie asked about things to do in the area. I cleared my throat, snapped out of my hypnotic state, told her about the malls, a few clubs in Moreno Valley, Redlands and San Bernardino that weren't all that.

I said, "There are a gang of African-American groups and different functions going on out this way, but L.A. has a lot more going on, so far as variety, culture, and quality are concerned."

"L.A. sounds too big, too established," Perri said. "We're small-town girls. This sounds like a virgin area without much competition."

"Yeah." I nodded. "So far as a lot of black businesses, this is a virgin area."

She grinned. "A virgin area is my kind of place."

Both of them smiled at the same time.

Female conspiracy.

Natalie clicked a button on the television and picked one of the adult-only pay-per-view channels. A porno movie kicked on.

Natalie asked me, "Does this offend you?"

I shook my head. "Not at all."

Perri said, "Good."

On the movie, a shirtless, Gold's Gym–looking guy was by the clear waters of a teardrop-shaped pool. The stereotypical pool guy. Two young blondes, late teens, were at the opposite side of the deep end of the pool, tanning and reading *Wall Street Journal*s. They all noticed each other and smiled. A beat later, he was rubbing suntan lotion on their breasts. Another day in Bel Air.

How did this happen? I was back already. Had my Speedos on and was ready to take a dip in ho soup. Whenever I tried to do right and get out of the game, something always went wrong and sucked me back in.

Perri started brushing her hair, rocking back and forth, crossing and uncrossing her legs. She opened a soda and some squirted on her fingers. She sucked them clean. With her fingers in her mouth, her eyes tightened.

Natalie was all into the movie, which now had the pool guy and the two now naked women racing into a bedroom.

Perri licked two ice cubes before she let them roll off her fingers into a glass. She filled it with soda and walked over to me. She took the first sip, handed the glass to me, and asked a sultry "What's on your mind?"

I smiled. Held my thoughts in my head and smiled.

Perri laughed.

Natalie leaned forward on her elbows and watched the two girls handcuff the pool guy to the bed. She was studying more than enjoying the film. The TV was on mute, and Billie Holiday was playing on the radio. She twisted her head like she was trying to see the depth of his passage.

"How long are you going to be in town?" I asked.

Perri said, "Until Tuesday."

Natalie had her face in her hands. She yawned. On the tube, the girls' gray-haired parents walked in, suitcases in hand, and caught both their daughters with the pool guy. One riding his waist, the other bucking his face. The mother screamed, pulled her daughters to the floor, dragged the pool guy into her bedroom, undressed, and rode him in punishment. Bucking and slapping his face while he bucked back and cried. Payback. The daughters cried while their daddy got naked. They showed him what the pool guy had made them do.

Perri was making small talk in between her heavy breathing. Sweat popped out on her forehead, and she ran her fingers across her face and licked it off. She smiled at me. A look of lust.

That did nothing for me. I was here, but thoughts of the conversation I'd had with Jake, his misery, popped into my mind. How a night like the one I was living in had ruined everything for him for years to come, maybe the rest of his life.

Words from Pops filtered through, fell on my thoughts like rainwater falling through trees in a forest. Coins were jingling in my mind as well. *Find 'em. Fool 'em* . . . I smelled Daddy's cigar. Heard the gravel shooting from his tires as he sped away. Imagined the loneliness he must've felt when he was suffering on his deathbed, dying all alone.

My pulse quickened. I made myself snap out of that, and when I did, my mind went back to Darnell and Dawn. Wanted to know how heinous it had become after I fled the scene of a crime.

Integrity has a price tag. Respect. Responsibility. That's why the overlapping voices inside my head were driving me insane.

It's a good thing when a man starts to question things around him. It's a better thing when he starts to question himself.

"Stephan?" That was Perri.

"Yeah?"

"Would you like another soda?"

"I'm cool."

My eyes went back to the television. Then to the beautiful women in the room. I have to change that fucked-up part of me. All of this was always about the chase. It's the chase that makes a man high. That addiction. Change. Maybe I came here for confirmation. Or to simply extend my denial. Or forget another woman by being in the presence of two. But not even two could make me stop thinking about her.

I blinked, cleared my throat, focused.

Now in the porno flick, everybody was in the same bed.

Natalie's fake blue eyes were on me.

Out of the blue she said, "Do you?"

"Do I what?"

"Want me like I want you?"

Perri spoke up. "Now, don't be greedy. I want him too."

Any other time my dick would've been harder than Chinese arithmetic and I would've been across the room.

Natalie walked over to Perri. They kissed. In that moment I understood their relationship. Their marriage. Natalie ran her hands between Perri's legs. Perri arched her back and smiled at me. Natalie sang along with Lady Day and undressed herself with the rhythm. Natalie spread her legs, put both feet miles apart on the center table, lay back, and reached up for Perri. She was damn near crying, "Come here, baby. Come to momma."

Perri looked down at Natalie, then stood up and slowly wiggled her hips side to side, moved with the rhythm of an Indonesian belly dancer. Her housecoat broke free and parted.

Perri's massive penis plopped out and pointed at me.

*"Holy shit!"*

I dropped my glass, spat my drink out all over my clothes, couldn't stop coughing. I wiped my eyes, did a double-take, saw what the fuck I thought I saw the first time, then scurried to the far end of the sofa and gawked at her dick. It bobbed up and down like it was trying to hypnotize me. Surreal and illogical. At first I thought it might be one of those sex toys, but this was connected to her.

My head was so bent out of shape I couldn't move.

She rubbed her meat like she was trying to wish the genie out of the lamp. Perri glued her eyes to me, wagged her thang my way, licked her lips and grinned with some serious desire. I closed my mouth so fast I almost bit my damn tongue off.

Perri found her comfort on top of Natalie.

Big momma groaned. Perri boned.

I forgot how to blink, breathe, move, talk.

Perri made a motion for me to come join them. She made a gesture with the same fingers she used to make my soda, kissed at me with the same lips she'd sucked my ice cube with.

I fell-stumbled-tripped-jetted to the door and couldn't get the damn thing open. The locks clicked free, but the door stood firm. I was about to start kicking ass and fight my way out.

Perri laughed. "Don't push, *pull*."

I screamed, jerked the door open so fast I stubbed my toe. I limped and tripped out into the hall. I found my balance, then shoved my fingers down my throat and made myself vomit. All that happened before the door to their insanity could shut all the way. I hobbled down the hallway, left a lot of wails and laughter behind me that were silenced when the door clicked closed.

# 44 Chanté

Tammy tried to cheer me up with some humor. "Best female performance by yet another sister showing her booty off in an I-can't-stand-your-ass-because-I-like-ya-too-much drama goes to . . ."

I made a that's-not-funny face that stopped her cold. Through clenched teeth I snapped, "Knock it off, Tammy."

She laughed, winked at Darnell.

Without taking his eyes off Tammy, Darnell asked me, "Where did Stephan go?"

"Who cares?" That was me, uttering my turmoil.

Darnell and Tammy didn't care either. They touched so much, giggled so much, made eyes so much, it was sickening.

Minutes went by with me bouncing my leg, tapping the table, thinking about how much I despised that fool Stephan. Thinking of all the snappy comebacks and not-so-nice remarks I wish I had rained on him when I was close enough to spit in his eye.

How did I let him get the best of me?

It would be a cold day in hell before I gave my heart away again. I'd been hurt before, and that time was the last time. Seemed like when it came to a deck of men, I always pulled the wrong card. From here on out, my heart'll be in a safe deposit box. I'm becoming the mayor of celibate city.

God, I don't know what got into me. One second life was fine, then I saw Stephan hee-hawing and being all touchy-feelie, drooling all over those overdressed and so-damn flirty women, and I don't know. It felt like my soul was *sizzling*. I didn't remember moving, but the next think I knew I was flying out of the club, stepping up in his face.

I reached the bottom of my soda too quick, and my bladder was telling me that I'd had two drinks too many. All the dancing, all the moving bodies had heated the place up to oven status. Nonstop chatter blended with the band. Nature knotted my stomach, but I didn't take anything to ease the pain.

Stephan had left me so rattled. One minute I was a ball of fire, the next ice. I was dark and cold from the inside. I hated it when I felt that way, especially when it was over a man.

I never wanted to see him again in this lifetime.

But still, every now and then, I did a sly peek-a-boo toward the door to see if he had come back. A sister should always know where her enemies are lurking.

Darnell asked over the music, "What does she say about me?"

"Nothing bad," I said. My words were to him, but I constantly looked toward the glass front windows and doors of the club. I cleared my throat, said, "Darnell, for the record . . ."

"Uh-huh."

"I'm not down with what you and Tammy are planning."

"I'll file that opinion with the rest."

He stared at Tammy as she grooved with one of her admirers, a brother who had been bold enough to come over and ask for a dance. All night everybody had wanted to dance with Tammy. With the exception of one cross-eyed brother who needed to texturize his nappy hair, no one had asked me to shake my moneymaker, which left me somewhere between jealous and happy. Tammy was getting all of the attention. That was cool. I wasn't in the mood, and all I was doing was faking the funk.

Tammy came back from her dance, leaned over, and whispered in my ear, "Oh shit. Somebody's coming over here."

"Stephan's back?"

"Nope." Tammy waved at whoever. "You're gonna faint."

I turned around. Karen was slipping through the crowd.

The sight of her drained the last of my human spirit.

She was dressed in an orange spaghetti-strapped dress, hair pulled back into a shiny ponytail. She held her purse and jacket in front of herself, the move we did to keep our body parts from rubbing against other people, especially the men who wanted a freebie.

I said, "I guess the parole board had a hearing."

Tammy slapped my shoulder.

"You knew she was coming?" I asked.

"I invited her," Tammy said. "We need to resolve this before I leave for Paris."

In the pit of my stomach, nasty feelings were on the rise.

Karen hesitated, then wrestled through the crowd toward us. Toward me. Each step was deliberate, like she was waiting for us to wave her away.

Karen spoke her soft hellos to everybody.

I didn't say a damn thing. I sucked my tongue, held it against the roof of my mouth, shifted and looked away from Karen.

"How've you been, Chanté?" Karen asked.

"Fine. Considering how broke I am."

Tammy smiled at the refugee. "How you been?"

"I'm surviving. I'm a survivor." Karen shifted, then she addressed me, "Chanté?"

I said a testy "What?"

Karen's gaze bounced around the table. She told me, "I want to thank you again for helping me out. Everything's gonna be okay. They aren't going to do anything to me."

I said, "They're not pressing charges, is that what you're saying?"

"Right. They just wanted me out of there. I won't be working at Mervyn's anymore, but my job at the DMV is still tight. They don't know, so it's not in jeopardy."

"Good for you," I said.

Karen continued, "You should be getting your money back soon, Chanté. I'll give you the difference for the part the people at the company keep. The ten percent."

"Okay," I responded, that single word drawn out and lasting until I could get my next thought together. "I'll give you your stuff back then. As soon as I get the last penny you owe me."

"Have a seat," my cross-eyed admirer said, offering his chair to Karen.

"No, thank you," Karen said. "I'm waiting on somebody."

"Who?" I asked.

Karen answered, "Not him, Chanté."

With easy hips she walked away. I glared at the back of her head as she jostled through the crowd. My eyes followed her until she sat outside. By herself. A couple of guys stopped by her table, trying to get their flirt on. Karen raised a hand and blew them off before they could open their mouths.

I was still watching. Karen was still sitting alone. Every now and then I'd catch Karen looking my way.

"Infamous bitch," I mumbled.

"Chanté?" Tammy said, snapping at me like she'd had enough.

"What?"

"Meeting in the ladies' room. *Now.*"

"Whatever you have to say, say it here."

Tammy asked the men if they would mind leaving the table for a minute. Darnell headed toward the men's room. Cross-eyes took a stroll out in the parking lot. I was so glad he finally left.

Tammy's voice was tender. "She's all alone. She's been through a lot. Was locked up. Lost one of her jobs."

"The fugitive earned it. If it wasn't for me, she'd be locked up in Twin Towers fighting off lesbians day and night."

"So what?"

"And don't forget, you co-signed for this deal if my money don't come through."

"Chanté?"

"Kiss my grits."

"And forget you too."

Tammy hissed. "Please?"

"You begging?"

"If that's what it takes."

"Say it."

"I'm begging."

"Get on you knees."

"Chanté?"

"Kiss your grits?"

"Suck 'em till you choke."

"Why are you so soft on Karen?"

"I'm soft on you too."

"Why?"

Tammy hunched her shoulders. "Because we're all alike."

"I don't think so. I don't do sloppy seconds."

"For real," Tammy said. "We do stupid stuff."

"Not too tight to get with your friend's man."

"He wasn't your man. He curbed your butterball booty and left you blowing snot bubbles and slinging boogers on your birthday. Want me to act it out for you? 'He didn't call me. How could he do this to me? Woe is me. Nobody loves me but my momma, and she's in Australia breast-feeding kangaroos.' "

I laughed a little. "I didn't say 'woe is me.' "

"I improvised." She patted my hand. She said, "C'mon, Chanté. Tell the truth. She did see Craig first."

"And last."

"You shouldn't've been advertising and bragging about how good he was in bed."

I huffed, "He wasn't all that."

"Remember what you said about him being a two-dollar man?"

"I said buck fifty."

"Okay, a buck fifty."

I said, "You know I can't count."

I glanced toward Karen as I held Tammy's fingers.

"Chanté, please," Tammy said. "I'm going to Paris in the morning. I've never asked you for anything. I wanted her here because I want you two to make it right before I leave."

"I can't believe you invited her."

"I did. I've talked to her every day. So now you know."

"I don't believe she had the nerve to show her face."

Tammy said, "I know it won't be the way it used to be, but let's see what we can do."

I groaned.

Tammy said, "She's been through hell."

"Where the hell do you think I've been, huh? My life ain't been no Disneyland lately."

"Somebody's pissed off."

"Geesh. How could you tell?"

" 'Cause you use double negatives when you're mad."

"Shaddup."

She gripped my little finger and said, "Just be cordial."

I gave up much attitude, tsked. "Don't expect anything."

Tammy led the way. Karen was alone with a soda in front of her, watching clouds walk by in the sky, swaying to the music.

Another awkward moment was born when we stopped in front of Karen's table. Eyes roamed from person to person in search of feelings and words. I stared. Karen shifted. Tammy massaged one hand with the other. Everything was vague.

"Who you waiting for?" Tammy asked.

"Nobody. I didn't want you to have to make excuses for me," Karen admitted. "I wanted to be woman enough to see my sistas and ask for forgiveness face-to-face for what I did to us."

My breaths were so short I could've used Primatene.

Karen tried to smile. "I miss hanging with both of you."

I kissed Karen on the cheek. Karen kissed me back.

We smiled. Painful, unsure smiles.

Karen said, "Sit down if you want. Actually, I want you to."

I copped a squat. Tammy smiled like she'd had a great day at the U.N. doing something significant for humanity.

"So," I exhaled, "they dropped the charges?"

Karen pulled a folded newspaper clipping out of her purse and handed it to me. Without touching Karen's hand, I picked it up. It was an article from Riverside's *Press Enterprise* on the military "implementing disciplinary actions and imposing monetary fines against Craig Bryant." He'd pled guilty to all charges and was "facing correctional custody or Leavenworth" plus a guaranteed dishonorable discharge.

I was stunned. So was Tammy.

This victory was supposed to feel good, but it didn't.

Karen looked so uneasy and childlike as she apologized in ten different tones. I listened, said very little. Watched her shift and suffer inside her own skin.

Tammy said, "It's getting late. I'll be leaving soon."

Karen asked, "For Paris?"

Tammy shook her head, spoke softly, "Darnell and I are going to have a few moments together before I leave."

I asked, "Nervous?"

"As a virgin about to be tossed in a volcano."

Karen asked, "Why nervous?"

I said, "Duh, hello. She's leaving so she can get her freak on with a married man."

Tammy made light of it. "Well, if you were leaving town, wouldn't you be trying to get hooked before you hit the road?"

Karen didn't comment on that. I didn't say any more. I guess that Karen and I had had our own indiscretions. Our own regrets.

Karen asked, "Who's the sista who keeps staring over here?"

I asked "Who?"

She motioned behind her, toward the parking lot and a couple of big trucks. She said, "She must've left. She was right there when I came out a minute ago. She was upset, staring at y'all."

Tammy's eyes were on Darnell. His eyes were on hers.

Tammy said, "It's a good thing I'm going to Paris."

I asked, "Why?"

"I'd be so in love with him I'd start thinking about babies and PTA meetings and learning how to microwave chocolate cakes."

All of us actually laughed at the same time.

The band came for Tammy. She was going to do a few more songs before she left with another woman's husband. The band was going to party hard until damn near two a.m., but Tammy was going to be rocking somebody's headboard and screaming a different song at midnight. In other words, at the stroke of twelve, she'd be getting stroked.

We all bumped through the crowd and headed back into the warmth and alcoholic fragrance of the club. Tammy held Karen's hand. Grinned and held her close. Karen walked a few steps before she glanced back at me. She was as uneasy as I was.

She stopped, left her eyes on me as she said, "Tammy, why don't you go ahead and go inside? Sing your songs."

I nodded.

Tammy's eyes went from Karen to me before she said, "Don't get ugly, okay?"

At the same moment Karen and I said, "We'll be fine."

We walked toward the movie theater, away from everybody, then stopped close to the driveway that led to Foothill Boulevard. By then Tammy's voice followed us out into the dark, telling Porgy how much she loved him. She sang with so much desire. So much that it touched me. Jarred me deep within. Softened me up.

I pushed my lips up into a nervous smile. I offered, "Come and get your stuff from my house."

Karen kicked the pavement with her feet, then shook her head. "Not until I give you the last penny."

"Please?"

"No. I don't want your charity."

"At least come and get the television. I hate to think you're sitting up in there with no TV."

"Well, I do miss *ER* and the *X-Files*."

"And *Ally McBeal*."

"You like that crap. I hate that show."

I insisted, "Follow me home and get your idiot box."

"Let me think about it. I'll call you and let you know."

I paused, admitted, "I still care about you, Karen."

"I love you too, Chanté. And I've *always* respected you."

"Stop it."

She said, "Can you keep a secret? It's about me."

"You're pregnant?"

"No."

I said a reluctant "Okay."

"Chanté," Karen was struggling, "I've always been jealous of you. You've always had it going on. Independent. Secure. You own property."

"Geesh. Thanks for the compliment."

"I'm still stuck in a damn box in Riverside. Short on my damn college credits. Got so many bills I don't know when I'll ever go back and get that weak degree from a junior college. Don't know if I'll ever see the inside of a real university."

"You can do it."

She shrugged. "Your folks are there for you. If I had to wait for my people, I'd still be in jail."

"Well, bring up everything, why don't you?"

"Chanté, listen." Karen had a painful smile. "I've got the floor."

"No, you listen. You've been engaged *twice*."

"Three times."

"Even better. That means *three* men wanted *you* the rest of their lives."

"I was engaged to the same guy twice."

"So what? I haven't been proposed to once. All I ever get is propositioned, never a proposal. I can get a j-o-b at Moss Adams, but I can't even keep a boyfriend. Guess my dating DNA is screwed up, or I'm boyfriend-impaired or something—"

"Chanté, let me talk—"

"Karen, my life ain't all that. If you want it, I'll give it to you. Bills, raggedy car, heartache, bunions, and all."

"There you go again. Always have to have the last word."

I stuck my tongue out. "So."

Karen was serious. "But not this time. Give me that. The last word. Don't yadda yadda yadda when I'm speaking my heart."

I shut up and braced myself. I've never been a big fan of truth, especially when it was my truth.

She said, "You've changed. You've become rude. Bitchy. Self-centered. Arrogant. Spoiled to the teeth. And worse of all, promiscuous."

My eyes lowered to my feet.

Karen added, "Things I wish I could be most of the time."

We chuckled a bit.

She said, "Slow down. Please? I want you to outlive me. At least try to. 'Cause I'm sure as hell trying to outlive you."

Silence.

I said, "Thanks."

A cappella, Tammy was singing another song. A poem, actually. Images. Telling how a black woman often overlooks her own beauty, how she thinks her brown body has no glory.

Nobody in the area was moving. Everybody was listening.

The words were so strong, I wanted to cry.

I said, "In a few she'll be leaving with Darnell."

"So, she's actually going to do it."

"They're going to a hotel to finish celebrating, or should I say start consummating."

Karen shook her head. "She has the fever for him."

I muttered, "Just like I have the fever for Stephan."

"Do you?"

"Yeah. I'm back in love again. You just don't know. I got the fever and it's making me crazy. I haven't been in love with anybody since Craig, which was a waste of good emotion."

It became very uncomfortable. Karen cleared her throat and shifted away from me.

I asked her, "You love Craig?"

"Yeah. I had the fever for him."

"I see."

"But jail has a way of making a woman reevaluate her life."

Silence.

It became a lot more uncomfortable.

She tensed up, gripped her purse. Trembled a bit. Then she exhaled and loosened up a bit. It was coming, I felt her emotions rolling out of her in waves.

"Chanté," her voice was fractured, deliberate, "you've always said things to me that hurt my self-esteem like no one else ever has."

"Words, Karen." My voice was hardly there, fading and unclear, static-filled like a Walkman that had weak batteries. "They were just words."

"And a rope is just a rope, until it's around your neck."

I asked her, "What about the things that you've said to me?"

"I've only said things that would help you."

I told her, "That's the same thing I did."

"I only wanted to give you empowerment."

"I wanted you to be empowered too."

More silence as Tammy chanted and chilled the air.

With a whisper I asked Karen, "Do you think I'm a fool?"

"What do you mean?"

"The things I do. The things I've done."

"Sometimes. But hey, if the woman who wrote *Ten Stupid Things a Woman Does to Mess Up Her Life* can end up with naked pictures out on the Internet, I don't think we're doing too bad."

"True."

With sadness she said, "At least you haven't been incarcerated."

I said, "Just because you can't see the bars doesn't mean I'm not in-carcerated. Sometimes we create our own prisons."

We listened some more.

Then Tammy was done. While everyone stood and applauded, Karen and I blinked, sniffled at the same moment, came out of whatever reality Tammy's words and emotions had created back into our world. Into this cradle of humanity. Both of our eyes had teared up. Not from crying. I don't think that we'd blinked while Tammy was singing.

We saw Tammy getting ready to leave with Darnell.

I wiped my eyes and said, "We better get back to the party before we start crying."

"Or fighting."

We chuckled a little. Not much.

A tingle, an electric sensation ran through me. A surge that said everything would be better. Not all right, but better. We gave each other a single soft kiss.

I said, "One more thing, Karen."

"What?"

"A secret between me and you."

"Okay."

It was hard for me to say, but I confessed, "Ten."

She only looked confused for a second; then her eyes sparkled when she knew what that number meant.

Karen admitted, "Eighteen."

I was surprised. My mouth dropped open. "Eighteen?"

"Yeah."

"Damn, Karen."

She added, "Nineteen if you count Victor."

We laughed.

"Eight-fucking-teen." Karen's words rode on a sigh. She picked at her nails, said, "Would you believe that? Lost my virginity in the back-seat of an abandoned car that was parked on a side street. Lost it to the guy who turned me on to pot."

I suggested, "Why don't you quit getting high?"

"Man made beer; God made herbs. I know who to trust."

Some laughter.

I ran my hand over my wild mane and told her my story. "I was damn near out of college. In the backseat of a car at a drive-in. A damn Eddie Murphy movie. Not a romantic movie, a damn Eddie-Murphy-telling-ten-minutes-of-fart-jokes movie."

Karen chuckled, "Well, at least you got a movie."

I was quiet.

She asked, "What you thinking?"

My tone was sad. "Wondering who number eleven is gonna be. How many nights he'll last. How it'll end."

"Yeah. I feel you."

We didn't say anything else on the subject.

The impulsive side of me took over. The check that Thaiheed had given me, I signed the back of it. I pulled out my checkbook and wrote another check for five hundred. I made Karen take them both.

I told her, "Maybe this'll help. Pay down some of those bills."

She was reluctant to take my help, but her eyes told me she was in a serious bind and she needed it much more than she'd ever admit. Her eyes were misty, voice was cracking when she said, "I'll pay you back."

"Pay me back by getting back in school. Do it for me. Just two or three classes, and I'll call it even."

"Chanté—"

"Just think about it."

"Okay. Then do something for me."

"What?"

"Slow down. Outlive me."

We shared one more hug, then headed back to the party.

# 45 Darnell

The hotel faced the mountains. It was a clear night. A sky filled with a million stars.

We were kissing.

Touching.

I had to think of all the things my wife had done to keep the dreams alive. She had sat up a lot of nights and helped me study. Had been patient. Had put meals at my side, kisses on my face while I studied through the night. Had allowed me to be an absentee husband. I owed her a lot.

And even if I disagreed with some of her ways, I had to consider the commitment I had made to a higher power.

To honor and love my mate until my bones turned to dust.

In the true scheme of things, relative to the length of my marriage, I'd known Tammy for a metaphorical fifteen minutes. An intense fifteen minutes that felt more important than the last six years I'd given Dawn. Some people you could be with forever and never love completely. Others you could be with a short time and feel like you've loved them a lifetime.

That's not fair. Not fair at all.

Honey. Condoms. Massage oils.

Dim lights. Jazz on the radio.

Not much on Tammy's flesh.

Not much on mine.

We stared at the bed. Then at each other.

I looked outside, at the heavens. The sky was lit up with a million eyes that were waiting to see what we were going to do.

Somewhere, an angel sighed.

I said, "We can't do this."

"I know."

"I want to."

"Me too. Believe me, I do. Save me, Darnell."

"Let's save each other."

A moment passed. A moment with me holding her close to me.

She asked, "Why can't you? This ain't one of those Viagra moments, is it?"

We laughed a little. When I was at my lowest, with a simple sentence she'd brought me back up.

I wanted to say that my wife didn't deserve this, but I told her the other reason, the one closest to my heart. "You deserve better than this."

"Thanks," she said. "I know what this is about for me."

"And that is?"

"Well, the way I see it, every person I meet might not be the one, just the one I learn from while I wait to meet the one. On an emotional level, you've raised my standards a helluva lot. I didn't know I could feel like this for somebody."

I told her, "You've done a lot for me too."

"I'm gonna look for your handsome face in crowds all day, every day," she said sadly, "and I'll dream about you all night, every night. I'll dream about us kicking it in a villa on a hill so high that it'll be warmed by the stars."

"Wow."

"I wish you could come to Paris. I'd sing all night, then make love to you all day."

"Sounds good to me. I'd write all night, then rest so I could have the energy to make love to you all day."

Tammy winked at me, said, "We'd make love so much your wee-wee would have carpal tunnel syndrome."

We laughed. Then we kissed. That ten-minute kiss absorbed the laughter the way a sponge absorbed water.

I asked, "What do we do now?"

"We try to pretend everything is normal when it isn't."

I smiled. "I'm good at that. Projecting a sense of normalcy to everybody around me."

She said, "Another thing we have in common."

"Pretending is exhausting."

"Very."

She pulled away and led me to the dresser. Tammy picked up her diamond earrings, put one in her ear and gave me the other.

She said, "Keep this."

"No, these are my gift to you."

"And this one is my gift to you."

"I can't take this."

"You can and you will. Give it to me when I see you again."

"You're not coming back."

"Let's just say I'm creating hope. Something for me to look forward to. I'll keep this one in my ear and think about you every day. Maybe I'll get famous and you'll see me on TV. I'll do the Carol Burnett thing and tug on it so you'll know I'm thinking about you, that my heart will always want you, Darnell."

I closed my hand around the earring. Held on to the hope.

She said, "I wish we were more like our friends."

"In what way?"

"In search of true love but would settle for a midnight romp."

For a while she held my face in her hands, and I held her face in mine. We stared at each other like we were memorizing the details. Like we'd never see each other again.

She let me go, went in the bathroom, closed the door.

I stood near the door, said, "Tammy?"

Her word came on top of tears: "Yeah?"

"Sing. You sang me to you, now sing me away."

"What do you want to hear?"

"Whatever's on your heart."

"That'll be easy." She cleared her throat. "Darnell?"

"Yeah?"

"You pray?"

"Yeah. Not as much as I should, but I pray."

"Next time you do, ask God why he sent me my fine-ass-intelligent-black-man soul mate and let him be married."

Soft chuckles came first from her, then from me.

I said, "I have a few questions of my own, too."

Tammy stopped laughing. "This must be my punishment."

"For what?"

"You know my pains and my secrets. You know."

She started humming out her emotion. The vibrations that came from her soul ran through me, dipped into the crux of me.

Tammy said, "I'm not coming back out."

"I know."

"I'm not coming back from Paris."

I told her, "You can run, but you can't hide. You'll take it with you."

"I'm not hiding. Just choosing where I want to be miserable."

Silence.

"Bye, Darnell."

"Bye, Tammy."

I whispered, "Thanks for everything."

"You too. You've been incredibly supportive."

I pulled my pants on, wiped my eyes and sat on the bed.

"Love you, Darnell."

"Love you, Tammy."

"I'll send you postcards."

"I'll write you letters."

"I'll write you poems."

"I'll write stories about you."

We said that, made those promises, but we knew we had no way to get in contact with each other.

"Just write those books," she told me and blew the sorrow that was stopping up her nose. "Follow your dreams."

"Then I'd have to follow you."

"Hush."

Sniffles came from the other side of the bathroom door.

She sang, "Ne Me Quitte Pas . . ."

Her voice was haunting. Crisp and clear. Sounded like a twenty-piece orchestra was backing her up. I shivered.

Ne Me Quitte Pas

Tammy's words were almost crying, begging.

Ne Me Quitte Pas

I dressed.

I went to the bathroom door, put my hand up to the wood, imagined that she was on the other side doing the same as she sang. I imagined both of us reaching for the doorknob at the same moment, then both of us letting go. Her tears on that side. Mine on this. I kissed my fingers, then put that kiss where I guessed her face was, at the spot I felt her voice coming through the strongest. Her vibrations ran through the wood straight to my heart.

Every step was so heavy as I walked to the hall door. It was so hard to move away from my heart. The door felt heavier, almost impossible to open. Then too quick to close.

An angel's voice followed me down the hallway.

*Ne Me Quitte Pas . . .*

It felt like I could drive a hundred freeways, cruise a thousand streets, and never find my way home. But I did.

All the way my mind was on the forever that I had stood before God, my pastor, my family, and promised. People leave out the human factor. We evolve, change. We reinvent ourselves a million times over. The things we want today might be the things that we want to forget about tomorrow.

I looked at the earring in my hand. Hope.

Maybe I was lost. So confused I really couldn't distinguish between reality and fantasy. What Tammy offered was fiction, my marriage wasn't.

The inside of the garage was dead quiet. Tammy's voice lingered inside my head. I sat there holding onto the diamond earring. My gift to her, then her gift to me.

Inside, Dawn was on the bed. I didn't see her, but I heard her shift around, get up, then take a slow, skeptical walk up the hardwood section of the hallway.

I tossed my keys on the marble counter in the kitchen.

On the kitchen table was an open EPT box.

My mail was propped up against the pregnancy test. Car note. Insurance. Another a letter from another publisher in the Big Apple was in the pile. I picked that up first. It was already open.

Like all the others, the letter was brief. Sweet.

But different.

They liked my book. They wanted to talk to me ASAP.

I closed my eyes with the weight of the irony.

Words.

I heard them.

I heard what Dawn had said before I left this evening, what she'd done to rattle my psyche, her effort at making me impotent.

*"Darnell, what time will you be back?"*

*"I haven't left yet."*

*"I know where you're going."*

*"Do you?"*

*"Yeah, I do."*

*"How do you know?"*

*"I know a lot of things."*

*"No doubt."*

*"What time will you be home?"*

*"Don't know."*

*"Maybe I should be asking if you're coming back tonight."*

*"You've never asked that before."*

*"Never felt I had to. Are you?"*

*"Don't know."*

*"Before you leave, there's something I should tell you."*

*"I'm listening."*

*"My period is late."*

*"How late?"*

*"Late enough."*

*"I see."*

*"So take that with you, Darnell."*

My wife's silhouette was facing me when I raised my head.

She had on jeans, a pair that looked as wrinkled and worn as I felt. A yellow bra that contrasted with the beauty in her flesh. No makeup. Ashen face. Swollen eyes.

Pages of the novel I had been working on were in her hands.

She raised my labor of love to her chest, held it to her heart, and whispered, "This is good, Darnell. It's damn good. I never knew. I mean, I had no idea that you could do this."

I hesitated, spoke softly, "Thanks."

Dawn cleared her throat. She said, "Borghese."

"What does that mean?"

"It's the name of the perfume I smell on you."

Tears grew in her eyes.

Dawn whispered, "I saw you dancing with her tonight. I saw you holding her. I saw her holding you. I saw her kiss your face. I saw you kiss hers. I saw more than I could bear."

I opened my mouth to say something, but she put two fingers to my lips, shushed me.

She reached her hand out to me and said, "Don't explain. Just come to bed. There are things I need to tell you."

I didn't move. "What do you have to tell?"

"What I've tried to tell you a thousand times before—"

"Which is?"

"But either you didn't listen, or my pain didn't interest you enough to notice. There is a lot inside me. It's burning. I love you, Darnell. I love you more now than I did the day I married you. It hurts for me *not* to tell you."

Conversations like the one we had always start with a preface. Dawn told me, once again, about how things had been when I was in law school. The pressure and demands from law school have destroyed many a relationship. The song that Dawn always sang was playing again, at the most inopportune time possible.

My perceived shortcomings were again brought to life. For four years I'd been too busy for the marriage. Never home. A husband in absentia. She had been forced to carry the load of the household.

Home and school. Husband and student. I couldn't be at two places at the same time. Something would suffer. And like my wife, the law was a jealous lover. Unforgiving. Impatient.

Her master plan had been to marry, have a child within three years, and about a million other things. Decisions she had made on her own. Things that we never talked about before we were married. Things we should have addressed before we exchanged rings. Maybe sooner. Before we exchanged bodily fluids. Maybe before the first time we shared a tongue dance.

In a tone that said it all, Dawn said, "I was lonely."

"Explain."

"Don't make me say it."

"Say it."

"I was susceptible to someone filling in the hole that was growing in my heart. I was a puzzle with a missing piece."

That stung. I finally understood.

She told me that her affair happened while I was studying for the bar. During the last week I stayed at a hotel and crammed for the test with a group of people. Space and opportunity. Long before that the loneliness had made her feel like she was dying. The attention she needed, the compliments that make a woman feel like a woman, all of that came from a loan officer. She wouldn't say who. All she would say was that was then, that her indiscretion was a thing of the past.

I didn't ask her to explain any more than that.

She'd had an affair long before I'd even considered doing so.

Eyes. Our eyes were on each other.

Dawn said, "I figure that what you did with her tonight, well, I brought that on myself. Let's forgive each other and move on."

I should've corrected her, let her know that she was rowing in that boat of adultery by herself, but in so many ways I had too. Tammy had touched me with the slight of her hand, and I felt like I'd loved her a thousand times.

Dawn put her fingers on my face. Her hands were damp, trembles came from deep within her. That was when the tears came, when her shoulders slumped and her weight shifted to one foot. She held me, dropped everything that she was holding and wrapped her arms

around me. Her nose was deep in my chest, inhaling the scent of another woman.

She moaned. "Say something. Please. Say something."

I cleared my throat.

I flinched, blinked. I hadn't blinked for a long while.

Softly I asked, "Why didn't you tell me this yesterday?"

# 46  Stephan

Shelly's didn't look the way I thought it would, not at all. Quite a few
people had left, but there were enough around to make it feel like late-
night after hours. Balloons, streamers, everything was still in the
Mexican palm trees. Banners danced with the breeze that was bringing
a hint of the smells from the strawberry and cow fields to the south.
Here and there brothers and sisters were strolling, exchanging smiles
and numbers, trying to get their romance going. I expected that ambi-
ence after everything had settled down, but there were no whispers
about any kind of pandemonium. I'd passed by a couple of people I
knew who were down near the coffee house. They said that nothing
had jumped off. No angry wives had come to claim their husbands.

I wondered what the hell had happened in my absence.

I followed the soft sound of the music.

Darnell's car was gone. So was Tammy's.

I heard her arm filled with silver bracelets jingling before I saw her.
Chanté and Karen were leaving the club, looking exhausted and running their fingers through their hair at the same time, avoiding the
pack of scavengers who were trying to get their last-chance mack on.

Chanté saw me and stopped in her tracks. Her dark lips didn't part.
Her arched brows were still.

I looked at her without compunction.

Short skirt that hugged her with possessiveness. Tall block-heel
shoes. Silver bracelets. Blue sleeveless blouse open just enough to show
off her tight belly and that silver earring in her navel. Wild hair that
was moving with the breeze. Intelligent as night is dark. As beautiful
as the sun is hot.

She glared with probing eyes that said she was through with me.
The way her judicial gaze was slamming on my face made a lump as

big as a fist pop in my throat. Just like that, she had used her powers
to chill the light breeze.

She was so complicated.

My life had been so complicated.

So I kept it uncomplicated.

I opened my arms, plain and simple.

Before I could open my mouth, her frown dissolved into a smile.
She opened her arms and came to me, bracelets jingling all the way.
Slow steps toward my wide-open wings. Then she had the softness of
her chest to my chest. I folded my arms around her like it was home.
She shifted side to side. I felt her tremble in rhythm with my own.
Heavy breathing as she squeezed me.

Then there was calm.

Karen sashayed right by us. She said, "Take care of yourself, Chanté."

"You too, Karen."

We stood and held each other for a while.

She said, "So, Mr. Hyde has turned back into Dr. Jekyll."

"I was about to say the same thing to you."

She asked, "Where you been?"

"Went to visit Marilyn Manson and Ellen Degeneres."

"What?"

I asked, "Where's Tammy?"

"Her and Darnell should be doing the shout right about now."

"You're joking?"

"Nope."

"They left together?"

She nodded.

I left that at that.

While people walked by, I kissed Chanté. Kissed her lips. Her face.
Let my lips warm up that butterfly on her flesh that I missed. She kissed
me back. No resistance. No smiles to make this seem not so serious.

She hugged me tighter and put her head deeper into my chest and
mumbled, "Sorry."

"Me, too."

We savored that moment of forgiveness.

She whispered in my ear as she kissed the side of my face, "Roses
are red, violets are blue, Stephan Mitchell, I love you."

I kissed the side of her face.

She asked, "What you think of my impromptu poem?"

"Don't quit your day job."

"Jerk."

"Jerkette."

She smiled a little.

Music wafted down from the club. We rocked side to side. Without Tammy's voice this place seemed so plain. Hollow like a big house that had large rooms, wooden floors, and no furniture.

She whispered, "We need to talk."

I nodded.

She said, "I've got to think about my future."

"Uh-huh."

"Every day we get older."

"That's a law."

"Can I stop by your place so we can talk for a while?"

"Okay."

"Just talk. Nothing else."

"Okay."

"I think it's time for me to listen to my friend's wisdom and slow down."

"So, you're slowing down?"

"Stopping would be better."

\*   \*   \*

Juan and Rebecca were coming out of their place when me and Chanté walked up my stairs. Juan had on jeans. Rebecca had on a short dress. I couldn't see any panty lines.

I asked, "Where're you lovebirds going at two in the morning?"

Both of them smiled. It was a naughty smile.

They held hands and headed wherever they were going.

I watched them. Watched the way they touched each other. The subtle glances. Communication in silence.

After they disappeared, Chanté was still looking in the direction they went. She set free a heavy sigh, a groan.

I asked, "What's wrong?"

"I wonder if I'll have to wait as many years as they did to find what they've found. That would really be depressing."

I thought about my daddy. "Yeah, I guess it would."

Chanté asked, "Why did you get a new door?"

"Termites."

"Stephan, termites don't just attack doors."

I stopped Chanté before she could get through the door, slowed her stroll and put my hand between her legs and squeezed.

She said, "Ouch. What was that all about?"

"Just making sure you're a woman."

As she stepped inside, a strange look came over her face. A deep, serious expression. Her head tilted like she was contemplating. I could tell that she was in a reflective mood.

I asked, "What's the matter?"

"You said 'a woman.' "

"And?"

She shrugged. "Just thinking. Feeling. I have a long way to go up that road to get there, to be the kind I know I can be."

"You're a great woman."

"Negative, not yet. My voice rings out in the tone of a woman. I feel pain like every other sista I know, or every sista who will be. I sure as hell can make love like a woman. But every third day I fall apart like I'm my daddy's little girl."

I felt solemn after she said that. I admitted, "So far as being a man, same thing here."

She quizzed, "Any idea how to get there?"

"Manhood is a process. It's not overnight. You train yourself to act a certain way and hold yourself accountable."

She said, "Same thing goes for being a woman."

With a slight bob of my head I said, "I guess."

"Want to walk that road together?"

"For how long?"

She shrugged. "Awhile, if not forever."

"Do I hear an escape clause?"

"I wouldn't have it any other way."

We stood at the door and kissed for a while.

I asked her, "What do you want to do right now?"

"First tell me what you want to do."

"Love you."

"Good thing we don't judge a man by the size of his thoughts, or there'd be no men left to judge."

"Ouch. That was sexist."

"I'm learning."

"What do you want to do?"

"I want to sleep in your space. Put on one of your T-shirts, some of your paisley boxer shorts and a pair of those big, thick socks and cradle my head in your lap and sleep."

"Sounds good."

"But first I want to feel you swelling inside me."

"Thought you wanted to slow down."

"Tomorrow. Change is hard."

"Tell me about it."

She spoke in a wispy tone, "If I had never been in love, I wouldn't crave the wonderful, crazy and euphoric feeling it gave when it was working. If I had never had sex, I'd never ache for the eroticism while I worked it with someone I wanted to have my heart. If I had never been heartbroken, I wouldn't fight the feeling of love when it came."

"You're fighting it?"

"I wouldn't be fighting the feeling now. So much betrayal from so few people has left me so jaded."

"I understand. You don't have to be ashamed of what you feel."

"I know. But sometimes I am."

"Don't be. Not with me."

"If the truth be told, Stephan, I have to be honest."

"Okay."

"My failed relationships were built with an oatmeal foundation. I want something solid. That thang called l-o-v-e has made a social call, but never really moved into my life. Love should be one hundred percent and not graded on a curve."

I let her know, "You're getting deep on me."

"I'm emotional. Very. So the intensity I get from loving somebody I'm in love with is remarkable. Damn near uncontrollable. I love hard, love deep, love long."

We kissed for a while.

I told her, "Love is like finding fresh water. I want to drink of you, Chanté."

"Good, 'cause I'm thirsty too."

She opened the curtains, let the light from the street light outside my window shine through the vertical blinds. I turned back the sheets nice and slow. I took off my shirt while she pulled off her silver bracelets. Tied her hair back.

I said, "Leave it down."

"It's already sweaty."

"I like it wild."

"You don't have to comb it."

"I'll comb it for you."

"Ooooh. Next you'll be painting my toenails."

"Never know."

I readjusted the pillows and watched her satin bra fall to the floor. She stared at me and set free a soft sigh. Unsnap. Unzip. Down to her thong panties. Then to her dark and beautiful flesh. Flesh to flesh. A long embrace. I was that animal again, smelling her. She was smelling me.

She started giggling.

I asked, "What's funny?"

"Nothing. Don't frown like that."

"Was I frowning?"

"It was a cute frown."

"Why were you laughing?"

"I was looking at your buck fifty—"

"My what?"

"Your thing-a-mah-jig."

"And?"

"It was moving side to side, real slow."

"So?"

"I started thinking about a windshield wiper."

The morning sunrise was as beautiful as the glow in her eyes. I had a strong feeling of melancholy. Things were on my chest.

I talked to her about my daddy. It wasn't easy sharing myself, but I did my best. I told her about the last time I saw him on that humid day down in Mississippi. Let her know that the man who used to be my daddy's best friend was now my stepdaddy. Told her how he did things for me, like teach me how to fix cars, the trips to Disneyland, things he did not because he liked or loved me, but because somebody had to step in and ease the burden my daddy had left behind. Didn't know where I'd be without Pops. I guess I was trying to say that I owed him a lot. Told her how I never got a chance to say good-bye to my daddy. I had to tell her all of that because Daddy had come to me in a dream and I woke up feeling heavy, stopped up with emotion.

I admitted, "I'm afraid to die alone like he did."

She asked, "You crying?"

"Nah. I don't cry."

"Then your eyes have a leak."

"Get some duct tape."

Her voice was feather soft. "Let me hold you."

"Let me hold you back."

"I never knew you could be like this."

I asked, "Like what?"

"So yadda yadda yadda."

I masked my emotions with a manly chuckle.

She traced her fingers around my chin. "I like this side of you too."

I still missed him. Guess I always would. Missed him, but not his wisdom. I was on another road now.

Life would get busier, more crazy, and I wouldn't see Jake for a while. A few times our paths would cross and we'd hang out in L.A. Catch a party at Little J's. Duets. Hook up at the Shark Bar. Club Fifty. Or on the Avenue of the Stars.

All of that would get old. It always did.

Without Charlotte in his life, Jake wouldn't have any reason to keep coming out east to hang out in the Inland Empire. A few months after the dust settled, he'd be on television. A fire broke out on Fairfax

Avenue, at the Cienega Apartments right behind LA Hot Wings. That sudden blaze burned down a section of the building that faced the fire station.

Jake would be the one who ran in and saved three children, then came back out. But he'd say that he heard the voices calling him. Voices of other children. No one heard those cries but him. Other firemen tried to stop him, but he ran back into the jaws of the flames.

There was silence.

The type of silence that surrounded death.

Then Jake burst through the smoke, like Wesley Snipes in an action movie, coughing, hanging onto two crying children, one in each arm. He collapsed, but after a good dose of oxygen and a few days in Cedar Sinai, he was okay. In every newspaper, he was a hero. The man of the hour.

Every time I talked to him, he asked about Charlotte. A tentative smile of regret lived in the corner of his lips, on the surface of his eyes. She never asked me about him. I never talked about him in front of her. Every year, at Christmastime, Valentine's Day, and on her birthday, without fail, a dozen long-stemmed roses would show up on her doorstep. Flowers and a card that had no signature.

Dawn had a miscarriage before Darnell's first book was published. The first one was the bomb. In the second one I'd see some of all of us, too much of me between the pages. Things that I'd done that didn't look too cool on paper. Not everybody could stand looking in the mirror. Darnell was still working at the FAA during the day, then writing at night.

Dawn threw book parties at their house. Side by side, she and Darnell would smile and be the perfect hosts. Sometimes I would go, a lot of times I didn't. Dawn didn't get along with Chanté, so that made it uncomfortable for everybody.

One day Darnell called me and asked to give him a ride to LAX. He told me he had to catch a flight to Phoenix to handle a trial against an airline carrier. Something about a hidden shipment. He left his car at my condo early that morning. At LAX he had me pull over at the Tom Bradley Terminal.

I said, "This is the international terminal."

"I know."

"It doesn't have planes that go to Phoenix."

"I know. But they have planes that go to Paris."

We sat and digested the moment. Darnell stayed motionless, in a trance, then he pulled down the visor on his side, opened the mirror, and stared at the diamond earring that sparkled in his left ear.

"Paris?"

"Yeah."

"You coming back?"

He shook his head.

I asked, "You thought about this?"

"Yeah."

I nodded.

He handed me the key to his car. The key to his house. A note was already mailed to Dawn. It said, "Don't look for me."

I wished him luck. He did the same to me.

He said, "I'll be in touch."

"Okay."

"Hug Chanté for me. Hug her twice for Tammy."

"Hug Tammy twice for Chanté."

He walked away, blended with the multiethnic travelers, and disappeared into the terminal.

I'd check on Dawn. Sit with her from time to time. In her eyes I'd see her grief. Then one day I called her and got a message that said her phone had been disconnected. I stopped by and a For Sale sign was in the yard. Her job let me know that she'd gone back to New York.

As the man said, So it goes.

Once in a while I'd pull up at a red light, and a sista in a white blouse, or sweatsuit, or jean jacket would be sitting in the car next to me, head bobbing to the beat, smiling and laughing with the brotha she was riding with. She'd turn her head and it would be Samantha. Or Toyomi. Or Brittany. Or somebody whose name was vague, someone whose smell had been gone from my life for a lover's lifetime.

For a quick sec, we'd make eye contact, see the familiarity that would take us back to those brief twinkles of pleasure; then her eyes would dim with the reminder of an undeserved heartbreak, and her face would lose its joy. She'd turn away as if she didn't know me, start back to laughing and smiling along with the man at her side.

Her laughter wouldn't be as loud. Her smile, not as strong.

The light would change.

Then she'd vanish with the winds.

I'd feel sadness every time.

A lot of things had been ruptured, but life repairs itself.

Pains lessen.

Wounds heal.

Scars remain.

Whether we want to or not, we stop clinging and move on.

I'd always remember my daddy, but I'd forget about his misguided wisdom. I'd stop jingling the change in my pocket.

# Author's Note

Thanks to the Creator. Much love.

Okay, it's 1:31 in the A.M. on Friday, January 8th. I was sitting up at my P.C. working on another book (in other words I'd been coming up with ways to mess up some other folks' lives—heh, heh), when it hit me that I hadn't done my acknowledgments for *Cheaters*. Yikes! In case you're interested, I started working on this novel right after *F&L*, before *MIMC*. Actually, one of the subplots in this one is a (demented and extreme, that's how I like it) twist on something that happened in *F&L*.

People always ask me where my ideas come from. The truth is, I don't know. I can see people saying good-bye in an airport, play "what if" and come up with a decent short story. Seems like for every book, peeps (I don't know) ask if "that's you or somebody else." Well, since I make 'em up, I guess, in some ways, pretty much every character in the book is me. But at the same time, they aren't me. Just plain old imagination in overdrive. The idea for this little puppy came one day I was looking at my phone bill, and saw all of the services I had listed: Last Number Redial, *69, Call Forwarding, and it hit me how much people use those little old services to, well, cheat.

Then my imagination took off like ... hell, put in your own metaphor.

Anyway, as I was wrapping up *F&L*, I didn't wanna do the same kinda book again. I wanted to do something one-hundred-eighty degrees from that. So, the peeps in *Cheaters* are the folks that the characters in *F&L* wouldn't date. Well, maybe prior to Tyrel, Shelby would've gone out with Stephan, but not for long. And Lord knows what Chiquita would do. (Before I forget, Charlotte is the same girl from *Sister, Sister*. Debra is the same character from ... well, if you've been keeping up, you'll know. There will be a test at the end of the semester.)

In some ways, I was writing about the bad guys. The ones with weaker morals. With habits that are so hard to break. And about the consequences from those habits. No matter what we do, it always catches up with us one way or another. It's about people. Real people. And it's not a book that answers why anybody cheats. (Just like *MIMC* wasn't a book that was meant to explain "why brothers go out with white women." Lawd haf mercy. Did ya see the word FICTION on the cover? LOL. I wish y'all could've read some of the e-mail people sent me. Yikes!)

So, anyway, making up new peeps is the fun part of my gig. New drama. New suspense. New freaky deaky (girl, did you read the part about Obispo?) scenes. I get to be creative without anybody peeping over my shoulder. That's cool too. Well, nobody other than my wonderful editor, Audrey LaFehr, who works overtime watching my back and making sure the final product looks good. She can tell ya how bad I need grammar check! And John Paine steps in and tells me what SUCKS and what's a keeper. I mean that in a good way. It's all in the rewriting. (So you writers with bad English and Works-In-Progress that need a lot of massaging, don't be discouraged. There is hope. Follow that rainbow until you get to that pot of gold. Just don't ignore the IRS man who'll be standing there ready to take half of it!) Genny Ostertag, thanks for taking all of my requests for books and just answering the phone with a friendly voice. You be cool like that.

And of course my agent (who has been in my corner since day uno) Sara Camilli always reminds me to pay my taxes and take my vitamins. She's a dream. And yes, Sara, I am working on the next book. For real. I'm serious.

Question: Dang, can't a bro take a five-minute break?

Answer: Not if he wants to be good in this biz. I'll rest when the big sleep comes along. I'll snore through eternity.

A lot of mornings I have to get that stress out of my body, so I have to thank my gym rats and running group for sticking with me (sometimes waiting on me) while we put in the miles and run the streets of Baldwin Hills, Crenshaw District, and Culver City: Dwayne and Evelyn Orange, Richard Scott, John Marshall, Mike, Sam Jones, Sam Gardner, Carl Williams, Jodie Little-Williams, Juanda Honore, Glenda Greene, Karla Greene, Vince and Wanda Owens, Raymond Bell, Victor Miller, Ron Streeter, Malaika Brown, Lawrence and Brenda Doss, Melanie Miller, Neiko, Tracy, Stephanie "Miss Thang" Swan, Sheila Cooley, Stephanie Myers.

Shout out to my peeps at 24 Hour Fitness on Century Boulevard: Evelyn Orange, Taj Fatiji, Tonya Marshall, Maria Quesada.

To my family, who have been my sunshine on my cloudy days: Dwayne Keith and Monica Pigues, Kevin Darnell Pigues.

All of my love to MaDear. Mrs. Virginia Jerry. Nothing keeps a man straight like a grandma with a warm heart and a good back hand. She's raised her kids, her kid's kids, her kid's kid's kids—she is the family tree. The firm foundation that keeps us from washing away when the rain comes on strong.

To my fav uncle and aunt, Darrell V. and Carol Jerry—love you!

My adopted Cali family: Brenda Denise Stinson, Gina Watkins, Chiquita Martin, Tiffany Royster, Danielle Moore, April and Rick Williams—Love y'all!

To the Fances: Tyrone, Taylor, Delia, and Devin—the girls are growing up so fast!

Pat and Twyla Hiendl, out at SAFB! Miss you guys!

To my boys who kept food on my table in the lean years: Audrey Cooper and Robert "Bobby" Laird. Thanks for the umpteen years of West Coast friendship!

Thanks, Linda Hughes, Larry Newsom, Jerome Woods, Randy Ross, Hazel Harrison, and everybody at the International Black Writers and Artists/Los Angeles for the support, starting way back when I only had a short story. Who would've thunk I'd do all these books?

Thanks and hugs to the writing crew I've met on my journey down this yellow brick road: Lolita Files, Sheneska Jackson, Tajuana Butler, Jerry Craft, Kimberla Roby, Benilde Little, Tina McElroy Ansa, E. Lynn Harris, Franklin White, Van Whitfield, Timmothy McCan, and Colin Channer (I taught him all he knows about the biz. He'd be selling fake watches and bean pies on Crenshaw if it wasn't for me!).

Much love to all my cyber-buds in Black Voices and Net Noir! Hugs to my peeps at Mosaic.com. Ron Kavanaugh is the man!

Melanie Richburg, Monica Mingo, Dawn Bryant—Whassup!

Thanks to the book clubs! I can't thank you enough. All of you were the bomb! You really came out to support a bro! Shout outs to Diva Readers, SWAVE Book Club, Sisters with Books, Nubian Book Club, Imani Book Club, Room Full of Sisters, Pages Book Club, Tabahani Book Club. And these are just the tip of the iceberg.

Okay if I accidentally forgot ya here's your chance:

I wanna thank _____ because you know I couldn't have written this book without their _____. S/He was my inspiration and without her/him, I'd be at the unemployment, screaming, "WHAT DO YOU MEAN YOU DON'T HAVE ANY JOBS! DON'T MAKE ME GO POSTAL UP IN HERE!"

Feel free to e-mail me: EDICKEY142@AOL.COM. The Web page is www.ericjeromedickey.com.

Okay, now it's three a.m.

Bedtime for Bonzo.

*Eric Jerome Dickey*